Every SCAR Tells a STORY

Victoria K. Mavis

and

Angelo R. Senese, Ed.D

Archway Publishing books may be ordered through booksellers or by contacting:

Archway Publishing
1663 Liberty Drive
Bloomington, IN 47403
www.archwaypublishing.com
844-669-3957

ISBN: 978-1-4808-9394-8 (sc)
ISBN: 978-1-4808-9395-5 (hc)
ISBN: 978-1-4808-9396-2 (e)

Library of Congress Control Number: 2020914607

Print information available on the last page.

Archway Publishing rev. date: 11/04/2020

This book is dedicated to my family members and friends—
both close and separated by the miles or years.
Their love, silent strength, perseverance, and belief in me
have taught me how to live life large,
forgive regardless of circumstance,
love unconditionally,
and remain steadfast in my search for the truth—
which ultimately sets us all free.

—Victoria K. Mavis

Contents

Introduction

The first thing people notice about Liz is her metal crutch. Then they typically ask, "What happened?" Embarrassed by her awkward gait and angry at such a bold and personal question, she used to answer vaguely and with an edge. But something in her has changed. She's at peace now, accepting life for all its injustices and limitations, while granting forgiveness, love, and grace to those who have wronged her the most.

I've known Liz for more years than she may have known herself. She was a child born in the 'sixties who grew up in a rural community and should've died at the age of four from a tragic accident. But she didn't. I watched her grow from the day of her childhood trauma through all of life's chapters, many of which are recounted in exacting detail in *Every Scar Tells a Story.*

I've also known Rhonda for several years. She's a life coach who worked with Liz to help her reach her greatest potential—and in the process, she unleashed her own. Through their work together, Liz's and Rhonda's daily, relatable blemishes are brought to these pages as they grow into inspiring role models connected in a mission to harness their own vision, will, and resilience to overcome their biggest fears and all of life's hardships.

Of all the challenging life stories I've ever heard, Liz's is the one that brings me to tears when I think of her lifetime battle of acceptance based on her abilities, rather than her physical walking disability. If you ever meet Liz, you'll see what I mean. Her ability to balance tragedy with grace, fear with strength, hopelessness with resilience, and self-absorption with compassion for others is inspiring to all who meet her.

But why believe me? After all, I'm a bit biased, since I've known Liz almost our entire lives. Of one thing I can assure you: readers following her chronicles may attribute her inner strength to God, a higher power, fate, or the universe. The unassailable point, however, is that despite its source, everyone has a choice whether to follow their mission or to let hardships, their needs, or their wants get in the way of such accomplishment. You can do it Liz's way and choose to rise above, or you can choose something else. In the end, it's always your choice.

One final disclaimer: The authors do not suggest to any reader what life purpose their creator had in mind for them. Rather, they can only encourage each of you to embark on your own path of discovery, just as Liz did. They challenge you to begin today by following one brave woman's relentless journey to fulfill hers; in doing so, may you find the strength and clarity to pursue yours. For it's in the journey, not in life's possessions, that our heart is truly filled and we are blessed beyond imagination.

~Victoria K. Mavis and Angelo R. Senese

1

Conquering the Unpleasant

Rhonda Jackson peers through the slats of the white shades on her front office window, catching herself staring as she notices her client in a new way. She's never watched Liz walk for more than a few seconds at a time. She notices her methodical limp, her stoic expression, the jerking sway of her long blond hair, and her crystal blue eyes. What's so interesting that Liz focuses all her attention on the ground? Her intensity and her stride suggest a cold, detached drone. But that's not the Liz that Rhonda has come to know. She's seen her demonstrate great people skills, a depth of intellect, truth, and emotions that most people never display. Rhonda is in awe of her level of transparency.

Liz winces as she nears the seven wooden steps, surrounded by a handrail, eyes darting from the ground to the door and back to the ground again. Her left hand clenches the rounded crutch handle, the gray metal cuff gently scraping the top of her forearm, as she shifts her weight to the right leg and steps up with her left, then does the opposite for the next step. Although Rhonda is accustomed to physical endurance as the result of years of running, she is exhausted watching Liz walk; the crutch reminds her of a ski pole pulling Liz along as if she's scaling an uphill slalom.

As she nears the landing, Rhonda pulls the front door open. The wind swirls into the foyer, whipping Rhonda's shoulder length red hair into her face. She brushes her hair aside and welcomes her client with a bright "Liz, come in!"

Liz nods soberly and shuffles her way into the beige foyer while tracking in remnants of the damp outside.

"How was the beginning of the Visionary Course?" Rhonda asks.

"It was good," Liz replies curtly.

Detecting annoyance in her tone, Rhonda says, "We'll talk more about it later, I'm sure." She then spins around and heads purposefully toward her office with Liz trailing behind.

Mrs. Taylor looks over the top of her blue-framed eyeglasses from the mahogany desk outside Rhonda's office. "It's so good to see you again, Liz!"

"You, too," Liz replies warmly. "How's that grandson of yours?"

"He's getting bigger every day. In fact, you can see for yourself soon enough. He's visiting today. Shortly, he's going to help me make pies. Now, please excuse me, ladies. I must get to the kitchen and start baking," says Mrs. Taylor.

Rhonda nods in approval and watches as Mrs. Taylor, a five-foot, heavyset woman, with short gray curly hair, slowly heads for the other end of the house.

"Rhonda, if you don't mind, I'd like to use the restroom before we begin," says Liz.

"By all means; you know where it is," Rhonda replies as she points down the hallway.

Liz limps past the desk to the door on the right and stands her crutch in the hallway corner to enter the bathroom. Watching her, Rhonda is mentally preparing for their session. From their previous meetings, she knows today is a critical point that could either set her client back into the dark recesses of her past or lead her on a path to personal freedom and peace. Rhonda then returns to her office, sits in her high-backed black leather chair near the room's perimeter, which faces the entrance door, and scans her meeting notes one last time. Within minutes, she hears the thumping of Liz's crutch on the hardwood floor. With her back to the wall, she looks up at the entrance and calls to Liz, "Come in and make yourself comfortable. I already got you a water; but if you want a cup of coffee—"

"That's fine," Liz says, as she sets down her steel forearm crutch and phone-sized burgundy, leather purse. Seated in her usual place on the charcoal tweed sofa across from Rhonda, she nods that she's ready to begin.

Rhonda focuses her attention on her client, who is seated far back in the sofa, arms crossed, coat and purse beside her, and crutch at her feet.

"Liz, I want you to know that today will be difficult. If you have to stop to collect your thoughts at any time, please do. I have as much time as you need." She takes a last sip of coffee and places the mug back on the small round mahogany table to her right.

Waiting on her response, Rhonda observes Liz staring at her feet, the left pointing straight ahead and the right tilted at an inward angle, like a small watch hand indicating eleven o'clock. Her footwear reminds Rhonda of army boots that are scuffed and worn from months of battle. How long has Liz had to wear a buildup of the sole on her right shoe? With every passing minute, Rhonda's concern for her client increases. If she doesn't quickly get to the heart of what happened in Liz's past by the end of today's session, Liz may never be able to express how she got injured; thus their work becomes a futile exercise.

Rhonda breaks the aching silence between them. "Liz, I know you have private reflections about what happened, and trying to work through it in your head can be therapeutic to a point.

However, in our work together, I you need to tell me the truth of what happened, or it's pointless to continue."

"Rhonda, I'm trying; however, since I live alone, that's when I think about it the most. It doesn't make sense for me to call someone only to dump about my past, so I keep everything inside, and it continually loops in my head like a bad horror show rerun."

Rhonda gently prods, "I understand. Let's agree when we meet that you will bring up anything significant that you've recalled since our last session, and you agree to verbalize all your thoughts while we're meeting."

Liz cocks her head to the right. "I can do that." She draws a deep breath. "So here's what happened." She bites her lip. "There was an accident when I was four years old. I fell from a hayloft and landed headfirst on solid concrete; now I'm like this."

Despite Liz's reluctance to detail her past, Rhonda is intent on pressing as far as she needs for Liz to reveal the complete story of her tragedy. She studies her client, who has tears forming at the corner of her eyes, and asks, "What part of your childhood accident is the most difficult for you to talk about?"

Liz's body stiffens and her lips purse as she speaks in a rising voice. "All of it. I'm sick and tired of telling the story; then there's nothing else. Do you know how many hundreds of times I've recounted that day?" Liz is all but ranting. "It's not just friends, but strangers will come up to me and ask, 'What happened to your leg?' without even getting to know me first; then they walk away. They don't ask others, 'Why do you have black hair?' or 'Why are you six-four?' I just want people to accept me for who I am without having to know my life story."

Rhonda guesses her client to be in her early fifties; which means she's lived with the effects of her accident for close to five decades. How many times over the years has she's tried to get help for the emotional scars that it caused her? Leaning forward, Rhonda blurts out, "I understand life has been difficult, but you have to change your perception; otherwise you will continue to make your own misery."

Liz clenches her left fist as her voice hits the highest pitch that Rhonda has ever heard. "Change my perception? You make it sound as easy as changing my underwear!"

Rhonda lifts her chin as she draws back in response to Liz's rejoinder.

Liz rages on, "Tell me how it feels when kids continually mock the way you walk, or when people stare at your leg and avoid eye contact when you walk by. Then there's the date when guys only want to 'be friends'"—she makes air quotes around the phrase—"once they see you walk. Oh, and I'm sure you remember how attractive you felt when asked if your leg prevents you from having sex."

Rhonda blinks as she rests her hands on top of the blue notebook in her lap. "Liz, if you want my help, you need to be honest with me, rather than hurling your painful memories. The decision on where we go from here is yours. I'm going to get some more coffee and give you a few minutes to think about what direction you want to head in our work together. When I return, I hope we can pick things up and move forward. Are you okay with that?" she asks.

With glowing red cheeks, Liz says, "Yes."

"Great. Do you want me to get you a cup?"

Liz, head hung low, replies, "An adult beverage would be so much better."

Rhonda reflects on her comment, unsure whether it was a joke. Smiling, she replies, "Hmmm, maybe if it was after five o'clock, that might a possibility, but for today. How about if I get some of the black stuff with a shot of cream instead?"

With lips still pursed, Liz shakes her head. "Sure. It really doesn't matter anyway."

Deciding to leave before the discussion spirals further from her planned agenda, Rhonda gets up and heads towards the kitchen, glancing towards Liz as she calls over her shoulder, “I’ll be back in ten.”

“I’ll be right where you left me,” says Liz.

Walking through the foyer, lined with doors to the left and right, and a winding staircase in front, Rhonda can’t help but question if Liz is ready to unlock the keys to her past.

2

Five Months Earlier

Rhonda sips her chai latte with nervous energy. Why did Justin insist she meet with Liz Harris? Is she some power broker who can benefit Rhonda if they connect? She looks out the café window onto the snow being blown down the ice-crusted sidewalk and reflects on her love of this place; despite the bitter January weather, it's always warm at Coco's, with its brown walls tastefully decorated with paintings and photos by local artists and music playing faintly overhead. "Mmmm," she says as she takes another sip, breathing in the warm scents of nutmeg, vanilla, and cinnamon.

Her mind wanders to the time she met Justin Saylors at her first business mixer meeting she attended at Coco's after starting her coaching business. She was attracted to him the moment she saw his six-foot-three muscular frame, golden skin, and jet black hair from across the room. When their eyes met, she instantly felt connected to the soul behind his dark brown, almost black eyes.

That night as they quickly struck up a conversation, it left an imprint in her mind that would last forever: his slightly graying temples, the curving of his lips as he smiled, and the heaviness in his tone as he spoke about his business.

Since then, Rhonda and Justin had become trusted business associates by meeting whenever Rhonda stopped by Coco's for coffee between client appointments. As their relationship grew, he spoke of his vision for Coco's. He wanted it to be a place where people got more than coffee and sticky buns. They'd come up with the slogan, "Coco's: Where everyone gets coffee, connected, and a conversation."

Rhonda's smile is short-lived; she vacillates between the joy she has in watching Justin turn his dream into a reality, and her disappointment in knowing their time together is based in business—although she'd like it to be more. Despite knowing that they can never be more than friends; Justin is her greatest love. Justin—good, kind, married Justin—fills the void in Rhonda. She enjoys the lightness of his laugh, the way she feels when they talk, the fact he challenges her to be her best self.

Even when they argue—which they do quite often, given their strong personalities—they never go more than a day or two without talking. One of them always picks up the phone; the relationship is bridged, and they move onward. Like the time they fought over the best way to get others to take accountability: Justin's approach was telling a third-party analogy in hopes that the other person would see their behavior and be willing to rectify it; Rhonda preferred using direct questions to get the person to identify what in their behavior was wrong. Although both are acceptable strategies, they overcame this conflict when each tried the other's approach and was able to acknowledge its merit and move onward.

A crash from the kitchen twenty feet behind startles Rhonda. She cranes her neck and spots a tall blond woman with pale ivory skin, stumbling near the back entrance, muttering apologies. She wears a long black suede coat and clutches a purse in one hand and a mop handle in the other.

Rhonda notices the sway of her long blond hair as the woman limps toward her but assumes she took a nasty fall on the ice-covered parking lot and dismisses further concern. She turns back toward the front entrance, a glass door with the word *Welcome* etched on the outside in gold and black and a baseball-sized jingle bell dangling from a short, brown leather strap on the inside door handle; she hopes Liz arrives soon because her schedule is packed today.

Just then Rhonda hears a *thump-thump* behind her and turns to see the blond woman a few feet away. She quickly scans her from head to toe and realizes she's carrying not a mop but an arm crutch, which she's using to walk. Her mind flashes to the muscular dystrophy posters she remembers from the early 'sixties. At last she realizes the woman is not hurt—she's disabled.

Justin approaches from behind the blond woman, the warmth of his cheek-stretching smile visible as he moves to her left side. "Rhonda, I want you to meet Liz."

Rhonda stands, forces a smile, and extends her right hand. "Pleased to meet you."

Liz slowly raises her right arm, wrist drooping and fingers slightly bent, and accepts Rhonda's handshake.

As Rhonda holds her limp grip, it reminds her of holding a dead fish. Knowing Justin would never forgive her for offending one of his patrons, she tries to mask her obvious look of repulsion by centering on Liz's facial features: her crystal blue eyes, high cheekbones, and thin, slightly smiling pink lips. Their shake ends, and Rhonda sits.

"Liz is interested in learning more about your services," Justin says as he pulls out a chair for his guest.

Liz leans her crutch cuff against the wall, puts down her purse, takes off her coat, drapes it on the back of her chair, and slowly lowers herself, wincing, to the seat.

"Well, I'll leave you ladies here to talk," Justin says, returning to the kitchen.

Liz calls after him, "Thank you for cleaning up! I promise I'll be more careful next time."

Facing Rhonda, Liz takes a deep breath and blurts, "Ever since Justin told me that you're a life coach and that you helped him, I've been looking forward to meeting you."

Although her initial impression of their meeting leaves Rhonda with feelings of discomfort, she puts aside any reservations and jumps into her coaching approach. "Liz, I apologize. Justin didn't give any details; rather he just said there was someone he wanted me to meet."

Liz says, "He said you could help me on personal issues related to my business. Lately, I want to give up."

"You shouldn't despair. I'm sure it's not that bad."

"That's easy for you to say. I've given everything to be professionally successful, sacrificing a personal life and family, and now trying to save a failing business. If it wasn't that I've invested all my retirement savings into it, I'd close it tomorrow." Her eyes meet Rhonda's. "Justin mentioned that after you worked with him on a few personal issues, his business started to grow. I was hoping you could do the same for me."

As Rhonda takes this in, her internal voice is screaming for her to quickly turn away before she gets further involved in a situation that reminds her of Phillip, her fraternal twin, who died as a result of a disability caused at birth.

"I'm not sure I'm the person you need," she says in a monotone. "It sounds like your business is the main priority. I think a business adviser would be better suited to get things back on track for you."

With a frown of disappointment, creasing brows, and tears forming in her eyes, Liz says, "That might be the case if I could concentrate on it. I can't with all these personal issues constantly battling in my head."

Why did I tell Justin I'd help her? Rhonda thinks. Out loud she says, "I really don't think I'm the person to help you right now."

"Please hear me out," Liz begs. "I keep thinking of all the bad choices I've made: career, finances, and relationships. It seems whatever I touch ends up in disaster. I'm scared to move forward with anything. Some days I just want to quit life or run away, but I'm afraid my problems would find me."

Despite her visceral reaction to the desperation she hears, Rhonda tries to mask a tone of arrogance as she states, "In my line of work, we refer to that as 'changing seats on the *Titanic*.'"

"Then you can help me?" Liz pleads one last time with arms outstretched on the table between them.

Rhonda puts her left hand to her face, covering her lips, while her right hand taps fingers absently on the table. Pushing through her discomfort, she says, "It's not a question of whether I can; it's whether I have the time. The issues you raise are ones I normally work with people on; however, I'm not sure I can fit you in with my current caseload." Reaching in her purse, Rhonda removes a business card and lays it near the glass of water in front of Liz. "Since Justin referred you to me, I do want to help. How 'bout this? Please contact me to schedule an appointment to talk in more detail. If I find that I can't help, I'll give you the name of an associate who can."

Liz abruptly sweeps the card up and into her purse; she places her hands on the table to push herself up, gets her coat on, and slings the purse strap over her right shoulder. She reaches for her crutch and says, "I'm sorry. I didn't mean to waste your time."

Rhonda puts out a hand to stop her. "Liz, wait a minute! What makes you think you wasted my time?"

"You don't have to be nice about why you don't want to work together. I've had it my whole life; I was a fool to expect you'd be different. Now I need to leave before I get a parking ticket." Liz bites her lip as tears begin to stream down, smudging her black eyeliner. "Thank you, Rhonda."

Although this may have been the outcome that Rhonda personally wanted, she is disappointed by her own lack of professionalism in handling her reaction to Liz, which she knows was triggered by certain aspects of Liz's physical likeness to Phillip. In order to save face, Rhonda extends her hand for Liz to shake.

Ignoring it, Liz turns and limps toward the door.

Rhonda feels a little surprised and angry, but she also realizes there must be something seriously wrong with the woman. She is quickly drawn out of her thoughts by methodical scraping on the rust-colored, tile floor; watching as Liz's black, military-style boots march awkwardly toward the exit. As the right boot lifts off the tile, its tip draws a semicircle outward to the right. It makes a scuffing sound when it lands. The door closes swiftly behind Liz, and the ringing bell sounds faintly for a few seconds.

Rhonda analyzes Liz's walk; it's like someone kicking a soccer ball, the way she swings her right foot around with its elevated shoe. Rhonda is still seated as her breathing begins to slow, her chest feels heavy, and she can't hear; she's about to pass out. She lowers her head to the table so she doesn't tip over; then darkness surrounds her.

A few moments later she hears muffled voices, the clatter of coffee cups, and a familiar voice. Rhonda opens her eyes to see Justin's brown-black eyes staring at her from across the table, in the seat that Liz just occupied. "How long have I been out?" she asks.

"Less than a minute. How are you feeling?" His black brows crease with worry as he asks.

"I'm fine, really. I must have overheated with this sweater on." She tugs at the neck of her green turtleneck.

"Sit here and rest for a few minutes. I'll be back with more coffee."

"That'd be great," she says sheepishly.

Immediately, she's concerned that she isn't doing all she could to stay fit; despite her workout routine and low-carb diet. Her doctor has told her that stress or physical trauma can bring on her fainting spells; however, it'd been years since she last experienced one. The last time was during a medical procedure she had when married to Ken; but she attributed that occurrence to being an emotional train wreck about their impending divorce.

It hits her. Liz pleading for help was the same as Rhonda seeking guidance in her failed marriage; she just wanted someone to listen. Guilt settles in as Rhonda knows she pushed a desperate Liz away, just as Ken did to her on the day they separated and Rhonda moved out of their micro-mansion and into a two-bedroom apartment of her own.

Several years earlier, it was her first day of work when Rhonda met Ken—her boss's best friend—at orientation. As the two of them sat that early Monday morning at the oval, twelve-foot conference table filling out their new hire paperwork, Ken's focus was all on Rhonda. His boyish charm, red-blond wavy hair, hazel eyes, freckled skin, and witty humor charmed their way past her guard. But he had one flaw—his wedding band. Despite the rumor she heard in the following weeks that he was soon to be divorced, she classified him as a professional workmate for all time.

It was about a year later when they were working on a project together that she noticed the wedding band was gone, as well as his laughter. As they worked into the early afternoon to meet their Monday deadline, he suggested a working dinner so they could finish that night and have the weekend to themselves. She agreed, feeling no concern; working dinners were common at their company. However, she became apprehensive when he called her an hour before they were to arrive at the restaurant and switched the location to his house. He said he would order pickup, as it was impossible to get a reservations on a Friday night, and without one, there would be at least an hour's wait—valuable time that could otherwise be applied to their project.

Any concerns she had about meeting were overshadowed by two thoughts: First, they had worked together for a year, discussing only business ever since orientation, and second, like the rest of the girls in the department, she was curious if his house was as big and gorgeous as the rumor mill suggested. Ignoring faint misgivings, she accepted.

Too much wine that night led to conflicting emotions and a physical relationship Rhonda wasn't ready to handle. And she while briefly wondered if she would lose her job if she declined his sexual advances, any reticence was swept away by his boyish charm.

By the next morning, she found herself facing two paths: independence (something she knew and did well) and security—though that came with strings, as she'd soon learn. On the drive home, she considered what life would be like with Ken; he was intense about business, as she was, and they seemed to reach the same conclusions about situations, which to her indicated a likelihood that they would seldom disagree and instead stand united. Although he was fourteen years older than she, his jovial nature, sense of adventure and travel, and unconditional love for his son filled the void she had felt since the death of her parents and sibling, which had occurred years earlier. Life with him would afford her a princess lifestyle, no financial worries, a successful man's undying affection, and a family.

Considering the pros and cons, she was sorely tempted, but she did have reservations. As their brief dating continued, she was caught up in events that masked her true feelings. They played great together—from their nightly workout at his home gym to their regular competition in marathons. Then every few weeks he whisked her away on weekend excursions to exclusive resorts and spas around the country; lavished her with shopping trips where he bought her clothing, shoes, and jewels; and took her to the finest restaurants, barring no expense on food and drinks. She was caught up in a lifestyle that was too good to be true.

Then one night he proposed marriage. She confessed that she wasn't sure she loved him and suggested they should live together first. Always the strategist, he countered that it didn't look good for an executive like him to be single; he assured her that she would learn to love him, and if it didn't work out, they could get a divorce.

Leaving on the night of his proposal, Rhonda knew the truth—she didn't love him—but she needed to decide whether she could live with what was essentially a business transaction as long as there was an escape clause. The next day she accepted his offer. Shortly thereafter, the three-carat solitaire engagement ring arrived, followed by a new Mercedes convertible and a walk-in closet filled with designer clothes, shoes, and jewelry; the trade-offs were her independence and spirit, and both slowly eroded, one argument at a time, until there was nothing left. Rhonda had become her husband's handmaid.

Rhonda shakes off the distant memory of her failed marriage as Justin returns, two full black coffee mugs in hand. He sits across from her wearing blue jeans and a white buttoned-down oxford; his hair in a perfect cut, an inch long to frame his oblong face. If she didn't know he was her age, forty-nine, she might guess he wasn't a day over thirty-two. The creases in his forehead gather as he asks, "Better now?"

She puts her hand to her head and runs her fingers through her shoulder-length auburn hair and down the back of her head to her neck. "Not really."

"Can I get you anything else?"

"Not unless you can rewind the past and let me have a do-over."

Moving toward her, he asks, "How'd it go with Liz?"

"I appreciate you referring her to me; however, I'm not sure I have time to help her. I did agree to meet with her and talk more to see if I can work her into my caseload."

"Really, Rhonda?" he snaps with gritted teeth. "Are you seriously so busy that you can't take on a new client, or is it something else, and your caseload is a convenient excuse?"

Rhonda purses her lips; he knows her too well. "I told you I will meet with her and see where we go. That's all I can commit to at this point. Besides, I didn't get a good feeling on the chemistry between us."

"How could you? You didn't give her more than five minutes."

"Justin, why are you questioning me on this?" Surprise and a touch of guilt creep into Rhonda's voice. "Besides, she's the one who stormed off," she says, pounding her fist on the table a little harder than she intended.

"When we first decided to be accountability partners, we agreed that if one of us thought the other was wrong, we were to speak up. So I'm saying I think you're wrong on this one. You rushed to conclusions; you're not giving Liz a fair chance." He pauses and looks around the coffee shop, tables half-filled with chatting customers. "Can I be candid with you?"

"You mean that wasn't you being frank?" Rhonda tries a wry smile. "I think I want you to lie to me on this one."

Sitting on the edge of his seat, he raises a finger and points it toward her. His smile disappears, and his eyes narrow. "I'm not sure what your personal issue is against Liz, nor do I need to know. But you need to get honest with yourself; give her the same consideration you would give anyone else. If you decide after that not to work with her, I'll let the matter rest."

Rhonda scoffs at his statement. She believes he's like a dog with a bone when it comes to helping charity cases; he grips bitterly to the end. She asks, "What makes Liz so special that you want me to help her?"

"That's a fair question," Justin replies, softening. "From the day I left home to join the service, I knew I was destined to help others. Early in my Air Force career, I had a serious accident; I was scaling a wall about twenty-five feet up, and I fell."

Rhonda reflexively muffles a gasp.

He says, "People who witnessed it said my body hit the ground and bounced five feet up. It's a miracle I lived; I was lucky that only my back was broken."

"Oh, Justin," she murmurs, her eyebrows drawing inward as she studies his broad shoulders.

He asks, "Do you know how humiliating it is to be a young, virile man who has pretty nurses come by only to put you on a bedpan and wipe your ass?"

She smiles.

"I can laugh about it now, but back then it wasn't funny. One time they gave me a strong narcotic because the pain was horrendous. I was constipated for days; nothing could loosen me up." He blushes. "I remember this beautiful nurse stopped by; I was thinking about asking her to visit me after her shift, but all she wanted to do was put me on a portable toilet seat and come at me with some kind of scooper."

"What'd you do?" Rhonda asks anxiously.

He winces. "There was nothing I could do, except lean forward and joke my way through the procedure, hoping she wouldn't remember that every time she saw me."

Rhonda laughs hysterically. "I'm sorry, Justin, but the visual of that is hilarious."

A wide-eyed Justin says, "I actually tried poking fun, so to speak, at the pooper scooper, but I don't think she saw the humor. I never saw her again." He looks away.

"Great story, Justin," she squeaks, clutching her side, still laughing. "But I don't get the connection to Liz."

"Rhonda, I was blessed. I could have been a paraplegic or worse. I remember being distraught; wondering if I would ever walk again or enjoy a woman in my arms. Now, I haven't trod Liz's path, but I do understand some of her inner struggles and doubts. If it wasn't for the help I got from friends and family while I was in the hospital, I would have given up or found a way to commit suicide. However, I wanted to live and make a difference. I wanted to give back for all that was given to me."

Rhonda bites her lip and looks up.

"Right now I see the person who needs our help is Liz," Justin says. He pauses and asks, "What are you thinking?"

"I'm thinking I hate you! I suppose you want me to work with her?"

He smiles. "I want you to do the right thing." He raises one hand to grip his chin.

She leans as far back in her seat as she can, her eyes piercing his unflinching stare. "Hmm. I'll reconsider, but I'm not promising," she says.

"Why are you so resistant to work with a person who has a disability?" he demands, drumming his fingers loudly on the table between them.

She bows her head and looks down. "She has more issues in her life than I have the resources to deal with right now." She hazards a look at Justin's face but can see that he isn't buying.

"I'm sure you'll make the right decision. And someday, you'll have to tell me the real reason for your reluctance," he says.

Rhonda knows that he's right; someday she'll have to get honest with him. But today is not it.

"Okay, lady. You can sit here if you want, but it's time for me to get to work. My barista called out sick, which means I have to start adjusting some things to get ready for the midday rush."

She smiles at him. "Have a good day, Justin. I'm sure I'll see you later in the week."

He stands and walks down the back hallway to the kitchen. Why couldn't it have been him that she married? With the chemistry they have and her love for him, she's confident they could've made it work for a lifetime.

3

More than Just a Social Security Check

Nearing the end of the snowbank-lined block of Victorian homes, which have been converted into offices for doctors and lawyers, Liz spots her car, a white Elantra. The closer she gets to it, the angrier she becomes at Rhonda, with her catlike green eyes, for refusing to help her. She regrets asking Justin to introduce them and wishes she could just forget the whole matter. After throwing her crutch in the back seat, she gets situated in the driver's seat only to find that she can't see around the two vehicles boxing her in, a red Jeep Cherokee and a black Ram truck. Given her physical condition, she's unable to twist her neck lest dizziness set in, so she slowly starts to reverse watching through her rearview mirror, hoping there's enough space for her car to clear. She hears a thud; her left foot slams on the brake, and the nightmare returns with the jolt.

She imagines: the freefall that lasts forever … the thump of her body hitting concrete … warm liquid oozing … the color red. She shudders, frozen in time and tied to a tragedy by sounds and images that have haunted her since early childhood.

She pulls herself back to the present and inches the car forward. She gets out to inspect for damage. Finding there's not even a scratch on the Ram's front grille guard, she slides back into her seat and drives away without further incident. Today's bump is yet another reminder of the many hurdles she cleared to gain and protect the independence that driving affords her. Despite learning to brake with her right foot to get her driver's license as a teenager, today she uses both feet, to make sure her left foot can stop the car in time.

On her way home via the busy interstate, her mind wanders to a time before her driving days. During her childhood, her parents always insisted that she do everything for herself—despite any physical hardships on her end. Why couldn't they have been a bit more empathetic to her condition, instead of scolding her when she did her best? Countless circumstances prove that no one understood her—not even those she was closest to: walking to the school bus with her mother yelling after her to stop dragging her leg, working in the garden and being chastised for not using both hands to pick vegetables when she only had the dexterity in her left hand to do so, visiting relatives and having her mother remind her in front of everyone in the room to "bend her knee."

When Liz was in her late thirties, a doctor explained that her injury caused permanent damage, with the "bend your knee" signal getting lost somewhere between her brain and the right side of her body. Since that day Liz wondered if that knowledge would have kept her mom from making the threat she often gave when she felt Liz was being disobedient: "If you don't bend your leg, I'm going to get the cattle prod that we use on the cows and use it to get you to pick it up."

As Liz grew, she came to believe that if her accident had occurred with today's medical technology, they could've fixed her as a child, like they did with Lindsay Wagner in the television series from the 'seventies, *The Bionic Woman.* Instead, she grew up in a world that shunned her difference. Once she took a bad fall in the middle of a busy downtown sidewalk lined with sales and hurried shoppers at Christmas time. Her mom looked ready to spank her, but instead she sternly yelled through a gritted smile, "Get up, brush off your knees, and keep walking." That day Liz shamefully did just as she was told, silently passing the many onlookers who whispered she should be institutionalized. Her skin had grown another layer of toughness by the next morning.

Liz shifts her thoughts to meeting with Rhonda. Why was she willing to believe that Justin, a businessman she'd recently met, would understand her life enough to recommend someone to help with her personal circumstances? With growing doubt that her life can be turned around, Liz sees the ugliness reveal itself in her contempt towards others when she becomes defensive.

She arrives home and parks behind her apartment, a forest green, two-bedroom duplex built in the 'fifties. As she slowly exits the car and inches through the narrow snow-lined alley between the yard fences toward the back porch stairs, her crutch tip slips on black ice. She lurches forward but quickly regains her balance. Scared that she could break her hip and freeze to death if she isn't careful, she finds her thoughts leading her to yet another regret—not moving to Texas when she had the chance and instead following her career with her former husband to Pennsylvania, where the weather is hardly better than Michigan when it comes to the hazards of snow and ice.

Annoyed that it takes her three times as long as a normal person to get somewhere, Liz puts her head down and forges toward the house. Several minutes later she is safely on the wooden porch. She steadies herself as she inserts the key into the lock, hearing howls from behind the white door. She says, "Geez, you'd think I had left for days. It's barely six o'clock." Then she coos toward the closed door. "Mommy's almost there! Hang on another minute."

She walks inside and flips on the light to the coral kitchen, lined with refinished oak cabinets and a bronze bistro table with one chair. The cries suddenly stop; her two long-haired gray felines circle empty food bowls on the floor. She closes the door behind her, puts her purse and keys on the counter, and quickly limps over to retrieve the cat food container. She pours a generous amount into each dark blue plastic bowl. The cats devour their morsels as if they hadn't eaten in a week.

"I know, Mommy's bad as she left her girls alone again." She smiles warmly catching the sudden phantom whiff of warm chocolate-chip cookies, fresh out of the oven, baked by her mother to try to make her feel better. The sound of her cats meowing pulls her out of the memory. Both cats crane their necks to reach her hand, which she uses to pet them.

From the day she and Timothy rescued the cats from the humane society, as six-week-old furballs, she has referred to them as her girls. Now, the three of them enjoy a nightly routine of watching television together, just like she did with her own parents. They, too, play games—Chase the Mouse, though, has replaced Monopoly—and they all sleep in the same big, comfy bed. The cats wake her each morning for breakfast, and their daily routine starts all over.

She looks at them lovingly and whispers, "With Timothy gone, you're the only family I have."

She sighs as she picks up her purse, limps past the cats, and heads through the cozy teal living room to her office, a ten-foot nook facing the street with bay windows and white molding lining its front. She leans her crutch against the desk and drops her coat on the back of the chair. Emotionally exhausted, she sits down and turns on her computer to tap out a few emails.

She writes, "Justin, I'm so sorry for the mess I made this morning. Let me know how much I owe you for the broken mug. I must have tripped over something on the floor. On the other matter, I appreciate you introducing me to Ms. Jackson. Take care. ~Liz"

Then she quickly sends another: "Ms. Jackson. It was a pleasure meeting you today. I look forward to meeting again soon and hope we're able to work together. I'm pretty open for the next week. Please let me know what works for your schedule. Thank you. ~Liz Harris"

She turns off the computer without looking at her inbox and goes to the kitchen. She pours a glass of cabernet sauvignon into her favorite purple-stemmed glass and returns to the living room to relax.

The cats, done with their dinner, join her in their customary places—Abbey near her feet and Ruby beside her on the couch.

"Whatcha think, kitties?" she asks. "You've had a rough day too? I know it's exhausting to chase your mouser all day."

She picks up the gray cloth mouse with nibbled pink ears and tosses it across the room. Ruby, the smaller of the twins, leaps down and chases the toy, skidding to a stop inches short of the far wall. She picks it up and returns to Liz and gets a pet; they repeat the drill time and again, until Ruby wanders off toward her water bowl.

Abbey begins to wheeze, and after a few minutes of hacking, coughs up a hairball next to Liz's feet.

"That's great, Abbey. You cough it up, and I have to do cleanup. If only I were a cat, maybe it would be that easy for me to get rid of a past that's choking me."

After cleaning up the mess, Liz returns to the couch, intent on watching TV. Surfing through the channel menu, she finds her anger rising for the second time today in response to her brief encounter with Rhonda.

Could Liz's leg have been the reason why Rhonda refused to take her on as a client? If it was, why does that always make a difference with the people Liz meets? Perhaps things would've been different for her had she gone on permanent disability when she was in her twenties, rather than pursuing paid work. In the long run, it's questionable which means afforded her a better quality of life. All she knows is the one she chose—a life and career filled with opportunities and daily hurdles, some of which are caused by her disability while others are not.

Her anxiety building, Liz thinks about her business and many other things that need fixing in her life. She's at the brink of exploding if she doesn't talk to someone about what's bothering her, but who can she trust? Liz closes her eyes and tries to relax. Can she trust Rhonda, or will she judge her like everyone else?

4

Door to the Future

A week later, Rhonda, with hair pulled back and dressed in blue athletic gear from her midday run to Coco's, is reviewing notes in the sparsely filled coffee shop when a smiling Justin approaches her table with two piping-hot cups of coffee and an inviting black-checkered plate of sticky buns.

"Hey, Rhonda! I know these are normally for breakfast, but they looked like a great afternoon snack today." He's grinning like a schoolboy as he sets everything on the table.

"I do agree, although it might cost me an extra run to burn the calories off."

"Oh, I don't see that you have much to worry about." He winks.

"It might seem that way, but I work hard to keep the pounds off. If I didn't control my eating and exercise, I'd easily weigh more than three hundred pounds."

He scoffs. "I find that hard to believe."

"Yep, many people do, especially when I tell them I once tipped the scales at two fifty-six."

His eyes open wide. "Wow. When was that?"

"My late teens, following the deaths of my parents, a period in my life when I sought comfort in things—and people—I later regretted."

"Such as?" he prods gently.

She bites her lip. "The usual vices: eating, drinking, shopping, sex. I drew the line at crime—no theft, violence, or drugs for this girl."

Justin, always one to go with the moment, takes a bite of a sticky bun and looks at her curiously, "What turned things around?"

"A lot of things. The main one was that a coworker convinced me to start counseling. A few months and a lot of work later, I was on my way out of the darkness and into the light of my future"

"I'm glad you got on the right path; otherwise, we wouldn't be sitting here. Anyway, you didn't come here to recount the past. What can I help you with?"

"Justin, I've been doing some soul searching—you know, about Liz."

"And?"

"You were right in our last meeting. There's something else. Working with her would force me to face a part of my past that I'm not ready to deal with."

"I'm listening."

"There are some family issues I still need to reconcile. Part of my reaction to Liz was because meeting her reminded me of being bullied for stuttering as a kid."

He cocks his head and purses his lips. "You never mentioned that before. How'd you fix it?"

She laughs. "Silly, you don't 'fix' stuttering. It took remedial instruction with caring teachers and work with speech therapists to help me develop and refine my communication skills. I was one of the lucky ones; it only took me until the end of third grade to overcome it."

He leans forward. “Hmm. I understand, but I’m confused. What does that have to do with Liz?”

“It’s complicated.” She struggles to organize her thoughts. “As a kid, I was labeled ‘stupid.’ Being face-to-face with Liz brought back all my childhood fears and emotions. My past—and the pain I suffered as a child—became as real with Liz that morning as if I were a little girl again. I acted like a child and withdrew.”

“That makes sense,” Justin says, rubbing his chin. “I guess I have my own version of that from when I had my accident, but it’s been so long ago, I rarely even think about it. However, I do recognize when something happens to put it on my radar.” He pauses to take a sip of coffee. “It’s fortunate you outgrew your situation. Liz probably can’t forget hers. I’m sure she’s reminded of it with every step she takes.”

Rhonda draws a deep breath and flips a lock of red hair behind her ears, showing off her new diamond stud earrings. “I can’t imagine what that’s like; it was difficult enough living with mine through third grade.”

“Well, do you think you can help her?” he asks as he takes another bite.

She looks up and then back to him. “Somehow I knew you’d get back to that. There’s a part of me that still doesn’t want to, but it’s the right thing to do. I’m not sure it will be effective; I sense she’s still holding back.”

“Rhonda, think about it. Would you divulge the intimate details of your entire life to someone you only met for five minutes? Hell, we’ve known each other for three years, and this is the first time you’ve told me about some of your past. You might want to cut her some slack on this one.”

Her cheeks flush with embarrassment. “You’re right. It will take time for her to trust and open up.” She smiles at him. “I’m not sure why it happened today, but for some reason that charm you have worked, and I was able to cough up a few hairballs.”

"You can butter me up this time, but I know your tactics. You're hoping that next time I'll apologize for something stupid I did because you were nice to me today. Now, what's this hairball thing?"

She laughs. "You told me once you had cats, so I'm sure you know what hairballs are."

His eyes roll. "I mean in people."

Should she tell him? She knows he's going to ask at some point about hers, and she can't lie to him. She responds, "It's a term I thought of recently when I was watching TV and saw a commercial about cats. I consider hairballs to be thoughts or feelings you can't or won't express; but if you don't, they'll have a damaging effect on your life. Like how a hairball could be harmful if a cat never coughed it up."

Justin turns to look toward the kitchen and then returns his attention to her. With a blank stare he leans back in his chair and asks, "Hmm. Can you give me an example?"

Knowing she can never mention the feelings she has for him, she attempts to cloak her biggest hairball. "Well, this friend of mine is in love with someone, but she can't tell him because he's involved with another woman. However, it's killing her not to say anything. If only she could express it or get rid of her feelings for him, she'd feel so much better that she might actually be able to start a relationship with someone who is available."

Frowning, he asks, "How long has she had this hairball?"

With a look of anxiety she can't conceal, she retorts, "Too damn long."

"What are you going to advise her to do?"

"We're working through that right now. It's gotten so big that if she's not careful, she can hurt others if she randomly coughs it up. But she also needs to get rid of it to get on with her life, as there's no hope in sight for a relationship with him."

He smirks. "I see. Be sure and tell me what happens. I may have a few hairballs myself that I'll ask for your help with someday. First, though, I want to hear the end result of this hairball exorcism."

As he laughs, she forces a smile, clutches her hands, and looks toward her lap. He has never given her any reason to believe that the feelings she has toward him are mutual. Although she has tried countless times, she can't seem to get him out of her heart and instead continues her pattern of self-destructive behavior by fantasizing that someday she might have a chance. She tilts her head slightly up and studies his relaxed pose and wide grin through her bangs.

She briskly changes the subject, "Anyway, getting back to Liz—I'm meeting with her this afternoon."

"I knew you'd do the right thing."

"Thank you, Justin, for holding me to my commitment to help others—even if I didn't enjoy it at the time."

"Rhonda, if I punched you in the nose, you'd thank me and say, 'It's too small anyway; now it will swell up and look better.'"

She covers her mouth and stares, trying to avoid taking the bait which could easily lead to an argument. Then she warmly smiles, knowing that if he can't accept her acknowledgement, it's his problem. To be true to herself, she must still always give it.

He continues, "Since we didn't meet as planned the other day, do you have time for a quick chat about the café? I have something new that I need to run by someone."

She unfolds her hands and puts them on the table. "Of course I have time for you. A lot has changed over the years. Coco's has grown to become a real community hub! What do you want to do with it now?"

"Actually, I'm not sure I want to continue," he says, taking her aback. "I took it over temporarily when I retired from the Air Force, since my in-laws were in failing health; I never intended to be here for the rest of my life."

"Is there something else you'd like do?"

"If only it were that simple. Since we own the building and rent out the extra rooms, well, I rely on that rental income as well as the income from the business to support my family."

"Okay. If money weren't an issue, what would you like to do?"

He smiles. "Photography." He points to a twenty-by-thirty-inch photograph on the wall in the back hallway. It shows a little girl stooping to pet a cat. The photo is in black and white except for the fluffy blue angel wings the girl wears.

"That's yours?" she asks with a note of surprise.

"Yes, and my little girl, too."

Taken aback at the reminder of his marital status, she swallows hard, trying to suppress all emotion. "That's good work, Justin. I'm sure there's something you can do with your talent."

He rolls his eyes again and sighs. "Maybe, but who's going to buy pictures of my kids?"

"You just have to think it through, like you did with Coco's." She looks around the room, making mental notes of the work it took to get the business to where it is today: the building renovations, determining customer preferences, creating a menu, advertising, pricing, and portion control. She further suggests, "Maybe photos that you display for sale at Coco's."

"Perhaps someday, Rhonda. For now, though, I have to take it one day at a time and figure out the path immediately ahead of me."

She knows well enough that's his signal when he doesn't want to talk about things any more. Trying to change the subject, she asks, "Do you remember when we first met?"

He waves his hand breaking out in laughter. "How could I forget? Like clockwork, you would come in and sit in that booth over there." He points to his left. "I always recognized your long red hair and those green eyes peering into a book or over a stack of papers, even as I served you coffee."

"Some days, I don't think much has changed since then."

"Sure it has. I've seen you open up to others, help business owners and community leaders, even if you don't get paid for it."

Rhonda inhales. "Free advice for a life coach is tricky; I often chalk it up to goodwill and community service."

"It'll come back to you. I know it has for me."

"It's starting to. But for my business to move forward, I have to either become better at managing all aspects of it or hire someone to perform the roles I'm not real good at."

"Now that's exactly where I'm at, and what I would like to talk about today," he says.

She glances skeptically at him before taking another sip of coffee. "What do you have in mind, Sir Justin?"

"Coco's is beginning to do an incredible amount of business, and I need more help. I've advertised and haven't gotten any takers. I know your resourcefulness, so—any suggestions?"

"What about a high school intern?" she asks as she digs in her purse to pull out a business card.

He takes a bite. "That has possibilities."

"Aah, here's the person to call—her name is Katie." She hands him a white business card with large, black print. "I met her the other day at the beauty shop. She works with the high schools and uses state funding to get students with disabilities trained with work skills."

His eyes narrow, "Before I do that, I need to know why you didn't want to work with Liz, but it's not a problem for you to refer others to someone who may have a similar issue."

She purses her lips. "I never said I didn't have my own head trash; that's an issue I'll need to keep working on."

"Fair enough. So going back to the conversation about my hairballs—"

She looks at her new Fitbit watch and grins. "Oops. Too many hairballs, too little time. Gotta call it a day, Justin. If I leave now, I'll make it just in time for Liz, and you of all people understand and respect the value of being on time."

"I do! In fact, in the military we were taught that if you're not fifteen minutes early, you're late."

Rhonda dashes out, intent on avoiding future hairball discussions with him.

5

One Memory from Personal Destruction

Rhonda's office is located ten blocks from Coco's in a beautiful gold Victorian house with black shutters. She originally purchased the building with the intention of running a bed-and-breakfast, but after visiting friends who had done the same thing in upstate New Hampshire, she modified her plans a bit. She has kept the downstairs as her living area and office, except that her bedroom is upstairs with three soon-to-be-renovated suites. Her plan is to provide short-term rentals to individuals going through a divorce or relocating to the area for work.

She was fortunate to quickly find her first renters, the Taylors, a retired couple who needed a place to stay for a few years. They trade room and board for Mr. Taylor's help renovating the house; he works at his own pace and according to her budget. Mrs. Taylor is paid to clean and provide light clerical support for Rhonda's coaching practice.

Rhonda's career started in a Fortune one hundred company, where she started work in human resources as a benefits specialist. Although she enjoyed it, she quickly found her way to the training side of the business, where she consulted with managers on skill and professional development. Eventually, she became known as an industry expert in her field. Despite her professional success, a series of corporate closures left her out of a job but not without a plan. She took her expertise in leadership development and started a life-coaching business within days of losing her last corporate job.

As a life coach, she quickly found initial success as she worked every imaginable hour to build a caseload. She still leverages every personal contact she makes to grow her business. With little distance between her personal and professional lives, a normal day begins early with a visit to the gym or a run. Each minute thereafter is dedicated to work, and she ends each day late in her study, either preparing for the next day or else reading.

Today is no different. She's been home only long enough to change out of her gym gear and get settled in her office when the main door opens, and she hears scuffing and banging on the hardwood floor. From the sounds of the footsteps, she instantly knows it's Liz. She calls out from her office, "Please come in."

She gets up as Liz reaches her office doorway, framed by white molding and beige colored walls on both sides. As the women face each other, Rhonda subtly observes Liz's physical composure; she is almost four inches taller than Rhonda's five-foot-six frame. Although they are both a similar slender size, Rhonda's body is more muscular and shapely than Liz's. Compared to Liz's looks from afar, Rhonda can tell up close that the left side of her body is significantly more developed and muscular than the right.

"Good to see you again, Liz." Rhonda motions. "Do you want to sit on the couch?"

"Sure. That's fine," Liz says, slowly making her way across the room. She lays her crutch on the dark brown hardwood floor, takes off her coat and lays it on the couch, and slowly sits.

Rhonda scrutinizes every detail of her crutch; positioned as a seeing eye dog, obediently waiting by its master's heels, the steel straight frame, topped with a gray metal arm cuff at the top and an oversized yellow rubber tip at the bottom, has a matching gray handle about twelve inches below the cuff with which she aids her walk with her left hand.

Finally Rhonda looks into her sea-blue eyes, vivid against her ivory complexion and blond hair. She says in a calm tone, "When we met at Coco's, I wasn't sure I had time to help you. However, I have reviewed my caseload, and after today—if you still want to work together—I'll be available for the times we schedule. However, before we start, I want to give you the ground rules for our work."

With a guarded expression on her face, Liz says, "Okay."

Rhonda looks her directly in the eyes. "Just to clarify, my role as a life coach is to help you identify your goals and to develop an action plan to achieve them. However, to begin that work, we often must visit what you've done so far, which involves to some degree looking at your past. Often in doing so, clients find it helps to seek additional services from another professional, such as a psychologist. If this happens, I can give you a name or two of someone you can see."

Liz cocks her head. "I understand."

"Also, it's essential for you to share complete and accurate information in response to my questions and in all the work we do together; I promise that I maintain confidentiality with our discussions. Does that sound like an approach that will work for you?"

"It does at this point."

"Good. And remember, we are only working on personal situations. If I ask questions about your business, it's to get an understanding of how that impacts your personal life; in no way does it mean I'm providing advice on the business. Is that clear?"

Liz swallows and settles back into the couch. "Yes."

"Great. Then let's begin." Rhonda clears her throat. "Liz, when you alluded to things in your life going the wrong way, which circumstance do you feel is causing you the greatest level of stress right now?"

Liz closes her eyes momentarily and draws in a deep breath. "It started earlier this year when my former mother-in-law called on New Year's Day and told me my ex-husband, Timothy, had stage four cancer. I was surprised, but not shocked, at the news. He passed away a few weeks later of liver, lung, and brain cancer."

Liz covers her mouth as her eyes swell with tears.

"In the end, he gave up on life. It's my fault; I should have saved him. Instead, I let him smoke and drink himself to death," Liz says with a quaver in her voice.

Rhonda, skillful at extracting bits of conversation to expand the dialogue, says, "Liz, I'm a little confused. When we met, why did you initially say that personal matters were affecting your business?"

Liz seems incredulous. "I can't think of it any other way. Lately, when I try to work, I can't concentrate; instead, I dwell on my personal life and failures. If I try to resolve my personal situations, I'm drawn back to work and can't face my life. I feel like a hamster running on a wheel." She glares at Rhonda. "I'm scared I'm going to wind up penniless and living out of a cardboard box under a bridge."

Wondering where her thoughts of desperation came from, Rhonda asks, "Why do you feel that way, Liz?"

Liz groans as she folds her arms across her chest and looks at her work-style black boots, wet from the outside snow. Slowly she says, "Nothing's working right now. I've hit this similar low point in my life before, only I never bottomed out like this. I have a history of hiding my problems from others, and when I can't take it, I distance myself by destroying relationships and opportunities that are in front of me."

Liz hides her face with her hands and continues, "The list is there: broken relationships, bad financial decisions, job changes, and failed business ventures. What else needs to happen before there's nothing left of me?" She lowers her hands, and tears are streaming down her cheeks. "Can't you see I'm tired of doing it all myself? I want to find a way to solve it while I still can and to grow, rather than dwindle and die, which is what I feel I'm doing."

Rhonda ponders where to begin. "Liz, I want to take you back to your comment about business and personal life being related; it's very insightful of you. Many people think that problems only affect the area of their life where they occur—as if there's a contamination chamber that can be locked down when life gets bad, while the good compartments remain intact. Life is not a series of partitions; every area is interconnected. When one thrives, it gives lifeblood to the rest; when one fails, it takes a toll on all, and there's potential risk of absolute failure."

Liz nods pensively.

"Although you feel overwhelmed by several life events right now, we're going to start with the one that's bothering you the most—your relationship with your former husband, Timothy."

Liz peers down at her crutch, nervously shuffling her black boots in the water droplets surrounding them. She blurts, "Timothy was an alcoholic. It came to a head after he had been laid off and refused to get a job or quit drinking. I snapped; I gave him an ultimatum with a six-month deadline. At the end of the time, when he hadn't met my conditions, I kicked him out and put the house up for sale in order to pay off our debt. He moved back to Missouri with his former wife. That was three years ago; I never saw him again."

"There's a lot there," Rhonda says sympathetically. "What part of your relationship with Timothy bothers you?"

"It's complicated. As I said a few minutes ago, there's so much I've ruined in my life. He's just the tip of the iceberg; perhaps if you have a few years, we can cover the rest." Liz taps her left boot on the floor as she bites her lower lip.

Rhonda scribbles in her notebook, *Iceberg—Is that sarcasm or Liz's truth?*

"It's not going to be easy or quick, Liz. The decisions affecting your personal life are deeply rooted and connected through events of your past. It will take time to discover the underlying cause and create an action plan to rectify it."

Liz clenches her left fist. "I have to do something! The agony I have is enormous. I honestly feel it's choking me at times," she says, raising her hand to her neck to rub it.

Rhonda tilts her head, and her hair falls around her shoulders, "How long have you felt that way?"

"It comes and goes, but I guess it started when I was a child. Maybe by the age of eight, by ten for sure, it was there."

"Can you describe an incident that gives you the choking feeling?"

Liz stares at the wall to the left of Rhonda; her eyes glaze over.

"From the earliest I can remember, I hated going to the barn to do chores, especially by myself. Whenever I walked through the center, I would feel tightness in my chest and have difficulty breathing. There were certain areas I wouldn't step near because bad things could happen; I'd get really scared, always looking over my shoulder. I'd finish my chores as fast as I could and run outside to safety. Within ten feet of feeling the outside air, I could breathe again."

Leaning in, Rhonda asks, "Why do you think you felt that way?"

"I don't know," Liz replies as her stare is unflinching.

"Do you have that same feeling now?"

"Somewhat. The more I talk, the worse it seems to get," Liz says.

Rhonda reflects and quickly realizes Liz is reliving her anguish because she hasn't identified the real problem yet, only symptoms from an underlying issue. She's unsure what the cause is or how deeply it's buried in Liz's past, but her hunch is that it's far removed from Liz's relationship with Timothy.

To speed their work, Rhonda decides to take a different course at this point than more discussion. She leans back and taps her pen to her cheek. "We're going to change this up a bit. For us to have a starting point with Timothy, there are many questions you need to answer. I've found it works best when I give clients a questionnaire, and they write out their answers. Once it's completed, we can meet to discuss."

Liz turns toward her and nods.

"I recommend you do this as soon as possible. Ideally, we would meet within two weeks to review your answers. Otherwise, life happens, making it easy to delay or avoid altogether."

Liz clenches her teeth and then asks, "How long will it take to resolve my issues?"

Sensing that Liz is counting on a quick solution to her anguish, Rhonda responds, "That depends on your level of diligence in getting it done. I have some clients who are able to answer the questions within a week, and then we create an action plan. Then there are others who take several months. The key is willingness to be honest with yourself and to look at all areas of your life."

"I understand."

"Great! Now, if you'll excuse me for a moment, I'll get a packet for you."

As she walks out of the office to the black metal file cabinet near Mrs. Taylor's desk, Rhonda imagines what Liz must be facing right now, knowing where every skeleton is buried but not sure she is strong enough to dig them all up. As she pictures decomposed bodies rising from the ground and walking toward Liz with arms outstretched, she imagines Liz grabbing her crutch as if it were a sword and striking them all down—once and for all.

Rhonda beams with the belief that her client is a diamond in the rough with an inner strength that allows her to overcome what most people are unable to face. Through their work she's encouraged that they will discover the source of Liz's strength so she can unleash it in others and perhaps even in herself.

Returning to her office, Rhonda observes a relaxed Liz. She hands her a large manila envelope, about a half inch thick. "Be sure and look these over when you get home. I think you should begin in the relationship section, since resolving your past with Timothy is foremost in your mind. After that, work to complete the rest of the questions, one section at a time. Write down any memories that are not related to the questions. When you can, call or email to schedule a time for us to meet again. If you have questions in the meantime, please contact me directly." She pauses. "Do you understand what I want you to do?"

Liz stands to put on her coat. "Yes, I do. Thank you for your time." She picks up her crutch, slings the purse over her shoulder, and then clutches the envelope.

The women walk a few feet into the foyer, and Rhonda says, "Be careful. I saw the weather online, and snow might be turning to sleet this afternoon." Rhonda shakes Liz's hand, turns around, and starts back toward her office. There are a few shuffled footsteps and a sudden screech, she quickly turns to see Liz falling forward, twisting her lower body to the left, and landing on her butt. Instant fear overcomes Rhonda; she runs to help as Liz lies on the floor, face up with legs sprawled, the envelope near her, and her crutch a foot away.

Liz murmurs, "I'm sorry. I can do it myself." Rolling to her knees, she grabs the legs of a nearby wooden bench and clumsily pulls herself to her feet, straining her upper arms from the weight of her whole body. She brushes off her skirt and reaches for her crutch.

Rhonda picks up the envelope and asks, "Are you okay? What happened?"

Looking disgusted, Liz replies, "The floor must have been wet from the snow I tracked in, and my crutch slipped. I'll be fine. Really. I've fallen hundreds of times."

Liz takes the envelope from Rhonda and resumes limping, but more slowly, toward the front door. Rhonda follows, furtively looking for wet spots and unconsciously holding her breath while watching Liz walk.

When Liz is finally outside and safely down the steps, Rhonda bids her farewell and slowly closes the door. Turning to her office she realizes her insensitivity to ask Liz where she had parked or to watch as she walked to her car. She brushes all concern away, confident that Liz parked in the handicapped-accessible spot at the end of the block that no one ever uses.

Walking into her office, she sees the red digital clock by her computer. It's five thirty, and she knows that once again she's not going to be on time for her business dinner. She spins around and hurries upstairs to her room to change outfits, hoping that the group will not kick her out for always being late.

6

The Unanswerable Question

As Liz trudges on the snow-covered sidewalk toward her car, parked a few blocks away, the snow gets heavier and starts to accumulate, making the walkway slippery. If she falls again, she might not be so lucky and get up easily, as she did in Rhonda's foyer. Eyes forward, she spots a young couple approaching from behind a nearby parked car, holding hands as they laugh. As they get closer, their levity ceases, and the young man holds the woman close to him.

She thinks, *Wow, does he think I'm going to attack them with my crutch?* She tries to smile her way into their hearts, cordially greeting, "Hello."

Her words are returned by stares of cold righteousness.

When the couple is several yards behind her, the laughter resumes; she turns to see them walking hand-in-hand on the sidewalk, lined with trees drooping from heavy snow accumulation.

The farther she limps, the more she wants to be respected as a person and not as a disability. She longs for someone who'll be able to look beyond her awkward gait, to see the dimples in her cheeks or the twinkle of her eyes. Then the hairball returns, filling her lungs and throat.

For Liz, apprehension about her leg never ends. At one of her former jobs she was told she wasn't friendly enough for a particular promotion. The feedback the manager gave her was "You always walk with your head down, and you don't smile at people."

She winces at the memory. Was it really that? Or was that her way of saying Liz's leg bothered her? Does she have any idea how difficult it is for Liz to walk without tripping? She hoped that manager would break a leg someday so she could know a few of the struggles that Liz has to deal with. She lost the promotion because she couldn't walk and smile at the same time. Thank God she can walk and chew gum!

Despite the thick skin she's developed by watching strangers avert their gaze, Liz remains self-conscious when friends and family avoid looking in her direction until she's standing still or seated; she's afraid they're repulsed at the sight of her struggling to do what comes easily to them.

Nearing her car, she catches the attention of two teenage boys playing in the snow, in front of a three-story slate gray office building. They stare at her and then turn away, snickering. And just like that, she's back in her twenties on a brisk winter day, walking downtown on the riverwalk, between the snow-covered yards in front of newly built condos and the half-frozen canal nearby, when she came upon two similar teenagers.

"What's wrong with your leg?" one of them asked.

Her head spun around like Linda Blair in *The Exorcist.*

"Nothing," she growled. "What's wrong with yours?"

They cowered and quickly ran away in response to her boldness.

She bites her lip at the absurdity of still getting angry after all these years over those boorish boys. Smiling, she envisions meeting them today, only this time asking, "What's wrong with your brain, idiot?"

Although Liz has so far successfully ignored the heaviness of her feet and the growing pain in her hip from the walk, she can't help but fixate on inconsiderate, nondisabled drivers who park in handicap spaces. If only her hands had been free; she could have keyed the car parked in the handicap spot near Rhonda's without a permit. Perhaps if there were parking tickets she could put on windshields as she walked by, it would discourage the "violators." But how would they read? She grins. It's the perfect tagline: *Being an inconsiderate moron is not considered a disability.* Had she thought of it years earlier, she could have retorted to the driver who yelled at her one sunny day at the beach, "Parking one space over won't kill you," as he jumped over the door into his red 'fifty-six Thunderbird convertible and sped out of the only accessible parking space.

Rational thought returns to her. Despite the joy she would get from calling people out for their selfishness, she would never go through with it, as her wrath would give others a reason to retaliate against those who need handicap parking the most.

All thoughts of solving the accessible parking problem subside as she finally arrives at her car. She tosses her crutch in the back seat and slides behind the steering wheel. Exhausted and soaked from melting snow that accumulated on her coat, she peels it off and finds her mind wandering back to childhood as she cautiously drives home.

When Liz was a child, it wasn't called bullying, but that's what it was.

Growing up on the farm, she had no one to play with. Maybe that's why she considered the trees to be her first friends. Lining the driveway between the old farmhouse and the cow pasture stood the seventy-five-year-old maple and the tall white pine, forever majestic in the loneliness of her five-year-old world. The first time she told her older adopted siblings, "These are my friends. They talk to me," the other kids laughed.

The mocking continued whenever they caught her in childlike conversations with them. Then the taunts: "Lizzy is weird and talks to trees. No one's going to like her, and she's going to grow leaves."

She was so humiliated that one day after school she ignored the trees on the way into the house. They were whispering her name, asking her to stop and play. Despite how badly she wanted to rush to their big, strong branches, to be protected from all harm, instead, with the onlooking white and brown Guernsey cows listening from just beyond the reach of their branches, she shouted at them, "You just want them to make fun of me!" Then she hobbled as fast as she could to the back of the house, away from their voices begging her to sway in the gentle breeze and dance with them. She didn't know which upset her more: that they would never play together again, or that her mother would yell at her for getting her new shoes dirty from dragging her feet as she hurried on the dirt driveway.

Young Liz cried on the rickety back porch steps, while she picked off loose chips of white paint, until one of the recently abandoned cats started rubbing up against her leg. Like her, she figured the cat was from the city and looking for a friend. The orange tabby wouldn't leave her alone. She started petting it and named her Sandra, after a redheaded girl who'd befriended her in kindergarten. She figured the cat could be her friend since no one told her that she couldn't talk to cats.

Liz arrives home safely. She struggles to get out of the car and then grabs her crutch and purse and limps through the back alley, between twin green rental houses with no yards, to her back porch. Once inside, she greets and feeds the cats. Looking at the trail of melting snow she's tracked in, the familiar choking feeling returns to her throat, and she gets a paper towel to wipe up the floor.

She pours a glass of wine and takes it to the living room with Rhonda's envelope under her right arm. Putting both on the oval glass top table, with antique silver stand, she sits and quickly sifts through her memories.

Could writing after all these years reignite the passion she once had for composing poetry? Back then, she wrote about the triumph and tragedy of others. Yet she's never put ink on paper about her accident or her feelings about being adopted. Can she face those memories today and not have her hand betray her heart? Or has that time already passed?

Liz pulls out the twenty-five-page questionnaire. Although she's initially overwhelmed by the sheer mass of questions, she glances over the first page to find each one has a large blank space under it in which to write her response; at once the task seems less daunting. She begins immediately recording her answers.

Number 17 stops her: "When did you first experience romance?"

The details are as clear as if it had happened yesterday. Liz's first love was Jeff, her new pastor's eldest son.

> We met the summer after his freshman year at college and spent summer afternoons talking about the world outside our small hometown in Michigan. He was nineteen; I was barely seventeen and positive we were destined to be together. Three weeks before he was to return to school, I wrote him a heartfelt letter which told of my deep affection for him and my desire to spend the rest of our lives together.
>
> I wrote of our kisses; the way he made me feel special as he held me in his eyes and in his arms. I wrote about the dreams we shared on those warm

summer nights. I carried the letter with me for days, debating whether to give it to him.

One afternoon, we met at our usual spot, a park near where we both lived. My heart was anxious as I watched for a sign to give him the letter. He asked what I would do when he went back to college. That's when I gave him my letter and ran behind our bench to a row of trees. With my back toward him, I waited for him to come get me after he read of my love for him.

Five minutes passed, then ten, then fifteen. I came out from behind the trees, and he was gone. On the grass was the crumpled envelope, still sealed. Why didn't he open it? I scoured the park, but he was nowhere to be seen.

My heart felt betrayed.

In the days that passed, I heard nothing from him. Each day I went to the park at our normal time, hoping he would be waiting for me; all I found was disappointment. I was too embarrassed to ask his family where he was.

Despite my humiliation, I scanned the pews every Sunday hoping he would be there. He couldn't have died, could he? Surely if there was an accident, his father would have announced it during the service.

Eight weeks later, I saw him at church. I stopped dead in my tracks. He was walking my way, his face beaming as he said, "Liz, about the day in the park—"

Then seemingly from nowhere, a tall brunette, wearing a short skirt and skinny legs, walks up and slides her hand into his.

He blushed, still grasping her hand, and said, "This is my fiancée."

I was mortified; the blood drained from my face as I bolted past him toward the bathroom. He caught up with me, grabbed my arm, and said, "I tried to tell you I was going back to school."

I felt my voice rising uncontrollably. "I thought it was to study."

"Look, Liz, we had a great summer. I really like you a lot. If it wasn't for her, maybe we'd be together. I never meant for it to get that far with you."

"You lied to me!" I said, pulling away from him.

In a defiant tone he answered, "I never lied. You never asked if I had a girlfriend."

"Go to hell," I said as I charged into the bathroom and dropped to my knees in the first stall. Without even closing the door I began vomiting until the dry heaves stopped. I was fortunate no one else entered while I was in there.

When I came out a half hour later, I could hear his father delivering the sermon. I looked at the bulletin and saw the topic was "Living an Honest Life." I tossed the paper in the garbage on my way out of church. As I drove away, I vowed never to give my heart to a man again.

Liz sips her wine, the woodsy coolness easing her bitterness a notch.

She always wondered what would've happened if Jeff had read her letter. Would he have married her instead? Or would he have made fun of her? She felt cheated that he never gave her a chance.

She thinks next of Timothy and asks whether she really loved him. Instantly, her heart knows the answer: she shouldn't have married him. It was a matrimony of mutual convenience; he was looking for a caretaker, and she was tired of being alone on holidays and weekends. After Jeff, she had given up on love and decided it was better to settle for someone rather than no one.

She takes another sip and stares into the cherry red liquid before placing it back on the table. Then she continues with the questions about her relationship with Timothy.

As she settles into bed that night, surrounded by her girls in their four-poster bed with a white draping canopy and matching white quilt with purple lacing, her final query is about her work with Rhonda. Does she understands Liz's challenges or what she has gone through? Can she really help her? Rather than deliberate further, Liz closes her eyes, pets her cats, and drifts off to sleep in hopefulness.

7

Welfare of Others

Running to her business meeting, Rhonda is preoccupied with images and sounds of Liz that she can't get out of her head: Liz's body sprawled on the floor after she fell, the way her right arm lay limp at her side, her ugly worn and tattered boots, and the scrape of her foot across the floor.

She shivers from the chill of the night as she calms her inner disgust at the thought of her new client. She crosses the threshold into the Italian restaurant, lined in burgundy walls and redwood molding, with green ferns hanging near the ceiling at the room's perimeter, reassuring herself that working with Liz may benefit her as much as it does Liz—it will build her repertoire of skills so she can work with others like her.

Rhonda drapes her coat and earmuffs on the back of the only empty chair at the table—hers. Although she missed dinner, she's not too late for dessert or the start of the meeting. Over the next forty-five minutes or so, she drifts in and out of conversations that are openly flowing around the table. Suddenly, she hears Justin call her name from the head of the table. He asks her, "We haven't heard from you yet. What's new in the coaching business?"

She stares at the empty bottle of chianti near his almost empty wineglass, to avoid eye contact in hopes of masking her annoyance at him. "Well, I recently began working with a new client who presents personal challenges for me. I'm not really sure what the next step will be."

"Is there anything the group can do to help?" he asks after taking a last bite of tiramisu.

"I don't think so. I have to reflect on it, and I may ask the group for suggestions next time we meet."

Justin nods, and with no further business on the agenda, he wraps up the meeting. As everyone stands and exits the restaurant, he keeps pace with Rhonda. "Can I give you a ride home and spare you getting snow-covered?" he asks.

She throws him a guarded look and hesitantly accepts.

Once they're in his silver Lincoln Navigator, he turns to her and says, "Okay, spill the beans. What's going on, Rhonda?"

"That didn't take long," she snaps with her hands folded in her lap.

"Listen, I don't have a lot of time. I want to see my kids before they go to bed," he says as he starts the engine and begins to drive.

"Fine." She throws her hands up. "When I met with Liz today, everything seemed to go well as long as we were talking. When she got up to walk, though, I felt a certain anxiety in my chest, and as she was leaving, she fell."

He gasps. "Was she hurt?"

"I don't think so," she quietly replies.

"Did you check?" He glances toward her and quickly returns his eyes to the road.

"Not exactly. At the moment it happened, I was caught off guard. Besides, she got up by herself, saying she was fine, and then she left." Rhonda finds her tone more defensive than she likes.

Justin's voice rises. "That doesn't mean she didn't hurt herself! Did you walk her to the car or watch to make sure she made it okay?"

Her body tenses, and she continues to stare into the windshield. She knows she could have done more to help Liz as he suggests. Independent Liz might not have wanted that, but if Rhonda had offered— her conscience would be clear, knowing that she'd done all she could.

He cuts her thoughts short. "If someone without a disability had fallen, would you have acted the same way?"

"Justin, I think you're wrong. I believe that she may have felt babied because of her disability if I did much more. However, your challenge makes me realize that what I missed was the chance to help her get to her car. She might not have accepted, but I should have offered just the same."

He grins, breathes in, and puffs out his chest. "I'm glad you realize I'm always right."

Her lips purse as she rolls her eyes and nods, shaking off his manner, which seems to be more than a pretense of arrogance.

"Can I ask you another question, Rhonda?"

"Sure," she responds in a deflated tone.

He grasps the wheel firmly and leans forward. "Do you think you're prejudiced?"

She pauses. "I don't think so; there are just certain types of people I don't like to be around."

He loosens his grip on the steering wheel. "Ya know, I read an article the other day about unconscious biases. To summarize, it stated that the feelings we have toward groups of people can play a strong part in influencing our judgment and treatment of them along a scale from fair and equal to unfair and unjust."

She cocks her head and smiles. "I think that's called discrimination. Besides—that's a tension that's been centuries in the making."

"Precisely. My point being that we all have that some unconscious bias or UB as I call it, and we need to bring it to the surface, so we can view each person as an individual, instead of a stereotype that we've unfairly judged."

She quickly throws the implication of his challenge back. "So what's your UB?"

He scoffs. "SAs and DAs."

Her jaw drops. "What's that?"

"Smart-asses and dumb-asses."

She giggles, caught by surprise.

His rant continues, "To me it doesn't matter if your skin is white, black, or purple, or if you were born in the US or a foreign country. The folks I have little tolerance for are those who choose to be stupid—so that's my UC."

Dumfounded at his outburst, Rhonda stares out the windshield, with wisps of snow and ice in its corners. In all their meetings, she's rarely heard him swear or say negative things about anyone. In fact he never gossips, and she respects that in him. Seeing his passion on the topic, she's forced to look into the mirror of semiconsciousness; she sees her UC clearly for the first time. Finally, she whispers, "I'm not sure I can get beyond my own family issues to do that."

He arrives at her house and parks in front. He turns to her. "The past can be upsetting; however, if you want to alleviate your clients' issues, you need to push beyond your comfort zone and face their imperfections—or in the case of Liz, her physical deformities." He takes a deep breath. "Rhonda, it may force you to dig deep inside to discover what you're afraid to reveal to others."

A knife pierces her heart; she winces.

"Rhonda," he says softly, the concern evident in his voice as he rests a hand on her shoulder, "you can tell me anything, and I promise I won't judge you. I may challenge you, but I will never judge."

"I believe you, Justin. I'm just not ready yet to talk about it. When I am, we'll have the conversation—I promise."

She quickly puts on her royal blue earmuffs and exits the car, running through two inches of freshly fallen snow and up the front steps, to escape to her world of solitude. Safely inside, she watches him drive away.

She goes to the kitchen to pour a glass of wine and then walks down the hall and into her private study, across from her office. She lights the sandstone fireplace, leaning for a moment against the mantel of dark oak to reflect on the day's events. So much has happened over the past few weeks—the handicapped woman, arguing with Justin over Liz, passing out, memories of her failed marriage. Her thoughts return to Justin; she could have easily crossed the line tonight if she had mistaken his friendship for the romantic love she hoped for.

As she sits down in her charcoal leather chair and matching ottoman to enjoy the crackling fire, the pit in her stomach grows as despair overcomes her. She takes a long sip, leans back, and closes her eyes. Given her professional training, it's uncanny for her to have these feelings for Justin. It's time to address them before she does something she'll regret. She gets up and walks to the bookshelves on the back wall where she finds a blue composition notebook. On the cover is written "1979–2002". She grabs that along with her current journal, a purple composition notebook, returns to her chair, and flips the pages of the blue one until she gets to the page marked, "9/15/1981." She begins to read:

> I met Paul when I was thirteen and my family lived next door. He was the middle of five boys and exactly a year older than me. I loved him ever since we sat next to each other on the school bus. We were best friends—until SHE agreed to go out with him. We never spent time together again—and then he visited me six weeks ago.

I knew he was getting married, so I wasn't sure why he wanted to see me. While we talked and had a few drinks around the kitchen table, he confessed that he was making a mistake. I listened and tried to focus him on what he wanted for his life, the same as I always had done in the days of our early friendship.

And then he leaned forward and kissed me. I was still in love with him and had longed for that moment, but not this way. I was furious and yelled at him to make a choice—be honest and call off the wedding or go through with it and live with his decision. Hurt and angry, I stormed into the next room. I heard his footsteps start toward me, then abruptly change direction and head for the outside door. There was silence for a few seconds, and then the door slammed, and muffled footsteps went down the outside stairway.

I had one last chance to run to him, throw my arms around his neck, and tell him I loved him; but would it have made a difference? Before I could decide, I heard the whining sound of his car engine as he headed down the back alley toward the street. I ran to the window to see his face through the windshield as I peered out from above; then he drove out of my world forever.

He got married yesterday. He was always the obedient son who couldn't stand up for what he wanted but did what others though he should. Maybe someday I'll be over him and pray for his happiness.

Rhonda stops reading and reflects on how Paul and Justin are alike. They're both taken, which represents the challenge of winning the impossible. Holding on to the stem of her glass, swirling its contents, she watches red trails of wine snaking down the inside. She takes a long, thoughtful sip, savoring the faint black cherry flavor. She picks up her purple journal and writes: "Don't feed the monster!"

Focusing on her scribbled handwriting, she knows that her continual interaction with Justin is feeding her own monster, thereby sabotaging her happiness and chance for love. Despite her belief in "love at first sight," which she felt with Justin, she needs to set boundaries on her heart and her actions and only pursue relationships she has a chance of winning. For her to do that, she must change how she thinks of Justin and interacts with him.

She shakes her head and begins talking out loud. "Rhonda, the real challenge is, will you wait for someone you know you'll be happy with?"

She sets her glass on the gray square end table and watches the last of the embers slowly burn to ash. Sleep quickly overtakes her, and she begins to dream: Paul's in her apartment having a drink and bends forward to kiss her. She jumps out of his reach to circle behind the table and stand facing the kitchen cabinets. With tears streaming down her face, she orders him to face the truth. When she turns; there sits Justin.

Rhonda wakes up with a start. Wrestling with her insights from earlier in the evening, she confirms to herself that it's time to break her obsession with Justin.

8

The Peace of Forgiveness

Three weeks later, the packet of Rhonda's paperwork still sits, incomplete, on Liz's desk. She picks up a few of the pages, ready for an emotional journey into the past.

It's been a painful few weeks as she has reflected on her marriage, looking at the cause of the breakup. She always knew they were together for the wrong reasons but hoped they would become good enough friends and lovers to hold it together when things got tough. However, they were both to blame for falling in love with someone else while they were busy arguing about who was right. For Liz, it was another man; for Timothy, it was a bottle of Crown Royal. In the end, neither her encouragement for his dreams nor his concern for her physical welfare was a strong enough bond; their lack of commitment and love for each other was their undoing.

Overwhelmed by memories of a lifetime of bullying, bad decisions, and broken dreams, she quickly flips to the next section, which is designed as a timeline to review all significant life events. Although she doesn't want to be defined by her disability, she can't help blaming her shortcomings and the negative events in her life on her leg. She scans the questions while muttering to herself, "I might as well answer 'my leg' or 'my accident' for all the questions and save myself time."

She looks at her leg, bites her lip, and remembers the time her mother yelled at her when she fell while they were grocery shopping: "Get up and stop feeling sorry for yourself."

Brushing off the paper as if to ease the past, Liz reflects on each question. Suddenly, a cat jumps onto her desk and sniffs the pages.

"Hey, Ruby, does that smell good? Perhaps you need a treat."

She looks at the wet nose print on her paper, quickly shriveling the dry edges that surround it. "That's it! I'll tell Rhonda the pages got destroyed." She hoots. "The cat ate my homework!" Still chuckling, she calls Rhonda's assistant, Mrs. Taylor, and makes an appointment. She then scans her responses and sends them via email to Rhonda.

Liz wakes up late the next morning to four inches of snow on the ground, and it's still coming down. She limps downstairs to feed the cats and turns on the TV to hear the weather forecast. She makes a cup of coffee and takes it to her desk to check her email, only to discover that all her client appointments for the day have been canceled due to weather.

The TV weatherman announces, "Snow tapering off by ten o'clock this morning with gentle winds through Sunday."

She limps upstairs to change clothes. The cats are on the wood-stained windowsill, watching snowflakes flutter by. "Well, kitties, it's eight o'clock and the weatherman says it's going to stop soon. The snowplows have already gotten started, and roads should be clear by noon. That gives me plenty of time to dig out of this mess and get cleaned up for Rhonda's."

Abbey looks at Liz and then back at the falling flakes.

She pets both girls, puts on a sweatshirt and insulated pants, and goes downstairs to don the rest of her snow gear: heavy boots, winter jacket, scarf, earmuffs, and gloves. Looking out the front of the house, she's relieved that she parked in the street the previous evening, as this means she only has to make a path to her car as the landlord always takes care of plowing the back alley, provided her car isn't blocking it. She grabs the snow shovel by the front door, limps outside, and gets to work, starting at the front steps.

Liz has perfected her own method of snow removal; she stands in one place, bends over, gets a shovel full of snow, throws it over her left shoulder, then moves a step and repeats the process. Since she can't bend her legs to lift with her knees without getting off balance and falling, her back and arms do all the work. Fortunately for her, the snow banks are high enough for her to prop her crutch as she clears a path to the street.

Once the sidewalk is clear, the fun really begins: cleaning off her car. With extreme caution so she doesn't slip, she uses the same technique around her car as she did on the sidewalk. She worries that someday she may slip and fall while shoveling around her car and fears that another car—or worse yet, a plow—will run her over. Just in case, she decides to watch each driver who approaches, monitoring for their alertness of her.

Two and a half hours after she started, Liz is finished shoveling. The task takes her three times as long as the neighbor to complete. Despite her strong independence, she regrets not getting up earlier; she knows her kind neighbor to the left would have offered to help her shovel out before he went to work, cutting her time down immensely.

She walks inside her toasty apartment, her fingers so numb from her soaked, freezing gloves that she barely can feel her fingers. After doffing her snow gear, she takes a steaming hot shower and gets dressed to leave.

On her drive into the city, Liz notices freshly plowed white snowbanks along the road. She fears that she will be met with the same plight she often experiences. Snow and ice piled along the curbs and intersections can make them death traps for her; worse, handicap spaces may have been packed with snow by the plow operators because they were the only places they could find for it.

Two hours later, she turns off the interstate and is two blocks away from Rhonda's office when she spots an empty parking space between two snowbanks, each almost as high as the top of her car, near the next intersection. It looks like there's enough room to fit between them; she decides to take it, as there's no guarantee she'll find a closer space.

It takes her three tries, but eventually she slides into the space resulting in each bumper having only inches to spare before hitting the snowbanks. The curb and sidewalk surrounding the parking meter in a two-foot radius are covered with snow and ice. With no safe way to get there, she decides that getting a ticket is a lesser risk than a broken hip or back. She quickly surveys the street to find the safest path. Grabbing her purse and notebook, she opens the back door to get her crutch and locks the car. With determination, she limps to the end of the block where she safely crosses to the sidewalk. Traversing a shoveled but snowy path, she finally arrives at Rhonda's office and enters up the freshly cleared steps and into the front foyer.

Rhonda, dressed in black yoga paints and an oversized brown and black sweater, greets Liz as she returns to her office from the kitchen. "It's good to see you, Liz. I hope all has been well since we last met."

"It's been just delightful," Liz responds sarcastically. Her hip is throbbing in pain from shoveling earlier, and she's still chilled from being outside as long as she has been today.

"Come in and we'll get started," Rhonda says, ignoring Liz's tone.

Liz enters, puts down her belongings, and sits.

Rhonda faces her intently, lips tightly drawn together. "Liz, I'll get right to the point. I don't understand what you did. I reviewed your paperwork and although there are certain questions completed, most of them have either 'will explain' or ditto marks as your answer. I thought you were clear with the instructions I gave, but what you did doesn't match what I instructed."

Liz gulps at Rhonda's harsh reprimand. She protests, "I understood, Rhonda. But it didn't work for me that way; I adapted it for what I was able to get through right now. If I had to answer everything, you'd never see me again."

"That's a bit different than I'm used to."

"I've completed the section with Timothy, and I'm ready to close that chapter of my life and move on. However, it will take time for me to confront the rest."

"Okay." Rhonda draws her hand to her chin. "I'll need a few minutes to review. Mrs. Taylor made fresh coffee and corn muffins. They're in the kitchen if you want some."

A frustrated Liz slowly gets up from the couch, grabs her crutch, and heads toward the door. Can't Rhonda see how awkward it is for her to carry coffee without spilling or understand the embarrassment she feels when she drops a cup in someone else's home?

When she returns a few minutes later, she leans over and carefully sets her coffee cup on the table in front of the coach. A few drips appear on the spotless walnut brown hardwood floor. Bending down to wipe it up, she notices a trail of droplets leading from entrance door to the table.

As she turns to clean it up, Rhonda says, "Don't worry about that. Mrs. Taylor is doing the floors today, and she'll get it."

"Are you sure?" asks Liz in an apologetic tone.

"Yes, I am." She pauses and meekly asks, "Liz, I know you're capable, but would it help if I carried your coffee?"

Liz blushes with embarrassment. "I don't want to trouble you. If you have a travel mug or something with a lid that I could use, it would prevent me from spilling."

Rhonda taps her pen on her cheek as she surveys the room. "I have a better solution. How about if I move the coffeepot right over there?" She points to a small round glass-top table with a vase of silk purple hydrangeas on it, located in a corner just behind Liz. "That way you can get it when you want."

Liz's face lights up. "That would be great. Then I won't have to worry about spilling again."

"It's something I've thought of doing before to make it convenient for everyone. By next time, it should be taken care of." Rhonda writes in her notebook. She continues, "Now, on to you. My plan is to explore multiple areas to determine which obstacles are getting in the way of your life. Once you share the feelings of your past, it will have the same effect as cleaning a wound. At first it hurts; then it begins to heal. In time, you will bring closure to all areas affected this way; however, since your relationship with Timothy is what brought you to me, and that's the section you fully completed on the questionnaire, let's begin there."

"I'm ready," says Liz as she stiffens and throws her shoulders back.

"Is there anything in particular that's still bothering you about your relationship with him?" Rhonda asks as she shifts back into her chair and crosses her legs.

Liz looks down at her black boots, weathered from two years of wear and wet from the morning's walk. Then she rocks her shoulders slightly as if to shake away her feelings. "Yes, there is. I feel guilty about his death. Looking back, I realize he was on a path to self-destruction long before we met." She frowns. "My part was that I could have stopped it if I had gotten him the support he needed to turn his life around."

"I'm curious. Your responses indicate you helped Timothy in areas such as starting his music recording business. Is that correct?"

Liz looks up at Rhonda and stares intently. "Yes."

"If you helped him in those areas, why didn't you with his drinking?"

"I did by pointing out what needed to be changed, but I was determined I wasn't going to do it for him. He had a history of never making decisions, so life decided for him; then he blamed others for the way it turned out. I believe he needed to make a choice for his life and then put a plan into action to achieve it."

"Do you think he was an alcoholic?" Rhonda asks.

Liz's head jerks back. "Yes."

"What makes you say that?"

"Isn't that what it's called when a person drinks and can't function in life? Timothy got to the point where he couldn't deal with anything without first drinking a six-pack." Her checks glow at the thought of his horrific drinking binges: fits of rage alternating with complete apathy for daily tasks like shaving or bathing. What if Rhonda asks about the private details of their love life? Will she have to embarrass herself by recounting that she chose to sleep in a separate bedroom because she still wanted sexual intimacy with him, but he had no physical interest in her—not even kissing or putting his arm around her while they sat on the couch together watching TV?

Rhonda asks, "What about you?"

Her question jolts Liz back into the conversation. "Me?" Liz bends forward and asks indignantly, "What about me?"

"Your responses indicate you drank regularly. Do you believe he thought your drinking was a problem?"

"How could he?" Liz asks defensively. "I always worked and financially supported both of us." Her eyes brim with tears as she says softly, "I've always been proud that I never asked anyone to do what I wasn't willing to do myself." She sniffles. "I realize now that I betrayed that with Timothy."

She looks away for a long moment at the various paintings tastefully hung on the office walls; the one of a couple holding hands and walking near a canal with gondolas reminds her of the good times they enjoyed in their nine years together—many of which involved alcohol. She lowers her head and says, shamefaced, "A glass of wine is the only way for me to relax. It lets me pretend I'm normal and fit in, if only for a moment." The words linger on her lips. Does this make her an alcoholic?

With tears streaming and her head hung low, she continues, "I wanted him to leave; I couldn't take the pain of being with him anymore. We fought daily about him getting a job; he'd argue that making minimum wage would upset me so he didn't even try looking. The more excuses he made, the less respect I had for him. It got to the point where I nitpicked at everything. He reacted by drinking and shutting down more; it was a constant spiral downward for both of us. We had slept in separate bedrooms for the previous two years. His mistress was found at the bottom of a bottle; I eventually found relief in the arms of one of his friends. I should've helped Timothy with his addiction; instead, I put the bar too high for him to even attempt, and I watched from the sidelines as he gave up."

"Which part of that makes you feel guilty? Having an affair, or watching him fail?"

"Both. However, my greatest guilt is that I lied to him on his deathbed."

"How so?"

"When I learned that Timothy was in his final weeks to live, I sent him a letter. After reading it, he asked his best friend to get me to call him. I did. We talked and cried. Right as we were getting ready to hang up, he asked about the person I had the affair with. I denied there was any involvement between the two of us; I thought it was best to leave it alone rather than open an old wound while he only had days to live."

Liz sees Rhonda wiggle her nose and purse her lips as she goes on taking notes. *What's she thinking?* She decides it's best not to ask for fear she'll open yet another can of worms she can't contain.

Rhonda says, "Liz, forgiveness and resolution will come over time for the way you feel about Timothy. You took an important first step by telling the truth of what happened and what your responsibility was in the situation. The key is to learn from it and to react differently in the future.

"Part of the process as you examine this and other situations is to review your motives. Peace doesn't necessarily come immediately upon confession, especially when you can't seek forgiveness from the person you wronged. However, over time it will be there."

"I hope you're right."

"I want to take you back to the statement about being normal."

"Okay." Liz takes a deep breath.

"Why do you think you're not normal?"

"Isn't it obvious?" Liz stares at the floor, trying not to look at her knee and thigh.

Without hesitation, Rhonda answers, "No."

"It's my leg," Liz responds, pointing to it.

"Oh. Why does that make you think you're not normal?"

"It doesn't work as well as the other one."

"Liz, if I can ask, what happened?"

"Can we talk about it later? I'm not ready yet."

Rhonda smiles softly. "Yes, but the longer you wait, the harder it becomes. I have a few more questions about Timothy, and then I have something for you to work on before we meet again."

Liz relaxes and leans back into the couch.

"You were very honest with the questions that you answered," Rhonda says. "Is there anything you see now that you could have done differently going into the marriage with Timothy that would have strengthened it for both of you?"

Liz thinks long and hard. Finally she answers, "Not expecting him to fulfill my every need."

Rhonda cocks her head to one side. "What do you mean by that?"

"I agreed to marry Timothy for companionship. He filled a

hole in my heart that I'd had since childhood. I liked him, but I wasn't in love; I hadn't loved anyone since high school. He represented the opportunity to be with someone versus no one. I never wanted to be alone; yet, ever since I was separated from my sister as a child, I have been."

"What happened?" Rhonda asks, surprised.

Liz looks down at her semi-dry boots and feels the coolness on her toes. "I was given up for adoption at the age of four. It's probably wrong to look at it this way, but the events surrounding my adoption and early childhood made me believe that it wasn't possible for me to have a lasting marriage and children."

Rhonda puts down her pen. "Did something happen as you grew up that made you unable to conceive?"

Liz, still torn by her decision to remain childless, recounts, "It wasn't physical. I couldn't bear the thought of bringing a child into the world, knowing they might never live with one of their parents or siblings again, as I didn't. In fact, my adopted mother never stopped reminding me that I would end up like my biological mother."

"What did that mean?" Rhonda asks with a frown.

Liz props her chin on one fist and looks upward. "Probably more than I could understand at such a young age. The only thing I recall is that she would say it in the same judgmental breath when she talked about my mother having more than five husbands."

Sensing that Rhonda will press for more details than she cares to recount, she puts on her best annoyed face, biting her lower lip, pulling on her earlobe, and wincing. She studies Rhonda to see if it worked. It must have; Rhonda is flipping through previous pages of her notes. Noticing the intensity in Rhonda's face as she stares up from her notepad, Liz braces herself for more interrogation about her family choices.

"Going back to Timothy, do you believe that maybe you were searching for something else and mistook it for companionship with him?" asks Rhonda.

Partially relieved, Liz relaxes at the direction Rhonda is steering with her question. She tilts her head. "I have at times, but I don't know what. The hole seems to never get filled; companionship and love worked for a while, and then I had the hole again. Logically, if the hole was companionship, why wasn't my relationship with someone enough to make me happy?"

"Liz, you may hate me for this, but I have to ask: do you love yourself?"

How can Liz respond to that question without appearing egotistical or conceited, as her mother used to describe her? She chooses her words thoughtfully. "I was taught that is selfish; you are to put others first in life."

Rhonda looks her squarely in the eyes. "Liz, what I mean is do you realize that you're very special and you deserve to be loved, not only by those around you but by the most important person in your life—*you*?"

As she contemplates Rhonda's words, she's moved. It's been decades since someone has expressed similar sentiments about her. The last time she can recall was when she was in her early twenties; her parents came to visit and took her to dinner. As they dropped her back to her apartment, her father expressed his pride over her accomplishment in working full-time and getting a degree—both done without their money or support.

Liz is pulled back to the present at the sound of Rhonda clearing her throat. "In those terms, I'm not sure I do realize that," she says softly, a bit chastened.

"Self-love is about getting in touch with yourself, your well-being, and your happiness. Once you achieve that, then you can push through any limiting beliefs you have and live a life that's filled with happiness and joy, despite life's circumstances. So let me ask again: do you love yourself?"

Liz lowers her head, closes her eyes, and shakes her head from side to side as she answers, "No."

"Do you believe this is connected in any way to the story about your leg that you keep avoiding?"

Liz inhales deeply. Although she knows it had to happen, she hates Rhonda for continuing to prod about her leg. If she answers truthfully, the floodgates will open and her past will come rushing out, like water through a broken dam, drowning her and others in the sea of regrets that fills her life. She exhales, opens her eyes, and nods in agreement.

Liz watches Rhonda take notes as her tears begin to flow. What will Rhonda think of her when she knows the truth of her accident?

Rhonda presses on. "Putting everything we've said today aside, I want you to summarize what's in your heart right now."

Liz clenches her fists. "It aches in some areas, and it's empty in others." She looks stoically at Rhonda.

"Liz, you need to let go of what's holding you hostage. It's in releasing the truth that you reconcile past events. Letting emotions naturally detach leaves you in peace."

"If I knew how to do that, I would," she pleads.

"It's not easy, but I'm confident we'll get there," says Rhonda.

"By answering the questions?" Liz asks.

"That's where it begins."

Liz scrunches her face. "There's so much, it's going to take years to write."

"Let's put the questions aside and focus on the main events that give you the greatest heartache," Rhonda gently suggests.

"It hurts to go there," Liz says, with a twinge of fear.

"What's it worth to be at peace with your deepest pain and fears?"

Priceless, Liz thinks. Out loud she says, "You have a good point."

Rhonda rustles the stack of papers on her lap. "I can tell from your answers that you've already begun this; however, I want you to put a laser focus on it. When something upsets you, I need you to track your feelings to what exactly causes you to react. For instance, when I think of cooking for others, I get upset. When I explore it further, I realize I'm not upset because I have to cook; what upsets me is the memory that as a young woman, I could never cook what I wanted. My mother was a control freak who needed to be in charge of everything. Now maybe that's not the best example, but to me it makes sense of why I don't want to cook; I saw it as a chore, rather than an expression of creativity and helpfulness."

"I understand," Liz says.

"The key to this working is identifying when you are in the midst of an emotional reaction to the past. Begin by noting what caused the emotion. Then separate it from the present, rather than burying your feelings along with your memory. Doing this will keep you from getting trapped in the rabbit hole leading to nowhere."

Liz smiles and nods in agreement.

"Great!" Rhonda says. "Now, one more thing. I'm giving you a notebook, and I want you to record when you get upset or highly emotional over something. Think of it as a sort of trigger journal. This will help you identify destructive feelings that we can work to remove. Then you will be able to develop the self-love I was referring to."

"Does that mean I don't have to answer the questions anymore?" Liz asks.

"Not for now. However, we'll come back to them at some point."

Rhonda goes to her desk and gets a yellow composition book, walks back, and hands it to Liz. "When you get upset, simply jot down what happened, when it occurred, how you felt, and what you did in response. Then periodically, we'll discuss what you note and identify what life choices you may want to start making differently."

Rhonda hesitates, "Do you have any questions?"

Liz reflects; she has hundreds but doesn't want to risk asking any of them for fear it will open up another part of her past that she doesn't want to talk about. She refocuses on why she came to Rhonda in the first place—to make the pain of her past disappear. Screwing up her courage, she says, "Actually, I do have one. I mentioned that when I was with Timothy, he filled the emptiness in my heart, and then it was empty again. Since that's always been there, is there something wrong with me?"

"I don't think so, Liz. I believe we all have the same emptiness, or 'hole' if you will, at some point in our lives. What matters is whether you seek to fill it internally or externally. When you choose an external source, like a person or an addiction to something like alcohol or food, it's bound to backfire and leave you sad or disappointed."

Liz bites her lip, studying Rhonda intently.

"Your emptiness can only be filled by you, and what fills it is uniquely different for each of us," Rhonda adds. "I mentioned self-love. There are many definitions for it, but I believe it's the foundation on which each of us develops our own inner strength. You've probably heard that you can't love others if you don't love yourself?"

"Yes."

"By the time we next meet, explore why you don't love yourself."

Isn't it obvious? It's my leg! Liz thinks. She responds simply, "I will."

Rhonda smiles. "Liz, are you clear with what you need to work on at this point?"

Liz summarizes: "Yes. I need to identify those events in my past that cause me to react emotionally and record everything I can about them in my journal. While I'm at it, I need to explore why I feel the way I do about myself."

"Exactly." Rhonda nods and adds, "Also, be sure to track your feelings back to the original event that caused them, not the event you are reacting to. It's most likely the memory of the past that prevents you from moving forward."

Liz stands up, puts on her coat, and grabs her belongings. "Rhonda, I'm glad you forced me to work through Timothy, even if I didn't enjoy it at the time. Now with that out of the way, I'm confident I can concentrate on the bigger issues, like fixing my business."

Rhonda pierces Liz's stare. "Although you're making good progress, remember we have a long road ahead, and it will get more difficult before we reach the end."

"You're telling me this for a reason?"

"Well, sorta. Once progress is made, some people think they can go it alone the rest of the way; however, changing one's life direction doesn't work like that. The best results are gained when you follow through with recommendations steps until the end goal is met. The key to accomplishing this is open and honest communication."

"Hmm. Thank you for explaining that, Rhonda. I'm going to journal a bit tonight, so I'll email you if I run into any problems."

"You can also call my cell anytime. Enjoy your weekend!"

9

Wear Clean Underwear and Tell the Truth

Liz is standing in front of the steps outside Rhonda's office when she notices the snow quickly turning to rain as droplets of melting ice accumulate around her boots. She sighs in disgust, hating the weatherman for being wrong. How is she going to get safely home? The roads will become slick very quickly given the current weather conditions. Limping to her car, she comes up with the plan to get a hotel room in the area and work on her journal; rather than risk landing in a ditch or getting in an accident.

She reaches her car, still sandwiched between mile-high snowbanks, and instinctively looks at the windshield. "Phew! No ticket. It's my lucky day!"

Liz calls to ask her neighbor to feed the cats, and he agrees. Then she begins to drive toward a hotel that's near Rhonda's office. Determining the key essentials for her emergency stay over, she throws caution to the wind of her mother's warning to always wear clean underwear—since she only needs a toothbrush and a few other toiletries—so she looks for a drugstore. Besides, who's going to know she didn't change her underwear? Certainly not her mother.

Located at a busy stoplight intersection, there's a drugstore to her right, adjacent to a pizza parlor and surrounded on the other three corners by various fast food places. She pulls in the entrance and drives to the front, furious to find the two handicapped spots filled—one with snow, the other with shopping carts. The next open spot is four rows back. Remembering the driver who told her that parking a few spaces over wouldn't kill her; she hopes he was right and that she can walk safely in the sleet. She opens the car door, struggles to get her feet acclimated to the ground, and then carefully balances to get out of the driver's seat. She grabs her purse and steps aside to open the back door. Removing her crutch, she shuts the door, puts her arm in the cuff, and begins to limp forward. Immediately she steps into a puddle choked with melting snow and ice. She shrieks, "Shit! I totally missed that!"

She reminds herself to be more aware of her surroundings; she could easily slip and fall. She shivers, debating whether she should park somewhere else, but decides it would take too long to move the car, and there's no guarantee she'll find a better space. So she assumes the position: head down, crutch firmly in hand, and eyes watching every step. She veers to the left to avoid the large puddle and then forges ahead.

Once inside, she dries her feet and crutch tip as best she can on the black rubber mat directly in front of the entrance, and walks toward the shopping carts immediately to her right. As she pulls out a cart, she drops her purse in the front and her crutch—arm cuff down—along the side. Slowly making her way past the cosmetics and into the travel section, Liz never takes her eyes off the floor, which is a minefield of wet spots that could easily send her tumbling at any moment. All items safely in her cart, she heads back to the register and gears up to do something she hates: speak up.

"Did you find everything you needed tonight, ma'am?" The cashier has bleached blond hair and dark roots.

"Actually, I'd like to see the manager, please," Liz requests.

The clerk shouts over the intercom, "Code thirty-two at the front register, please, code thirty-two." Liz pulls her cart to the side while other customers pay for their merchandise. A few moments later, a Hispanic man in his mid-thirties with a stocky frame, short, straight hair, and matching black eyes approaches from the photo counter in front of the candy and cigarette aisle near the register.

"Hello, ma'am. I'm the manager." He looks at her crutch and the items in her cart and asks with a touch of annoyance in his voice, "What can I help you with tonight?"

She smiles and says, "Sir, when I came in, there were no handicapped parking spaces available. One is filled with snow and the other with shopping carts, so it was difficult for me to come into the store."

He looks out front and says dismissively, "We can't control what our patrons do."

Her jaws clench. "Maybe you can at least speak to the company that clears the lot and ask them to put the snow in another spot. You can also educate your patrons to obey the signs."

With tightly gathered eyebrows, he answers, "If I did, they would never shop here again."

Years of pent-up frustration come rushing out. "And you think I will?"

"That's your choice," he says, folding his brown arms across his chest.

Liz throws up her hand in frustration as her voice rises. "Do you even care that you're losing business from people who need those spaces to shop here?"

He scans the aisle between her and the back of the store. "I don't see a lot of disabled people in my store, so I doubt that's true."

She clenches her left fist. "Maybe you're not getting those

customers because they're going to more accommodating stores. It doesn't take much; just reserve a few more spaces for people like me."

His blank stare meets hers. "There is nothing more I can do," he says with finality.

"Really?" Liz grabs her purse and crutch and quickly limps toward the door, leaving the cart with merchandise by the counter.

"What about your items?" the young cashier calls out.

Liz throws a glance over her shoulder and yells, "Sell them to someone who needs your products more than I do." She then pushes her left shoulder into the front door to open it, uses the tip of her crutch to keep it open, and storms out.

Lizzy, be careful and slow down, she tells herself.

Somehow she gets to the car safely, despite her rage, and opens the back door, throws her crutch in, and slams the door shut. She yanks open the driver's door, tosses her purse to the other side, and plops into the driver's seat. But after the car starts, she suddenly lets go of the wheel to wait until she's calmed down. *No accident getting to the car; let's not have one on the road.* She leans back, closes her eyes, and takes a deep breath. Will Rhonda be pleased she finally spoke up? Just then she's startled by a knock on her window.

Liz jolts upright to a face peering at her: a man's brown eyes, dark complexion, and black and gray hair, dimly lit by the overhead lights. She rolls the window down and asks in a calm manner if she can help him.

He smiles and says, "I heard you back there."

"I'm so sorry," she says, turning red. "I shouldn't have made such a scene."

"I disagree," he says. "You have a right to be angry. If more people like you would speak up, maybe things would change. What's your name?"

She sees he's wearing a brown trench coat and a top hat and assumes him to be about her age. She gulps. "I'm Liz."

Leaning on her car door, he confidently says, "Liz, I'm Jim. I suggested to the manager that he immediately resolve the situation by getting his employees to clear the carts from the handicapped spaces. Then I left my purchases behind too!"

Dumfounded, she stammers, "Aa-aah, I never thought of that. I'm so accustomed to it that I only think of enforcing the signs. But your way is so much better!"

He smiles. "That's your blind spot. When we're used to solving a problem a particular way, it's often difficult to see other solutions."

"I'm glad you shared that, Jim. Thank you. I'm gonna try that next time and see what happens."

"You're most welcome, Miss. Liz. Now, make it a great evening," says Jim.

Extending her left hand, she shakes his, and he leaves.

Taking one last look at the handicapped parking spaces, just outside the front entrance, she sees the store manager, dressed in a brown coat and gloves, hands on hips, looking up at the sign, down at the carts, and then up again. He collects the carts and pushes them toward the store. She's in awe; realizing that getting someone to do something they resist may depend entirely on how the request is made. Liz drives away anxious to tell Rhonda about the incident; a few minutes later she arrives at a hotel.

Driving up to the brightly lit lobby, she's worried there won't be handicap parking and she'll have to repeat the drugstore parking lot escapade. Luckily, she finds an open and plowed handicapped-accessible spot just outside the covered awning for the loading zone. Beside the entrance door is the next best thing: an adjacent bar, where she can have a drink and relax from her stressful day.

After checking in, Liz heads to the bar through an inside entrance from the hotel and orders a cabernet sauvignon. She scans the dark burgundy and walnut colored room and notices a fireplace off to the left, with a few overstuffed black chairs and gray end tables nearby—the perfect spot to hide and write without interruption.

A few minutes later, as she's deep in thought with the journal on her lap, the bartender quietly places her drink on the table next to her. Staring at the blank pages, she cringes at the thought of recalling her past yet again; but then she recalls Rhonda's insistence that writing about it can take her pain away. Liz begins scribbling bullet points that recap her day, according to Rhonda's instructions to track her reactions back to the feelings associated with them.

She sips her wine and stares into the orange and yellow glowing flames of the electric fireplace as if it were revealing her past. Tears sting her eyes as she writes:

> I was ten when I stole a Boston cream donut from my aunt's house. I took one bite and spit it back into the bag because it was spoiled. Then I hid the bag in the wood stove in the kitchen. I wonder if she ever knew it was me.
>
> I was thirteen and it was four days after my first hip surgery. Mom and Dad brought me a bouquet of flowers—pink roses with orange and yellow gerbera daisies. When I asked why they hadn't visited me the day before, they remained calm as they told me Grandpa had died and they were at his funeral. I cried so hysterically that the nurses gave me extra sedation so I would sleep. Ten days later, I returned home in a body cast; the summer passed painfully slow without Grandpa to laugh and play with. He and the cats were my only friends. After that, I had only the cats.

Liz puts her pen down. She makes the connection between lying about the donut, her parents lying about her grandpa's death, and her lying to Timothy on his deathbed; they're all about being deceitful, even if for a good reason. But what does that have to do with her leg? Instantly, she has her answer. To be honest means she would have to break her promise with her sister, Carla, and tell the truth about how the accident happened.

Liz has a fuzzy recollection of the night she and Carla made their secret pact. They were in their early twenties and had been drinking, somewhat heavily. She seems to recall that Carla confessed that she had pushed Liz while they were in the hayloft, which is what caused her to fall. She was in horror; how could her bigger sister have done such a thing?

More drinks followed with outbursts of anger mixed with sobs and slamming doors. Within hours, Liz had decided that to avoid hurting more people, they should continue telling the story as the family had told it for years: that Liz had missed a step and fallen down the ladder. They sealed their agreement with more drinking—until Liz passed out.

In the morning, she woke to an empty apartment and the worst hangover she ever had, along with doubts about Carla's confession. What she remembered from the night before was consuming massive shots of tequila, which is not Liz's friend, as well as watching sci-fi movies while playing a game of Clue. All those factors coupled together would explain how Liz came up with the crazy tale that her "sister did it in the barn."

Although her heart and head yearned to know the truth; they were at opposite ends of the spectrum; her head believed Carla's confession; but her heart couldn't accept it as the truth. From that day forward, she vowed never to ask Carla to recount it. Instead, her heart prevailed; Liz continued to live and tell the story of her accident as it had been pieced together since early childhood.

Continuing to stare into the fire, she changes the direction of her thoughts and focuses instead on what she believes is the true issue causing her agony—her leg. First, she visualizes the day she was walking as an eight-year-old to the milk parlor while the barn cats followed her. She yelled to the sky, "What's wrong with me?"

Then she heard a booming voice, "It's your leg," as the cats rubbed against it, meowing as if to acknowledge her pain.

As the fire roars, Liz recalls one heartbreaking memory after another. Tears run down her cheeks. She brushes them aside with her arm, but not before one drips on the page, causing the blue ink to blur her words. She takes a break and turns her attention to the bartender, who is busy brandishing a cocktail shaker over his shoulder while talking to patrons. From his profile she can see the flashing whiteness in his eyes and teeth as his wide smile shows off both, in stark contrast to his black skin and blacker band collar shirt and dress pants.

He serves the drinks and scans the room; he points to her glass and then to the bottle of wine. She gives him a thumbs-up and watches him pour another glass and bring it over. As he scoops up her empty and heads back to the bar, Liz returns to her journal.

A few minutes later, she is startled when a tall medium-built man with sandy brown hair and hazel eyes, wearing a gold university class ring on his right hand, points to a nearby chair. He asks, "Do you mind if I share the fire with you?"

Slightly irritated, Liz lets her native politeness prevail. "No, of course not." Then she pointedly returns to her writing, wiping away any remaining evidence that she had been crying. She can feel his stare and finally looks up.

He smiles gently and asks, "Are you a writer?"

"No," Liz says, annoyance in her voice.

"Perhaps you should be," he says obliviously. "You sure make quick work of that notepad."

Realizing his interest is not in the fire but in picking her up, she studies him closely. Flattered at his attention and attracted by his looks, she pauses in her work for a moment. With a half smile she says, "Maybe someday." Then she closes her yellow journal and says sweetly, "I'm Liz Harris, and you are?"

"I'm Joe Clark. Pleased to meet you, Liz."

She turns slightly in her chair to face him more directly. "Are you staying here tonight, Joe?"

"No, I live nearby. I didn't have anything to eat in the house, so I stopped by for a few drinks and a bite to eat," he says as he swirls a shot of Jack and Coke around the ice in his glass. He takes a sip and sets it on the table between them.

She scans his hands for a wedding band, relieved when she doesn't see one. She dismisses further thoughts of his attachments and instead yields to a keen interest in getting to know him. "Well, Joe, what do you do for a living?"

His face lights with a smile, and his chest puffs out. He responds, "I'm a contractor specializing in the restoration of older homes."

"I bet that's fun," Liz says and means it. "What do you find is the most rewarding part of your job?" With that question, they move headlong into further conversation that quickly moves from their respective careers to their family heritage, personal interests in restoring furniture and gardening, and then ending with their beliefs on religion and politics—which they both agree should never be part of family get-togethers, in order to avoid the fights that naturally ensue.

Several hours later, a mesmerized Liz is entranced with her newest acquaintance, a charming and witty man, one of the few she's been able to engage with who doesn't talk about sports or drone on about himself and his accomplishments.

The bartender interrupts her reverie. "Last call! Can I get either of you anything from the bar?"

Joe looks at their empty glasses, smiles at Liz, and asks, "Do you want another drink?"

Her homework—and leg—long forgotten, she focuses on her current situation: talking and drinking with a man at a hotel bar that she's barely met. What's next? Will he suggest they take their discussion and nightcaps to her room? Or should she end things here at the bar, while she is safe and before she does something she'll regret in the morning?

"No, thank you. I've had my limit for the night," she replies.

"Please bring me the tab for both of us," Joe tells the bartender.

Liz blushes. "You don't need to do that."

"I've had a good time talking with you. I don't meet many women who talk about something besides shopping or their ex. Besides, it's the least I can do since I interrupted your evening of writing."

She's falling for the dimples in his cheeks as he smiles and his eyes twinkle.

He slides a gray business card with black print onto the table near her empty glass. In a manner that seems a bit rehearsed, he says, "Call me if you know someone who needs work on their house"—he winks—"or if you are in town again. Maybe we can meet for drinks or something else."

Does "something else" mean a movie, dinner, or having sex? Before she can decide, his words quickly cut her thoughts. "I can escort you out if you'd like."

"Sure," she blurts.

Liz quickly recoils as she's brought to the point of truth: he doesn't know about her leg—they didn't talk about it and he didn't see her walk. Will her having a limp make a difference in his interest in her, as it always seems to with others? Will she have to explain what happened? Will his smile turn to a look of shock or disgust as she has frequently seen in other potential suitors?

Considering the late hour of the night and with very little time to explain everything, she decides it's a conversation best left for another day. Tonight she'll go to her room without him accompanying her;

next time, she'll tell him about her leg, if not somehow in advance. In an apologetic tone, she says, "Oh, I forgot. I've got to send a few emails while I have good reception on my phone. Go ahead, since you have to drive home and all. I don't want to keep you."

She extends her hand along with her business card. "It was fun talking, and I'll keep your services in mind. And next time I'm in the area, I'll call and perhaps we can meet."

He kisses her hand. "Good night, Liz."

Caught off guard, she hesitates. "Good night, Joe."

He leaves through the front door to the outside. She journals a few entries from tonight, mainly to make the best use of the next several minutes; thereby giving him ample time to get away before she heads to the hotel lobby.

Ten minutes later, she gathers her belongings and limps through the doorway into the hotel. Remembering the never-purchased toothbrush, she decides to ask the front desk rather than wait on housekeeping at this later hour. She limps toward the counter and stops dead in her tracks as she sees Joe turn from the reservation agent and face her.

She's breathless from fear. Why is he here? What she's going to say when she has to walk in front of him?

His face beams with surprise as he walks over. He says, "I just left a message for you to meet me at nine for breakfast."

Before she can respond, his eyes shift from her face to her crutch. His look turns somber, and he cocks his head and asks, "What's the crutch for?"

She lowers her head. "I use it to walk."

All expression and color drain from his cheeks. After a long pause he responds, "Oh."

Instantly, her heart sinks to its lowest level, as she knows what's going to follow. She's heard that "Oh" response countless times, and it always means one of four things: disappointment, embarrassment, being uncomfortable with her disability, or the biggest—she'll never see him again. Experience has taught her that he, like the others, can't handle her truth—and some days neither can she.

A woman taps her shoulder from behind and curtly asks, "Are you in line for check-in?"

Liz apologizes and awkwardly limps a few feet to the left while every inch of her body feels his stare.

The woman rushes past with rolling luggage and high heels loudly clicking on the marbled gray and white tile floor.

Liz turns to Joe and sheepishly says, "Breakfast would be great. I'll see you then?"

With eyes fixated on her crutch, he says, "Sure. I left details at the front desk."

"Great. I look forward to it."

Joe leaves as she waits in the middle of the lobby. Once he's out of sight again, she limps forward, gives the desk clerk her room number and asks for a toothbrush and toothpaste.

The desk clerk returns with the items, hands her a sealed envelope marked with the hotel's return address, and says, "Ma'am, I was just going to call you and let you know this was here. It was left by the man you were just talking with."

She boards the elevator alone, her leg always seeming to get in the way. Pressing the button for the tenth floor, she whispers, "Maybe this time it won't."

The next morning Liz wakes with thoughts of the previous evening. She checks her phone for the time and begins to panic. It's ten after eight and she only has fifty minutes before she meets him. Maybe her Mom was right; a girl always needs clean underwear.

Forty minutes later she arrives in the lobby to see that the three-foot round wall clock above the front desk reads 8:52 a.m. She perches on a brown high-back chair near the bar entrance, trying to calm her racing heart before he walks in.

Five minutes pass. She stares at her black boots, now dry and lined white by salt residue from last night's snow and ice. What else is Joe going to ask about her leg? How much detail will she need to go into?

Another five minutes go by, and another ten. The clock reads 9:12 a.m.

She rereads the note he left her, clinging to the words that he'll appear: "Liz, I'd love to see you for breakfast. Please meet me in the lobby at nine o'clock. I'll be the one wearing a smile and holding memories of a great evening. If it doesn't work for your schedule, you can leave a message on my cell. Hope to see those deep blue eyes of yours then! ~Joe"

Liz pulls her cell phone from her purse; no texts or missed calls. She can excuse his running late because the roads are a mess from last night's storm, but not to call and tell her he's been detained is simply inconsiderate. When they meet, she'll find a way to diplomatically let him know so he can be mindful of it for the future.

She clicks on the camera app on her phone and takes a selfie. Opening the Facebook app, she posts the picture with the comment, "Waiting on a new friend."

Within minutes, there are several "likes" and a comment from Carla. "Sis, what are you doing at a hotel at 9 a.m.? I hope he was worth it! LOL!"

Liz laughs as she replies to Carla's post: "Time will tell. At least he can hold a conversation beyond the normal pickup lines that we single women hear. Will tell you more later."

She looks at the clock, which now reads 9:35 a.m. Worried, with her head hung lower than normal, she limps to the front desk and asks the clerk in a strained voice, "Excuse me. Has anyone left a message for Liz Harris?"

"Not since I arrived at six this morning," the clerk says.

Liz thanks her and heads in humiliation toward the elevator.

The silver-mirrored doors are just beginning to close, so she sticks her crutch in between to stop them and looks up. She whispers, "Please, open up so I can get out of here." The doors spring open; she gets in and pushes the button for the tenth floor.

Behind the walls of steel, Liz breaks down and weeps bitterly. Fortunately for her, the elevator stops on her floor without anyone else boarding. She stumbles down an empty corridor leading to an emptier room. Swiping the door lock with her card key, she enters and collapses on the bed, crying herself to sleep.

A few hours later, a knock at the door wakes her; she bolts up. The clock reads 12:01 p.m. Did he come back to meet her?

She gets her crutch and limps to the door. Squinting out the peephole, she sees a woman's distorted face: puffy brown cheeks with black hair, black eyes darting to the side, wearing a white pant suit covered with a green apron; it's the housekeeper. "Give me ten minutes and I'll be out," Liz shouts.

The woman responds in Spanish, and Liz answers back, "Gracias." Hoping that her response was appropriate, she has a fleeting thought to someday brush up on her high school Spanish.

An hour later, she is driving home and still reeling from her latest dose of reality. She reviews the previous evening; how did her heart get so far off track to fall for a guy who lets a little thing like her crutch prevent him from meeting her? After the night they had at the bar, getting to know each other, they should have been able to talk about her leg so he understood her condition before deciding to run off. But that never happened—she never talked about it.

Always fearful about people's reaction to her, she never knows if it's best to bring her leg up in conversation or let others ask if and when they want to. And in the case of Joe—she waited an hour or so too long.

She recalls being mortified when a former boyfriend was asked by one of his friends if she could have sex. After that, she thought they were both jerks. Her seriousness turns to a short giggle as she realizes that no matter what, men always seem to have one thing on their minds.

Turning serious again, Liz pushes beyond past events that made her feel rejected. She sets the cruise control, and within moments, her memory is of playing at recess as a child. She daily wandered from group to group trying to fit in while kids would either laugh and point—or worse, mock her as she walked by. Despite the game at hand, she was never invited to play or picked for teams.

Reflecting on Rhonda's advice, she digs deeper and sees a pattern. The more she got picked on, the more she threw herself into schoolwork, trying to be accepted for her academic accomplishments. She never wanted to be smart; she only wanted to be liked and accepted for who she was—not rejected for what she couldn't do.

Her thoughts return to the previous night: relaxing with Joe in front of the roaring fire and deep into conversation. How would Rhonda suggest she bring her leg into the conversation with Joe before things went too far? And then it hits her. She semiconsciously hides the issue, pretending it doesn't exist. Her spirit sinks as she realizes that Joe and probably others question her level of honesty and genuineness when she does this.

Within minutes of turning off the interstate she pulls into the back alley, parks the car, and dials Rhonda's number to book a time to see her the following week.

10

Do as I Say

Rhonda arrives a few minutes early to the Coco's, where she's arranged to meet Justin before her appointment with Liz. She's fortunate to get her favorite table near the back; she often loses it to other customers, who also seem to prefer that section of the café. Looking farther, she wonders who Justin is with as she spots him chatting with two women near the kitchen. The older one is wearing a long black coat, and the younger one has a blue ski jacket and holds a matching knit cap. He escorts them to Angela, the barista at the front register, and then approaches Rhonda's table with a bowl of vanilla ice cream on top of a freshly baked cherry tart. He sets it in front of her and sits down.

"Nice to see you've expanded the menu with one of my favorites," she says with a smile.

"Yep! So far it's been a hit with everyone."

"That's great," she says and then pauses. "I hate to be nosy, but who were those women?"

He winks and grins. "C'mon, Rhonda, don't lie. You love to be nosy. The young lady, Chloe, is a recent high school graduate working with the local rehabilitation office. Today she's doing a job shadow to see if hospitality might be a career for her. If so, there's funding for on-the-job training to teach her the skills she needs. The other woman is her job coach—you know, from the card you gave me."

"Ohh," she says, things starting to click. "I forgot about that."

He rolls his eyes. "Can't you remember anything that's not associated with your Facebook posts?"

"Hey, there are worse people than me! At least I don't text during a dinner date like a lot of people I see. Anyway, let me know what happens."

"I will. Now what can I help you with?"

"Liz will be joining me shortly. I may want to invite you over before we end to ask her to do something."

"What's that?" he asks

"I know you've taken the same Visionary Course that I did, so I'd like you to tell her about it and ask her to attend."

He huffs. "I don't understand. You've been a course mentor, and you're working with Liz, so why can't you do it?"

She sighs. "Justin, you know how obsessive I am when it comes to work and things being done a certain way."

He grins. "You might say that."

She leans into her chair, staring intently at him. "Well, rather than get on a new methodology, I want to stay on track with the tools I've given her, and I believe the course could greatly speed up our work."

"Go on," he says with a nod.

"Liz mentioned that she adapted the way she completed some work I gave her—even after my explicit instructions." Her lips purse tightly.

"Ha!" he says with a laugh, bending forward with folded hands. "Knowing your compulsive nature, I bet that really infuriated you."

She studies his arms: sleeves rolled up to his elbows and a black and blue checked shirt dusted with flour up to his shoulder. Then she looks deeply into his brown eyes. "More than you know. But later, when I was considering the difficulty she has walking with her shoe lift, I realized that she's been adapting things her whole life; since that's the way she sees the world, I can't expect her approach to be the same as mine."

Justin pops out of his seat and says, "I'll be back in two minutes!"

As he hurries to the kitchen, Rhonda digs into her ice cream and cherries, pulling most of the crust to the side of her plate. She hopes he's not going to come back and talk about his wife.

He returns carrying several colored poster papers. Flashing a victorious smile, he lays them on the middle of the table; each page is a collage of magazine pictures.

"I remember that homework assignment! I hated it," Rhonda says with a groan.

He winks again. "That's a coffee conversation for another day. Since you're familiar with the assignment, these are my beliefs which have haunted me for years. Here's an example of what I refer to as 'I'm a failure.'"

She scrutinizes the pictures in order to draw her own conclusion: a man pushing a cart of suitcases and boxes down the street, an ankle chained to a pole, a headless mannequin, and a chain link fence with one side open blowing in the breeze. Rather than comment on her interpretation, she asks, "How can you say that, Justin? You've had a successful military career and now own a business that's growing. Plus, you have a gorgeous family. It's a nice life; you're far from a failure."

He bows his head. "First, all is not what it seems. I've hinted that things are bad at home; I just haven't told the extent of my misery. I love my kids and I can't live without them, but my marriage is in shambles, and I don't understand why I couldn't make it work."

"Oh, Justin, I shouldn't have said anything about your personal life. It isn't any of my business."

"It's not that, Rhonda. My heart aches all the time, and I don't know what to do. If I leave her, I'll lose my kids; if I stay, I'll lose me."

She pauses. "As a friend, I'll be there for you."

He looks at her gratefully. "Thank you. I need your help saving my marriage."

She winces at the tug in her heart. "I'm not a marriage counselor."

"I know, but you're my best friend and the only person I can confide in."

Rhonda, caught off guard, isn't sure that she's ready to be his confidant on this matter. She says, "If that's what you want, I'll do what I can."

"Thank you, Rhonda. I won't ask much—just that you understand what I'm going through." They both stare at the table; she feels the gravity of the moment. He wipes a tear from the corner of his left eye. "Back to how this worked for me. When I did what the instructor advised—put 'seems like' in front the belief that I'm a failure, and then read the words—it seemed to ease my emotions over it. Over time, I've been able to replace the phrase with more positive statements like 'Success will find me today.'"

"That's great work in such a short time," Rhonda says. "As a mentor, I've learned that everyone has similar beliefs running through their minds as if they were factual, when in actuality they're false perceptions of our reality." She looks back at the pictures. "Can you tell me what these mean?"

"Okay." He points to a leashed dog walking on a treadmill. "This represents how I feel held back. I'm always trying to go forward but never advancing. The result is that I'm tired, frustrated, and ready to give up." He then points to a bare-chested man who is breathing fire and carrying a briefcase near a swimming pool.

"In this one, I think of a guy who is on the brink of both success and danger—a calculated risk-taker."

She points to a sandcastle of a king's head with children peeking out from under his beard. "What about this one?"

"I didn't see it before, but given what I just told you about my marriage, I think it represents that I'm hiding—both from people and events in my life."

"That's understandable. You're facing tough decisions that would make most people want to run and hide."

He stares intently at the pages. "I guess my testimony that the course works is that it's helped me find the means to talk about what I couldn't express before—even if it means I blurt it out to a business associate."

His words dampen her spirits like a wet rag, downgrading her from his best friend to a mere business associate. She sighs. How long they will play their little cat-and-mouse game before she tells of her true feelings for him? Changing the focus of their conversation, although she knows the answer, she asks, "Interesting. I guess this means you're a visual learner?"

"Yep," he says

"Aah. Well, my version of your failure belief is 'I'm not pretty enough.'"

He chuckles. "Yeah, in our class we noticed that most everyone had their own version; it begins with 'I'm not' and ends with 'enough.'"

She looks at him. "So what's your story?"

Disappointment clouds his face. "I guess it goes back to my parents. When I was in high school, I ran track. Although I was good, my father only saw me race once. At the end of the meet, he said to me, 'You're wasting your life, Justin. Put your focus into something more meaningful.'"

Without thinking, Rhonda touches his hand. He pulls away. She blushes, embarrassed at her display of emotion toward him. "I'm sorry, Justin. How good were you?"

He sighs. "I placed second in state competition. Never good enough to take first, though. My coach always said it was in my head, that I was much better than the guy who beat me."

She shifts in her seat and looks out the front windows of the café onto a busy, snow-covered sidewalk. Then she looks back at him. "And what did your mom say?"

"She was too busy working and raising three sons and a daughter," he says matter-of-factly. "Besides, my father wasn't nice to her either." He folds his hands, leaning his elbows on the table, glances up and then returns his look to her. "If she disagreed with him, she put herself and her children at risk. For me, that was until I turned sixteen and began to fight back."

She changes tack. "Well, I think since you enjoy the course so much, and it's helped you in ways you never imagined, you're the best one to tell Liz about it," she says with a tone of encouragement.

"Okay," he says with a wink. "I'll let you have your way on this one, but the next is mine."

She smiles. "Great! When's the next guest night that Liz and I can come to your course?"

He looks at the calendar on the far wall and then responds, "The twentieth. It's next Saturday night. You girls can ride with me if you want. It'll make it easier for all, especially considering Saturday night is a tough time to find downtown parking."

"That's a wonderful idea, Justin."

His cheeks flush. "I really enjoy having you as a friend, Rhonda. Now, I have to get back and finish Chloe's job shadowing for the day. Flag me down when you're ready to spring the news on Liz; I should be able to spare a bit of my wit and charm." They smile, and he leaves.

She feels thrown headlong back into her late teens—different guy, different time; but still torn between being lovers and just friends. If she's not careful, her reactions will only continue the unhealthy trend of obsession she seems to have for unavailable men. Her lament fades as Liz enters the restaurant and makes her way to the table.

"Hi, Rhonda!" exclaims Liz.

"Hi, Liz." Rhonda waits while Liz leans the cuff of her crutch in the corner which keeps it standing. She winces as she slowly sits. "Are you okay?" Rhonda asks.

Liz forces a smile. "Thank you for asking. I have a lot of pain today, partly because of the weather. I'll be fine in a few minutes."

"I'm glad you called to meet so quickly after our last appointment. It sounds like you had a few discoveries with your journaling."

Liz nods. "You might say that."

"Have you completed any more questions?" Rhonda asks eagerly.

Liz hesitates. "No-o, I haven't had time."

That's okay for now, Rhonda thinks, surprised by her own compassion. "Tell me about your adventures since we last met," she says.

Liz plunges in. "It began right after I left. I decided to stay at a nearby hotel and stopped at a drugstore to get a few things first. There was no place for me to park, so I took matters into my hands and spoke to the manager about it."

"That's great, Liz! I'm pleased for you. How did you feel about it?"

Liz cocks her head. "Well, it didn't go exactly as planned. The manager told me he couldn't do anything about where customers parked their cars or where the snowplows put the snow. I reacted sort of badly. I made a scene and snapped at him, leaving behind the items I was going to purchase."

"Really?" Rhonda exclaims.

Liz grimaces. "That's probably the 'bad Lizzy' coming out. Anyway, there was this gentleman who suggested to the manager that they train their employees to focus on clearing the carts from my space. As I was leaving, it was being done. I was astonished; I never thought there were others who supported me."

"Liz, it goes beyond you. It's the right thing to do for everyone, whether they have difficulty walking or not."

"Hmm. I never thought of it that way," Liz says.

Impressed and encouraged by Liz's new behavior, Rhonda asks, "What else happened?"

"I met a guy.

"That's great!"

"Not really. He may have had potential, but things never really got off the ground."

"What happened?"

"It's complicated," Liz says sheepishly. "The short version is I sort of lied to him. And whether telling the truth would have fixed it or not, I'll never have the chance to find out if there could have been more."

"Liz, my experience is that relationships are complicated. In regards to the guy you met, there is no one thing that makes two people attracted to each other at the same time or in a manner that they stick together for a lifetime. However, a lot of little things can build a solid relationship and can even lead to love. If these are not established as cornerstones of the relationship, you have a shaky foundation that will not pass the test of time or life trials."

"What are they?" Liz asks, picking up her pen as she opens her yellow journal and presses pen to paper.

Rhonda muses, privately reflecting on her own love for Justin. "I can't speak for everyone. For me, it starts with friendship and builds from there. Respect, honor, and holding someone's needs before your own. At the end of it comes love. If you're lucky enough, you'll get someone who loves you at the same time, just as you are—so there's nothing to hide or make up."

Liz asks, "So Rhonda, does he feel the same way you do?"

Rhonda forces a smile. "I'm not sure whether he does or not. We've never talked about it."

Liz puts down her pen. "Yeah, I had my own version of that

with Jeff. After I recorded it in my journal the other night, I realized that although I poured my heart out to him, it didn't mean he wanted to hear it or was open to accept my feelings. But how can you not talk about it? Telling him may make all the difference in the world about him committing to you."

Rhonda's heart aches; but she says the words anyway. "Some situations may make things worse when you speak the truth. In my case, there's a good reason why I can't tell him."

"Oh, I get it," Liz says, more than a little snarky. "It's okay for you not to tell the truth, but you expect me to tell the truth about my leg in all situations. Sounds like you're not exactly practicing what you preach."

"I hate clichés," Rhonda snaps, her anger rising at being challenged.

"Aren't we really talking about two sides of the same coin?"

Rhonda crinkles her nose. "Very funny."

"Rhonda, with all due respect, I value your expertise and recommendations as a life coach. However, you don't know what my life has been like or what I've faced." She hesitates. "Try taking one of your shoes off and walking around like that for a week. Then you'll know just a smidgen of how my world has been and can advise on full leg disclosure, or the proper response to make when someone asks about it—because, trust me, everyone will ask."

Rhonda mentally simulates what it would be like to have Liz's walking disability. She responds defensively, "We don't always need to walk in another's shoes to empathize. Sometimes our experiences provide us with insights to understand others."

Liz listens and nods in agreement.

Rhonda says, "I'd like to take a different approach to your situation. In these conversations, since you are seeking professional advice from me as a coach, my response needs to always be on that level. What I said to you a minute ago was personal in nature, and I should have left that out of this discussion. Please accept my apologies."

"I do, Rhonda. I only ask about it because I want to be inspired by a happy ending. If you love someone, you get it back someday, don't you?"

Rhonda sits on her hands, debating what to tell Liz to give her hope. "I can't give you assurances like that. However, loving someone begins by accepting them for who they are and loving them regardless of what they do or don't do. It's wanting the best for them and loving them with all their flaws—not for what you might get from the relationship."

Rhonda heaves a deep sigh. "Start with a friendship, no expectations, and grow it from there. You'll know when the time is right to turn the friendship into something more." She pauses. "It's not only your timing but also his. When people like each other but things don't gel, it usually means one of the parties isn't ready to move ahead for whatever reason. But you have to be willing to try again and determine where and when you need to take different action. Begin by understanding what you could have done differently in your other relationships."

Waiting on Liz to respond, Rhonda begins heeding her own advice; she must change the way she thinks of Justin for her feelings to change, and it must begin today. Until now, she has been selfish—thinking only of having him in her life and not understanding what that would do to his family, his children, and his business. If she truly believes that loving him means wanting the best for him, she will have to set aside her thoughts of a romance with him. She closes her eyes and clenches her teeth.

Liz breaks into her private reflections. "Perhaps if I had said something earlier to Jeff about the feelings I had for him, I might have been the one he chose," she suggests.

"Could be, but there are no guarantees." Rhonda lifts her right index finger. "There's one thing you can count on—people aren't mind readers. If you want them to know what you think or feel, you need to tell them and be willing to handle their reaction."

Liz scrunches her face as she bites her lips. "That's just my problem: honesty that reveals my innermost thoughts and feelings. People often get offended or hurt when you're straight with them."

Rhonda shakes her head. "Honesty plays out differently in various situations. There's factual honesty, like answering the question, 'Did you walk here today?' There's emotional honesty, like telling someone you love them; and there's thinking honesty, like believing you have the right answer to a situation. Considering these, the only one that is not debatable is factual honesty. The others are your interpretation of life and circumstances."

Liz asks, "So if telling the truth would hurt someone you love more than keeping it a secret, why wouldn't you be quiet about it?"

Rhonda props her chin on her palm. "I can't answer that without knowing all the specifics. However, I do know keeping secrets can hurt both parties—maybe not immediately, but over time, guilt from the cover-up often creeps in. Or once you do reveal the truth, the other person wonders what else you've been hiding. Deception by any means is like a cancer to some; it eats from the inside out."

"Ugh." Liz rolls her eyes. "How does a person know the right thing to do?"

"I always say it this way: You have to be able to live with your decisions and sleep at night. If you can't, then find a way to resolve the issue before it becomes a bigger mess for you." Rhonda observes her with folded hands, and head bowed.

Liz is staring over Rhonda's shoulder at the wall behind her, hands folded. Softly she says, "I'm afraid of who I would hurt by pursuing the truth. I may have to die with it on my soul, rather than destroy the life of someone I love."

Rhonda lets the words sink in, quickly realizing this is not where she planned to end their discussion. Feeling like she has fourth down with her back to the end zone, she decides to punt. "Liz, before you leave, there's a conversation I want to work through with you. It may seem difficult, but it will empower you in facing your past."

Liz grimaces. "Go ahead."

"Back to the question that we started with. Since people you meet often ask questions about your leg or your crutch, I'd like you to start thinking of a possible response that leaves you feeling upbeat and positive."

"I've tried, and there's nothing that doesn't evoke pity or disgust. Why do they have to ask anyway?"

"It's our natural curiosity to figure things out. When you get a birthday present that you think is the greatest, such as jewelry, what do you do?"

"I wear it and enjoy how it makes me feel special. I have fond thoughts of the person who gave it to me."

"Try shifting the way you view what you have." Rhonda holds out her hands as if to give Liz a package. "Think of it as the greatest present you've been given, wrapped with a big red bow on top. If that were the case, how would you feel about your leg then?"

"I'd show it off." Liz pauses. "But it's not. You don't know what I've suffered or—"

"Or how your life has been affected. You're right, I don't, and neither does anyone else. However, my guess is that it could've been much worse."

Liz stares at Rhonda's arms still stretched before her and swallows hard. "I get your point, but I don't know if I can do that. There's too many bad memories and feelings related to it."

"For now, I simply ask you to try shifting your view."

"I'll give it some thought."

"Perfect. We have a few more minutes. There's one more thing I wanted to mention to you. There's a program called the Visionary Course that I think will help you work through some of your past issues. It may accommodate your personal style better than the questions I gave you. A lot of the coursework helps you see your past in a way that's similar to what we just went through: shifting your perception on your greatest present." She looks around to see if Justin is available. "It's an extremely powerful course that both Justin and I have participated in, and I've been a class mentor for it."

Liz cocks her head to the side. "Really? Why didn't you mention it before now?"

"Until you spoke about adapting my questions, it didn't come to mind. It's also something I haven't participated in for a few years, so I guess it simply wasn't on my radar. Anyway, I'm going with Justin next Saturday night as a guest to refresh on some things I learned. Would you like to join us?"

Liz's eyes widen. "I'm game for anything to get through this part of my life and move on to something new."

Rhonda claps her hands. "That's great. I'll make arrangements and will get the details to you shortly. In fact, here comes Justin now."

As if on cue, Justin arrives at their table with a young lady at his side. Her medium length brown hair is pulled back in a ponytail that bounces off her shoulders as her head slightly nods from side to side. She wears large-framed blue glasses and stands about five-foot-two.

"Chloe, I want you to meet two of our best customers. This is Rhonda and Liz," he says.

Chloe stares blankly as Rhonda and Liz extend their hands.

"It's okay, Chloe," Justin explains. "In the business world, we greet each other with a handshake."

Chloe reluctantly accepts the handshakes.

"Chloe is part of a job-study program, and I invited her to observe what goes on here for a day to see if she might be interested in working for a coffee shop," Justin says.

"Yes-s-s," Chloe says. "My j-j-job coach thinks this might be something I could d-d-do."

"Well, Chloe, working in a place like this is a great start," Rhonda says. "We hope you find the day very interesting."

"I have al-r-r-ready," Chloe says.

Liz watches as Chloe turns and hobbles away.

Justin asks, "Liz, before you leave today, can I speak to you for a few moments about something else?"

Liz answers, "Sure. We were just wrapping up."

"That's perfect," Justin says. "I have to talk with Chloe before her job coach picks her up; then I'll be back." He leaves.

Liz whispers to Rhonda, "Did you see her walk? She looks like me, except that she's considerably younger and doesn't have a shoe lift. What do you think happened?"

Rhonda smiles. "Does it matter?"

Liz blushes with embarrassment. "No, I just thought. Er, there goes that curiosity you were talking about. I guess I have it too." She laughs.

"Laughter is a great sign of recognition," Rhonda says kindly. "Well, I've got to go, and Justin should be with you shortly. I'll be in touch on the details for the course, and if it works, we can all ride together."

"Great! I'm looking forward to it."

Rhonda puts on her coat and walks to the front by the glass bakery display, where Chloe is watching Justin as he bags up an order of cookies and shows her how to ring them up on the register.

Liz notices raucous laughter as Rhonda leaves, waving to her on the way out. She then turns her attention to Justin's interaction with Chloe; she can tell by his expression that he's explaining the job of waitressing. Within minutes Justin goes in the coat closet to the left of the bakery display and returns with Chloe's coat. She walks outside to meet her job coach, and then he heads over to Liz.

Before he can sit, Liz blurts, "I wish when I was her age, people had been as helpful and accepting to me as you just were with her. Maybe if they had, I would've thought of my leg as Rhonda suggests—the greatest gift that I'd been given."

"You know, Liz, I had an accident when I was in the military," Justin says, sitting down. "People who saw it thought I should've died. I remember lying in the hospital, and whenever I started to feel sorry for myself, I would always see someone who was worse off. Yeah, I had it bad, but I knew someday I would walk again—so I figure every day I'm this side of the pavement is a blessing."

She covers her mouth, and they sit in silence for a few moments.

"Anyway," Justin starts again, "back to business. I appreciate that you can spare a few minutes."

"My pleasure. What can I help you with?" she asks with hands folded on top of the table, near Rhonda's half-empty dessert plate.

He leans forward, almost whispering as he speaks. "Since you're a human resources consultant, I need some professional advice. I know you're familiar with hiring laws and such. I really like Chloe and want to give her a chance; however, I'm not sure she can do the job, and I don't want to violate the law by doing anything I'm not supposed to."

"What position are you considering her for?" she asks, tapping her fingers on the table.

"Busing tables and washing dishes. Chloe says does this at home without a problem, but when I asked about carrying dishes from tables to the kitchen, she got a frightened look and said something like she doesn't do that well."

"I know what that feels like." Liz evaluates the floor layout: distance between the tables, the size and height of the nearby bus stand, and the twenty-some foot hallway leading beyond it to the kitchen. "I have an idea. What about getting her a serving cart she can push? Do you think that might work?"

He strokes his chin that has a slight five-o'clock shadow. "Hmm, it's very possible. We don't have one, but it would be easy enough to purchase. Maybe I can have her try it first, just to make sure she can maneuver back and forth."

She smiles. "Great idea, Justin. If she can, I think that would work, and you'll be legal."

"Perfect! Now is there anything else I need to do?"

She smiles. "For now you've met the spirit of the law by offering a reasonable accommodation for her to do the job—which is purchasing a serving cart. However, in the future, if it doesn't work, or other accommodations are necessary for her to do her job, that's when you'll want to get additional advice. Also, I'll get you a list of questions use can use for interviews and such so you don't ask the wrong thing and get in legal trouble for that."

"You've been a godsend, Liz!" He taps on the table near her outstretched hand. "I will keep you informed on what happens with her and look forward to getting your questions."

"Great! I look forward to hearing about how it works out."

Driving home, beside the piles of dirty, melting snow along the interstate, Liz lets her memories drift to a time long forgotten by many—but not her: the occasional acts of kindness she received as a kid. She can't see their faces; she only remembers the ones who made her feel accepted by their actions or their words: There was the bus driver who waited for her to sit before he drove off; the older girl on the bus who slid next to the window so she could have the aisle seat; and Mr. Snitz, her favorite teacher, who encouraged her to take college-prep classes.

Then it hits her. On many levels she's still acting as a child—being silent, sometimes petulant, and never asking for special favors because of her leg. Have things changed? Should she be treated differently? Does she want to be treated differently? Does she want someone to carry her purse or coffee?

"Yep," she says out loud. "That's exactly what I want, or maybe I just need an adult sippy cup so I don't spill."

She shifts to her familiar obsession about her leg. Although it would be pretty great to help Chloe or others so they don't have to go through the bullying and humiliation that she suffered, she still has her leg to deal with. She can't very well help others if she can't get over what's happened to her. She remembers Rhonda's advice from their most recent meeting: to track her feelings to the original event that caused them rather than the event she is reacting to.

"All righty, I'll try it now," Liz says, speaking to her burgundy purse with shoulder strap draping to the floorboard, as if it were Rhonda sitting next to her. "When people meet me, and I'm seated and talking, they don't notice my leg. When I get up and walk, either the conversation ends or I'm asked what happened and then forced to recount my accident." Her words trail into thoughts: she hears the thud from her fall, time stands still, and she experiences the accident all over again, as if she were still four years old. If only she could make the thud disappear, she wouldn't react so negatively.

She imagines Rhonda's voice retorting to ask what part of that bothers her. Liz says, "I'm afraid they're going to make fun of me because of my walk. When I meet people, they assume I've had an accident and it's temporary. When they find out it won't get better, their attitude moves toward pity or shame."

Rhonda's voice whispers in her head, *Aah! That's how you learned to perfect the skill of avoidance.*

"Rhonda! I can't believe you said that!" Liz shouts at the purse. "There are actually hundreds of reasons and thousands of people to thank for that. And by you poking, I just may have to add one more to the list." She shrieks, "Now quit!"

Wincing, Liz puts her left index finger in her ear to soothe the pain from her words reverberating in the car. Then, silence.

She is encouraged. She bites her lip and speaks aloud again. "Rhonda, it's a stretch to fathom I can answer all of your questions, and yet I feel if I don't, I'll never resolve my issues. Either way, I'm not sure how much longer I can wait before I have to tell you the truth."

11

Inner Strength to Rise Above

Saturday evening, in a three-story brick building in downtown Philadelphia lined with windows on each floor, Liz joins Justin and Rhonda at the guest night for the Visionary Course. The beige-colored room is large enough to seat three hundred people in classroom style. The rows are separated into sections of a hundred, each with ten rows of ten metal chairs. A dark brown podium stands at the front of the room, and brown tables line the back wall. There are three mics evenly placed across the room between the podium and the front row.

As the instructor, Tony, begins to speak, Liz realizes she is in a place like no other she has experienced. The mood of the room is warm and inviting, filled with hopeful eagerness that started from the moment she walked in the door and was respectfully greeted by graduates of the program, who gave her a name tag and escorted her to a seat of her choosing. Although the only people she knows in the room are Justin and Rhonda, she feels accepted for who she is by everyone she meets.

Watching Tony, she is reminded a bit of a famous country

singer in the way he commands the stage: six feet of endless energy bouncing from side to side of the room, while engaging his audience in every word he speaks. He has an athletic build, short brown hair, and blue eyes and is perfectly outfitted in a pair of blue Dockers, a white shirt, and a brown sports coat. His silver alligator boots are a match for the power he exudes with each word he speaks.

As the night progresses, she hangs on to his every word as if each were a mystical key to her future happiness. A keystone of Tony's message sparks Liz's attention when he sits on a bar stool, one leg on the floor and the other on the rung above it, and says, "We're all going to die someday. The difference in our happiness will be the life choices we make between now and then," and then he drops the phrase, "The challenge is to live every day as if it were your last."

Tony's words spur her to contemplate what she wants her life to be: running barefoot in the grass … living on a beachfront … having enough money to not worry about making a living … having a family … owning a design company.

As his words fade into the recesses of her consciousness, she imagines her future: a crippled old woman sitting in her room with cats at her feet and empty cans of cat food on the floor. She shudders at the thought. That could be her if she continues on her current path—age sixty-five, housebound and alone, her cats feasting on her body when she dies.

The image fades, and another appears: a much younger-looking woman with silver-blond hair, surrounded by laughing people. Instantly, she determines that life is possible for her—a vibrant woman with a passion for living, surrounded by friends and family, making a difference in the lives of others. As the image fades, Liz isn't sure what changes she needs to make to get the second life, but she's willing to give it a shot.

Once again her thoughts are interrupted by Tony's voice: "What prevents you from going after what you want is often the self-doubt that continuously loops in your head."

Liz closes her eyes and finds herself a child again. She and Carla, two little blond girls eighteen months apart yet always mistaken for twins, sitting in the front yard at the farm picking dandelions. Freshly planted fields stretch behind them, a pasture full of milking cows to their left, and the old white two-story farmhouse with wraparound porch to their right. Those were happy days, until the accident changed it in the blink of an eye. That day at the hayloft, all was well—until she fell on her head from twelve feet above, landing on a cement floor—blood—a coma—paralysis—months of therapy—learning to walk again. She shudders thinking that's all her life has centered on, the aftermath of her accident.

As Tony scans the audience, his eyes stop on Liz when he asks, "What would you want your life to be remembered for?"

With a furtive glance to her right, Liz is relieved to see Justin and Rhonda are focused on Tony and not the tears filling her eyes. She always wanted to show the kids at school that she could be just as good as they were, to make an impact that changed the world. But nothing she's done begins to come close to that vision. Without a successful career or children to leave as a legacy, she's discouraged by how she believes she will be known—her leg. Then intuition kicks in. It's not her leg; rather, how she's triumphing over the tragedy that can make a difference—that's her true legacy.

Justin is leaning toward her and whispers, "Hey, Liz—"

She flinches and then absently asks, "What?"

"You didn't fall asleep, did you?" Justin says in a teasing tone. "Tony told us to break into groups and talk with each other for ten minutes about our future vision. Then we'll have a little break before the social event."

"Go ahead without me. I'm having trouble with my contact; I'll be back shortly," Liz says. She grabs her crutch to stand and then limps toward the bathroom, eyes heavy with tears. She reaches her destination quickly and locks herself in the handicapped stall. Sitting on the commode, directly facing a mirror and sink, and a baby changing table to the left, she buries her face in her hands and whines to nobody in particular, "I can't do it."

Her anguish turns to silence. How she can move forward if she relives the emotion of her tragedy every time she tells the story of what happened to her leg? She has another vision: She's walking. All that's behind her is a grayish-white smoke, almost like a battlefield. She looks down at her feet, the tips of her toes at the edge of an abyss. Directly in front and beside her is black. Across the distant horizon, there's a bright shining star with radiant beams streaming into the darkness. She knows her future is over there, but she's afraid. What perils lie in the darkness, waiting to destroy her? What if she falls into the abyss?

Liz looks up at her likeness staring back from the mirror; she imagines the old woman again and realizes that living the remainder of her days stuck in the past will only cause more suffering—for her and others. The image fades to black; the vibrant lady returns. There are no guarantees for her future. Even though she fears the path may be difficult or uncertain at times, she must move ahead. The lady's impression grows faint.

Liz looks at her worn shoes and declares out loud, "I gotta stop wasting energy on things I can't change; I'll live the fullest life I can, starting right now."

She stands and stares at the reflection of her legs as she limps forward. She always avoids watching reflections of her walk because she thinks she looks gross. Is that the truth or just her self-loathing? Liz studies her features in the mirror—her blond ringlets falling in front of her ears—her blue eyes that stare into the souls of those who look—her nostrils, the right one slightly smaller than the left—her scar—

Her eyes instinctively dart away, but not before she hears that all-too-familiar sound—*thud.*

Why'd I have to look there? She moans and tightly closes her eyes is if to keep the images and sounds of her past from ever creeping back into her consciousness. She grips the sides of the sink, watching the faucet drip into the washbowl. It's time to head back before someone comes looking for her; but first, she splashes water on her face and pats her cheeks until they're dry and rosy to remove any trace of tears. She gets to the auditorium just as the group is getting dismissed.

"Liz, I was just coming to look for you," Rhonda says. "Is everything okay?"

Liz gulps. "Yeah. My eyes are itchy from my contacts or perhaps sinuses, so I rested them for a bit. I didn't think it would take so long."

"Great! Now that you're here, the fun can begin. You'll love it. The theme is Vegas Night."

"Oh, I didn't bring any cash with me."

"You don't need any. All games are centered on conversations about your life, as opposed to gambling."

Liz hoots. "That sounds like fun!"

Justin walks over and says, "C'mon, girls! They said the games are in the room down the hall, and we could look around while they finish setting up. They should be ready in fifteen."

"You two go ahead," Liz says. "I'm going to wait on a bench over there." She points to an adjoining hallway, lined with alternating office doors and long wooden benches. "I'll be back by the time the games begin," she calls over her shoulder as she walks away.

Shortly after she eases herself onto the furthest bench from their room, Tony approaches carrying a blue notebook binder; he nods and enters a few doors before where she's seated. A few moments later, he reappears empty-handed and walks toward her. He stops and glances at her name tag. "Hi, Liz. Do you mind if I sit by you for a bit?"

A little flustered, she responds, "Of course not. Have a seat."

She moves her crutch from her right side to her left and turns to him as he sits. "I want to thank you for tonight, Tony. Your presentation was inspiring. It really gave me a lot to mull over."

"You're very welcome," he says with a bright smile. "But I have to ask you a question."

She shudders in frustration, knowing it's going to the same as everyone asks her—to tell them what happened to her leg.

He asks in an upbeat tone, "Since tonight's session is part of the Visionary Course curriculum, what vision did you create for yourself?"

Pleasantly surprised by his query, she replies, "Being an inspirational speaker."

He claps his hands together. "Oh, that sounds wonderful! What's your subject?"

Her gaze drops to her shoes. "The struggles of my life."

He looks past her to her crutch as if seeing it for the first time and says, "That's a great vision. People want to hear a speaker with passion, one who leaves them with an array of experiences and emotions—from the depths of sorrow to the pinnacle of euphoria. Your message of overcoming tragedy can be an inspiration. Others will want to know how you did it, to help them or their loved ones."

"How do you know what I've had to overcome?" she asks.

He shakes his head. "Liz, I don't know your exact journey. However, growing up, I lived with an aunt who had polio—her walk was similar to yours. Over the years, I became aware of some of the struggles she had to overcome."

She taps the gray plastic lining the cuff of her crutch. "That's what everyone guesses happened to me, but it didn't."

He looks into Liz's eyes, which have filled with tears. He says, "Daily I see people who get stopped by the smallest things. They quit. Yet, like my aunt, you haven't. Otherwise you wouldn't be here tonight. You see, the conversation about changing your life path is not a common one; it takes inner strength to follow it. That, coupled with overcoming your physical challenges, indicates to me that you're an amazing woman."

Tears are streaming down her face.

He takes a Kleenex from his coat pocket and hands it to her. "Why are you crying?" he asks, looking a little worried.

"I'm afraid," she says quietly. "If I tell what happened, it puts my life and the lives of those I love in the public eye—where they will be scrutinized and judged, leaving everyone in my story vulnerable."

"Liz, the point is to craft your message in such a way that you are empowered when you tell it."

She cocks her head, bites her lower lip, and glances upward. "Okay, I can work on that over time."

"Great. Then would you like to register to attend the next course?"

She surprises herself by confidently saying, "Yes! I think I would." Just then she sees Rhonda and Justin motioning from down the hallway for her to join them.

Tony turns his head to look to the hallway behind him. "Ha! It looks like your friends are ready for some fun," he says. "I'll have the team call you tomorrow, get you registered, and provide all the course details to you at that time."

"Tony, thank you for everything. I'm really looking forward to the course."

He smiles and shakes her hand to leave. "Now, go have some fun with your friends, and remember—what happens in Vegas, stays in Vegas!" They both laugh as he heads off.

Watching him walk down the hallway, Liz isn't quite sure why he singled her out to talk to, but she is glad he did. She feels honored by the perspective he shared with her. She struggles to her feet, puts her arm in the cuff, and limps after him, meeting Rhonda and Justin by the game room door.

"They're almost ready for us," Rhonda says.

Justin asks, "Liz, did you register for the course?"

Liz's face glows as she grins. "I wasn't going to—but then I figured it's about time for me to start doing things differently. Besides, if being in the course helps me and Rhonda work together without me having to answer more of those questions, that alone is worth the cost!"

Rhonda smiles. "Actually, we can put our work on hold until you get to a certain point in the course. Since the course has homework parties, maybe Justin can be the graduate who keeps you on track—at Coco's, of course."

"Will that mean I'll be busy baking sticky buns at all hours?" asks Justin as he throws Liz a wink.

"It may," Liz says with a sly smile.

"Hmm, that'll actually be good. I'll put Chloe in charge of it," says Justin.

"You hired her?" Liz asks, beaming like a gleeful child.

"Yes, I did. Your advice helped immensely. She begins next week, and I'm really looking forward to working with her and her job coach."

Rhonda turns to Liz. "I'm curious. What vision did you create from tonight's course?"

"I was afraid you'd ask that," Liz says with a sigh. "Tony asked me the same thing."

"And?" Rhonda asks in an impatient tone.

Liz clears her throat and declares, "It's to be an inspirational speaker."

Justin's eyes open wide, and he gasps with enthusiasm. "I can definitely see you doing that!"

Rhonda smiles. "That's a bit surprising. I look forward to seeing how that develops for you."

"Well, it'll take a lot of work for me to craft the message and practice my delivery. Then again, I definitely know the subject matter well enough—me," says Liz with a grin. Then she hesitates before asking Rhonda, "What vision do you have for your life?"

Rhonda responds in a mysterious tone, "I've decided to pursue a life with the man of my dreams."

Justin cocks his head and gulps. "Well, that's new news! I wish you and him the best."

Liz offers a cheerful encouragement, "Me too, and I look forward to hearing more details."

Before there's time for further comments, they hear shouts coming from the game room. Justin says, "Ladies, that's our cue. Let the fun begin!"

All three walk into the room together. The tan walls are lined with eight-foot brown tables; each topped with a different game. Game hosts, garbed in white shirts and black vests, stand nearby ready to assist in the play. Participants are beginning to mingle in the room and gravitate toward their games of choice. Rhonda and Justin head for keno while Liz makes her way to the blackjack table.

A woman close to Liz calls out, "Here's a place for you! C'mon and join us for the next hand."

Liz limps over and is greeted warmly by a woman called Cynthia. The women laugh like old friends as they play a few rounds and engage in conversation with other players on what they learned about their lives and future from the course. As Liz watches Cynthia, she can't but help notice the plainness in her facial features and that she's significantly overweight—Liz guesses by a hundred pounds or so. Yet there's something about her that Liz finds absolutely stunning. Is it her energy? Her sincerity? She's so carefree and at ease with everyone. *Is that what people mean by being comfortable in your own skin? If it is, I'm determined to be like that someday.*

As the dealer starts a new hand Liz decides her aching legs need some rest. She starts to leave but first turns to her newest acquaintance. "It was so good to meet you, Cynthia. Maybe we'll run into each other again."

As she slides her arm through the crutch cuff, Cynthia asks her, "Did you sign up for the course?"

Liz nods to confirm.

Cynthia says, "Me too! Hey, I know we just met, but do you want to be roomies? My mother lives in Manhattan, and I'm sure it will be fine with her if we stay for the weekend at her apartment."

Liz is dumfounded. "I don't know what to say."

"Say yes!" Cynthia begs.

Liz purses her lips and laughs. "Okay, yes!"

Cynthia hugs her goodbye and says, "Sista, I'll be in touch to confirm all the details."

Liz walks away, feeling thrown a bit off-kilter by her newfound friend and level of confidence. As she meets Justin and Rhonda at the double brown exit doors leading to the main entrance, her heart overspills with enthusiasm for the new path on which she is about to embark.

12

The Will to Overcome

Liz has eight weeks to prepare for the opening weekend of her course. Although lodging has been secured, the logistics of traveling to and around New York City are proving to be particularly challenging since she will not driving into the city but rather relying on public transportation and walking to get everywhere. Each morning Liz reviews her to-do list, and by the end of each day, she checks off at least one item. Obstacles that at first seemed insurmountable gradually work themselves out.

Finally it's the night before the course. She reviews her list once more and believes she has it all under control: the neighbor will feed the cats, she's packed everything in a rolling suitcase, she'll use her old fanny pack to carry her wallet and other small items, she has a backpack for the course materials, and she has a new travel mug from Coco's with a handle that fits on her wrist, so she can easily carry beverages without spilling.

She goes to bed early, pleased she decided to book the 11:20 p.m. bus into the city so she'll beat Friday afternoon traffic. Despite her expectation of a good night's sleep, she tosses and turns as she agonizes about the upcoming trip. Doubts stream through her thoughts: What if she can't pull her luggage from the terminal to the taxi area? Or walk to the restaurant for breaks? What if she arrives late and has to sit up front and everyone stares as she limps to her seat? What if Cynthia asks a lot of questions about her leg? What if—?

She cuts her thoughts short. "Kitties, this is crazy!" she says to Abbey and Ruby, who just sit and stare as she laments, "I need to let go of my worries and let life happen. All will be well."

As if to second that emotion, Ruby walks over to Liz's left hand and lies down. Liz starts petting her and quickly drifts off to sleep.

Late the next morning, Liz arrives at the bus station parking lot, which appears to be filled to capacity. Instantly she's alarmed that there are no open handicap spaces. Frustration and anxiety quickly set in. There's an attendant nearby, and she drives over and flashes her handicap-parking placard for him to see. He says, "Ma'am, you can park by that red car." He points to an unmarked area of the lot to his right. "Place your handicap placard in the window, and I'll let the manager know I authorized it for you."

Looking up from his name tag, a relieved Liz says, "Thank you, Mr. Rodriguez."

She parks as instructed and trudges with her luggage toward a line of people waiting for her bus. She has fifteen minutes before the bus is due to arrive, and there's no way she can stand that long. The only place to sit is a bench near the front of the line; she fears if she sits there, that's going to upset everyone.

Voices scream in her head, *Stay to the back of the line!* while another whispers, *Sit on the bench and wait for your turn to board.*

She vacillates for a few moments and then decides to forget appearances and sit down before she falls down. She limps with her luggage to the black iron bench ten feet from the curb at the bus loading zone, ignoring people's icy glares. She's sure they're all thinking she's pretty nervy cutting to the front of the line when they were there first. She plops down and stares at her shoes as the minutes drag by until the bus finally arrives.

Once the doors open, the driver hops out and stands at the side of the bus by the luggage compartment. Liz rises and waits in place. After the fifth person boards, the driver, a five-foot-seven, slender man in his forties, wearing a Mets baseball cap, walks over to her and asks, "Why aren't you getting on?"

"It's not my turn," Liz says.

"Of course it is," he responds, taking the handle of her purple suitcase. He rolls it toward the blue and white bus, and she obediently follows him. He raises a hand to stop the others boarding long enough for Liz to get up the steps. She's relieved to see the first seat open and quickly sits so passengers can continue to board. He then loads her luggage into the storage compartment.

On the entire two-hour ride into the city, Liz is overcome with different emotions. The driver and the parking lot attendant were so kind to her; that's never happened before when she traveled. Can it really be as simple as asking people for help when she needs it?

Her face flushes with embarrassment and then anger as she recalls previous travel difficulties. When she was in her early thirties, she tried to preboard a flight from Los Angeles to Indianapolis when the gate attendant barked at her, "We only preboard preferred customers. Besides, you're not handicapped, so get to the back of the line."

That day Liz swallowed her humiliation and obeyed, the way she always does. Waiting at the back of the line, she held back her tears as tightly as she held on to her luggage, her gut twisted in knots. Although she didn't walk with a crutch back then, it was apparent to onlookers that she needed a little extra time to board. Liz vowed to send a letter to the CEO of the airline but never did. Once again she didn't have the courage to explain her leg without fear of coming off as a whiner.

When the bus pulls into the terminal, the driver turns to Liz and says, "Miss, if you can wait until everyone gets off, I'll help with your luggage."

"That would be great," she says, not quite able to describe her feelings toward his kindness.

After everyone debarks, Liz picks up her crutch and slowly descends the steps. Her luggage is already standing by the curb. "Here's your bag," the driver says.

"Thank you. My weekend is off to a good start because of you." Looking around, she's puzzled.

"Do you need help?" he asks.

"Yes. Do you know the way out of here?"

"Yes," he says and gives her directions through the main terminal.

Liz heads off, slowly and carefully pulling her luggage while scanning the ground for obstacles. As she approaches an exit sign, she sees an escalator and lets others past, waiting for a big clearing before she gets on. Putting her left foot on the escalator step that's flat to the ground, she hoists her suitcase with her right arm and is instantly thrown off-balance as the stair rises. She lunges for the moving handrail and grabs it with her left arm still in the crutch cuff. Ignoring the fear of falling, she rebalances her suitcase and crutch and, then shifts her focus to scan the approaching brown tile floor as she nears the top. Glancing down as the rolling step slides against the main terminal surface, she takes two steps forward—off the escalator and onto the floor—and stops. Her heart beats quickly as she takes a sigh of relief.

Once her luggage and crutch are repositioned, she continues limping through the terminal, looking for a place to sit down. Why aren't there more benches for people like her who need to rest? She sighs and continues walking despite the growing pain in her feet. Her chest tightens as she passes each exit that's not hers. Did she take a wrong turn? It didn't seem that far away when the driver gave her directions. Some days she swears she couldn't find her way out of a paper bag!

She stops to lean against a light blue concrete wall between two food stands to rest her aching legs and feet. Spying an exit sign in the distance, she estimates there's only one hundred steps or so before she reaches the street, where she can hail a cab. She takes a deep breath and resumes her slow limp to the sidewalk outside the bus station.

She is pleasantly surprised that it looks just like the New York she's seen on TV: tall buildings and swarms of people facing forward or down, some talking on phones or texting, few making eye contact. She limps toward the street, looking for a yellow cab. Her throbbing feet and blisters on her hand make continued walking an even greater struggle; she's afraid she can't go any further. What would people do if she sat down in the middle of the sidewalk to rest? Before she can explore that thought, a taxi pulls to the curb beside her. She shouts through the open window the address of where she wants to go.

"That's only two blocks away," the driver snorts. "It won't kill you to walk it." He takes off chasing another fare as she gapes in disbelief.

Before she can recover, another cabbie pulls over. She looks at his seemingly kind eyes and sheepishly repeats her plea. He smiles and nods for her to get in. She clumsily puts her luggage and crutch into the back seat and climbs in next to them. It feels good to sit, if only for a bit. Fifteen minutes later, they're at her destination.

She slowly gets out—after tipping him generously—and surveys the building in front of her: a gray marble ten-story structure, lined with rows of black tinted windows. To the right is the restaurant she saw online, within fifty feet of her building. With the raised sidewalk leading to it, she will need to be careful or she could trip and fall. Lately the gentlest of inclines have seemed to her like climbing Mount Everest, as her mobility has significantly worsened in the past few months. She brushes that worry aside and focuses her attention on a respite she hopes is behind the entrance doors: a quiet place to get off her feet and relax for a while.

She limps past double glass entrance doors and about twenty feet ahead locates a small lounge with a comfy leather couch and surrounding tables and chairs. She settles in for the remainder of the afternoon, taking a pain pill and propping her feet on her luggage. For the first time since boarding the bus, she's calm. She closes her eyes and recounts all that happened on this leg of her journey.

Suddenly, she hears a woman's high-pitched, boisterous voice. "Liz, wake up! It's time to get ready for a new life!"

Her eyes bolt open; it takes her a couple of seconds to register her surroundings. Facing her is a plump woman with fair skin and short blond hair, cut in a pixie style, and accented by red eyeglasses; it's Cynthia. Liz shakes her head and drowsily asks, "What time is it?"

Cynthia guffaws. "Girlfriend, it's almost three-thirty. What were you doing? Snoozing?"

Liz rubs her eyes. "I-I must've fallen asleep. The last thing I remember it was a bit after two."

"Well, now that I did my job and woke you up, we have thirty minutes before class begins, and I want to get with a few people before we start. I'll meet you at the end of class, and then we'll go to my mom's."

"Okay, thank you, Cynthia." Liz straightens up on the couch and tries to figure out her next challenge—finding an appropriate seat in the classroom. It's exhausting to continually plan how she's going to get places—and today's journey has been no exception. Although she's come far, she's overwhelmed by thoughts of what lies ahead. She wishes she had never come; it would have been so much easier for her to stay home and keep living her miserable life. She chides herself for believing Tony that night when he said she could create a better future. She looks around quickly, considering reasons—and options—for a quick escape before it starts.

13

A Stranger's Helping Hand Gives Hope

Liz looks toward the classroom entrance, and standing nearby is a flip chart. Bold handwritten print says that doors will open at 3:50 p.m. Participants are starting to line up in the hallway, all of them busy talking and laughing. What will it take for her to laugh again in the company of others the she did with her dad as a little girl or to have friends she can hang out with who don't ask about her leg? Can the course make all that happen?

She mutters under her breath, "I hope so; it's my last chance."

She struggles to her feet and, with her head down to watch the steps in front of her, starts walking toward the crowd. Five steps in, she sees a familiar pair of silver alligator boots with navy blue Dockers. She glances up to see that it's Tony; his smiling brown eyes and dimples welcoming her. "Hi, Liz!" he says, extending his hand.

She shifts the crutch to her other hand, flips her left hand upside down, and shakes his hand firmly. He looks at her oddly. "Did you have any trouble making it here today?"

Should she regale him with her woes—her blisters and sore legs and all the crap she had to deal with to get here? Or just focus on what she needs for now?

"Probably no more trouble than most," she responds warmly. "However, as far as class tonight, I do need something."

"Sure. What can I help you with?"

She scrunches her face. "Would it be possible for me to get in the room a few minutes early to get a seat?"

His eyebrows knit as he looks down at her purple paisley luggage and says, "Absolutely. Do you need any help with your bags?"

Liz, embarrassed by her request, doesn't want to risk further humiliation by having him carry her luggage. After all, it's hers, and she should be able to manage it, or so her mother always told her. But her hand and feet are killing her, and since he did offer, maybe it's not a shame for her to accept.

"Thank you, Tony, that would help immensely," she confidently says.

He grabs her things and leads the way inside. Parking her luggage along the back wall, he asks, "Is this okay?"

"It's perfect. I appreciate you so much, Tony."

After he leaves, she scans the room. It's much smaller than the last one they met in, seating a hundred or so people in classroom style. The thinly padded black metal chairs are grouped in two sections, each with ten rows of five chairs. Facing the front of the room, she decides that the aisle seat in the back row on the left-hand side is perfect for her to get in and out easily, and her crutch will fit under the chair as to not attract attention or trip her classmates as they walk by.

She puts her brightly flowered backpack on the chair to reserve her spot and heads to the ladies' room before things get started. By the time she returns, the doors are open. Surprised that the room is half-filled, she's glad she got in early. She settles into her seat unobtrusively and stares straight ahead, avoiding all conversation and instead imagining where the weekend might lead her: a new life, a new love, freedom from the pain of her past.

As Tony starts the session, any reservations she had about attending are quickly erased. His relaxed manner and delivery ease her fears, and for the moment she is filled with peace and acceptance; she begins to let go of the past. Today is the first of many that will change her life. Knowing she needs to shift her distaste for meeting people and having them inquire about her leg into something else, she listens intently to Tony's presentation—but that's not a topic he mentions.

Her mind wanders. She surveys the room to find Cynthia, who's in the middle row to her right, nodding as she watches Tony speak and busily takes notes. How can Cynthia be so carefree, fun, and relaxed with people that she leads discussions with her small team, while Liz finds herself emotionally guarded and detached from the chatter around her? She returns her focus to Tony, intent on finding the part of his presentation that connects to her personal situation.

As the evening unfolds and various participants share their feelings and experiences from the mic at the front of the room, Liz is often compelled to join them. Then her interminable doubts intrude. She can't walk up there. If she did, they would stare at her just as they did that day in the airport when she was ordered to the back of the boarding line. Her head's insistent she will never share her feelings in front of everyone.

The course wraps up at ten. Liz feels a burning in her soul to break out of her past, to throw away her disability as easily as she might toss her crutch. She's previously been at this emotional fork in the road; it led to people who tried to use religion to heal her leg. But it wasn't that simple, at least not for her. Believing in God and all his blessings never made the reality of her leg disappear. Although she's not sure this course will give her heart that peace either, she has to try. She decides to take the fork to the left—trusting there's something other than herself to make a stand for, a cause that gets her out of her chair when the pain becomes so great she doesn't want to move. She sighs as people gather near her to discuss plans for the morning, but she doesn't utter a peep for fear they will ask about her leg.

Cynthia walks out from behind her and asks, "Are you ready to go?"

"Yeah, I'm beat," says Liz. "It's been a long day."

"There should be a cab nearby that can take us to my mom's. Can I grab your luggage?" Liz looks at the blister on her hand and wants to accept, but she doesn't want her new friend overloaded with bags. As if reading her mind, Cynthia says, "I took the bus last night and stayed over, so my luggage is already at Mom's."

"Okay, then. Thanks!"

Twenty-five minutes later, they arrive at a gray marble forty-story high-rise. "This is it!" Cynthia says happily. "C'mon, let's get settled into our digs for the weekend. Mom's gone, so we have the entire place to ourselves."

They drag themselves out of the taxi, through security clearance, and up the elevator to a two-bedroom apartment on the thirty-fifth floor, overlooking the Manhattan skyline and the Hudson River. Once inside, each of them quickly changes to comfy pajamas. Sitting facing each other on the guest bed, legs folded yoga style, they start their "big girl" slumber party with chips, dip, water, and lots of laughing.

After a few icebreakers, Liz fears that the conversation will lead to areas she's not yet ready to discuss with Cynthia; she takes the initiative by shifting the banter about their personal lives to today's experience: Tony and the course. She begins with her observation that Tony is extremely skilled, and although his words have connected with others, which she saw from their heartfelt sharing at the mic, his message hasn't yet resonated with her.

Then Cynthia boldly takes over the discussion, leaving Liz to listen intently. She reveals that her goal for the course is to find a way to provide a stable home for her preteen twin boys, pending a separation from her husband, and explore a bisexual lifestyle.

Two hours into it, they take a break to refill the water glasses and get something sweet to finish off their evening. Returning to the bed, their conversation shifts to what they have in common: they're the same age, they were raised by someone other than their natural parents, they love to cook, and they have traveled to Paris. By the time Liz's head finally hits the pillow at three o'clock, she discovers she has a new friend. Sleep finds her quickly—every muscle aching from her exhausting day.

The next morning, the ladies are up and out early to catch a cab to the course. Once in the room, Liz quickly settles into her comfortable routine of distancing herself from others. She sits in the same seat at the back of the room; she's the last to leave for breaks and the first to return. She tucks her crutch under her chair, out of her classmates' sight and her mind. As the day progresses, a growing chink in her emotional armor allows her to engage with others a bit more than she's previously experienced; the lowering of her guard has begun.

That evening, as participants return from dinner, Tony announces, "We're going to have a social hour to end the day's events."

Wait, what? Liz thinks. *They're serving drinks here?*

"The theme of the night is summer camp," Tony says. "It's designed to bring fun and play to life through conversation, and it's built on our day's coursework, expressing emotions or thoughts through play or art." He puts on a baseball cap. "Go quickly! Get on a team for our first activity—the three-legged race!"

"Aw, shit," Liz quietly mutters.

She hated playing games as a child—especially that one; her team always came in last. And tonight's theme only reminds her of the many activities she couldn't do at camp as an eight-year-old with a disability: run races, swim, or canoe. Her camping excursion ended with the spotlight on her, the gimp, who made her team lose at softball by striking out with the bases loaded. She fumes at her reality: no one ever has an icebreaker or team activity that isn't based on physical abilities—all of which serve to spotlight her limitations.

She scans the room for Cynthia and finds her surrounded by others at the far end of the room, hooting and hollering with surrounding teammates. She starts shrinking away, intent to find the nearest bar to drown her anxiety but then realizes it's not an option. She would be lost in the city with nowhere to go as soon as she walked out the door. Frowning, she walks to the nearest group and quickly gets paired up with a man she's only seen from afar; he's a few inches taller than she, with short brown hair and green eyes and a muscular build that could easily carry her in the race.

She looks him in the eyes and sheepishly says, "Hello, I'm Liz."

"Good to meet you, Liz. I'm Sam," he says. Spying her crutch, he adds, "And what's your friend's name?"

She blushes. "Er, I guess I never named him."

"Well, he looks like a Steve to me," he says.

Her attitude perks up a bit. "I just hope Steve doesn't mind if I leave him behind for a few minutes."

He winks and says, "Since he's your biggest supporter, I'm sure he'll understand."

As they line up, Sam and Liz are the last of six couples. Her heart is beating out of her chest. She whispers in his ear, "Can you change our place in line so we're not last?"

He gives her a quizzical look and then talks with the couple ahead of them. They switch places. Sam and Liz are now fifth instead of sixth. Sam bends to tie her right leg to his left when she notices a problem.

"Can we switch sides?" she begs. "I have better balance that way."

He scoots around her and loops their legs together while Liz's anxiety grows. She watches nervously as four pairs go ahead of her, signaling that she and Sam are next.

As he puts his muscular arm around her waist to support her, she can feel the rapid beating of her heart. Their turn arrives. With every step, she tries desperately not to drag her leg and cause them both to fall as they awkwardly limp forward. About ten feet in, her right shoe catches his, and they jerk ahead; his grip on her tightens and keeps both of them from falling. He quickly regains his footing and rebalances her; she takes a deep breath and they continue.

They stop when they reach the wall. He asks her to stand still while he gingerly steps around to her other side; she shifts her left foot on the floor as he repositions both of them to head back. She now hears the shouts from the crowd and overcomes her urge to look at the faces by keeping her head down and focusing on the ground ahead of her. With ten steps to go, they finally have a rhythm of walking that she's comfortable with. A few moments later, they've crossed the finish line to raucous cheering.

Sam unties their legs, and they watch the last team finish. "Sam, you did it!" she shrieks. "We took third out of six!" He smiles and returns the ankle tie to the game coordinator.

Liz gets her crutch and wanders toward the back wall, to reflect while waiting for their next event. She admits that although her summer camp memories were painful, today's race was fun. For the first time, others didn't act any differently towards her because of her leg.

Tony breaks her thoughts by announcing, "Our next activity is campfire stories. Everyone gather 'round and take a squat where you want." He looks at Liz, "If you would rather have a chair, feel free to get one; there's plenty scattered around the room."

Liz quickly decides this is her kind of camp: telling stories around a campfire. If only they could roast marshmallows and make s'mores, she'd be in heaven. She smiles at the thought of warm, gooey treats as she limps to the nearest chair and drags it to the outer ring of the circle of participants formed on the floor, with Tony perched in the middle on a wooden stool.

Tony says, "Now tonight, we're going to tell a story of collective folklore. Someone starts with a sentence or two, and then the next person adds their sentence or two, and the story continues until we've gone all the way around the room. You can say anything you want, and for those of you who have difficulty expressing certain statements, this is a great way to do it with no one knowing if it's truth or fiction."

The audience laughs, and Liz relaxes at the prospect of an activity where her leg doesn't influence the outcome or become its focal point. Thinking of what she's going to say when it's her turn, she hears bits and pieces of the story, separated by outbursts of laughter: "On a dark eerie night eons ago … she put him in her shoe box and tied a string around it … his skin turning green from cosmic dust …."

She gets so caught up in the laughter as the story turns into a bizarre collection of memories, thoughts, and wishes for the future that she almost misses her turn. Without giving much thought, she blurts out, "And the little blond girl had a bad accident and almost died."

Despite her expectation that everyone would gasp at the truth of her words, they are received with laughter, as if it were a good joke she had told. The story continues around the circle, coming to an end a few minutes later. Then Tony gives instructions for the next morning's arrival and dismisses the group.

"Wasn't that fun?" Cynthia asks as she walks up to Liz. "If you want, we can do more of that tonight when we get back to Mom's."

Liz smiles as they exit the building and says, "I think I've had enough storytelling for one night."

Cynthia walks into the street, lined with rushing headlights, to hail a cab while Liz waits by the curb. She sees Sam in the shadow of the building, ambling toward her with his hands in his pockets. He's wearing a black leather jacket and matching cowboy hat. "Where are you two headed?" he asks gamely.

"To Cynthia's mom's apartment," Liz says. "We're staying there for the weekend. It's got a beautiful view near the top that overlooks the city."

"Oh. Well, it was good to meet you tonight," he says, turning to walk in the opposite direction.

Liz says, "Hey, Sam," and he stops. "Thank you for making my request happen back there—you know, the race and all. Having it end the way it did meant a lot to me."

He shrugs. "You're welcome. It was really no big deal. I'll see you tomorrow. Good night, ladies." He tips his hat and quickly disappears into the crowded sidewalk traffic.

Cynthia motions to Liz. "Here's our cab. C'mon."

On the way to the apartment Cynthia says, "I didn't mention anything last night, but I wanted to before the weekend is over and I forget."

Liz gulps in fear.

Cynthia turns toward Liz with a pursed smile and says in an encouraging tone, "You really give me hope."

Liz is puzzled. "I don't understand."

"Last night I told you about my kids, but I didn't tell you that they each have a learning disability. Being with you this weekend and imagining what you've done to succeed in life—well, it gives me hope for them. Now I know they can have a quality future—get jobs, fall in love, maybe own a house someday."

"Cynthia, I'm not that successful, and my marriage didn't work out."

"It's not what you didn't do that inspires me; it's what you did. Whatever it took to get you here is nothing short of amazing. Most people without your hardships would have given up rather than make the journey."

Liz feels the blood rush to her cheeks. "I almost surrendered plenty of times, including yesterday when I was ready to quit the course."

Cynthia smiles as she touches Liz's arm. "But you didn't. You keep going. Like the Energizer Bunny."

They both laugh, and Liz's eyes tear up. "Thank you, but you really don't know me."

"Maybe not," Cynthia says pensively. "But if your life has been anything like my boys', it's been hard on you."

"Yeah, it has," Liz agrees.

"I know you said you don't have children, but I still see you as a mom. Doing the hard things because the little ones might be watching. If you give up, then they surely will."

The talk goes silent, with each woman left to her private thoughts. Liz is starting to realize what might be her life's mission: to be a role model for people like Cynthia and her boys, who may not believe they can have a great life. But since her own mobility is getting more and more difficult, how can she continue for someone else when she may not be able to continue for herself? Liz puts all thoughts aside and gets lost in the glow of the passing city lights.

The next morning, while riding to the course, Cynthia has an important question but not the one Liz has always dreaded. She asks Liz, "Who was that guy talking to you last night when I was trying to hail us a cab?"

"That's Sam. He was my partner in the three-legged race."

"He's cute," Cynthia says with a sly grin.

"Yeah, but I think he's taken," Liz says.

"That may be, but he can just be a friend. He seemed to like you, and Lord knows, we all need friends in life." She gives Liz a wink.

I could use a few new friends, Liz thinks. *Especially ones like him.*

They arrive at their destination, and the taxi driver lets them off within feet of the front door. Once inside, Liz is shocked to find the room assembled into fourteen circles of chairs instead of rows arranged auditorium-style. In the middle of each circle is chair with a stack of paper on it.

Liz is about to sit in the seat closest to the back of the room when she notices Sam near the front. Why couldn't he sit back by her?

She looks at some empty seats near him. If she chooses to sit there, she'll have to walk in front of strangers. She stays put at the very back circle in the room and waits.

Standing in the front of the room, sandwiched by two tables on each side, Tony catches everyone's attention by announcing, "I know some of you are concerned that we moved your cheese, er, your chair." Laughter fills the room. "What we're going to do next is get you into homework teams."

Oh no, not him too, Liz thinks. *What is it with these people and their damn homework assignments?*

He then instructs everyone to join a group based on a nearby city where they can meet regularly to work on class projects. To speed the process, each circle of chairs has a preselected town printed on a paper taped to the chair in the middle. While Tony finishes giving directions, Liz cranes her neck to look around the room, hoping to find her town, but most are in New York or New Jersey.

Then she spots "Lancaster" near the middle of the room; she is relieved, as this is where Rhonda is, which will allow her to coordinate any appointments they have with her homework parties. The class gets up as instructed, and people begin assembling into new groups. Liz picks up her crutch and limps to her new circle. She sits down, waiting on Tony's next set of instructions.

From behind her, a man enters to sit next to her. She turns to see who it is and is welcomed by a grinning Sam. "Hi, Liz," he says and then bends his head toward her crutch, "and you too, Steve."

Her apprehension about being with new people, who might ask about her leg, quickly fades at his outward acceptance of her and her sidekick. Smiling, she asks, "Is this where you live?"

"I'm a bit to the east, but I work a lot in the area."

"I'm glad you're in this group, Sam," she says. "At least that's one familiar face for me."

Tony interrupts, "Great. Now that you're all in your groups, I want to go over your class projects. Take a sheet of paper from the middle chair, and please follow along."

Liz reaches forward and feels pain in her hip. She winces.

"Here, let me get it for you," Sam says. "My arms are longer." He easily gets two pieces of paper and hands one to her.

"It will seem confusing at first," Tony says, "but there are two main projects you'll be working on throughout the Visionary Course. The first one has to do with making an artistic expression of your life. Think of it as an autobiography done pictorially. I like to call it the pixography."

A man at the far side of the room asks, "Is that a word, Tony?"

The audience laughs, and Tony chuckles. "In the Visionary Course it is, as well as anything else you want to create. Anyway, moving on. Your pixography can appear any way you want, but it must include the items listed on this sheet of paper."

Liz scans the list: people, places, events, and pictures. It should be relatively easy to assemble, as all her memories and memorabilia are packed in a box located in the basement, waiting to be vividly recalled.

"And the second project has to do with those limiting conversations you have in your head. You know what I mean—the voices that stop you from doing certain things or cause you to do something else."

A woman near Liz asks, "Isn't that logic, Tony?"

"Perhaps. Or maybe it's something you told yourself as a child in order to be protected. Like the belief, 'I'll never love again.'"

Liz feels a knife pierce deep in her heart, knowing she told herself exactly that many times. However, with the remnants of a broken heart and the passing of the years, it has morphed into the conviction that she'll never find the man of her dreams.

Tony continues, "We'll get deeper into your projects at the homework parties, and each group will work with a mentor who's familiar with the course syllabus. I'll email everyone this week the name of their mentor.

"Now to finish the course for today, I'd like people to come up to the microphone and share what they've learned this weekend or what they now see as a possibility in their life, based on the work we've completed so far."

Liz watches as one participant after another goes to the podium to share. She lowers her head and stares at her shoes. She wants desperately to find the courage to get up there, but she doesn't know what she might say. Further, she'll have to walk in front of everyone to do it. Just then she sees Sam as he stands and walks towards the front of the room. Her curiosity is piqued.

Standing chest and shoulders above the podium, wearing jeans and a faded denim jacket, Sam takes the cordless mic and begins. "Friends of mine called last night and asked why I was in the Visionary Course. I couldn't give them an answer before hanging up. So I thought about it all night, tossing and turning while I tried to put it into words. I find that today, I'm even more confused than I was on Friday night when we started. Like many of you, I've had a successful career, playing high school sports and coaching school teams. When I was in college, I joined a macho fraternity. Excuse me, ladies, but guys, you know the kind: keg parties, pranks, women, tough images, and testosterone, lots of testosterone."

The audience chuckles with acknowledgment.

He looks at Liz. His raspy voice continues, "In college, I met a young man who needed my help, and it changed the way I've responded since that time to those in need. I've been blessed to do everything that's been on my 'bucket list,' from becoming a teacher, coach, and school administrator to traveling abroad. I'm not sure what's next, but I'm going back today knowing that I make a difference in this world. And Tony, I have you to thank for that."

Sam returns to his seat next to Liz, who whispers, "I was about to go up, but you're a tough act to follow."

He looks at her stoically. "I simply said what was on my mind, for a change, rather than holding back," he says.

She sighs. "I wish I could do that."

"Why don't you give it a try?" he suggests.

She nods and starts to stand. He grabs Steve and hands it to her. Liz limps to the front of the room, where she is second in line. Her heart races with anxiety; she's sure it's going to beat out of her chest. And just like that, it's her turn. She slowly steps to the mic and looks over the audience, settling initially on the calming presence of Tony, who smiles and gives her a subtle nod.

"I almost left Friday night and again last night before we started the three-legged race. But a friend here convinced me to stay."

She looks toward Sam's seat and finds an empty chair.

"But I so desperately wanted what Tony promised—that is, I could create the future of my dreams. Throughout this weekend, it became evident that I've allowed life's circumstances to stop me. I quit building what I wanted a long time ago. However, sometime during the past forty-eight hours, I've come to believe that this course can help me push beyond those self-imposed limits. Like others who have come up here to share, I don't know what's next, but so far I've clarified the direction I need to head—and it's utterly different than what it was last week or even Friday when we arrived. I appreciate everything people shared over the weekend, and I look forward to spending the rest of the course with each of you." Liz nods at Tony and returns to her seat.

Sam returns to her side. "I saw you from the back of the room; you were excellent," he whispers.

Her heart warms; she smiles and whispers in return, "I simply learned from those who went before me."

"Okay," Tony addresses the room as the final speaker retreats. "Remember, everyone attends monthly homework parties, and we'll be together again in a few months. Good day, safe travels, and start living into your vision!"

The room buzzes as people stand and say their goodbyes to one another. Cynthia runs up to Liz and breathlessly asks, "I forgot to ask, how are you getting back?"

"The same way I got here: the bus. It leaves at 3:10 p.m."

"Hey, I have a bus to catch too," Sam says. "We can walk together, if that's okay with you."

Liz looks at Sam and then Cynthia and says cheerily, "I guess I have an escort."

"Is that better than being an escort?" Cynthia asks, prompting all three of them to laugh. She reaches out to hug Liz, positioning her arms so Liz stays balanced, and says softly, "Be on your way now, my friend."

Liz looks at Cynthia with a heart full of appreciation and says, "You put bright spots into a challenging weekend for me, Cynthia. Thank you very much."

"You're welcome. Now scoot, or you'll be late," orders Cynthia.

Liz turns and heads for the door with Sam, who grabs her luggage and rolls it together with his out of the building. Stepping into the warm spring air, he quickly asks, "So where do you call home?"

"Hmm. Good question," she replies. "I was raised in Michigan."

"And? It sounds like there's more to the story."

"You make me realize I don't know where it is." She pauses. "Do you know what I mean?"

"I think I do. I used to think it was where family and friends were. Now I think it's where my heart's at peace."

She nods in agreement, and they continue to talk their way to and through the bus station. As they arrive at Liz's bus, which is near the end of the terminal, Sam hands over her luggage and asks if he can help with anything else before he goes.

"No, thanks, but Sam, you have been a godsend. I can't thank you enough for all you did."

"Just remember in our homework parties, I'm not the brightest bulb on the strand when it comes to artsy things. So you'll get your chance to pay it back sooner than you might think. Now get on your bus, and get home safe!"

"I will," she says with a broad grin, secretly hoping he'll ask for her number. The bus driver interrupts her thoughts as he takes Liz's luggage and stows it in the storage compartment. Liz thanks him and slowly climbs the stairs, carefully grabbing onto the left handrail while holding her crutch in her right hand. She sits in the front row and leans her crutch against the window.

As she looks out at Sam walking away, disappointment sets in. Why didn't he ask for her number to stay in touch? She dismisses it with the realization that she'll see him in a few weeks, and he's sure to ask for it then. She situates herself for the ride home, closing her eyes and dreaming of the last forty-eight hours.

Thoughts of everything she's gone through this weekend spin in her head: the group activities, games, challenges, and conversations. As they do, answers to Rhonda's questionnaire become clearer. Could that be a coincidence? Or did the coursework simply crack the code in a different way to let her face those traumatic memories?

Then there's everything wrapped up with her leg; first and foremost is walking. It will always be difficult for her, but with Sam, Tony, and Cynthia wheeling her luggage, the walks were bearable. Perhaps all she needs is a personal assistant, or to ask for help when she has difficulty.

And then there was Sam. He didn't care about Steve, her constant companion, or so it seemed. Why is he different than others, able to accept her so easily? Maybe someday she'll get the nerve to ask.

What about her behavior? Trying to mask her walk is like trying to hide the pink elephant in the room. She smiles, knowing that it's stupid to believe that people will stop asking about her leg simply because she hides her crutch or doesn't walk in front of them. If she wants a life that's different, then she needs to alter her actions—starting with everything that has to do with her leg.

She already cherishes her new friends, Cynthia and Sam, each with their unique perspective. First, there's Cynthia and the way she openly talked about her children with their disability, and then Sam's levity about her crutch. She smiles at his brilliance; giving it a name made it friendly rather than stiff and shameful.

As she reflects more deeply into her past, her eyes well with tears. She recalls being eight years old again, sitting in the largest desk, all the way in the back of the classroom. Back then, swivel chairs connected to the desks, and she was too fat to fit into the smaller ones. Every time she walked to the front of the room, kids would mock her, point at her leg, laugh, and call her names. Sometimes they would trip her or throw books onto the floor in front of her. The teachers mostly ignored such behavior or dismissed any scuffle as an accident. She remembers one occasion when the teacher pulled her aside after class and told her she needed to get tougher skin. Later that night, when she cried to her parents, instead of defending her, they told her not to create a scene and make the best of it.

Liz presses deeper. What more could she have done when she got picked on? Then she puts it all together. She's still practicing what she was trained as a child to do—grin and bear it. Although she had no voice as a child, as an adult she should be speaking up instead of being silent about her leg and what her needs are—just as she did when she asked Tony to escort her to the room early. Although her mom would have said she was taking advantage of his kindness, as an adult she is responsible to determine the help she needs and ask for it.

Her thoughts pause as she turns to view the city's skyline fading in the distance. Although she was scared at the start of the three-legged race, the way Sam and the rest of the team made her feel, and the fact that her team placed well, lessened the pain of her childhood camp memories. Is it possible that reenactments such as that could help her triumph over the past and overcome her fears?

As she applies what the course has taught her so far to her future, she concludes that life isn't made up of weekends or parties with people committed to changing their lives. She's challenged to create a way to consistently break out of her past, in order to sustain the life she envisions. If not, she'll remain stuck with the mind-set she had on Friday when she arrived. And the first step of this is breaking out of her silence about her leg.

Thankful and with a fresh perspective, Liz shifts focus to the world in front of her as she looks outward to enjoy the ride home.

14

Let Me Grieve

Rhonda peers at her client through the shades on her office window. Liz is approaching from the sidewalk to the left, lined with blooming purple irises, and orange and black poppies. Why does she always stare down and look angry when she walks?

As Liz nears the seven wooden steps to the entrance, Rhonda quickly reviews her planned next steps: to focus on the positives that Liz has and to leverage them—her friendliness and intelligence, her high level of transparency, and her eagerness to overcome the agony of her past. Together, these attributes make a strong foundation on which she's confident that Liz can turn her situation around.

Rhonda opens the front door and greets her brightly.

Liz smiles and limps into the foyer, following Rhonda to her office. She sets her crutch and purse down, taking her usual place on the sofa. After a bit of not-so-productive conversation, Rhonda decides to get some coffee, hoping it will help both of them restart their work session.

"Liz, I understand it may be painful for you to tell me about your past; however, that's where we need to begin today."

Liz stares at her feet and after an achingly long pause says, "I'm sick and tired of telling what happened. All I want is to change the past; to never wake from the nightmare again—to walk barefoot in the park while holding hands with the man I love, like everyone else does."

Rhonda gently responds, knowing that the right tone and words are needed for Liz to continue to open up. "All in due time, Liz. However, first we must start at the beginning of your story."

"It's complicated. It begins with an explanation of my family life."

"Then go ahead and start there."

"My sister and I were born in Ann Arbor, Michigan. Carla is eighteen months older than I, and we were inseparable as little girls. In our early years, we were frequently left unsupervised by our parents and assorted babysitters. By the time I was three, we were already part of the foster care system and had lived in several foster homes. Our parents decided to go their separate ways and give us up for adoption."

Bothered by this brief account of Liz's early childhood, Rhonda creases her brows. "Why did they do that?"

"Here's what I was told: My father was getting married, and their family plans didn't include children from a previous marriage. My mother was single and couldn't afford raising two young girls on her own. As it happened, there were relatives of my biological mother who had two teenagers: a boy and a girl. They wanted a bigger family but couldn't have more children. When they learned we were to be put up for adoption, the cousin and her husband signaled interest, and arrangements were made for us to live with them in preparation for our adoption."

She pauses to take a sip of water from the bottle that Rhonda earlier placed nearby. "It was in the spring, a few months after I turned three years old, when we arrived at their farm two hours away from our home in Ann Arbor. We were city kids who had grown up playing in the streets of our neighborhood. Everything in the country was a new adventure, a new opportunity to explore as we became accustomed to farm life. For us girls, it was all about raising chicken peeps and picking dandelions. By late summer of the following year, the formalities of our adoption were just about complete.

"Then came that fateful day in mid-August." Liz shifts in her chair and sips more water, eyes glassy with tears. "Before I go any further, it's important for you to know that I don't remember any of the details. In fact, most of my life up to about twelve months after the accident has been pieced together from either family photos or what I was told by different family members over the years."

Is she saying that to avoid taking responsibility? Or is it in fact the truth? Brushing aside her doubts for the moment, Rhonda says, "That's okay, just tell me what you know."

"The day was special for us. At lunch it was announced that we were to go with the older men to the hayloft, which stored hay to feed the cows in the winter. We were told to play nice with each other and stay out of the way; if we did that, we'd get ice cream when we finished. I can only imagine how we screamed with excitement—ecstatic that we had treats and a new place to play all on the same day!" Liz smiles.

"What was everyone else doing? You know, your soon-to-be siblings and mother?"

"Lawrence, the oldest, was in Cincinnati visiting his aunt with a few of his cousins, and Gail was picking fruit at the local orchard." Liz pauses reflectively. "As far as Aunt Helen, I guess she was busy with housework, but in all our conversations I never remember her saying what she was doing at the time."

"I didn't mean to butt in earlier or appear rude," Rhonda says. "I won't do it again. Please continue, Liz."

She takes a deep breath, her eyes fixed to Rhonda's left on a mural showing a lighthouse with waves breaking against the boardwalk and people walking along its path. Liz begins, "We'd always wanted to go up to the hayloft, but it was off-limits. That day, though, we were fearless at our opportunity to explore a new playground. At the lunch table, we were reminded that we were never to go up there unless accompanied by an adult.

"After lunch, we ran to the barn and eagerly waited for the men while standing on the concrete floor at the base of the twelve-foot wall ladder leading to the hayloft. When the two men arrived, they sandwiched us between them—we were like a conga line, with our grandfather first, then Carla, then me, then Uncle Norman—as we climbed to the top of the ladder and through a four-foot opening to the hayloft. Once we were up there, they escorted us to a haystack in the back corner and told us to stay there."

Liz continues, "We played for what seemed like hours, rolling around, chasing the cats, and climbing on the bales of hay. Eventually, we got tired and began fantasizing about our treats—ice cream bars from the local ice creamery. We decided to find out when we could have them." She chuckles. "I'm sure Carla was the brains behind the operation, as I was always the foolhardy one who carried out whatever missions she cooked up."

"Anyway, I told the men that I needed to use the bathroom, so they took me down the ladder. Uncle Norman told me not to climb back up without help. I said I wouldn't and ran across the yard and into the house. Once inside, I went to the bathroom and then asked Aunt Helen about the ice cream. She seemed annoyed, showed me the treats, and then shooed me out of the house. I must've forgotten about what Uncle Norman had said, because when I got back to the barn, I went up the ladder to the hayloft by myself."

Liz closes her eyes for a second as a frown wipes away her smile and her brows knit, accenting the worry lines on her forehead. "What I didn't know was that Uncle Norman, Grandpa, and Carla had left the barn and gone to the tractor garage. Carla tells me that when she saw me running across the yard to the barn, she yelled to me, but I couldn't hear her over the tractor engine. She told Uncle Norman she had seen me go to the barn, and he sent her to get me and bring me to the tractor garage."

While Liz pauses for more water, Rhonda is mentally processing what she's heard. So far, it sounds like Liz was set to have a normal childhood and—with her future family—to have the foundation for overcoming any negative effects from living in foster care.

Rhonda looks at Liz, whose cheeks are wet with tears, and dripping onto her blue jean skirt, she asks, "Are you all right?"

Liz mumbles, "Yes."

"Are you ready to continue?"

She nods and lowers her head. "I've often wished that I could relive the next five minutes of that day, as it altered the course of everyone's lives. When Carla arrived, she yelled up the opening that I was going to get in trouble for being up there. I hurried to climb down and fell from the top of the hayloft to the concrete floor below. I landed on my head."

Rhonda covers her mouth as she gasps. "Oh my God!"

Liz pauses. "Within minutes, the men ran in and saw my limp body surrounded by a pool of blood. The older man, Grandpa, scooped me up while Uncle Norman got Aunt Helen, and the two of them drove me to the country hospital twenty minutes away. I was then transported by ambulance to a critical care hospital two hours away. I was in a coma, and the prognosis was dismal. I had suffered a severe neurological injury to the left side of my brain. The doctors said it was a miracle I was alive. They prepared the family for the reality that if I survived I would most likely spend the rest of my days in a vegetative state."

Rhonda is overwhelmed by a rush of emotions: an extreme sense of tragedy and loss, followed quickly by the euphoria of bliss. The corners of her eyes grow moist. "But you survived …."

Liz wipes her cheeks, continuing to stare at her shoes.

Suddenly Rhonda relives her own personal tragedy—her brother, Phillip, forever lost in a world of his own by a disability that couldn't be overcome. For Rhonda, the bittersweet is knowing that Liz was given a second chance for a quality life—and her bother wasn't. Despite her resentment at the unfairness Rhonda perceives that life has afforded Liz, she suppresses any rising anger and returns all focus to Liz, intent on hearing the rest of her story and then pressing forward.

Liz continues, "When I eventually came out of the coma, I had effects similar to those of a stroke victim or someone with muscular dystrophy. I was paralyzed on my right side and had the vocal skills of an infant. It took months of therapy to retrain my brain; I had to relearn everything from walking to talking."

She hesitates. "I will never know what happened during those weeks and months when I was in critical care. I only know that when I finally came home, I wore a leg brace and a leather helmet, I stuttered, and I had a six-inch scar that framed my bald head from the top right corner of my forehead to the middle of my left ear along my hairline," she says, lifting her bangs to reveal part of her scar.

Rhonda stares in shock—her concentration solely on her client. The tragedy that Liz endured is inconceivable to her; it's a side of life she's known others have traversed, but she's never heard it expressed in such vivid detail until now. As the words resonate in her mind, a glimpse of the struggles that Liz has faced with her disability stuns her into silence. She finally speaks. "That's an amazing story. You're a miracle child."

Liz tersely responds, "I don't feel like a miracle right now. I feel like the ugliest person who ever walked the earth—like the hunchback of Notre Dame. I just want it to end. I want to be normal and have people not ask about my leg or pity me. I want to be touched by a man and loved for who I am—not made to feel like I'm part of a freak show. That's the miracle I want."

Rhonda pauses. "I believe we'll get there, Liz, but we need to take first things first. Are you good for us to continue with the past?"

Liz's face turns red, and she gulps. "I'm sorry for my self-pity. Please continue."

"Thank you, Liz. It will be okay, really." She hesitates. "Let's pick back up with what happened when you returned from the hospital."

"I went to live with my adopted family—Aunt Helen, Uncle Norman, and their kids; Carla was gone. My biological mother used to visit every year; sometimes she had Carla with her, sometimes she didn't. My biological father never visited me again."

"If you both were adopted, what happened to Carla?"

"That's just it. We were both supposed to be adopted. But my new parents were only allowed to adopt me, or so the story goes."

"Where did Carla go?"

"She stayed on the farm for a while after my accident. She wasn't allowed to visit me in the hospital. They only showed her pictures. Eventually, one of our biological parents came and got her. Carla spent her childhood bouncing from home to home—our birth mother's, birth father's, or uncle's family on our mother's side. The most she would stay at any one place was six months."

Silence falls in the room, giving Rhonda a chance to react to Liz's story, as opposed to her own. The initial sadness she felt at Liz's loss of family quickly morphs into hope of a bright future with her new life—post accident. Where did Liz's bright path get off track and lead to her current state of hopelessness and desperation?

After a few moments, Rhonda manages, "It's a wonder you lived. That's a lot to be thankful for."

Liz's words come at her in a blazing fury. "Thankful? *Thankful?* Until you suffer the tragedy that I have—facing unceasing physical and emotional pain—you can't grasp what I've gone through, and you never will. I don't see my life as a blessing to me—or anyone else, for that matter."

Recoiling at the bitterness in Liz's tone, Rhonda debates between getting her to center on the goodness of her life and creating a life plan based on that or allowing Liz time to whine about past injustices which she can no longer affect. She decides that whatever tack she takes, she has to be very deliberate to assist her—changing the words as necessary to keep Liz engaged in the discussion until she hits a point where she's ready to take positive action.

In an upbeat voice Rhonda says, "Liz, the fact that you lived, that you got a second chance—well, that's something some people never get. You may not see it that way, but your strength has taken you beyond the helplessness you felt as a child."

Liz cocks her head, and all emotion drains from her face. "I don't understand what you're referring to."

"I get that your physical condition has caused hardships. But I've met many people through the years, and I have never encountered anyone who has demonstrated as much resilience as you to overcome so many hurdles to grow into an independent woman who has worked her entire career helping others. In fact, most of my time with clients is spent helping them develop self-motivational strategies, but I don't see that as the case with you at all." She pauses. "The challenge, as I see it, is for you to decide what to do with that level of perseverance and self-direction to have a life that's fulfilling to you."

"You may see it that way, but I don't." Liz gazes at her shoes. "Rhonda, I get stopped every time I face another stranger who stares at my walk and asks what happened. With every man who only wants to be friends once he sees me walk, and with every employer who doesn't call back to offer me a job after an interview, I always wonder, is it because of my leg? I just want to be like everyone else." Liz sobs.

"You're not."

"But I want to be," Liz pleads.

"And I want longer legs."

Oh, my God. Did I just say that? Rhonda cringes at her analogy; it borders on being grossly insensitive in the conversation at hand. While deciding how to save face, she feels embarrassment burn deep in her cheeks—her own vanity, the length and shapeliness of her legs—brought on by a conversation with a client about that person's leg being disabled. How could she have been so thoughtless?

Humiliated, she bows her head as low as she can. "I'm so sorry for my choice of words; they were completely inconsiderate. Please accept my apology, Liz."

Liz seems to dismiss her words. "Rhonda, do you know what it's like to know you can never walk, shop, or travel without some major accommodation? My life's not easy, and a lot of people aren't up for the challenge. They want the simple version of a relationship. I'm sick and tired of everyone I meet having to know what happened."

She grimaces and sarcastically says, "I've actually considered recording my story and just playing it for people when they ask. Of course I'll smile while aching inside, and when it's over, we can pick up the conversation and maybe develop a friendship or perhaps something more."

"So if I understand correctly, you would say that your leg is a disempowering conversation, correct?"

Liz's eyebrows draw close as she scoffs. "That's an understatement."

Rhonda writes a note to make sure she comes back to that statement later. "I don't want to disregard what you told me today; there's a lot for us to review and for you to bring closure to. For now, though, I'm asking that you put the past aside so we can work on a few concepts going forward. Do you think you can do that?"

"Sure, I'll try," Liz says in an inspired voice.

"Great. I want you to consider this: You can't control someone's reaction, and in many cases, they are simply mirroring your expectations."

Liz purses her lips. "Can you give me an example of what you mean?"

"When someone asks what happened, you expect them to be put off by your story, right? Therefore, you probably deliver it in a negative tone; rather than being upbeat."

Liz nods. "I understand; but reality is that it always happens that way."

"In one of our earlier sessions, you challenged me to understand your life by taking my shoe off and walking around, didn't you?" Rhonda asks.

"Yes, I did, because that's the only way I know to help someone understand what daily life is like for me."

"Well, in one sense you're right; no one can empathize until they truly understand the world through your eyes, or in this case, your feet. However, for a shift to occur in your interactions with people, you need to give them a glimpse into your life in whatever manner is appropriate from their perspective—not yours."

"How else would I do it?" Liz takes a deep breath. "Besides, if I talk about it with others, how much do I have to share?"

"We'll work on that, Liz. When we get to that stage, it'll be easier than you think."

"This has been tough for me," Liz says. "I know you want to continue, but I'm done. I don't want to talk anymore."

"What's wrong?"

Liz pauses. "Ah, there's a lot for me to think about, and I need time to myself."

"I didn't mean to upset you," Rhonda says, "but we need to continue."

"I can't—I'm through." Liz grabs her belongings and stands up.

"Please don't go, Liz. I'm sorry that I pushed you so hard today. Let's continue by taking it a bit slower."

Liz studies Rhonda for a long moment and says, "It's too late for that. I've got to go. Thank you for listening, Rhonda." She turns and limps away.

Rhonda calls after her, "You're welcome. I hope to see you soon." She bows her head and looks at the notes in her lap; would she be as strong as Liz has been to face what she has gone through in her life? Or would she become a recluse wallowing in self-pity and collecting disability benefits without ever trying to work and support herself? She shivers, hoping she will never have find out.

With the sounds of Liz's footsteps fading as the front door slams shut, Rhonda fears that she may be failing her, as today's session was more about Liz recounting her past and less about actions that will result in a successful plan that she can create and execute for her life, spilling over eventually to her business. Liz inferred that she's worked with professionals in the past, yet nothing has changed, so is there something everyone's missing that has sidelined her efforts? Will she ever see Liz again, or will Liz be one of those clients who asks for Rhonda's guidance but isn't willing to undertake the necessary work to improve things? Rhonda hopes she doesn't have to wait long to find out.

15

Pictures Heal the Present

Two weeks later, Liz attends her first homework party at Coco's. As she nears the coffee shop, she drives past Rhonda's office. Regretting her dishonesty, she wishes she could have been strong enough to tell the truth about how the accident happened. However, since that may have been her only chance to do so, she worries that she may not be able to move beyond it.

Pulling into a handicap parking space close to the entrance to Coco's, Liz suppresses her anxiety by shifting focus to her next task at hand—the homework party. She walks in and sees Sam already seated in a booth at the back with black mugs and a matching carafe of coffee. "Hi, Sam, how are you?" Liz asks as she sits.

His green eyes flash. "I'm great, thank you for asking. Looks like it might be a short night, as it's just us; I got emails from the rest of the group, and they're all attending other homework parties this month."

"Oh."

"Where do you think we should begin?"

"Let's start by reviewing the assignment," Liz says, pulling the project instructions from her backpack. “When I read it at home, I was confused.”

“Okay,” he says, taking the instructions from her. “The first step is to create a scrapbook of your life in the form of a photo album or another visual display, which includes photos of yourself from each year. Then add notes of significant events that happened.” He pauses as the smile lines frame his slight smile. “Gee, that sounds easy.”

She responds, “I know. And I’ve started thinking about it. I know where all my old albums are located—”

“That’s all the homework we were supposed to get done for this month,” he says. “In fact, I didn’t bring anything with me tonight. I thought this was going to be a getting-to-know-each-other session, and since we’ve already done that, I guess we can go home.”

“Well, I’ve had a long day with clients, so I’d like to sit and chat a bit to relax if you have time,” she says.

Sam’s lips purse as he studies her. “I still have a lot that needs to be done before I call it a day. I don’t mean to be rude and cut things short. I’m game to stay if there’s more homework, otherwise, I’d rather get going.”

She abruptly picks up the homework directions and stuffs them into her backpack. “Good night, Sam.”

“I’m sorry if I was abrupt, Liz. It’s just part of the new me—speaking what’s on my mind, rather than swallowing it and getting mad at the way things turn out. I guess I have to work on softening my words a bit.”

Liz realizes that he’s not interested in her after all, because if he were, he’d stay and talk. “It’s okay. I’m wearing big-girl panties today.”

“C’mon, I’ll walk you to your car.”

“You don’t have to, Sam. I’m right out front.”

He throws his hands up and in a perturbed voice says, “You’re being silly now. I saw where you parked when you walked in; we’re next to each other. Let’s go.”

Once outside, they walk side-by-side to her car, and he opens the driver's door. Smiling, she brushes past him to open the back door and tosses her crutch inside.

"I'll try to remember that Steve doesn't like to ride shotgun," he says with a grin. "I always want to do the right thing as a gentleman."

Liz blushes as she closes the door and slides into the driver's seat. She thinks, *I should've thrown the damn crutch in the front. Now he thinks I'm difficult and won't want to walk me out again.* She says, "Thank you, Sam. Good night."

The following morning, Liz wakes to the unmistakable whine of hungry cats. Pulling the covers aside, she says, "You two make a great substitute for an alarm clock. I have to get up 'cause I can't snooze you!"

After feeding the girls and having her own breakfast, Liz goes to the basement, located off the kitchen near the dining room entrance, in search of childhood memories. She quickly locates the box where her keepsakes are stored on a dusty shelf; she wipes it off and carries it awkwardly to the staircase. To get it upstairs, she puts the box on the highest step she can reach and takes a few steps up, moving it further as she continues up the staircase. When she reaches the top, she puts it on a rolling chair and rolls it into the living room. She grabs the black and white floral cloth-covered scrapbook she bought last week and sets everything up on the dining room table. As she uncovers the box containing all her memorabilia, she's confident her assignment won't take that long; when she's done she'll have a mosaic of her.

Unpacking her memories, Liz is quickly drawn into the emotions of her yesteryears. She is saddened as she touches the remnants of a life that's no longer hers: the white lace-covered wedding album her mother made for her, dried flowers from her last garden, a CD of Timothy's recorded music, and a bottle of beach sand her father packed for her when she moved out of the house at eighteen—so she would always feel close to home. She then turns to the photos—more reminders—four different states in which she's lived, encompassing more than eighteen apartments and houses; friends, lovers, and business associates she lost touch with years ago; and decisions that didn't work out the way she intended, like throwing away a college education for a fresh start in a strange city or deciding to get married because she was lonely. Sorting through the photos to select for her pixography, she reexperiences the sentiments of each time and event.

By the end of the day, Liz's emotions are raw from crying her way through the years. That night sleep finds her quickly, with her beloved cats curled at her feet. In her dreams, she can't escape the flashes of life recounted earlier that day, each scene looping through her mind like a continuous video feed.

In the morning, she awakens with deep sadness. Just as she thinks she's going to stay in bed for the day, she hears the cats cry at the base of the steps and sighs. "Okay, I'll be there in a minute," she calls. Then she mutters, "Some days you two are needier that any child could ever be."

Limping down the tan carpeted stairs, she spies the girls pacing impatiently near the bottom landing, looking as if they'd be chiding her if they could. Once on the main floor, she limps into the kitchen, grabs their food from the counter, and bends to fill their bowls, all while clinging to her crutch for support. She asks her tabbies, "Do you girls think I'd ever forget to feed you?"

She looks at Abbey, the bigger of the twin cats. "You're getting chubby," she says in a teasing voice. "You're going to have to go on a diet or else exercise more."

She cocks her head. "Do they have a treadmill for cats?"

She laughs at the image in her mind. "Even if they did, I'm not sure I can pull you away from the food bowl that long, Abbey."

Then she prepares a cup of coffee, grabs a blueberry muffin, and makes separate trips to carry them both into the dining room.

She scans the round wooden table covered with partially completed pages of her pixography and piles of unused pictures. She's ready for the next step, which is to identify and record her self-defeating statements. This should be easy, since many of them are still swirling in her head from yesterday.

Sinking back in her chair, she says, "Let's see: 'I don't want to'—'It's not fair'—and 'They don't like me' are the top three that come to mind."

Writing on multicolored Post-it notes, her thoughts trail to whatever comes to mind next as she looks through the pages of her pixography. Hours later, she stops and reviews her work. There's an odd pattern; it starts with her negative reaction to something and ends in less than what she expected might result in light of the situation. For instance, when she got in a fight with her parents over what course of study she should follow in college, they withdrew their financial support when she announced she wanted to either be a doctor or a psychologist. Despite her conflicted feelings that much of her life didn't go as planned, she records all the self-defeating statements she has from the years in review.

"I've gotta break for a bit," she says out loud to the nearby cat.

She carries her plate and cup to the kitchen and heats up a few leftovers for lunch. When she returns, she sorts through the colorful pile of Post-it notes to match up the statements with the year they first appeared in her language. She takes the note with "It's not fair" and turns through the pages, stopping at "Age 6." There she sees a picture of young Liz walking to the bus on her first day of school, flanked by her adopted siblings. She sticks the note at the bottom of the page, as seeing the three of them boarding the bus together reminds her of the statement. Instantly, the longing she has had for Carla since childhood resurfaces, and she sighs.

"Yes, it wasn't fair that we were separated. It wasn't fair that I got adopted and she didn't. It wasn't fair that—"

Her words trail off as she glances at the next page, with pictures of her and Carla during one of Carla's annual visits. Next to them is a black-and-white photo of Liz sitting in the backyard swing hanging from the maple tree; she's alone, with a leg brace on, her shoulder-length white-blond hair blowing in the wind, and big, sad eyes looking at the ground. It must have been the spring, a year or two after her accident; Carla was already gone.

Studying the picture reminds Liz that every time she sat in that swing, she felt alone and depressed. Now, looking back on the entirely of her life, she understands why. This technique also helps her draw similar conclusions to other distressing times that she endured.

She continues her work of putting the Post-it notes on various pages, connecting many of her self-defeating statements to the pictures and memories in the pixography.

When she finishes, evening has come, and she prepares dinner for herself and the cats. Then she returns to her pixography, as if seeing it for the first time. The combination of pictures, people, events, and Post-it notes with limiting statements serves to once again summon emotions and memories to the forefront of her psyche. Who can help her sort out these feelings? Since she lied to Rhonda, it's not going to be her.

With weeks before the next course meeting, she can drive herself crazy fixating about the past. So she stows the unused photos in her keepsake box and closes the cover to her pixography.

As if instinctively knowing she's needed, Ruby rubs against Liz's leg and drops the cloth mouse at her feet. Liz reaches down and finds herself engrossed in a game of fetch, followed by an evening of mindless television.

16

Wishes to Change the Past

Weeks have passed, and Liz has an idea of how to mend things with Rhonda. Before she loses her nerve, she dials her cell phone.

The voice on the other end answers, "Hello, this is Rhonda Jackson."

After some pleasantries, Liz gets to her point. "This Friday our homework group is meeting for dinner near Coco's. I was hoping you and I could meet beforehand and catch up on a few things."

Rhonda says, "Oh, yes! I'm glad you called. I was beginning to worry since I hadn't heard from you. Friday would be great because I have something to talk to you about also. Oh, and Liz, I think I'll be at your dinner party. It seems your team, the team I mentor, and Justin's team have been talking for a while about having a big get-together, and they decided this Friday would be perfect."

Feeling left out, Liz asks, "Why didn't I hear about it?"

"I just saw it on Facebook, so you'll probably see the details shortly."

"How many people will be there?"

"Probably close to twenty. I know almost everyone who's

invited as I've mentored two of the three groups. I'm sure you'll know a lot of them also."

Friday afternoon when Liz arrives at Rhonda's office at the agreed time, four-thirty, she notices something's changed.

"Oh, you made a coffee station!" Liz says, eying the red single-serve Keurig atop the small black refrigerator, covered with rainbow-colored coffee mugs.

"Yep, and it's great—except I'm finding I drink a lot more these days, and I'm having to stop to use the restroom in the midst of client appointments." She blushes. "Would you like coconut crème or French vanilla?"

"Coconut, please," answers Liz, settling into her familiar seat.

"Before we begin, I wanted to make sure you're still coming to the dinner party," says Rhonda as she hands Liz her coffee.

"I wouldn't miss it for anything," Liz says, exuding excitement.

"There's something I'd like to talk to you about before we begin."

"Okay, I'm listening," Liz says, a little nervous.

"When we first met, your walk stirred up feelings on a personal level from my past that I wasn't ready to deal with. It's unprofessional for me to bare my problems to you, so I said nothing. However, as time went on, I knew I needed to talk to you about it. You see, you reminded me of my twin brother, Phillip, whom I haven't mentioned to anyone for more than twenty years. He was born with Group B streptococcal septicemia, also called Group B strep. Many infected babies don't live past a few years. In his case, he lived much longer. His symptoms resembled those of a person with severe cerebral palsy."

"So why did I upset you?"

"It was a knee-jerk reaction," Rhonda says, turning away in embarrassment.

"I'd think that growing up with it, you'd be more understanding."

"The only thing I knew was jealousy," Rhonda says. "He got all the attention from my parents, and I got none. His needs were more important than mine. In fact, when we turned seven, my birthday party was canceled because he got sick. At ten, I couldn't go to summer camp because money went toward his medical bills. And at sixteen, I had to skip prom because he was admitted to the hospital. The way I reacted was wrong, but I was too immature to see any other perspective."

"I didn't realize what your life was like, Rhonda," Liz responds, feeling for her. "How old were you when he passed?"

"It was the day we turned eighteen," she says sadly.

Liz leans forward. "If you don't mind, can you share what happened?"

Rhonda sighs, folds her arms, and begins, "We had a birthday party with 'seventies music, bright colors, flashing strobe lights, and two cakes—chocolate for me and lemon for Phillip. All the family and our close friends attended. Everyone cooed over him as you do with a young child. He grinned and cackled, and at moments you felt as if he was connecting with you. At the end of the party, my mother laid him down for a late afternoon nap. When she went to check on him for supper, he was dead."

"I'm sorry," Liz says woefully.

Rhonda looks away. "Not as much as I am. Every year on my birthday, I wished that I had been the only child so my parents would love me more and pay attention to me. That year as I blew the candles out on my cake, I wished that my relationship would change with my parents. The next day, both those wishes had come true, only not the way I meant.

"After he died, instead of having time for me, they felt so much guilt that a healthy family relationship was just about impossible. Mom could never talk to me again without mentioning his name. My father was silent and emotionally withdrawn for the most part.

Eventually, I stopped wanting to have a relationship with either of them. It was too heartbreaking to know I wasn't even second best."

"Can you change it with them now?" Liz asks hopefully, her eyes intently on Rhonda.

"It's too late. My parents both died in a car accident a few years after Phillip passed. As the obedient daughter, I did what was expected—I buried them, along with my memories, hurt, and anger. Seeing you, however, brought back the silent rage that had been growing in me since early childhood." She covers her eyes and rubs her eyebrows. "I was repulsed at the memory of Phillip. The anger I laid to rest all those years ago was quickly unearthed."

Rhonda moves her hand and peers straight at Liz. "The past doesn't excuse my current behavior and any thoughts you must have of my unprofessionalism. However, like you, my humanity rears its ugly head at times, and I can't always control it. I'm sorry—I hope you can understand and forgive me."

Liz reflects on her confession and feels a twinge of compassion. "I understand, Rhonda; really, I do. Is there anything I can do to help?"

"Before I answer that, there's a second part to the story," says Rhonda. "As a child, I too was born with a disability."

Liz's eyebrows crease. "You look fine to me," she skeptically says, silently comparing her disability to what Rhonda might have had.

"I was fortunate. I stuttered as a child, but with the help of speech therapists, I outgrew it by the end of third grade."

"Let me get this straight," Liz says with a huff. "Both you and your brother had disabilities, yet you resisted helping someone like me, because—"

"Like your past, it's complicated, Liz. Trying to sort through my emotions, I finally realized the shame and humiliation I bore as a child labeled with a handicap was at the root of my prejudice. It's as if the mere association with an individual who has a disability would bring back mine—as if it were contagious. I'm not sure if that even makes any sense to you."

Liz stares down at her scuffed-up shoes, the right one lightly covered with dried grass clippings on its two-inch black rubber buildup. "Unfortunately, it does. I've had those same thoughts and feelings myself—only toward others." She pauses. "Rhonda, I'm curious. Why couldn't you tell me that?"

Rhonda swallows hard. "I deliberately avoided talking about it so I wouldn't have to face the pain and humiliation again. When we met, it brought me back to that period in my life I've been trying to forget. By eluding you, I wouldn't have to face my own fears and shortcomings of the past. I hope you're able to understand."

"I get it," Liz says, lowering her head. Can she tell her the truth and trust that Rhonda will take it in a positive manner?

Before she can decide, Rhonda interrupts, "Are you ready to continue where we left off last time we met?"

Hesitant, Liz remains with her head bowed, vacillating between being truthful or just moving on. Finally she nods. "First, can I tell you what I've been working on?"

"Sure."

"Since you're a mentor in the Visionary Course, you're familiar with the homework, right?"

Rhonda nods in agreement.

"Over the past few weeks, I've been working hard on my pixography," says Liz. "I've already matched a few of my self-limiting or doubting conversations, as I think of them, to events in my pixography to help me discover why I react to certain events the way I do."

"This is great progress! Have you found that the pixography also helped with the questions I gave you?"

Liz stares at her in disbelief. "You said not to worry about the questions."

"I didn't mean forever, just for a few weeks."

"That's not what you said," Liz says, determined to resist.

"Well, it's what I meant. Liz, I feel like I'm pushing you on this. Last time we met, you said you were ready to resolve issues about your leg so we could move forward and work on your life; yet I don't see you doing anything on your end to help. In fact, I've been concerned and worried that if we don't get back to the work we were doing though the questions, we might have to start all over."

Liz, never a fan of stretching out the pain of getting caught in a lie, the way she often did as a kid, decides she might as well get the lynching over with quickly. She blurts, "I didn't tell you everything."

Rhonda's eyes fly open in shock. "What do you mean?"

"It didn't happen the way I told you."

Rhonda's voice rises. "The accident—you lied to me?"

Liz stiffens, hunkering back in the couch as if to be out of Rhonda's reach. She protests, "No! I wouldn't call it a lie."

Rhonda waves her hand up as in anger. "What would you call it, then?"

"I just didn't tell you everything."

Rhonda's lips purse and her eyes narrow as she asks, "Liz, let me ask you a question. Why did you want to work with me?"

"I thought you could help give my life direction."

"Wasn't I clear from the beginning that if I was to help you, I needed to know your story?"

Liz feels the anger in Rhonda's stare and mutters, "I understand that."

"Do you realize that our time working together may have been wasted? I'm proposing solutions, directions, and clarity based on a false foundation of your story. So everything I've told you, everything we've discussed, may not work?" She slams her pen on her paper.

Liz sits motionless in silence. Not knowing what else to say, she sheepishly says, "Okay."

"Okay? *O-kay?* Miss Liz, you need to think about this real hard because right now I'm not sure I'm the person to help you." She stands up and marches out of the room, her high heels clicking rapidly on the hardwood floor and her auburn hair whipping past her shoulders, while calling over her shoulder, "Have a good day."

Liz is shell-shocked. Even if she told her the truth now, she doubts that Rhonda could hear it and understand her side of things. She never should have said anything; she should have kept it to herself and just moved on.

She waits; surely Rhonda will return in a few minutes. Meanwhile, she studies every detail of the office, but her eyes settle on Rhonda's newest art addition hung above the Keurig. It's a photo of long fence posts lining a wheat field, each post topped with a shoe or a boot; some battered like hers, others in seemingly pristine condition, and some with names painted on them. For some reason, this real-life scene lightens her heart about her own footwear and lets her begin to think of them as something other than ugly.

Ten minutes later, Liz decides Rhonda isn't returning and reaches down for her crutch. Pain shoots through her hip. She struggles to stand and slowly limps out of the building, descending on the stairs carefully to her car, which for the first time—and maybe the last—is parked directly in front of Rhonda's building. She didn't expect it would end like this. Still, one good thing—there was close parking today! She gets in the car, wondering whether she should still attend the dinner. Hopefully, there are enough people to put a buffer between Rhonda and her—and if not, maybe she'll have cooled off by then.

17

The Peacemaker Prevails

Rhonda calls Justin from her upstairs bedroom while watching through the treetops as Liz gets into her car. First the back door opens, then the front, and then the car drives away.

She thinks, *What's taking him so long to answer his damn phone?*

In the middle of the sixth ring she hears a click and Justin's voice, "Hi, Rhonda. I'm finishing work now; can it wait till I see you at dinner?"

"No, it can't," she says, biting off the words. "I told you I didn't want to work with her."

"Wait, what? Are you talking about Liz?"

"Who else would I be referring to? Queen Elizabeth?" she nearly shouts.

"Whoa, simmer down," he says. "I've never heard you this upset before. What happened?"

"She lied to me about her accident."

"How do you know that?"

"She told me she lied, although she didn't refer to it as lying."

"Okay. What's the lie?"

Rhonda is outraged at his questions. She shouts, "I don't know, and I'm not sure I care. As far as working with her is concerned, I'm done!"

"You're giving up so quickly?"

His tone, even more than the continued questions, enrages her. "Justin, I've worked several months with her, and now we're back to square one. It's pointless for me to continue."

"I'm sure she did the best she could. You need to back up and understand why she did this. It's her issue, and you're taking it as a personal assault. Remember, you said she's an expert at adapting a situation to fit her needs. She's probably perfected it in order to survive; she doesn't even know she does it. I doubt it was meant maliciously."

"It doesn't matter."

"Rhonda"—now his exasperation is coming through—"what did you expect from her? That everything would move ahead smoothly, and you could give her life a new direction in a few quick sessions? Her situation, as most, has been a lifetime in the making. Besides, you know as well as I that for progress to be made in any program, you often have to take a step or two backward."

"It didn't include lying to me."

"Come on, Rhonda. You started building a relationship where you two could work together, and in few minutes of her doing something you didn't like, you both blew it up."

Rhonda stares at the empty spot where Liz's car was parked.

"You reverted to not working with disabled people, and she's back to denial and avoidance," says Justin. "You've both regressed. You need a break, and so does she."

"I need to quit," she says, not entirely for dramatic effect.

"My request is that you evaluate this from a business perspective and consider how it impacts her and your coaching practice before making any decisions in haste that you may later regret."

Silence—then Rhonda continues in a low voice, "I'm not sure

right now that I'm willing to give it another chance. I reached out to her the first time and overcame my reluctance. She's going to have to reach out next time if we're ever going to work together again."

"I understand," Justin says. "I'm glad you called and let me know what happened. We'll pick this up at dinner, okay?"

"Sure, I'll see you shortly."

As soon as Rhonda hangs up, she grabs her blue journal that's on the wooden bedside stand and writes frantically to release her anger in order to avoid lashing out at dinner to some innocent bystander:

> Friday, 5:00 p.m. Anger … Frustration … Disappointment … Why couldn't I keep my personal life and tragedy to myself? Why can't she follow instructions? Is it her or am I not being clear? If something doesn't change, I may need to find a new job.

With that, she puts the book aside, changes to more casual attire and a pair of running shoes, and darts out of the house. During her brisk jog to the restaurant, her mind is spinning. Should she confront Liz on their meeting or act as if nothing happened? Whatever approach she takes, it will set the stage for their next phase of work—that is, if they both decide to continue.

She arrives promptly at five thirty and makes her way to the bar in the back, where Justin and the others are assembled. "Hey, Rhonda," Justin says, "I think you know everyone except Sam, who's part of Liz's homework team."

She smiles and extends her hand. "Good to meet you, Sam."

"Likewise, Rhonda," he says.

"Oh, and here comes Liz," Justin says, as she limps from the bathroom with her long blue-jean skirt dragging the floor on her right side as she steps toward the opposite end of the bar, farthest from Rhonda. She scooches onto a barstool as the group continues to mingle around her, and Rhonda sits in silence, waiting on Liz to say something to her.

"We're ready to seat you now!" the hostess announces to the group. To Liz, she adds, "Do you need assistance?"

Liz blushes and says, "I'll be fine."

Nearing the table, Justin asks Liz where she'd like to sit. She scans the setup and replies, "Near a corner works best for me—preferably on the left since I'm left-handed."

"Here's a good spot," Justin says, pulling out a chair at the left corner, nearest to the wall, with a three-foot tall potted peace lily sitting on a white granite plant stand nearby. "Sam, why don't you sit at the end? Rhonda and I will sit over there." He points to the chairs to the right of Liz.

Rhonda leans toward Justin and hisses, "Did you see her while we were waiting? She won't even look at me. Yet she's carrying on with everyone as if nothing happened."

Sam nods.

Rhonda leans her head forward and catches Liz's glance.

Liz smiles.

Rhonda smiles back, quickly realizing that she too, is averting additional confrontation by giving the professional smile.

Within moments the waiter, dressed in a red shirt, black pants and matching tie, comes over. Liz orders off the menu while everyone else opts for the seafood buffet.

After the waiter leaves, Sam says, "I thought you said you wanted to have the buffet."

"I do," Liz says, "but the setup is a bit hard for me to get around."

Justin jumps in. "One of us can carry your plate for you."

"Maybe next time. Thank you for the offer, though," Liz politely says.

"It's easy enough to switch your order, and we'll all have the buffet," Justin insists.

"That's not—," Liz begins. "I know, don't argue with a man who's trying to be helpful."

He flags down the waiter and whispers his request. The waiter nods to Liz and says. "You can all get your food now, Enjoy."

As Rhonda heads to the buffet line, this discourse reminds her that the demand of accommodations on Liz's life is one of the core reasons why she came to Rhonda in the first place—to find a way to be normal, in a world where she perceives she isn't.

It's just the two of them, Liz and Justin, at the table; everyone else is in line for the buffet. Justin faces her and in a peaceful manner says, "Liz, you can tell me to mind my own business, but I know there's tension between you and Rhonda. She told me there was a misunderstanding and that you two aren't working together anymore. You need to think this through. I can tell you're close to a breakthrough on the matters we discussed that affect your business." He pauses. "Remember when you told me that you were having difficulty facing decisions?"

She nods.

"Well, it seems you've turned that around and probably a few other things too. So rather than being disheartened by a little bump in the road, why not continue?"

"It doesn't matter, Justin. It was only a matter of time before it happened. If it wasn't this time, it would've been at another juncture. It's best now before anyone gets hurt further."

"Why do you say that?" he asks.

"No one has ever been able to withstand the truth. I was an idiot to think she would be any different."

"Maybe. But you're fooling yourself if you believe you can

travel this journey alone. Perhaps it's time for you to go somewhere to sort things out?"

She considers his suggestion. "The only place I can go is home to Michigan."

"Then maybe it's time for a trip back there."

Liz is silent. Suddenly she asks, "Justin, did you do the pixography in the course?"

"Yes, why do you ask?"

"Well, I keep getting drawn back into the emotions of my past by pictures I put in my pixography, and I'm not sure how to go forward; I was hoping to talk to someone who can give me a bit more guidance."

"If it would help, we can meet for coffee, and I'll walk you through what I learned when I did mine." He pauses. "In fact, if you're like me, you might choose to use your pixography as a form of self-therapy after the course is over."

"How does that work?" she asks.

"Without having it here, it's hard for me to explain. It may be a bad analogy, but it's sort of like learning to ride a bike from a book—it doesn't work that way. You have to do it for yourself. Feel free to call me anytime, and I will find a way to meet with you on it."

"Thank you, Justin. That's very kind."

Just then, a server approaches and says to Liz, "If you're ready for the buffet, miss, I can carry your plate."

Liz smiles and looks at Justin. "Do you mind? This way you don't have to balance two plates plus side dishes and silverware."

"By all means! Whatever makes you comfortable," he says.

She graciously nods, gets her crutch, and stands up. She limps to the buffet line with the server following.

During dinner, Rhonda continues studying Liz, who is carrying on like everything is great. What part of her accident isn't true? Will they ever be able to talk beyond it?

As dinner ends, Rhonda concludes she's not the person that Liz needs to help give her life direction right now. Maybe at a different time or in a different situation she could help—but not now. And if Liz ever wants to continue, she'll need to change her ways for Rhonda to be willing to work with her again.

18

Memories That Keep Us Locked in Dark Places

The next morning Liz is having coffee and regrets from the previous evening, wishing she had handled things differently with Rhonda. But the point of no return came so quickly—when she couldn't go back and tell the truth or repair the damage she'd done. Is there ever a way to rewind the past and have a do-over?

Seated on the couch, she looks at the pixography on the coffee table, where it has sat untouched for weeks. The cats jump up, curl on either side of her, and promptly fall asleep.

Liz sips her coffee while fixated on last night's tiff with Rhonda. It reminds her of the last argument she had with her dad a few years before he died. The two of them never spoke again after she stormed off from the family picnic that day; it kept her from trusting him and wanting to be close—until he was on his deathbed. Then it was too late.

Liz closes her eyes as she remembers her father's final days:

Her father stared at her as if she was a stranger. Liz burst into tears and ran out of his hospital room, followed quickly by Gail, her oldest sister.

"What's wrong?" Gail asked gently.

"I-I didn't expect that he wouldn't know me," Liz stammered.

Gail took her hand, just as she had on Liz's first day of school, and escorted her to his bedside. "Daddy, Liz doesn't think you recognized her with her new hairdo."

He winced, visibly muster all his energy, and whispered, "Oh, I know Lizzy, even with red hair." He gave her a feeble smile, pinched her hand, and threw her his wink. She hugged him around the IV lines and sat by his side, determined to be there for the rest of his life—just as he had been there for all of hers.

Within hours, he lost the ability to utter even the simplest of words, and the spreading infection made him too weak to smile even if he wanted to. As his condition declined, her need for his forgiveness intensified. How could she have been so self-absorbed to disregard the lasting impact her actions had on others? She yearned to bridge the distance that had come between them, but the time for her confession had long passed. Liz could only express her love and appreciation to him.

As the end neared, the family left Liz alone with him. She felt like Daddy's little girl again—laughing at the memory of his teasing. She hadn't giggled like that for decades; neither had he. She took his hand, which had always been so powerful, and noticed its frailty under the weight of the needle taped to it. "Daddy, I love you, and I've missed you so much. I never planned to hurt you and Mom by the way I lived my life. I ask for your forgiveness."

She saw compassion and love in his eyes.

"I've never thanked you for the sacrifices you made to give me the life I have today. You've always treated me as one of your own children. Most of all, I'm grateful for your love, which I hold daily in my heart."

Tears streamed down his cheeks. She leaned over, brushed them away, kissed him for the last time, and whispered, "Don't worry, Daddy. Timothy will take care of me."

When she looked up, the worry that had creased his brow was gone. It was as if the clock had rewound the hands of time, and she saw him as her age, in his early forties. They were frozen in that moment with nothing between them but their love for each other—two hearts and souls connected forever.

The rest of the family came in shortly thereafter, followed by the chaplain to give Dad last rites. The nurse administered one last dose of morphine, and the family gathered around his bed.

Lawrence, her brother, began reciting Bible verses they all knew well. By the glow in her father's eyes, she could tell he was reciting the twenty-third Psalm with them. "… Though I walk through the valley of the shadow of death, I will fear no evil …." Everyone held hands and recited the Lord's Prayer, ending with a resounding "Amen."

Liz watched as her dad drew his final breath, the brightness in his eyes fading and his tears ceasing. The respirator that had breathed for him the last few weeks was eerily silent. The head nurse appeared, checked his vitals, and declared him dead.

She hugged her mother and slipped out of the room, her tears so heavy as she walked that she couldn't see the floor in front of her. Clinging to the glass wall between the lobby and the patient wing, she needed someone to grieve with; she called her husband, Timothy.

His response: "I can't deal with this."

The phone went dead; she sank to the floor, feeling abandoned, just as she did when they'd taken Carla away many years ago.

Soon there were soft footsteps, and she saw a black-clad man pushing a silver steel cart toward her father's room. A few minutes later he returned with a filled body bag on top of the cart's thin mattress.

The end of the cart, though, was radiant white; she saw her father sitting on the edge with his hands at his sides and his feet dangling down. She wanted to run after him, to hold him in this life, but she knew it was time for her to let go.

As she walked out of the hospital that afternoon, Liz inexplicably stopped in the gift shop. There, she found a birdhouse that reminded her of the one her dad had helped her build for sixth-grade carpentry class. This one had a green metal frame with glass walls and an opening in the top; at the base was a gold hummingbird hovering atop a bright flower.

He would have liked it; her father was fond of hummingbirds.

Liz pulls herself back to reality and flips through the pixography again. Her dad is pictured in every year of her life until he died. She turns to the year of her accident—1964. Since Liz has no pictures of what happened to her that year, she's followed Tony's instructions and found similar ones in magazines and on the internet. The images she chose showed children in critical care units and physical therapy centers. While medical technology has greatly advanced since her accident, these photos are as close as she can get for that time in her life.

As she studies each shot, she shudders, hearing the thud that always brings back the awful memories of her accident. What was it like for her dad that day, hearing Carla shriek in terror as he scooped her up from a puddle of blood and rushed her to the hospital, not knowing if she would survive? Was he haunted for the rest of his life too, as she has been?

She closes her eyes and imagines him smiling at her.

"I love you, Daddy," she says out loud. "I miss you every day."

With a sad sigh, Liz gets up and limps into the kitchen to clear her head. Despite her intent to take a break from reliving the regrets of her past, she can't escape the anxiety that's building up inside her; ready to burst if she doesn't talk to someone soon.

She looks up Justin's phone number on her cell and starts texting: "Hey, it's Liz. I'd like to take you up on your offer to work with me on my pixography. Tomorrow at Coco's?"

Waiting for a response, Liz inventories her past relationships. Why couldn't she be like Gail and Jeffrey, her sister and brother-in-law; who have the perfect marriage, children, and lifestyle? If she did, maybe her mom and dad would've been proud of her, too; but all she has are the cats—and her parents were never fond of felines.

Her phone beeps with Justin's response: "Love to. See you at Coco's at 2 p.m. Be sure and bring your pixography, and I'll dig up mine."

She's relieved knowing that Justin will help her sort through things in just a few short hours.

19

Pictures Tell the Story

Liz arrives at Coco's a few minutes early for her meeting with Justin.

On the way to her favorite booth, near the back entrance and rest rooms, she notices a white community board on the right wall, with a flyer advertising an apartment for rent posted among the business cards hung with red, blue, and yellow pushpins. It reminds her that she has forty-five days to either renew her lease or move out. Deep down she knows that moving is her only option; she must find somewhere to live that's all on the ground floor, reducing the hip pain she has from climbing the stairs, a place that will allow her to keep the girls.

Waiting for Justin, she notices a man sitting several booths away and looking her way. She feels as if she's seen him before, only not at Coco's. He has blue eyes and dark hair, graying at the temples, and wears glasses. Could he be the guy who stood her up at the hotel bar? He couldn't be—although she drank a lot that night, she would remember him.

Their eyes meet; he ducks behind his newspaper.

She looks back at her pixography and opens it. Before what's happening can register in her mind, she hears an unfamiliar voice, "Excuse me, miss, do you mind if I join you for a few minutes?"

Liz looks up at the stranger; his tall, muscular body standing next to the table with a tan coffee mug in his hand. She finds him overly striking.

"Oh," she says. "I'm actually waiting for someone who should be here shortly."

"I'll only be a minute."

She nods, and he slides into the seat across from her.

"I'm Lance. I know this sounds like a pickup line, but I've seen you here before."

Liz smiles politely, the kindness in her eyes perhaps encouraging him.

His face taut and wide-eyed, he says, "I find you very attractive, but I was curious what happened to your leg." He poses the question in a frank, unapologetic tone; his approach reminds her of a national news reporter trying to get the inside scoop on a breaking crime.

Her cheeks redden, and she struggles to curb her rage. She snaps, "Are you serious? *That's* the first question you ask me? Even if I found you remotely good-looking, it's apparent you're an idiot. Now, go share your stupidity and ignorance with someone else."

He jumps up and marches toward the door with her glaring after him. When she hears the bell faintly jingle after the door closes behind him, she remembers to breathe. Maybe she didn't handle that the best way, but she did stand up for herself without making a scene. Would Rhonda be proud of her for that?

Looking around to confirm that nobody saw what just happened, she notices the man's abandoned coffee mug and hopes Justin isn't too mad, since she's probably cost him a customer. With a shrug she returns to her pixography.

Feeling drained so early in the morning causes her to wonder if she drank decaf instead of regular. Then she realizes she's relived her entire life in less than thirty days. It may not seem like a lot to some, but for her, the emotions stirred by reliving her past and grieving for the first time over many losses have taken a toll, both mentally and physically. How much more will she need to endure to let go of the past?

Just then she hears footsteps, only this time they bring a smile to her face as Justin approaches with his pixography tucked under his arm.

"My parents used to have an album like that," she says, seeing its blue-and-gray checked vinyl cover.

"Really? I bought this when I got my first camera, and I never used it before, so I thought it would be ideal for our course project," he says, opening the front cover. She sees its true age from the discolored tops of the adhesive pages no longer sticking to the plastic.

Chloe is right behind him, pushing her rolling blue metal cart filled with hot coffee and treats. "Here you are, Miss La-La-Liz. I hope you enjoy your c-c-coffee and stickies."

"Thank you," Liz says. "Can I ask you a question, Chloe?"

"Sh-sh-sure."

"What's your favorite thing about working here?"

Chloe's face lights up. "It's M-M-Mr. Justin. He treats me with r-r-respect and forgives me wh-wh-when I'm stupid."

Justin blushes. "You're not stupid, Chloe. You're just learning new skills. We all had to learn at one time."

"I b-b-better get back to work, or I'll get fa-fa-fired," she says, smiling at him.

Liz watches her walk to the kitchen and says, "Chloe has really blossomed since you hired her. I think all she needed was someone to give her a chance."

"She has done extremely well," Justin says, nodding. "So where did you want to start with your pixography?"

Liz moans. "Looking at it makes me feel heavy, like I'm carrying around an extra fifty pounds and it's all in my chest."

"It doesn't look that big to me," he says with a sly wink.

"Oh, Justin!" she chastises.

"You set yourself up for that." He's grinning. "Besides, it's probably no different than what you ladies say about my buns."

They laugh.

He continues. "What other thoughts do you have on it?"

"There's so much in there that I want to talk to someone about, and I only have the cats, who bore easily."

He chuckles. "Hmm. Here's what my class instructor taught us to do, and it seemed to help. He suggested we work with someone and exchange pixographies. After looking at each other's life, the conversation naturally takes off from questions that come up or stories you're each compelled to share."

"That sounds good. I'm willing to try it," Liz says. "Here's mine."

"Yours looks better," he says handing his to her.

She smiles. "I think that's a self-defeating conversation. Should I give you a sticky note to put in your book?"

"You're too late," he says with a smirk. "It's already on my eight-year-old page."

Silence settles in as they get immersed in each other's albums. When Liz gets to the last page of Justin's pixography, she notices he's already finished with hers. "So what do you think?" she asks.

"What do you mean?" he asks cautiously. "It's your life. What part of it do you want me to comment on?"

"I want to rewind and alter a few of my choices. Don't you?" Liz says eagerly, hoping for agreement.

"I haven't gotten to that step yet. I'm still trying to wrap my head around all that's happened to get me where I am today and coming to terms with my role and responsibility in each situation."

Liz starts flipping through his book again, obviously searching for something. "I want this," she says, pointing to a picture of a man and woman embracing each other, sandwiched by two toddlers and a dog, and lots of boxes in front of a moving van.

"So do I," Justin says. "That was back when we couldn't get enough of each other. Now we sleep in separate bedrooms, and the only thing we do together is balance the schedule of taking care of the kids."

"I'm so sorry, Justin."

"Don't be. I learned a lot, and some of it has been what not to do. With young children in the picture, it becomes complicated. The short version is that my wife doesn't want to be married to me anymore; but she does want the security that marriage offers. As for me, I love her as much today as I did back then." He pauses for a sip of coffee.

"It doesn't have to end that way, does it?" asks Liz. "Can't you do something to bring her back?"

"I don't know the details of your past relationships," Justin says kindly, "but I can only say we both have free will and have made choices that led us in different directions. I'm not sure if it's too late to rebuild or not." Justin rests his chin on his hand.

Liz straightens up in her seat. "There are always situations that people must work through," she says, unsure if she's speaking to Justin or herself. "No one has a perfect marriage. At the end of the day, what matters is resolving your differences, so in the morning you can start anew."

"Is that the approach you've taken in your relationships?" he asks as his eyebrows narrow.

Her lips purse. "I have to admit—no. I tried, but the other parties weren't big on open communication, so I gradually stopped fighting, and the relationships fell apart," she says wistfully. "However, I did have great role models in my parents, who were married for over fifty years. Some days I wish I had their strength and had continued the battle when I was in my marriage."

"What about now?" Justin asks. "I mean, if you had a new life partner, do you think you could make it work?"

She sighs. "I doubt whether a man would be interested in someone who hasn't demonstrated they can be committed when things get tough."

"You know you can change that by demonstrating commitment in other areas," Justin says.

"There's an Achilles' heel of mine. The C word."

He cocks his head to one side. "Um, the sea word?"

"C as in commitment. Or should I say lack of commitment? Through my pixography, I'm realizing it's at the heart of some of the choices I've made."

Justin grins. "This is too funny. You have commitment issues, and I have overcommitment issues. Once I commit, I can't stop until it dies or I do. In fact, my motto has been 'Die first, and then quit.'"

She grins. "How's that working for you?"

He takes a deep breath. "I used to think it was great, but now I realize some things aren't worth fighting for or being right on."

Her fingers tap on the table. "Justin, you bring up an interesting point. Is it more important to be right or to let others win for the sake of the relationship?"

He cocks his head. "I'm not sure. It makes me question though, what might happen with my wife if I just stopped fighting and let her win some of the issues."

"I believe it comes back to what's more important to you: pride at being correct, or having a good marriage," she wistfully says.

He smiles. "You've given me plenty to mull over, Liz. I'll let you know if I find out."

She nods and changes the subject. "Justin, what do you think of when you see me?"

"That you're an intelligent, attractive woman with a good heart who's struggling to find her way. In fact, you remind me of

Dorothy in *The Wizard of Oz*, except you don't have those shiny red shoes." He smiles. "Liz, you're searching for what's already inside you. All you have to do is unleash it."

Peering out the front windows, beyond the sidewalk filled with pedestrians, she scans the distant horizon above the storefronts across the street, as if would reveal her answer. "I have to find it first; it was buried long ago, and I forget where."

He folds his hands and twiddles his thumbs. "What I believe is more important is what's in your heart. You have a good one; it's just a bit off track right now."

"I'm working to get it back on track. Our course has provided an opportunity for me to see where I went astray from me. I have to start making tough decisions and follow through if I'm going to change what my life looks like." She pauses and asks, "Justin, what's the biggest challenge you've faced as a result of being in the course?"

He leans in. "Probably being satisfied with what I have. Looking back, I've been so focused on where I was going that I couldn't stop and enjoy where I was. I always had to be on to the next activity and filling my calendar to leave no empty spaces. Now, I realize it's been my way of filling the voids in my relationships and probably in me."

She squints and bites her lower lip. "Do you think we have a hole in our heart that prevents us from being happy?"

He looks behind her to the hallway where years ago his in-laws began posting pictures of local high school students playing sports. "I'm not sure what to say it is, Liz. I thought the life with my wife and kids would be enough. Now I wonder what's next. If I don't have my family, what becomes of me?"

She studies his face, noticing every new line and crease caused by his worry and accented by his dark hair, slightly graying at the roots. "Justin, you're a good man, just like my former husband. In his own way he adored me, but I was trying too hard to make him into what he said he wanted to be—a man who followed his passion for music and became known for the songs he wrote. We got caught up in the petty things along the way, and we both lost sight of who we were to each other until it was too late to save our marriage. But you have time, Justin. She's still alive. Make her fall in love with you again."

He frowns. "It may already be too late for that."

"It's never too late." She looks up and then back at him. "A committed man once said, 'Die first, and then quit.'"

"Hey, that's my line," he declares.

She points back to the picture of his family on moving day. "Now it's time to start living it, my friend."

He smiles in acknowledgment. "Touché."

"Justin, can I ask you one more question?"

"Sure, as long as you're not going to sucker punch me again."

"I'm sorry about that," she says quickly.

"Don't be. I deserved it." He winks. "Go ahead and give it your best shot; what's your question?"

"Why have you never asked about my leg?"

Without hesitation, he looks into her blue eyes and responds, "It simply doesn't matter to me. What I believe is important is who you are as a person and what you do in this world to positively affect others. Looks fade, but the heart lasts forever. Take my marriage, for instance." His brows draw together. "I'd rather have a woman who wants to hold my heart than one who wants me to hold her purse and high heels while she's busy catching everyone else's attention. But that's just me, Liz, and what I hold to be important; it's different for everyone." He leans forward and taps the table. "The key is to surround yourself with people who value what you bring to the party."

She tilts her head, taking in his every word. "I'd better get going, Justin. I appreciate all your help."

"Thank you, Liz, for reminding me of what I stand for. I think

I lost that somewhere these past few years. Seeing the battles that you're facing gives me the strength to wage a few wars of my own."

She smiles, gets her crutch, stands up, and limps out of Coco's, the bell jingling through the closed door behind her.

20

No Pets Allowed on the Ground Floor

With the onset of late summer, Rhonda finds herself with a focus on cleaning, so to speak; but it's not her house. The business is at an all-time low, when typically her client load is booked beyond what she has the capacity to realistically deliver. In fact, since losing Liz as a client, she's also lost three others and had a 30 percent decline from the usual number of business referrals from the many contacts she developed since starting her practice.

Although not yet alarmed, she is concerned that if the trend continues, she will need to take other measures to support herself and the business. So she sets out to identify the root cause of the business decline and tasks Mrs. Taylor with sending out confidential surveys to past and current clients, as well as her referral sources. Her hopes are that the responses will provide clarity on what she can do to resolve the problem; but deep down she fears that it may be too late to save.

It'll take a couple of weeks for the survey results to start coming in, and Rhonda is impatient . She decides to get a head start by direct contact with one of her best referral sources that appears to be drying up—Justin. She reaches out to him; he agrees to meet and discuss her business—at Coco's of course.

Rhonda slides into her back corner booth at Coco's. "Good morning, Chloe," she calls toward the busing station, topped with a large square black plastic bin.

"G-G-Good morning, Ms. Ja-Ja-Jackson. The usual?"

"Yes, that would be fine, Chloe. Can you please let Mr. Justin know I'm here for our meeting?"

"Sh-sh-sure." Chloe limps to the kitchen and disappears.

Justin comes out shortly, his black baker's apron spotted with flour. He drops a plate at the busing station, takes off and folds his apron, then heads her way. Once seated, he leans back and stretches his arm out beside him. "Greetings, Rhonda. It's a surprise to hear you wanted to meet on your business; that's a first for us to discuss."

Her eyes drop as she forces a smile, wishing she hadn't asked him to meet. Deciding how best to begin, she looks out the windows overlooking the street and catches a glimpse of a woman limping from the building next door toward Coco's.

"Ugh! It's Liz. What's she doing here?" Rhonda asks while slumping in the booth. "I don't want to run into her. Can I use the back door?"

"You sound like my ten-year-old daughter," he says, exasperated. "Let me see what I can do. By the way, this is the only time I'll do this. Next time you'll have to confront your problems squarely in the face."

Justin greets Liz at the counter while Rhonda raises a menu to block her sight. Minutes pass. *What's taking him so long?* She doesn't hear Liz's boots. Peeking from behind the list of daily baked specials, she sees Justin and Liz nearing the front door; he opens it, and she leaves.

He returns to the table with a neon green flyer in his hand. "That's too bad." He frowns.

"What happened?" she asks.

"Liz has to move to another apartment soon. She's downsizing, so to speak, and having difficulty finding a place without stairs that allows pets."

Rhonda asks, "What's she going to do?"

"If she can't find an apartment to rent, she can stay with friends who have offered her a place to crash in the short term."

"What about the cats?" Rhonda asks as her heart fills with despair for Liz. "They're her family."

"It's heartbreaking," Justin says softly. "If she can't find a home in time, she'll have to give them up to another family or take them to the humane society." He looks at Rhonda. "And we both know what happens then."

"Oh no. If they're not adopted within a week, they're put to sleep. Either option will break her heart. At least if she can find them a home, she'll rest easier."

"Liz asked if I would post this flyer to help her find a new home for them. It's the least I can do; I'd take them, but my son's allergic to cats."

"Did she say anything about me?"

"No. Her focus was simply on her girls. Although her demeanor is hopeful, I can tell it's a big weight on her."

"More than you know."

"Why do you say that?" Justin asks.

"Liz probably compares giving up the cats to some of her own childhood experiences because—" Her words stop midsentence, and her gut wrenches. She's breaching confidentiality, ready to go way too far in divulging details that Liz has only shared in their private meetings. Hoping that Justin didn't catch her lack of judgment and business ethics, she redirects. "But Justin, we're here for insights you can give me on growing my business."

He shifts in his seat and growls, "What is it you want to learn from me that you don't already know?"

She's unprepared for his question and the attitude she's detecting from him; he's supposed to openly give her advice without her having to verbally grovel for it. She blinks. "Well, for starters, what do you do to make sure customers come back and others continue to refer your business?"

He puts his hands to his chin narrows his eyes. "What are you really asking me, Rhonda?"

Suddenly his frankness puts her off; he's seen through her, and she now must be truthful, or she may never learn what she needs to in order to fix her business direction. She takes a sip of coffee, clears her throat, and dives in. "It's embarrassing to admit this, but my business is not doing as well as it has in the past. Don't get me wrong—all is fine, it's just that I'm not picking up as many clients as I used to, and the ones I get are not a good match to what I do. I was hoping you might be able to shed some light on this, as I'm sure you've been through something similar at Coco's."

His smile turns to a look of grave concern. "Aside from our totally different business models, I would think that with your people skills, you could see what you're doing wrong and correct it. After all, who am I to give advice to a life coach?" he asks with raised eyebrows.

She stretches her arms across the table as if to bridge the distance she feels between them. "Justin, I'm asking because last year you were one of my greatest sources of referrals, and ever since Liz, you haven't sent a single person to me." She stammers, "You may not have met anyone who needs my services, but I thought I would check just in case you had concerns over Liz. I know things haven't gone as smoothly as I wanted with her, but it's not all me—she has a part in it too. I still think we weren't a good fit from the start."

"Look, Rhonda, I'll get straight to the point. I think you failed Liz, but I think the bigger person you're failing is yourself. You've changed, and professionally, I don't think it's for the better."

Aghast, she asks, "In what ways? I know that I've altered my strategy to work more on growing sales, but that's necessary for me to maintain the level of income I need. I don't see how this has been for the worse."

He snorts. "I'm not prepared to dig into every single detail, so let's focus on one—your handling of Liz."

Rhonda feels the hair on the back of her neck rise in defense. She growls, "Go ahead, I'm listening."

"As an adviser, you have two main commodities you sell: your knowledge and your confidentiality. I can't comment on the first, as I'm not in your private sessions with her, but you suck at the second; and that's the one that counts when I refer business."

Rhonda's cheeks are burning from the slap of his opinion. She holds her breath, hoping that's the end of what he has to say about how she runs her practice.

He continues, "You see, I believe that we can all grow our business knowledge, but ethics, business and personal, are part of your core makeup and behavior; ethics aren't easy to change because they're developed over time."

Sinking into her seat, she asks in a deflated tone, "But what about you? You always tell me things that you know about Liz, like today with her apartment search."

He breathes deeply. "The difference is that she's paying you for confidentiality in those areas of her life. Also—there's a lot we talk about that I never discuss with anyone. I've developed trust with her and others, as I exercise discernment on what I share and only do so in areas that I have permission. People have seen that—that's why they tell me their innermost thoughts and secrets: they know it will go no further, because I don't gossip."

Rhonda's head is reeling from Justin's critique. Quick to draw conclusions, she calculates the impact to her business; if others feel the same as Justin and her referral sources have stopped trusting her, to move ahead in business, she is practically at ground zero. She'll have to establish new contacts and referral sources, in addition to rebuilding the trust, if it's possible, that she broke with her current network. Both tasks mean it will take years to reach the income flow she needs to pay her bills.

Her eyes are filling with tears, and she sighs. "I wanted the truth; I didn't expect that."

He folds his hands and says, "I'm sorry, Rhonda. That's just one man's opinion. I could be wrong; that's for you to discover."

She rests her forehead in her hands and rubs her temples to relieve the headache that has suddenly set in.

He slowly asks, "Is there anything else?"

"There's not. I appreciate your candidness, even if I didn't enjoy the message. I guess I needed to hear it from someone whose opinion I respect."

Silence follows; then she can hear him getting up from the table. "I'd better go and see how the kitchen's doing. Take care, Rhonda." He taps the table as he leaves her in silence.

21

Circumstance Parallels Our Lives

Three weeks later, Liz is down to the final days in her apartment.

She's upset that despite her wide search, she couldn't find a place to live that would accommodate her physical needs and let her keep her cats. She tries not to think about tomorrow, the day the girls will leave for their new home with a man who answered Liz's ad.

That night while Abbey cuddles on the bed at Liz's feet and Ruby is curled by her shoulder, Liz reminisces about bringing them home for the first time. Timothy had insisted they go to the animal shelter, but she wasn't so sure she wanted another pet. He fell in love with them immediately and thought they would replace Raven and keep Zevon company. She didn't want to love them, but she did. Somehow through them, she was able to make peace about Raven's death, for not making sure she was safe while they were on vacation. She never thought the cats would get loose while they were gone. Once Zevon escaped, Raven found a way to follow. She crossed the street, looking for the neighbor she always watched from the window. But she wasn't streetwise. Liz had never prepared her for that; rather, she had protected her from every danger because Raven was deaf.

Tears spring to her eyes. If only she had boarded the cats, Raven would be alive today. As if understanding her torment, Ruby stands up and settles down over her heart. Liz brushes away her tears and pets her beloved cat with her wet hand. Did her parents and Carla feel the same anguish and remorse after her accident that she does with Raven? As her older sister, Carla always protected her, but that day she couldn't. Carla didn't know the danger in the hayloft any more than Liz did with the neighbor watching Raven. It broke her heart when Raven died, and it's breaking again to lose the girls now.

Liz shifts memories to her early childhood. It was the Christmas when she was eight, and Carla and her biological grandma came to visit. She was devastated after they left, standing outside in the snow watching the car drive away as Carla's face was pressed against the back window. Both girls had tears streaming down their cheeks. That's when Liz first asked why she wasn't good enough. Why didn't they want her?

She imagines the words *It's your leg* floating above her head as she restlessly falls asleep.

The next morning Liz rises early for her last day with the girls. An hour or so after breakfast, she tries to get them into their gray knee-high carriers with one-inch metal grid doors, but the ordeal is more strenuous than she expected. The first problem is securing them in one room. Once she's managed that, she spends an hour coaxing each one out of her hiding place. By the time both girls are in their carriers, howling in terror and frustration, she has only fifteen minutes to say goodbye.

She tries to comfort them, but she is just as scared and frustrated. With tears dropping onto the carriers, she reaches through the metal bars and says between sobs, "I wish it could be different. But I can't take care of you anymore. There's a nice man and his family who will give you a good home and love you. I want to take you out and hold you one more time, but I know if I did, I would never let you go."

Moments later their new dad arrives. He rushes them to his white Ford Bronco, where he places them in the back along with all their food, toys, medical information, and special treat instructions.

Liz watches the Bronco leave. She can see the carriers above the rear window; her girls' furry faces pressed up against the metal grids, looking longingly at her to rescue them. In that moment, she's eight years old again and watching Carla leave; she cries at the loss of her girls and her childhood with her sister.

She waves one last time and manages a weak smile. She whispers through her sniffles, "I'm never going to see you again; it would be too painful. But know I will always love you."

Limping into the house with tear-flooded eyes, she feels a tremendous loss. She puts her head in her hands and collapses on the tan suede couch. When she finally calms down, she's intrigued at the parallels between these two seminal moments in her life. Rationally, she can understand the dilemma her parents faced when they decided she was to be given up for adoption because they believed it was best for her. However, she doesn't understand why they couldn't see that it was the right thing to keep Carla and Liz together, just as it was better for Liz to keep the two cats together. If only Liz had pressed for the real answers when all her parents were alive, maybe she wouldn't have been haunted so long over her adoption and the accident. Then she remembers the thud; the sound of which is still too painful for her to confront and attempt to reconcile.

She packs up her feelings—disappointment, loss, rejection—as best she can and puts them in the corner of the dining room with the other brown, taped, boxes going into storage. Walking toward the kitchen, she hopes that the next chapter of her life brings clarity despite her heartbreak, which will last forever.

22

Transforming Self-Defeating Statements

Several months later, Liz is in her new home: a dingy one-room ground floor efficiency. She has only three hundred square feet of space and two twelve-inch windows, but it's within twenty minutes of Coco's. Her new surroundings daily remind her of being eighteen and living in her first apartment, a one-bedroom flat built on top of a garage. Back then she drove a '78 Plymouth Fury and ate twenty-five-cent mac 'n' cheese from a box.

Now she worries about how she will get her laundry done or carry groceries from the parking lot. Her current life has afforded her more conveniences than in the past, including a place and time where she can have privacy to reflect on her life. She hopes that this move will inspire her to create a new direction for the future.

Over the last few months, Liz has focused on developing new client relationships through the local business and service clubs. She continues with the Visionary Course, and now that she is not tied down with cat care, she visits out-of-town friends she's met in the course. Still, she misses the cats terribly and can't shake the guilt from giving them away. She is also mindful of her looming final course assignment as she struggles to complete it. She decides to call the course instructor, Tony, to get clarity.

Clinging to her iPhone she makes a bit of small talk and then gets to the reason she called. "I'm stuck on my next assignment," she says. "I've called others in the course, but no one can explain it in a way I can understand. I'm not sure what I can do to finish." She puts the phone on speaker and lays it on her desk so she can take notes if necessary.

"Aah," she hears Tony say with a slight echo to the call. "You're at the most difficult part of the course—creating collages from your self-defeating statements and connecting them to the events in your pixography. This step is extremely visual. That's why no one's been able to help you over the phone. What I recommend is that you call one of the mentors and request that they attend your next homework party. In fact, the one who comes to mind is Rhonda Jackson. She's trained very well in this technique. I'll text you her phone number."

Liz is silent. She thinks, *Doesn't he have anyone else?*

"Did you get the number?" he asks.

She looks at the message notification on her cell. "Yes, I did."

"I suggest you act quickly. There's still a lot for you to do to stay on track with the course."

After they end their call, Liz is left stewing over his recommendation. Surely he has another mentor available to help. Perhaps she should call him back and drop the course. Instead, to avoid being the drama queen on this matter, she does the only thing she knows: trudge ahead with confidence that her professionalism will keep the discussion on course.

She picks up the phone and punches in the number she knows by heart and gets Rhonda's voicemail. She leaves a message: "Hi,

Rhonda, it's Liz Harris from the Visionary Course. Tony suggested I call you because a few of us are having difficulty with the project assignment. We're hoping you could attend our next homework party and help us catch up. We meet at seven-thirty Wednesday night at Coco's. Please let me know if we can expect you, so I can tell the others."

Rhonda retrieves the message that evening and instantly explodes. She shouts into the phone in disbelief, "Really? She can't get someone else?" But she knows she made the commitment to help anyone in the program, even Liz, and she knows that if she keeps it professional, she can get through it.

The following Wednesday Rhonda arrives at Coco's with a box of materials and a guarded attitude. As she nears the table at the side of the room, she notices Liz approaching from the restroom while Sam is already seated. The three exchange greetings as Rhonda sets her box on the table, quickly unpacking the stack of magazines, blank construction paper, and glue sticks and spreading it all before them.

"Will more be joining us?" Rhonda asks.

"No," Liz says. "Although several wanted to, they're all out of town for the weekend."

Rhonda says, "That's fine. It'll allow us to get done quicker than normal. Now, where are you two getting stuck?"

"It's with the collages," Sam says. "We don't understand what's next or how it's different than our pixography."

"Got it. Many course participants get confused at this step," Rhonda says kindly. "The collages actually build on your pixography using the same concepts—pictures, words, self-defeating talk—to help you identify and remove hairballs that are blocking your life and relationships."

Sam cocks his head and looks quizzically at her. "I don't remember Tony mentioning hairballs. Did I miss something?"

Rhonda smiles. "My apologies. That's my term for thoughts or emotions we can't express but that end up causing havoc in our life."

"Oh," he says, "like the comments I wish I could say when people irritate me, but I hold back. Eventually, when I've had enough, I explode."

Rhonda nods. "Sort of like those. When people can't release their emotions, it can take a toll on their life. The result could be mental, emotional, or physical in nature."

"My mom has cats," he answers, "so I totally understand what a mess hairballs can create. I like the analogy. Don't you, Liz?"

Liz looks up from her course notebook. "I'm sorry, I was engrossed in my notes."

"Anyway, the hairball explanation is off topic," Rhonda says brusquely. "Back to clarifying your homework. When you encounter something at an emotional level that you can't express through words, you're going to use a technique involving visualization. Doing this will help release the emotions you can't otherwise express. Although you may not be able to immediately put words to your feelings, eventually you'll be able to identify them through this technique. Does that make sense?"

Liz and Sam nod.

Rhonda continues, "Good! Then from your pixography, I want you to select one self-defeating belief that you've identified through the sticky notes and want to eliminate from your head forever."

"That's easy," Liz says. "I'm not good enough."

Resisting the urge to dive deeper into Liz's statement, she redirects her attention to Sam and asks, "What's one of yours, Sam?"

"I'm stupid," he replies.

"Okay. Now on the back of this"—Rhonda hands each of them a piece of yellow construction paper—"I want you to write your statement at the top." She watches as they write the words. She resumes, "For the next part, think of your statement, and then tear out pictures from the magazines that you feel emotionally connected to when thinking of your belief. You should have between three and seven pictures per statement."

Liz throws her hands up and says, "I don't get it."

"The pictures aren't necessarily a logical connection to the statement," Rhonda says. "It's about getting in touch with your feelings through pictures. Just follow the instructions, and I'll be back shortly."

"Take your time," Liz replies without looking up.

Rhonda turns to the kitchen and sees Justin. They exchange waves, and he calls to her to sit down, that he'll be with her soon. She finds a booth some distance away and sits down.

A few minutes later Justin slides into the booth and looks across at her. He says, "Hey. How's it going?"

"It could be better."

"It looks like you two may be on the way to mending things."

Annoyed by his assumption, she says, "I wouldn't go that far. Liz called and asked me to attend a homework party to help with an assignment. Just because I did it doesn't mean we're working together again." She pauses to debate how much she wants to share with him about her recent business decision. Casting doubts aside, she lunges forward. "In fact, since I last spoke to you, I've thought a lot about what you said, along with other feedback I've received, and I've decided to pursue another coaching model for my career."

He tilts his head. "What does that mean?"

"I came to the conclusion that my strengths are better suited to areas of managing the business, rather than working directly with clients to identify issues and create strategies to move forward. So I've decided to return to traditional employment where I would be in charge of programs and a team of people, rather than having a business based on my direct involvement with clients."

"Hmmm. So, to put it another way, you're better at selling pies than making them," he says.

She reflects on his analogy and nods. "Precisely."

"I get that. It's the exact reason why I don't do certain things at Coco's, like my finances; my talents are more suited to other tasks involved in running the business, like baking and engaging customers. Besides, Rhonda, no one can do it all."

Feeling defeated, she lowers her head and says, "I'm finding that out, Justin. And for now I'll follow up with any commitment I've made but not take on any new clients or projects."

He nods and gives her a smile, which seems to convey that not all is as bleak as she thinks. Looking at the dimples in his cheeks, her heart remembers the love she had for him and feels its loss. Whether it's due to her still being angry at his critical business evaluation of her, or knowing she needs to stop chasing unavailable men, she senses the discord between them and despite her heartbreak believes it will lead her to pursue healthier relationships, both personally and in business.

His words break into her thoughts. "Does anyone need more coffee?"

She smiles. "Thanks, but we're still working on the carafe that was ordered earlier. Well, I'd better get back." She walks away, proud of maintaining her professional composure.

When she returns to the table, Sam and Liz are chatting about the pictures they selected for their collages. "Looks like you're done with that step!" Rhonda says like a proud teacher.

"Yes, and we're ready for the next one," Sam says.

Rhonda picks up the thread. "Now, on the back of the page, write any other statements you think of when you see the pictures."

Rhonda watches as Sam and Liz quickly write as directed. When she sees they're finished, she says, "Good. Now write the words *It seems like* in front of your main statement and each related statement on the back side."

Rhonda gives them a few moments and then asks, "Liz, can you please read your entire first statement again, with the new words added?"

"It seems like I'm not good enough," says Liz.

"Okay. Sam, how's that different than what she read a while ago?"

"The first one seemed factual; this one sounded more like an opinion," answers Sam.

"What about you, Liz? Did anything change?" asks Rhonda.

"Yes, it did! I felt defeated with the first one. The second time, it seemed like I didn't have to believe it if I didn't want to; it's a matter of interpretation," Liz responds, looking relieved.

"That's very good," says Rhonda. "Over time you will find you can shift opinions; you can't shift facts."

"Aah," says Sam. "I understand the way it works now." He turns to Liz and says, "Boy, I can't wait to dig in. With this, I can make all those negative thoughts I have disappear." He turns back to Rhonda and asks, "What's next?"

"All you need to do for the final course weekend is show up with your completed collages of six different self-defeating beliefs," says Rhonda.

"I can do that!" Sam says eagerly.

"Yeah," Liz agrees. "Should be a piece of cake. In fact, I could probably have twice as many and still have more left!" She smiles and turns to Rhonda. "Thank you so much, Rhonda. That gets us back on track."

"If you're both done, I'll clean up and you two can leave," says Rhonda.

"Okay" says Sam. "C'mon, Liz! I'll walk you to your car and carry your book."

"Thanks, Sam," Liz says, standing to leave. "And thank you again, Rhonda."

"You're both welcome. Now get out of here and enjoy the rest of your evening," Rhonda says in a tone of jocular command.

Sam and Liz smile as they leave. Rhonda watches them, wistful at Liz's chance for a relationship. She then returns her attention to the table, collecting her magazines, papers, and glue.

Outside in the cool spring air, with the wind gently blowing, Sam escorts Liz to her car at the end of the block. "That was a great meeting, Liz. I'm so glad you got Rhonda to help us."

"Oh, it was nothing," she replies, as if it wasn't torture for her to call Rhonda. "I was more stuck than you were."

"Well, I'm excited to create the collage from my statements, aren't you? Then I can make my self-defeating beliefs disappear forever! That's gonna—" He interrupts himself to look at Liz. "Penny for your thoughts?"

She hesitates, unsure of how he will react to her announcement. "You'll think I'm crazy," she says.

"I won't. I promise."

Just then they get to her car. "I have to sit, Sam. My hip is killing me tonight."

"Sure, sure. But I can only talk for a few minutes. Then I have to get going."

He opens both doors on the driver's side, and she hands him her crutch to put in the back and sits in the driver's seat. Then Sam runs around the front and hops in the passenger's seat. She leans to her right, turns the ignition with her left hand, and turns off the radio.

"Why do you start the car that way?"

She swallows hard. "Because my right hand's not strong enough to turn the key."

"Oh." He looks ahead silently.

She blurts, "I'm thinking about having my head shaved."

He cranes his neck toward her and cries, "Have you gone nuts?"

"Sam, you promised," she scolds.

"Well you didn't tell me you were thinking of doing something that ludicrous!"

"It's for a good cause," she pleads, even now seeing the streetlights dance in the rearview mirror outlining the blond locks that frame her face and shoulders.

"That doesn't matter," he says petulantly. "I like looking at women with hair." He sighs. "Okay, I'm sorry if I overreacted. What you said caught me totally by surprise."

"I got that," she says.

"I'll try to put the image out of my head for a few minutes." He waves his hands and slowly says, "Please explain to me why you're thinking of taking this unusual step."

She smiles at his attempt to be nonjudgmental, although it comes a bit late. "It's to raise funds for a national nonprofit organization that donates money for research to eliminate childhood cancer."

"Who in your family has cancer?" he asks.

"No one," she says gripping the steering wheel.

"It'd be easier to donate money than your hair."

"My goal is to raise other people's awareness. The organization has chosen this as its signature fundraiser."

"Can't you do something normal like walking or bowling to raise money?" he asks.

"Really? You've seen me walk. Can you imagine me bowling? Do you really think I'd raise any money with either of those activities?" She smiles, poking fun at her own situation.

He bows his head, "I'm sorry, Liz. I didn't think before I said that."

"It's okay. I know you didn't mean any harm."

He points to her head, "Will you do me a favor? Will you wear a wig or hat when we meet? If not, I don't know that I can look at you until your hair grows back."

Her reaction is disbelief at the shallowness of his comment.

How could be so narrow in his thinking as to make it all about her physical appearance? If that's the way he feels, then their relationship may go no further. She curtly replies, "That's too bad, Sam. Covering my head wasn't part of my plan."

23

Integrity: Doing the Right Thing when No One Is Watching

Liz looks in the mirror one last time. Will her presentation make a difference? Leaving the bathroom, she heads toward the hotel meeting area and crosses the threshold into the room lined with gold walls and brown and gold carpet, just as the announcer begins reading her bio. As she limps down the left side aisle toward the stage, she notices the twenty or so round tables of eight, covered with gold tablecloths, cups of coffee, and almost-empty dessert plates. Every head turns toward her, many people giggling and pointing to her rainbow-colored wig.

She confidently reaches the podium in front as the audience welcomes her with a round of applause. Liz looks over the crowd, smiles, and begins, "When one of my friends learned I was shaving my head as a fundraiser, he asked that I cover it." She points to her colorful locks. "However, this may not be what he had in mind."

There's some mild chuckling until she peels off the hairpiece to reveal her shaved pate and a large scar framing her forehead. An instant hush falls over the audience. One by one, people stand and clap. Liz feels herself getting emotional. She's not sure she'll be able to tell her story without breaking down; but she continues.

Ten minutes later, she wraps up: "I know what it's like to be different. I remember the feelings of a child who doesn't fit in but wants nothing more than to play with the other kids and be accepted. We can all help children with cancer or any illness. Simply do what it takes to help them enjoy their youth—whether it takes a minute, an hour, or their lifetime. I thank you for your time and for listening to my story."

Liz glows as she heads to nearby Coco's for her monthly homework party. She limps into the café, smelling the homey fragrance of nutmeg and cinnamon from Justin's signature eggnog lattes. He makes them year-round with homemade eggnog. Still beaming, she approaches one of the side tables where three of her classmates are already seated and asks whether they've heard from Sam. They all indicate they haven't. She sighs, shifting her focus to them, quickly forgetting Sam and becoming engaged in discussions of collages and pixographies and sharing self-defeating statements that they are wrestling with.

As the party breaks up, Justin's lanky frame approaches to ask Liz if she can spare a minute. He sits at the table, looks at her bright teal, purple, and black hat with matching purple golf shirt, and says with a smile, "You look majestic in purple!"

Liz perks up. "Thank you, Justin! What's on your mind?"

With smiling eyes he hands her an overstuffed white legal-sized envelope. "Several in town wanted to make donations to your fundraiser. You'll find checks and cash in there along with a list of donors and their contact information."

"Wow," she says, surprised that her efforts yielded such results. "I don't know what to say."

He runs his hand over his short black hair, revealing his slightly graying temples, "Words are not always necessary between friends."

She smiles and points to her head. "Do you mind if I take off my hat?"

"Of course not."

As she plucks the knit hat off, she feels the weight of Justin's stare as her eyes meet his. She turns her bald head, displaying the scar that runs from the middle of her forehead to right above her left ear, and notices his shocked look. She disarms him with a grin and says, "You probably don't see a lot of bald women."

"Actually just one, besides you," he says softly.

"Oh? Who's that?"

He looks away. "My sister-in-law. She was diagnosed with cancer three years ago; it's now in remission."

"I'm sorry."

He turns to face her. "There's no need to be. At first, I had difficulty looking at her. Once we talked about it though, I was fine." He continues, "I'm curious, how has being bald affected you?"

"I've gotten some stares and shocked faces. It's been challenging at times but no big deal. I think it's making me stronger in some ways."

Justin studies her face. "How do you deal with the shocked reactions that I'm sure you get?"

"When I realized people stopped talking to me because of my baldness, I came up with the idea to decorate my head. I went to a local costume shop and bought some sparkly rubber face tattoos shaped like feathers, teardrops, and swirls and the body glue to apply them. Everyone's response was that they were neat. I'm not sure why, but the tattoos seemed to reduce the tension and shift the focus from tragedy to one centered on art and giving back to others."

Justin sits quietly for some moments. "Liz, this is great work you've done on behalf of people with cancer. However, I'm curious for you to take it to the next level and apply it to where your life is headed."

"That's an excellent challenge, Justin. It's one I hope develops during my trip."

"Wait, what trip?" He looks stunned. "Where are you going?"

"I'm finally ready to return home for a while," she says, with a bit of melancholy in her voice. "There are questions I need to resolve, and the only place to do that is back where it started."

"So you're going to Michigan?"

"Yep, to see my mom and my sister Carla and to make a visit to where it all started."

She again feels his penetrating stare as he asks, "Does your family know you're bald?"

"Yes, and they have been very supportive since I told them."

"When are you leaving?"

"Tomorrow morning."

"When will you be back?"

"After I get the answers I need."

"I wish you well, Liz."

"Thank you, Justin. So do I."

24

Images Leave a Lasting Impact

Later that evening, sitting on her leopard print daybed facing the kitchen sink with side fridge and bathroom to the left and entrance door to the right, Liz reflects on Justin's question of where her life is headed next. She looks down at her shoes. What do others see when she walks? Do they feel the same repulsion she's felt from the few times she's caught a reflection of herself walking past a store window? Beginning in junior high and continuing through high school, kids called her Chester after the *Gunsmoke* character who limped. Perhaps if the actor who played the part had been Brad Pitt, she would have thought it cool to limp, rather than the embarrassment she endured being tied to his TV character.

She grabs her cell phone and starts typing: "Hey, Sam, it's me. Do you know of any job where dragging your foot is an advantage?"

She holds on to the phone like she's clinging to a lifeline. *C'mon Sam*, she thinks. *I know you can answer this.*

The phone chirps, and she breathes again. "Not sure of job, but there's soccer," his text reads.

She laughs and says, "That's it! Maybe my leg could help win the World Cup! Then everyone would see me as a heroine rather than a cripple."

She quickly taps out a response, "U R brilliant! Tks!"

As Liz puts the phone down, her thoughts drift to him. Although she initially thought he was interested in her, she has decided, based on his lack of contact with her since she announced her head shaving, that he isn't; this realization discourages her.

She gets out of her funk by shifting focus to his response—soccer. If she tells her story like she's the one who won the World Cup with her dragging leg, she might feel like the victor and not the victim every time someone asks about it.

Liz thumbs through her course notebook and finds the directions for the questions Rhonda gave her. She reads out loud the instructions: "Record the five W's: When, Where, Who, What, and Why." Reflecting, she concludes that this might help her develop a different response when asked the question about her leg, "What happened?"

Exhausted, she puts her notes on the only table in her apartment, her nightstand, and settles into bed. Trying to sleep, but instead visualizing herself with that guy at the bar who stood her up, she searches for how best to prepare him for why she needs a crutch to walk. In a flash, she has the answer—it's all in the introduction.

With her head on the pillow, she stares at the shadows on the ceiling from the nearby nightlight and practices her new opening line: "Hi. I'm Liz, and this is Steve; he's my biggest supporter."

With that revelation on her mind, she peacefully falls into a deep sleep.

Feeling well rested, Liz gets an early start the next morning. During the first thirty minutes of her twelve-hour trip, she reviews the itinerary in her head. She'll arrive at Carla's in time to spend the night, and then she'll wake up the next day and drive another three hours to see her mom and perhaps make a visit to the barn. She knows she can stay at Mom's apartment for a few days or up to a week if necessary and then return to Carla's in time to celebrate her sister's birthday.

As if giving herself a pep talk, she says out loud, "When I'm ready, I'll head back to Pennsylvania. But no matter how grueling the trip, I won't leave until I have my answers."

Passing the budding wildflowers along the freeway and exit stops, all of which she knows by heart, Liz feels refreshed by the warmth of the sunbeams shining through the open sunroof. The freedom she feels, coupled with expectancy at the upcoming Mothers' Day weekend, allows her to recall the painful vow she made years earlier when she was in a relationship. She desperately wanted to have children but was afraid they would turn out like her and have the lifelong heartbreak she's suffered—being rejected by her parents and separated from her sibling. So she made a pact with herself and took every step possible to ensure she never got pregnant. She also lied to those closest to her, blaming her "infertility" on a past medical procedure. The people in her life who should have prodded more never did; rather, they simply accepted her vague explanation of why she was childless.

After Liz hit thirty-something, her fears had been overcome; however, it was now too late to have a child of her own, or so she told herself. At length, she's figured that everything turned out for the best. Her siblings have wonderful families that Liz can visit any time, and Liz has a professional career and lives independently, proving she can do far more than the doctors and therapists predicted. However, notwithstanding years of soul-searching, life's journey has brought her to this destination: shedding almost every material possession, getting rid of her girls, and shaving her head bald. What's next on her road to inner peace?

Before she realizes she's driven that far, she arrives at Carla and

Patrick's house, a two-story brick ranch with white shutters; it's a little after six in the evening. She slowly gets out of the car, grabs her crutch from the back seat, and limps toward the house. She enters the green foyer, with stairs on the left descending to three of the bedrooms, a bathroom, and a family room, and stairs on the right leading up to the kitchen, living area, office, bathroom, and master suite. She proceeds up the stairs and straight into the kitchen. Looking around, Liz is bewildered that not even Gunner, the family Rottweiler, is here to greet her. Did they move and forgot to give her the new address?

Limping to the patio slider that is to the right of the kitchen, Liz sees Carla, a slender five-foot-eight blonde with long, wavy hair, walking barefoot toward the house from the back garden with Gunner at her heels. Liz opens the patio door as they get within a few feet of it.

Carla stops dead in her tracks as she spies her bald sister. After a few seconds, she steps forward, and the sisters share a warm embrace just inside the patio door. The dog sniffs Liz and wags his tail; she pets him obligingly.

Carla's crystal blue eyes stare at the scar on Liz's forehead. "I'll have Patrick get your luggage when he gets home," she says absently.

"That's fine," Liz says as she steps back and perches on her regular seat at the breakfast bar.

Before the sisters can begin to talk, Carla's four children, ranging from sixth to twelfth grade, troop in, one by one, each giving their mom and Aunt Lizzy a hug, updating Carla on their plans for the evening, and then heading downstairs to their rooms. On their heels, Patrick, Carla's husband of thirty-some years, marches into the kitchen loaded down with his gym gear.

"Hi, Liz!" he says as his six-foot-four husky frame with brown eyes and matching mustache leans over to give her a hug.

"We could almost be twins," he pauses rubbing his own bald

head. "If it wasn't for those blue eyes of yours, and my extra hundred or so pounds, people would never know you weren't my twin sister." They chuckle, and Patrick heads to the downstairs family room.

Carla sits at the bar across from Liz and says, "Sorry, Liz, for the turmoil, everyone just happened to arrive at the same time today, which is a rarity. Anyway, dinner is a couple of hours away, so that gives us some time until I need to start on it."

"Before we get into anything too deep, I wanted to know what your plans are for this trip. I mean, you're welcome here anytime, but when you called to announce your visit, there seemed to be some urgency about it."

Liz rests her chin on her folded hands and says, "I'll be here tonight and then leave in the morning to see my mom. When I get back, I figure we'll celebrate your birthday, if that's okay with you. I know you're busy, but I also need to talk to you about some things I'm going through associated with the course I'm in."

Carla studies the scar on her forehead. "You mean like the decision to shave your head?"

Liz looks at Gunner, kneeled by Carla's side. "It's not about my head; it's about our past. When the time's right, we can talk about it."

Carla replies, "I'm not sure the time is ever right for those talks, but we can always pour a drink and see where the conversation goes."

Liz smiles. "How about we catch up a bit first?"

Before Carla can respond, they hear a yell from the basement: "Mom, can you come here?"

"Oh! Excuse me, Liz. One of the kids needs something; I'll be right back."

Liz stands and limps over to the kitchen counter, where she grabs a coffee pod, drops it into the black multicup Keurig, and presses "Brew." She smiles when she spots the green and purple mug on the counter that Carla made with her name on it. When the coffee is finished brewing, she returns to her barstool.

When Carla returns a few minutes later, Liz can see that she's upset by the look of her flushed face, watery eyes, and pursed lips. She puts down her coffee cup and asks, "Is everything okay, Sis?"

Sitting across from her, Carla bows her head and blurts, "My kids are shocked by your scar." Before the words can even register with Liz, Carla adds, "I tried to explain what happened—"

Liz sees tears streaming down Carla's cheeks just as she thought they occurred the only other time they spoke of her accident—thirty-some years ago, the night in Liz's kitchen full of babble, libations, and revelations.

Her heart sinks in fear that she may not be able to get beyond her sister's upset. Her chest tightens as she breaks the awkward silence with the only expression that comes to mind: "I'm sorry."

Carla looks to be in shock. She haltingly says, "It's hard to see you like this; it reminds me of the pictures I saw after the accident—except you were such a little girl and the scar was so big."

Liz's stomach wrenches. "Carla, I don't know what to say. I wasn't there, so I have nothing to compare it to. I only know that by the time I got out of the hospital, you were already gone." Liz pauses in hopes that something in her words will relieve her sister's anguish. With a smile of encouragement, she offers, "If it helps, I can put on a hat."

Carla shakes her head. "It's too late for that now."

After a few moments of silence, Liz watches as Carla walks to the antique brown china cabinet, located on the wall between the dining room table and the living area; she opens the top stained glass door and removes the matching set of etched wine glasses that Liz gave her many years earlier. She then grabs a bottle from the adjacent wine rack, opens it, and pours them each a large glass of cabernet sauvignon. She motions for Liz to join her at the dining room table. Once Liz is seated, Carla raises her glass and says, "You have my undivided attention until I need to make dinner, so begin where you want."

Liz watches as Carla takes a big swig. Not sure how to ease into the conversation, Liz fumbles through her words. "As I've been telling you about the course I'm in—I'm at a point in my past where I'm left with questions I haven't been able to answer having to do with my accident and our childhood. I was hoping you could resolve some of them."

Carla's body jolts into a defensive position. "I, too, have my issues about our childhood, and you know what they are. I've tried to work through them, but it only gets worse. I suggest you save yourself torment and stop dredging up memories you can't fix."

"I can't afford to ignore it anymore," Liz says, her eyes pleading as she reaches for Carla's hand. "And neither can you. Please, Sis, I need your memory."

Carla clenches her teeth and closes her eyes. When she opens them, she nods.

"What do you remember about why we were to be adopted by Norman and Helen?" Liz asks as she leans in.

"Dad was getting married to someone else, and Mom could no longer take care of us as a single woman," Carla says, looking away.

"What happened before then?"

Carla sighs. "We used to have babysitters who would lock us in our bedroom and leave us there for hours. We had no toys to play with. There was one who always stuck us in your playpen and threatened us with a knife if we told our mother what went on."

"Do you remember anything about cranberries?" Liz asks leaning her chin on her hand.

"One day the babysitter with the knife was trying to find us something to eat, and there was only a can of cranberry sauce in the cupboard. When she went to feed it to us, you threw your bowl on the floor. She picked up the sauce, put it in the dish, and slammed it on the table in front of you telling you to eat it or she'd kill you.

She left the room with a knife in her hand," Carla said circling the base of her wine glass with her finger.

"What happened to her?"

"She married Dad!" Carla cries.

Liz bows her head, stunned; she never knew or even remotely suspected what Carla might have endured at the hands of her evil stepmother. She draws a deep breath and tries to add a touch of levity. "No wonder I cringe every time someone passes me cranberry sauce at Thanksgiving."

"You were only three at the time. You remember that?"

"No, I don't remember the actual incident. All I know is the terror I feel every time I think of eating cranberry sauce; it's good to know that now."

"Know what?" Carla shrieks. "That the psycho bitch was in charge of us?"

Liz shakes her head, upset at the misunderstanding. "That's not what I meant! I mean now that I understand what happened, it makes sense why I get sick at the thought of cranberry sauce. Knowing this, I can find a way to get past it."

"Perhaps I should serve it for dinner tonight?" Carla says, taking her turn at sarcasm.

"Er, maybe not tonight. But soon," Liz offers. "I'm new to this, but I'm sure it takes some time to overcome our fears from the past. In time, though, it just might be my favorite!"

Carla laughs. "I think that's a stretch."

Liz quietly debates her next question. There's so much she wants to ask Carla, but if she's not careful, she could violate the boundaries of their relationship; thereby losing her love and friendship.

"What do you remember about my accident?" Liz asks gently.

Carla's face is stoic, her words monotone as she repeats the story, parts of which Liz herself has cited hundreds of times. "We were in the barn playing, and you left to go to the house; I think it was to check on our treats. In the meantime, Uncle Norman, his father, and I went to the tractor garage. I was to be on the lookout for you. When I saw you run across the yard to the barn, I yelled, but you couldn't hear me over the sounds of the tractor engine. I told Uncle Norman; he said to get you and bring you back to the garage. When I got to the barn, you were nowhere in sight. I yelled at you to get down. You hurried and fell and hit your head. I ran to the garage and told them what happened. Uncle Norman sent me to the house to tell Aunt Helen. The next thing I knew, they were both speeding away in the car with you. I didn't see you again until months after you returned home."

"What happened to you while I was in the hospital?"

Carla visibly relaxes. "I stayed at the farm for a bit. A few weeks after the accident, our dad visited and there was a big fight between them. The next day, our grandmother on Dad's side came and picked me up; I went to live with Dad and his new wife."

Liz absorbs what she hears and asks her next natural question. "Where was our birth mom when all this happened?"

Carla sighs and bends down to pet Gunner. "I was told that she was working two jobs just to get by; she visited when she could."

Liz takes a sip of her wine and cocks her head. "What did our parents say to you about the fact that I never came home to live with them?"

Carla reaches for the stem of her glass and swirls it. "Dad didn't have to say anything; his new wife said it for him. Her words were 'They're your bastard children; I want no responsibility.' Mom simply said it was for the best since she couldn't take care of us as a single woman." She finishes her statement with a drink.

Liz's demeanor shifts. "Do you remember when I came to live with you after graduating from high school, and I asked if you could arrange for me to meet him?"

"How could I forget? You had that defiant look I've seen often through the years," Carla says with admiration. "Your request still strikes a chord with me." She mimics Liz's voice, "I just want to meet the son-of-a-bitch once to look him in the eyes and ask him why he gave me up."

Liz's eyes tear up. "I remember," she says with a nod, "those were my exact words."

Carla peers at her and asks, "Did you ever get your answer?"

Liz leans back. "Not exactly. We met at some restaurant, I with my Diet Coke, and he with a double shot of gin on the rocks. I asked why he signed the papers; he never directly answered, just talked of medical bills and then shifted all blame and responsibility to Norman and Helen and Mom. None of that mattered to me; I only needed to understand why he didn't love me enough to keep me. When he asked me that night if I wanted to meet the rest of his family, I was so happy to be part of his life that I mistook his attempt to reconcile the guilt he had with love for me. As you know, that opened a Pandora's box for more than just him."

Carla shakes her head and says, "Do I ever. His wife was infuriated. With you showing up, both of them had to explain a lot of things to their three children, who didn't even know he had another child. The kids were mad at you, and our stepmom was convinced you were there to lay claim to Dad's oil inheritance."

Liz wrinkles her nose. "Yeah, I thought so. She would often talk about Grandma's diamond ring and that it was willed to her, when you and I both know Grandma wanted you to have it since you were the oldest. In those same conversations, she made it clear that I would never get anything from him, dead or alive." Liz tilts her head and adds, "I could understand that, since legally he was no longer my parent. However, to this day, I find it incomprehensible that his children didn't know I existed. After all, his mother brought you to visit me every year at Christmas. There were pictures of us beside his family's picture on her mantel. How could the kids not have asked who I was? We even wrote letters back and forth when you were living at his house."

"And she read every one of them," Carla says with disgust.

"To proofread?" Liz asks, naively.

"No. To make sure I didn't tell you anything that was going on. You never received many of my letters because she destroyed them. She opened every letter I got from you and read it before giving it to me." Carla runs her fingers up and down the stem of her wineglass.

"You never told me that!" Liz says, almost accusingly.

"How could I?" Carla shouts. "She was the one with the knife!" She then takes a bigger swig.

There's deafening silence in the room while Carla goes back to twirling and Liz gathers her thoughts. Carla's answers have filled many of the gaps in Liz's memory, but she has more. Her main quandary is whether to press her sister for answers or to find another way to learn what she still needs to know to be at peace. She decides to try the second tack. But before she does, she has one more query.

"Carla, just one last thing," Liz pleads with outstretched arms. "I'm curious, what did you tell your kids about my scar?"

Carla recoils in her seat and answers with a stoic look on her face, "I told them how you fell, just as I recounted today. Now please excuse me, Sis. It's time to get dinner ready." And with that, she rises and heads to the kitchen; the conversation is over.

After supper, Liz and Carla convene in the living area, joining Patrick on the large brown L-shaped sectional couch with recliners on each end. Liz sits opposite Patrick, and Carla is in the middle. Intent on discussing his family's reaction to her scar, he says, his voice slightly breaking, "You know, I've seen your handicap for years, but seeing your scar shifts my perspective about the tragedy you suffered."

As Liz watches him lean back in his leather recliner, the room seems to ache with the echo of his words.

"With your head tilted that way," he says, "you look identical to my mom the day before she died."

Liz says, "Patrick, I'm sorry. I forgot."

"It's been a year, almost to the day," he says. "That may also be why the kids reacted the way they did; perhaps they're reminded of their grandmother and her last days with them."

Liz considers his words; how could she have failed to consider the emotional impact of her actions on others? She never meant to hurt Carla or her family.

Patrick interrupts her thoughts. "Liz, I find it amazing that you could hide the trauma over all those years and gracefully share your tragedy now."

Liz simply nods; nothing she has done so far on this trip has been graceful in her mind. Determining it's best to end the discussion before she spirals down further, Liz stands to leave. As if reading her mind, Carla pops up and says, "I'll go with you. I still have to get the futon ready and make sure all of Patrick's girly magazines are put away." She shoots him a flirtatious glance as she walks by, and Patrick pats Carla's butt.

"With you by my side, Babe, I don't need to fantasize about any other woman—real or in those magazines," Patrick says with a smirk.

Carla rolls her eyes and says to Liz, "He only says that kind of stuff when you're here, so someone will believe his lies. Everyone else knows the truth."

The girls laugh, and Liz limps toward him, leans over, and whispers in his ear, "I know you treat her like a queen."

She follows Carla down the green hallway to the guest room, also known as Patrick's man cave, filled with a futon, small side table, a writing desk and matching chair, a large-screen TV mounted on the wall above the desk, and a plethora of fish trophies and photos lining every wall.

While Carla unfolds the futon into a small bed, Liz ponders if she should ask her one more question; it's about her confession all those years ago—about Carla causing her accident.

Carla asks, "Is there anything else you need, Liz?"

In the blink of an eye, Liz decides not to cause further pain to her sister. She says, "Nope! Everything is great, Carla."

Carla hesitates. "Liz, about your accident—"

"Yes?"

"Either now or in the past, I've said everything I can about it. At this point, you know where to look for any other answers. However, be careful. What you seek to uncover may cost you in other areas that you're not ready to deal with."

Liz mentally notes Carla's seemingly odd statement and says, "That may be, Sis, but I need to put it behind me once and for all. Nothing I've tried over the years has worked."

Carla nods. "I do understand. One day, several years ago, I sought answers to my own childhood traumas. What I realized later was that I had been depending on others to fix it for me, waiting on those who caused me harm to say, 'I'm sorry,' or to visibly hurt as much as I had ached inside over the years. But that's not the way life rolls."

"What do you mean?" asks Liz. "People are supposed to admit their mistakes and fix them."

"Oh my dear, younger, naive sister—"

"You always start that way whenever you're going to spew your 'older, wiser' crap on me." Liz smiles. The sisters laugh and hug. "But seriously, Sis, how did you resolve it?" she asks, releasing from their embrace.

"I've learned that some people can't apologize; if they did, they couldn't face the consequences of their actions or the people they'd wronged," says Carla.

Liz knows deeply that's why she can never talk with Carla about what really happened. If she did, then she might not have Carla in her life, and her sister means the world to her. Tonight confirms to her for all time that she needs to let certain "sleeping dogs" lie and continue to tell the story as it's always been told—whether it's the truth of what happened or not.

Carla continues as her blue eyes meet Liz's, "I had a choice to make the day I faced my past. I could either continue to be a victim of it, or I could decide it was time to move on. It took me several years from that moment of choice to overcome the tragedy of my past, but when I did, I was stronger for it."

"I never knew that, Carla," Liz says, taking a seat on the edge of the bed.

Carla sits beside her on the floral comforter and grabs her hand. "Why should you? You've had your own matters to overcome, and I didn't need to burden you with mine."

"Yeah, but we're sisters."

"Yes, we are, and I love you for that. However, healing your past is always a journey for one. If you take anyone with you, they only become a prisoner. You're the only one who can make the choices that will lead to your inner peace."

"Hmm," Liz says, squeezing her hand.

"Liz, the only advice I can give you is this: The journey is dark and difficult at times. You can either get sucked into the past, where it gets darker and more difficult, or you can choose to walk toward the light found in the future. At the start of each day, you're the one who gets to choose. I hope you choose the light."

Liz bows her head, and tears well in her eyes.

Putting her arm around her sister, Carla says softly, "I wish you speed on your journey, Sis. I know it's been a long and bitter road for you." She hesitates. "Sometimes the forgiveness we seek is from ourselves for our choices and reactions. However, we don't see it that way as we are blinded by the actions of others."

With tears streaming down her face, Liz looks deeply into Carla's sea blue eyes—seeing herself in the reflection. "You mean the world to me and always have. I'm so proud to be your younger sister."

"And I so enjoy being the older, wiser sister you idolize!" Carla smirks. "Now, it's time for both of us to go to bed."

"You sound like such a mom!"

"That's because I am—just not yours!"

Lying in bed that night, Liz is determined to find an end to her nightmares. Determined that she will never confront Carla by pressing for more answers, she hopes that a final visit to the scene of the accident—the barn—will resolve the past that she believe keeps her from being empowered to deal with the common question asked of her, "What happened?"

Liz falls fast asleep but soon feels herself in a freefall, spiraling quickly to the surface below. A few inches before she reaches the concrete floor, she bolts awake at her own scream; her heart pounds deeply in her chest as she struggles to get her bearings. Her mind races, hoping it was only in her head and no one actually heard her shouts. What happens if she hits the ground in her sleep? Will she get so scared that she has a heart attack and dies? She shivers at the thought of not knowing.

Drifting slowly back to sleep, Liz shifts her thoughts to the cats. She misses them and hopes they're doing well. Maybe someday she'll drive by their new home and see them peeking out the windows, watching the birds like they used to do at the apartment. Do they miss her as much as she misses them?

25

Being a Victor over the Past

Early the next morning, Liz slips out of the house and gets on the road before the family awakes, to avoid further conversation about her head. She spends a leisurely morning getting to her mother's, which is normally only a three-hour drive, as she plans to explore every beach on the shoreline between St. Joseph and Grand Haven. Despite the beauty of each lake frontage she visits, her focus returns to sorting through emotions that surfaced at Carla's as she recalls one haunting memory after another associated with life after her accident; they all go back to the scar facing her in the rearview mirror.

For the first time since shaving, Liz is regretting her choice to do so. Until this point in her life, she had become so accustomed to people asking about her leg that she gave little thought to what their reaction would be to the scar on her head. Maybe she should stop and get a wig before she sees her mom, but doing so would undermine her reasons for shaving in the first place. She must be strong and break through her fears.

For distraction, she turns on the radio, but the only stations coming in are playing country songs about lost love, strong whiskey, and hard times. Figuring she may be postal by the time she gets there from further depressing thoughts, she shuts off the tunes and eagerly looks forward to her pending visit. She's not sure what she's looking for but convinced she'll know when she finds it.

As Liz approaches the front door of her mother's apartment, decorated with a wreath of pink and orange silk flowers and her name, MRS. HARRIS, on a metal plate beside the door, she's greeted with the wonderful smell of freshly baked brownies, her favorite. Before she can knock, the door swings open, and her mother greets her wearing a red and white checkered apron and a big smile, and they hug. "Come in! Dinner's almost ready."

Liz grins. Food and the kitchen table have always been central to her family; it's where discussions were held and relationships were built. But something's different this time. Standing at the kitchen sink, a few feet beyond and to the right of the front door, she watches her mom, who stands about four-foot-eight, a roundish figure covered with an apron. Her short white hair frames hazel eyes accented by bronze-colored wire-rim glasses.

As her mom puts finishing touches on the salad. Liz feels an unusual stress between them. "Mom, how have things been with you?"

"I've been better. My knee hurts, and I'm having trouble walking. I can't go anywhere, so I sit in my chair and watch my favorite shows."

Liz assesses the apartment's layout. Behind the sink there's a ledge, beyond that, the room extends into one large open area. On the left wall are doors to two rooms: a bedroom and a bathroom, then a rocker and matching recliner, both slightly turned inward to face each other. Immediately beyond the ledge are a small round kitchen table and two chairs. To the right is a couch with side tables on each end, and at the end of the room in front of the glass sliding door is the TV with surrounding bookcases.

"Why can't you get out?"

"Because it hurts too much to drive."

Liz's temper flares as she spies the walker tucked near the bedroom with a cane leaning on it. Her anger flares at the memory that her mother never allowed her to quit; rather, she always pushed Liz, as a child, to walk long distances or work in the garden without ever asking or seeming to care if she had pain in doing so. Liz deems her hypocritical for now justifying that it's okay to give up because of her pain. Despite her anger, Liz must let go of the judgment of her mother, or she may never move on.

She breathes deeply, centering on a levelheaded approach to encourage her mother as best she can. "There are plenty of people here who would gladly pick you up and take you somewhere; what about our relatives or your church friends?"

"I can't do that. It's imposing."

"Think of it as letting others be of service to you," Liz says kindly.

"You can sugarcoat it if you want; it's taking advantage of their kindness. I'll do without before I do that."

There's the source of Liz's independence and why her reluctance to accept help is so deep; her pride was bred at a very early age, and this is the ugliest form of it. Do others feel she's pushing their graciousness aside when Liz declines their offers of help as Liz does right now with her mom?

As she peers towards the kitchen table, covered with a light rust-colored tablecloth, she notices it's already set with the rest of the food. Mom interrupts her thoughts. "Liz, everything's ready; let's eat. There's plenty of time to talk later." The women sit, say the family meal prayer, and make small talk during dinner while the TV plays softly in the background.

As she chews her food, Liz is haunted by the strangeness of her mom. It's been easily an hour since she arrived, and Mom hasn't asked a thing about her or commented on her head. Liz can't believe her mother has no reaction; she always blurts out what's on her mind. Did she just forget, or is she too caught up with her own circumstances to care about Liz?

With dinner finished, it's time for her mother's favorite game show, *Wheel of Fortune*. Liz clears the table, saving the dishes for later, while her mother settles in her rocking chair and quickly gets caught up in the daily contest. Returning to the TV area, Liz tries engaging her mother in conversation, but she can't pull her away from the phrases that need solving.

As the closing credits roll, Liz jumps right in. "Mom, in a course I took, I did what's called a pixography to summarize my life. It's allowed me to face events such as my accident and confront my deepest fears, which I've struggled with for years. I'd like share it with you, as it explains why I made some of the choices that you and Dad never understood or agreed with."

"I'd like to see it." Mom's slightly pale, round face breaks into a smile at Liz's obvious surprise. "My next show isn't on for a few hours, so this would be a good time."

"Great. It's in the car. I'll get it."

"Be careful and don't fall!" Mom yells, almost automatically. "You're too big for me to pick up."

Liz stiffens, perturbed that her mom always has to say that when she walks; but she responds simply, "Okay."

A few minutes later, she sits down in the recliner next to Mom and hands her the album, with a recent picture of herself framed on the front. She explains, "Our assignment was to create a pictorial of our life. We had to record the names of people who were an influence in our life, the significant events that occurred, and pictures of ourselves and our life experiences for each year."

Liz helps her flip to the page she wants to use to illustrate. "Remember these little towheads?" Liz points to her and Carla in the yard picking dandelions.

"That was taken before your accident," her mother says as she turns to the page marked "Age 4." She studies the pictures: a child in a critical care unit of a hospital, a child with leg braces, and a child working with a physical therapist. "These aren't you," she says, confused.

"You're right. If we couldn't find pictures of ourselves in a given year, we were to get some from a magazine that represented us. I figured in light of my accident, these were the closest I could get to illustrate what that year was like."

"What are these little notes for?" Mom asks, pointing to a one-inch Post-it that reads, "I'm bad at that."

"Those are self-defeating statements we tell ourselves; they're associated with the age we first said whatever is on the note."

Her mother scrunches her face, pointing to the note which reads, "My BB Brain." She says, "I know that one very well. In fact, you probably got it from me."

Liz is astonished that her mom quickly identified that as hers. What other statements did she pick up from her?

Liz explains, "In talking to my classmates, we discovered we all have some version of these in our head. What makes a difference in our life is whether we understand they're just statements or opinions, or whether we choose to believe them as facts that can't be changed." As her mother slowly moves through the pages, sleepiness from two days of driving overtakes Liz. "Mom, I'm going to shut my eyes for a bit, if that's okay."

Her mother's stare never breaks from the book. "There's a lot here to take in," she says. "Go ahead and rest a bit. We can have dessert later."

Liz lies down on the couch and closes her eyes. Suddenly fear sets in as she realizes that parts of her life which she lied to her parents about are in that book. The biggest ones which would concern her religious mother are multiple live-in boyfriends, romance with a married man, and an alcohol/drug–related accident that she lied about as a young teen. Her heart races, wanting to grab the book before her mom has time to see everything. But it's too late.

Instead of trying to excuse away her past, she decides it's time to stop hiding and worrying about being judged. She drifts off to sleep with the knowledge that her mom loves her.

When Liz opens her eyes an hour later, her mother is still in her rocker, sitting still with her petite, wrinkled hands and long fingernails gently folded on top of the pixography on her lap. "I didn't know there were so many men," she says with a look of condemnation as she drums her fingers on the top of the book.

Liz knows enough not to take the bait, or it will turn into a full-scale war; instead, she observes, "Most of them were friends."

Her mother hands the pixography back and says simply, "The past is past."

The tension in the air goes far beyond an awkward pause. Hoping that comfort food will relieve the stress of the moment, Liz says brightly, "I'll make some decaf and dish up ice cream to go with our brownies after I do the dishes."

"That's perfect," Mom says with a tired sigh. "Now I need to rest my eyes for a few minutes."

Liz appreciates the respite in the kitchen, taking her time to do the dishes; but she can't shake the uneasiness that's building within her. Sharing her pixography with Mom was supposed to improve their relationship, not put more distance between them. Perhaps if she had taken a different approach, instead of dumping everything in her lap at once, they would now be uncovering the answers she came here to find, not sitting on opposite sides of the brick wall that her mom quickly erected.

Hoping that coffee and a brownie sundae will be the right setting for her mom to open up, Liz makes a pot of decaf; she pours two cups, carrying them in separate trips to the living room. Then she waits on the couch for her mother to wake up.

A few minutes later, Mom opens her eyes, looks at Liz and

then the coffee cup beside her, and asks, "Liz, are you ready for dessert now?"

"In a bit, Mom," Liz says rather boldly. "I'd like to talk first."

Mom looks genuinely confused. "I thought that's what we just did. What else is there to say?"

Liz proceeds carefully and gently. "I need to know what you remember about my accident so I can reconcile my memory."

"There's no need to think about that again," Mom says plainly. "As I said, it's in the past."

Liz is unflinching. "Not for me. Every step I take reminds me of it. The course helped me understand that if I don't talk about it or get answers, I'm stuck with the emotional trauma of it."

Mom's voice cracks. "You've heard the story hundreds of times before."

Liz pleads this time. "Yes, I've heard what's been told. Now, I need you to take me there with your memories. Help me recall everything just as it occurred."

"That was eons ago, and I'm an old woman," Mom says, without effect.

"I beg you to try, Mom," Liz says in a desperate whisper. "Please."

"Okay, but if it's wrong, don't blame me." Mom's eyes fill with tears.

Liz leans forward from her spot on the couch and draws close; she extends her arms out as if to surrender. "I won't. You're helping me."

Mom's thin, pale lips, surrounded by countless age lines, begin to move as she speaks softly. "Okay. You went up in the hayloft when you were told not to. When Carla yelled, you hurried down the ladder and fell. She came and got your dad and Grandpa, and we took you to the hospital. While you were in a coma, we didn't know if you would survive, and if you did, what your life would be like. Although the doctors gave limited hope, efforts paid off as you overcame most of the paralysis and learned how to talk and walk again."

As her mother takes a breath, Liz interjects, "How long was I in the coma?"

Mom pauses for a minute. "Hmm. I don't remember. But you were in the hospital for a long time. It happened in August, and we brought you home in time for Christmas. After that, I drove you to physical therapy, which was two hours away, twice a week. We did that for a year or so."

"Yep, I hated those trips; I always got carsick." Liz then remembers the end game. "Do you remember how I was lying when they found me in the barn?"

"I didn't see you. I wasn't there."

In a tone more demanding than what she wanted, Liz asks, "Where was Carla standing when it happened?"

Mom crosses her arms, "I don't know. I think she was inside the barn door."

"What did she say that she saw?"

"I don't remember. I think she said she didn't see anything—just that you fell." Mom curtly adds, "If you want to know more, you'll have to ask her yourself."

Liz knows the real answer—Carla was up with her when it happened. But where was her mom at the time? She's always been tough on Liz throughout the years, pushing her to overcome any obstacle in order to prove that there was no major impact on Liz's livelihood or potential. Could the reason be because she felt guilty, and that was how she reduced her own culpability? She always thought it odd that her mother frequently compared the effects of her accident to a cosmetic defect—when in actuality it was significantly greater than that.

Liz suppresses the urge to force her mother to face her own demons; rather, she asks in a childlike manner, "Do you remember why we were in the barn in the first place?"

Mom winces and smugly says, "Sweetheart, I'm too old to remember any more."

"You have to, Mom," Liz begs. "It's important to me."

Her mother's face is steely and her words harsh. "Your father never should've taken you up there."

Liz gasps, flung backward into the couch. "Did he say that?"

Mom is silent.

She rephrases the question. "Did you and Dad ever talk about it?"

"Only once."

"What was said?"

"I don't remember; I only know that he said he felt guilty."

Liz can't believe what she just heard. Incredulous, she asks, "And you never talked about it again?"

"In our day," Mom starts piously, "you didn't talk about your feelings."

Liz's heart begins to ache for her father as she absorbs the truth in her mother's words; he bore the guilt and shame of her accident alone and in silence all those years. She prays he was able to leave it this side of the grave in reconciliation the last time they met. Although she'll never know, she chooses to believe that's what he did. Taking a deep breath, she scratches her bald head gingerly. It all makes sense now; the sorrowful way looked at Liz whenever she struggled or shed crocodile tears for the injustices she faced because of her leg; he felt responsible.

She returns her attention to Mom, moving in yet another direction with her questions. "I know I've asked many times, but why were you not allowed to adopt Carla when you adopted me?"

Mom covers her mouth. "We wanted to. Your biological father wouldn't sign the papers."

Liz leans towards Mom and presses on. "Why didn't he ever visit me as my biological mom and Carla did? They visited yearly, sometimes every six months."

With her forehead buried in her hands, Mom defensively says, "We allowed visitation rights to both of your parents! Your adopted father and I felt it wasn't right to deny that since you had a memory of who they were. But once the adoption papers were signed, we never heard from your biological father again. Your mother would often call and say she was bringing your sister to visit and then not show up. You were always devastated when that happened and would cry for days. I stopped telling you she was coming until she pulled into the driveway."

After hearing this, Liz sinks further into the brown and black striped cloth sofa, as if to become a part of it.

Mom rubs her temples. "Sweetheart, I can't tell you anything else. I'm going to lie down; I have a splitting headache."

Liz gets up and goes over to hug her mom gently. "I know it's difficult for you to remember, but you helped me a lot, Mom. Thank you." She adds, "I'll be back in a while. I'm going to take a drive to the beach before it gets too dark. When I get back, we can have dessert."

"Okay." Mom stands and walks toward her bedroom without looking at Liz. "Be careful."

Liz gathers her purse and pixography and limps outside into the cool evening air. She gets into the car, places the book carefully on the passenger seat and drives ten blocks to the beach. She winds around the nearly empty public park and comes to a stop in front of the boardwalk that leads to a lighthouse.

Feeling melancholy, she opens the album to the page with an attached Post-it note reading, "I'm not good enough." Liz retrieves the blue folder of collages from the floorboard and finds the corresponding page. She looks at the four pictures that represent the statement and then looks back at her pixography. Her thoughts are blank. Who can she talk to that can help her sort this out?

She contemplates for a minute and then punches in the only number she really can.

"This is Rhonda Jackson," the voice on the phone answers.

"Hi, it's Liz Harris," she simply states.

"Liz, I'm surprised to hear from you. Why are you calling?"

Liz can hear the coolness in her voice. "I'm in Michigan with my family, looking for answers, and I need your help. I don't have anyone else to call. I feel my collages and pixography are key to understanding my past, and I need someone to help me put the pieces together. I know it's late, but do you have a few minutes for this?"

Rhonda declares, "I don't think I can, Liz. Goodbye."

"Wait! Don't hang up, please! You've got to try. What if I describe what I'm looking at?" Liz doesn't even try to disguise the desperate plea as she begs.

"Okay," Rhonda replies, sounding almost robotic, "I'll see what I can do. Begin by describing what you see visually; start first with your pixography."

"It's open to my ten-year-old page. There's a Post-it with the words, 'I'm not good enough.' On the same page is a picture of my sister and grandma."

"Got it."

"Then I have a collage titled 'I'm not good enough.' The pictures on it include a sad woman curled up on a bench, a running bull with a checkered victory flag, an aerial view of a crowd of people with a tree in the middle, and a pile of tires in an overgrown field."

"Which of those pictures do you have the strongest connection to when you think 'I'm not good enough'?"

"It starts with the woman on the bench."

"What does she remind you of?"

"How I felt rejected and ridiculed as a child and a young adult. The bullying by the school kids started in kindergarten and continued until the day I graduated from high school."

"How did they bully you, Liz?" Rhonda asks.

"They would mock and taunt me everywhere I went—the bathroom, gym, cafeteria, hallways, and at my locker; it was absolutely relentless. School was no safe haven for me," she says matter-of-factly as she watches the blue and white crested waves roll up on the sandy shore.

"What about friends?" Rhonda asks kindly, immediately easing the stress Liz feels from stirring up bad memories.

"I didn't have any public friends. To be seen with me at school would mean the person would be subject to the same ridicule I received."

"What about recess?"

"I despised it." Liz practically spits the words out. "No one wanted to play with me."

As Liz studies her collage in silence, Rhonda gently asks, "Which of the pictures are you looking at now, Liz?"

"The crowd of people with the tree."

"How is that related to recess?"

"There was no playground equipment I could get on, except for the big duck on a spring that the preschoolers played on." She scrunches her face. "The teachers would reprimand me and say, 'The ducks are only for the little kids.' Whenever I walked near them, kids my age would call me a baby. Even if I found something I could play on, like a swing, nobody wanted to play with me." She hesitates. "That's where I'm represented by the tree in the middle of the crowd."

"What did you do?"

"I would sneak into the school building, but teachers would usually catch me and make me go back outside. Once a teacher came out and told the girls they had to let me play jump rope. They followed her exact words and let me play; only I never actually got to jump because I was forced to hold the end of the rope during the entire recess. Eventually, I gave up on hold rope"—she giggles, trying to infuse humor into a dreadful story—"and tried to find other friends to play with, but I never did."

She pauses. "In retrospect, making the kids play with me compares to a team being forced to pick the worst athlete because of a quota. The kids hated me for it, and I despised being singled out in desperation."

"Did the teachers ever intercede in any other way?"

"They were nice to me, since I was a good student. Then I got taunted for being a teacher's pet; I couldn't win. I remember many days crying at the thought of going to school and begging my mom to let me stay home."

"Did you ever want to quit?"

"Every week. Especially as I got into high school. But I understood that education was a means to a certain lifestyle and personal fulfillment, so I was determined to finish." Liz looks at the collage again. "In fact, that's what the bull with the victory flag represents—finishing the race."

"What kept you going?" Rhonda asks. Liz knew she was guiding her toward the inner strength needed for her to climb out of her deep well.

"You mean besides my mom standing at the door and threatening to hit me?" She chuckles. "As a young child, I'm not sure it was the same each time. Mom regularly demonstrated a certain amount of tough love. I wasn't allowed to feel sorry for myself. By the time I got older, self-motivation was instilled in me, and giving up was never an option. I believed if I could get through what was directly in front of me, better opportunities awaited me on the other side."

"And what did you find?"

"I didn't always like what I found after each hurdle, but once I cleared it there was no going back."

"It sounds as though it left you a victor as opposed to a victim of circumstance."

Liz ponders this. "I never thought of it that way. I only looked to the next hurdle and kept pressing forward, figuring that someday I would become a success. And yet, I never have."

"That's a lot for one collage," Rhonda says. "It leaves us with one picture left."

Liz's voice deflates. "The pile of tires in the deserted field."

"Why did you pick that picture for this collage? It doesn't seem to fit with the rest."

Liz scrutinizes the page. "I'm not sure why I did at the time. However, in light of conversations I've had with my family these past two days, it seems related to the feelings I have over my adoption."

"Look at the tires one more time. Pay close attention to every detail about them. What adjectives would you use to describe what you see?"

Liz studies the photo—the dry field, weeds sprouting through and around the tires, the haphazard way they are all arranged. "Discarded, unwanted, and aborted."

"Great work, Liz. Now look at your pixography. What pictures or events have you depicted for the year where 'I'm not good enough' is posted?"

Liz's smile is as big as the waves in front of her. "Rhonda, you are brilliant!"

"What's the connection you made?"

"The picture I'm looking at—my sister and biological grandmother—was taken outside my house on Christmas Day. Right after it was taken, they got in the car and drove away. Then I went to my room and cried. When my adopted mom found me several hours later, she wanted to know what happened. My questions to her were: 'What's wrong with me? Why didn't my birth parents want to keep me?'" Liz continues, "In looking at it, I see the answer is on this page, 'I'm not good enough.' That's what I told myself that day and every day since, whenever I doubted my worthiness."

Rhonda pauses, clearly letting Liz's words sink in. "What's the tire connection?"

"To me, being adopted was like being thrown away by my parents; I guess I saw myself as a discarded tire."

After another moment of silence, Rhonda asks, "Can you now believe that statement, 'I'm not good enough,' isn't true?"

"It'll take some time to feel it in my heart, but I'm committed to getting rid of that belief," Liz says with renewed determination.

"One more thing," Rhonda says. "I know this is normally covered in the last weekend of your course, but I'm mentioning it now so when you get there, it will make more sense. There's something that's referred to as our 'unanswerable question.' My best explanation is that throughout our lifetime we ask ourselves the same question over and over, yet no matter what happens, we never get an answer that satisfies us. We continue searching, kind of like a dog chasing its tail."

Liz nods on her end of the phone, still taking in the beauty of the beach as the moonlight reveals the golden sand and blueness of the water with gentle whitecaps rolling into the shore in front of her.

"So in the case of your adoption, when you ask your question—"

"What's wrong with me?" Liz quickly answers.

"The answer according to your collage is—"

She asserts, "I'm not good enough."

"Then where do you lay the blame for your 'not good enough' feelings?"

Liz looks down. "My leg."

Rhonda asks gently, "Do you really believe that's true?"

"I'm not sure ...." There's a long pause as Liz retraces the sequence of statements she just finished, while following along with the images in her pixography and collages.

Rhonda breaks her concentration. "Consider this: In our head we have a series of beliefs that keep us safe. For instance, 'If I play with matches, I'm going to get hurt.' We also have a series of rules we tell ourselves in reaction to something that happened, such as 'Because I didn't eat my vegetables, I can't have dessert.'"

"Okay. I'm tracking so far," Liz says as she rests her head on the driver's side window.

"In your case, at the genesis of your self-image, the belief 'I'm not good enough' is so strongly tied to what happened to your leg that it's hard for you to see it any other way. If it hadn't been for your accident, you and your sister would've spent your childhood together, as well as the countless other things you wish would have happened but didn't."

"It's my convenient excuse for everything," she says, disheartened.

"It doesn't have to be, Liz. The choice is yours. Freedom and peace come by embracing your limitations, commanding the power of all your talents. You can continue to blame your leg for all your misfortune—and thus remain a victim. However, you didn't survive at age four to be that. Your life was destined for a greater purpose. Ours all are. At the end of each day, the choice is yours—victim or victor. Choose."

Liz scrunches her face. "I don't feel like the victor. Instead, I question what good I can make out of having a disability."

"Give it time and practice. Remember, you've perfected a lifetime of believing 'I'm not good enough.' It will take time to replace that belief with something that allows you to always live into your greatness."

"Thank you, Rhonda," Liz says, feeling a shred of optimism. "I'll try." Before they hang up, Liz has one more question for Rhonda. "Why did you answer the phone when you knew it is me?"

"As a professional, I am obliged to respond when someone reaches out."

The clinical response startles Liz. "Oh," she squeaks.

"Here's my one last question for you. What do you need to do while you're at home that's going to be the most painful for you to accomplish?"

Liz thinks, *Ouch—that was blunt of her.* She says, "Visit the barn." It's a simple response but tainted with extreme anxiety.

"Then make sure you do it before coming home. Otherwise, you may not work through this crisis, and it may linger for the rest of your life."

She gulps. "I will. I promise."

"Liz, this commitment isn't for me. It's for you."

"Why do you say that?"

"In order to honor yourself, you must keep commitments to you. Once you do this, you're able to honor others by keeping your commitments to them. It's important for you to have this as a personal cornerstone on which you develop all your relationships. Without it, you easily fall back into becoming a victim of life's circumstances."

"Wow. I have a lot of work to do, in this and many areas of my life. Rhonda, I truly appreciate your time today."

"Good luck, Liz."

"Thank you, Rhonda, for everything."

As Rhonda ends the call, she's pleased that she overcame the urge to tell Liz she was no longer in the coaching business or a course mentor and quickly hang up, leaving her with nowhere to turn. While she might have relished this end to her challenging work with Liz, it would have been short-lived. The "ethics" side of her consciousness would kick in, leaving her disempowered by her choice of acting in a less-than professional manner.

She turns her attention back to her computer, where she is in the midst of completing an on-line application for a job as regional manager at a national training firm. The strength of her candidacy, she believes, lies in her ability to quickly identify problems and trends, develop strategic and cost-effective solutions, and provide general guidance to team members who are proven self-starters. If she's successful getting this or any other new job, she will quickly be on her way to ending this turbulent chapter of her life.

26

The Lies We Believe and Tell

Lying on the couch that evening, Liz starts to plan out the next day. She believes if she can somehow get up in the hayloft, her memory of the accident will return. Her hope is that she can finally relive what actually happened, rather than continuing with her memory pieced together from stories told by family members.

Her thoughts are random: Playing with Carla and the cats in the hay … Running across the yard to check on their treats … The thud. She shudders. Despite her countless attempts over the years to resurrect that day's memory, her consciousness hasn't allowed it, just as it didn't with the knife-wielding babysitter and the cranberry sauce. She tosses and turns and eventually drifts off to sleep, dreaming of what the following day might bring.

Several hundred yards from the farmhouse, Liz pulls onto the dirt shoulder of the paved road and parks, looking at what has changed since her last drive-by visit decades earlier. She puts the car in gear and proceeds slowly toward the house. As she turns into the driveway, she remembers what her dad used to tell her: "In the country, only salesmen come to the front door. Everyone else enters through the back."

Most of her tree friends are gone, except for the trunk of the old maple she used to swing on, sandwiched on the left between the still-dirt driveway and the cow pasture. The house and farm layout has been redesigned since her last visit; the front entrance is now an exterior wall covered by overgrown evergreens, the back steps where she played with the cats are now a large patio, covered with blue patio chairs, a round table, and a kitchen-sized grill. The tractor garage where the men worked has fallen, and aged timber lies in piles near the corner beams; the surrounding buildings are in disrepair. The barn structure remains intact, the outside now a faded gray with a bright red entrance nearest the hayloft landing that seems to beckon her.

Parked behind the patio, she takes a deep breath, looks toward the sky, and whispers, "Please give me the strength to do this." She slings her purse strap over her shoulder, takes out her crutch, and starts toward the house. She gets ten feet from the car when she hears a deep voice behind her. "Are you lost, miss?"

She turns to see a man about thirty-five years old, short, with red hair, wearing denim bib overalls and a red and black checked shirt. Two young boys are beside him, and a little girl peeks from behind his left pant leg. She guesses the kids are all under the age of ten.

"Hi. I'm Liz Harris; I used to live here."

She takes a picture from her purse and holds it out. The man studies the shot of young Liz by the freshly painted barn, and then looks up at the faded building.

"I'm Devon," he says. "How can I help you?"

"Devon, this is a strange request, but I need to see your hayloft entrance, and I was hoping you'd let me in."

He gives her a quick once-over and glances to the barn in the near distance. Then, fixing his eyes on her, he asks, "Why?"

"I don't want to bother you with my life story, but it's important I get in there one last time."

She looks at the little blond girl who seems to be the age Liz was when she fell. "She's so little," Liz says, bending over to look into her deep blue eyes surrounded by her shoulder-length white-blond hair. For a moment she drifts back to the day when she was the four-year-old, clinging to a man's pant leg.

Devon's words bring her back to reality. "Yes, but they grow up so fast." He smiles.

She returns his smile and asks, "So can you please help me?"

"Let me get my wife to mind the little ones; I'll be right back."

He disappears into the house and returns a few minutes later with an older gentleman. "This is my dad. He owned the place before we bought it from him. He might be able to answer your questions," says Devon.

"Glad to meet you, Mr.—"

"Call me Harry."

"Good to meet you, Harry," she says, shifting her left crutch to her right hand and extending her left to shake.

As they walk across the yard to the barn, Liz looks to the right and asks, "When did you stop using the tractor garage?"

"We haven't used it for years," Harry says. "We now work on our farm equipment over there." He points to the newer building at the far left, behind the barn.

"Once we get the area clear," Devon says, grinning as he points to the fallen garage, "we're planning to put a swimming pool there."

"That's a great location, overlooking the wheat field." She glances to the left and adds, "I see the old milk parlor is still standing."

"We have a newer, bigger one, so we remodeled this for the kids to use as a playhouse," Devon says.

"I always wanted my dad to do that," she says with a sigh. "It seemed the perfect size, especially with the escape hatch on the side." She points to the half door in front of a four-by-four raised concrete slab that they used to store milk cans that were being staged for milking.

Once at the barn entrance, Liz stops to takes a deep breath. She's envisioned this moment for years, but now that it's here, she's a bit apprehensive about being ready for what might come from it. However, there's no going back.

As Devon opens the door, she transforms into her four-year-old self again. It's exactly as she remembers; the barn is dimly lit, with wings to the cow milking stations on the right and left, merging at the hayloft ladder directly in front of her. She slowly approaches and grabs a metal rung covered with an anti-slip coating.

"These used to be wood slats," she declares as she brushes the length of the one chest-high to her.

"We replaced those years ago," Harry says. "There was a girl who lived here and almost died because she missed a ladder rung. With our children running around, that was the first thing we fixed when we bought the place."

Liz turns to face Harry. "How do you know about this girl?"

"It's a small community, and people talk. They say she was a determined child; her parents were just as tough as they taught her to be. They were good people who fought for her quality of life long before there were laws for such things."

Liz's heart fills. "I'm that girl."

Harry smiles and says, "I figured."

Devon looks at his father and says, "If she's the one, who's the other woman who visited?"

"Someone else was here?" Liz asks, her mind racing.

"Yes, about ten years back. She was probably your age and had the same crystal blue eyes," Harry says.

"Carla," she whispers.

"I don't remember her name. She said she knew the little girl who fell," Harry recalls.

Liz takes another picture from her purse and shows it to him. It's of her and Carla, taken about fifteen years ago; they're sitting on the front steps to Carla's house. She asks, "Is this the girl?"

Harry studies the picture and says, "I reckon it is."

Liz nods. "That's my sister, Carla. Did she go up in the hayloft?"

"Yep."

"Can I go up?" she asks, now feeling eager.

"Are you able to with your crutch?" Harry looks worried.

"With a bit of help," she says.

At Liz's direction, Devon takes her purse and scrambles to the top of the hayloft. He grabs the crutch from her outstretched hand and grips it tightly as she climbs up the rungs, with Harry as spotter. When she gets to the top, Devon reaches down, grabs her left hand, and pulls her up into the hayloft. He hands Liz her crutch and she limps a few feet away from the opening that Devon is guarding. She slowly looks around and inhales.

Daylight illuminates the floor of the loft through open slats between the aged wall planks and a partially open door near the peak of the beams. Staring through the rays of light, she sees bales of hay stacked high on the far wall, with a few haphazardly strewn on the floor, and a pitchfork sticking down in the one closest to her. In the far corner are two barn cats sitting on top of full grain bags with rolls of yellow twine nearby.

She steps back near the opening, giving Devon a look of confidence and a thumbs-up with her left hand while it's still on the crutch handle. She looks down below; standing off to the left is the little girl clinging to Harry's pant leg. To the right is the cement that broke her fall; now aged with decades of dust and barn dirt. Its exterior, like moss on a rock, looks softened by years of wear. However, she's not fooled by that deceptive appearance; she knows the slate gray hardness of its unbreakable shell as its path slopes, leading to other parts of the barn.

She steps back a few feet and turns her attention to the barn walls, as if they could spark the return of her memory, but there's nothing new. Now what? The one thing she hoped to gain from this visit—remembering what happened—simply isn't happening, at least not in the way she had planned. Frustrated and determined, she can't give up; instead, she decides to give it one more try.

She deeply breathes in the barn scents. Her memory fills with the dank, humid air of freshly bailed alfalfa. She walks with her head down, returning within a few feet of the opening, and crouches as low as she can, which is about the height she would have been at the time of the accident. She imagines the trajectory that her body would have made from being pushed off the landing by Carla to the point of impact on the cement below. In her calculation, she would have landed on her head. Then she steps a foot back, which is where Carla would have stood. She imagines two little girls, standing toe-to-toe, one yelling and the other one with crossed arms—ignoring—

Suddenly, recollections of that day come flooding back into her consciousness, unmistakable—like choppy video footage of her from the 'sixties that she's never seen. Carla is dressed in the same hay-covered pink shorts and yellow T-shirt that little Liz is wearing. She looks into Carla's round five-year-old face, framed with a pixie haircut. Her sister is angry, her cheeks are aglow, and her lips are pursed as she yells and pushes on Liz's folded arms. Liz stumbles slightly to her left and then trips on the raised hay-covered wood threshold that lines the four-foot-square opening. Carla's hand stretches toward her, but already Liz is inches beyond her grasp; it's too far. Liz sees the ceiling beam receding above her, and then every brown ladder rung passes her by, upside down, until the last one—a few feet away is the oblong hay bale on the ground, twine broken, with remnants scattered around the floor—she hears a crack—then darkness falls—

Liz holds tight to her crutch and gasps as she is visibly shaken. Her gut wrenches in fear. In shock, she turns her back on Devon and silently limps to the far wall; her right arm and leg tremble as she tries to regain her poise. With eyes tightly closed and clenched teeth, she holds back the sea of tears, at least for now. How many years did Carla suffer from the guilt of a mistake that occurred in the blink of an eye? Or her father, every time he went into the hayloft? Or …

Her heart feels heavy from the truth, but she finally has the answer she's been searching for all these years: to see with her own eyes what happened. She turns her thoughts to Carla and the remorse she can only imagine her sister has lived with; and although tragic, she is thankful that in the split second it took for her accident to happen, Carla could only see Liz fall through the opening—which means she never saw the fear in her eyes as she hit the floor, a memory she's sure no one could ever forget.

For both these insights—Liz is forever changed in the moment and overwhelmed by what has been revealed in the past five minutes.

Regaining her composure, she stands tall in her knowledge as she shakes off the cold truth for the last time. Although every ounce of her heart rejected the memory of Carla's confession some thirty years ago, she can't escape its truth each time someone asks what happened, which is why she's always felt disempowered at her own lying answer, "I fell."

With tears forming in her eyes, Liz turns to Devon and asks, "Did Carla say anything when she visited?"

"I remember she wept." He looks away from her stare as if to give her a moment of privacy. Walking to the grain bags in the corner, he says, "She also left an envelope." The cats jump to the floor as he reaches beneath a roll of twine.

"She said that someday another woman might show up; if she did, I was to give this to her."

He hands Liz a plastic bag, discolored from the twine sitting on it. Inside is a beige stationery envelope with her name handwritten on the front. It is sealed on the back in red wax with an 'R'. Liz remembers that seal from the childhood letters she received, some of which looked like they had been resealed.

Liz tilts her head and says, "I took something a long time ago that should have been left here and I'd like to give it back."

Devon stares at her, looking perplexed. "Sure," he says.

"Can you please hand me my purse?"

Devon gives it to her, and she takes out a small black-and-white checkered flag on a stick. She walks to the grain sacks stored by the far barn wall. With tears streaming down her face, she proclaims silently, *Victory is mine!* Ceremoniously, like the winners in the Indy 500, her victory is declared as she waves the flag in the air and sticks it the middle of a ball of twine.

Her heart fills with peace from the freedom of her truth. Looking around for the last time, she bends down to pet one of the barn cats rubbing up against her leg.

Although she doesn't understand why it took a lifetime for her memories to return from that day, she quickly resigns herself to the fact that if it had happened at a different time or place—she wouldn't have been able to forgive Carla as she had so many years earlier.

Standing up, she wipes away the tears of her past, turns, and heads toward Devon.

"It's time for me to go. You've been very generous today and also when Carla was here."

Devon nods. He looks at her and then the opening. He promptly asks, "How you gonna get down?"

"I hadn't thought of that!" She hesitates and with a sly grin says, "I guess it should be different than the last time."

Their laughter eases her anguish from the silent tragedy concealed for decades within the walls of the hayloft and by a promise between two sisters to never speak of it again. Her heart lifts as she embraces the truth.

Devon has an idea. He shouts down and asks Harry to get the barn cart used to load grain feed into the bins. Harry obliges and places it at the base of the steps and stands on it. Both men then help Liz off the hayloft ledge and onto the cart.

Once safely on the ground, Liz gazes at the floor underneath her feet, remembering how she always felt traumatized whenever she had to walk near this section of the barn; she's leaving that terror behind today.

Her eyes twinkle as she says to the men, "If you don't mind, I'd like to say goodbye now."

"We understand," Harry says.

They all shake hands, and Liz heads back to her car. She puts her crutch in the back and gets in the driver's seat. She goes far enough down the road to be out of their sight and pulls over. Hands shaking, she opens the letter and reads it out loud:

> Dear Lizzy—I knew someday you'd find the strength to come here. I pray you're able to reconcile the pain of your memories from that day. I know you can never forget what happened, as you live with your injury every day. I can never forget either, that I caused it when I pushed you. You know I didn't mean to hurt you. I was just trying to get you to come down and you wouldn't.
>
> The only way I can live with what I did to you is to tell the story of your accident the way we agreed that night in your kitchen. Otherwise, always being reminded of the agony that I caused you would be so great, I couldn't face you. Know that I'll always remember, and I hope that by the time you read this, we've each found a way to forgive ourselves for this tragic mistake.
>
> I am forever sorry for that moment. I know by our relationship and the love you have for me that you've forgiven me many years ago.
>
> With all my love. ~Carla

27

Dreams Come True in Other Ways

Liz wakes early the next morning to the smell of freshly brewed coffee. Not wanting to get up just yet, she keeps one eye shut while quickly peeking around the room with the other; her mother is nowhere to be seen. Although the aroma is enticing, she remains curled up on the couch, her heart lifted by what lies ahead. Despite her desire for a do-over, she knows that last night's dream at the barn can never come true; the reality is that all family members felt some level of responsibility for her accident, although it never showed. For that, she must determine whether the reconciliation is hers to make or theirs.

Within a few seconds, she decides what happened to her all those years ago doesn't matter in the big scheme of things; what matters is how she's lived her life since the accident.

She visualizes one of her favorite pictures, a calm pond with ripples moving away from a purple water lily in full bloom. Every action she does or doesn't take has an impact and consequences, just as a pebble thrown into a still pond forever changes the water and what lies beneath its surface. How does she achieve victory and set herself free as she did in her dream, rather than continuing to be a victim in real life? What can she do to release the past, to move her heart beyond believing that everything she wants and doesn't have is because of her leg?

Liz reflects. The barn … the flag … a memorial … a new response to "What happened?" … forgiveness … the truth … What else can be done? Then she decides to begin with what she knows.

Liz limps to her mother's bedroom and knocks softly on the closed door. "Mom, are you okay?" she asks quietly.

"I'm not feeling well" is the faint reply. "I made you coffee, and there's fruit in the fridge and cereal on the counter."

"I saw them. Thank you! Can I get you anything?"

"No, dear. Do whatever you planned for the day, and hopefully I'll feel better in a while."

"Okay, Mom. Rest well."

Liz gets her journal and pixography then takes them to the kitchen table. She eats breakfast while writing frantically in her journal, not wanting to miss a detail of what she remembers from her dream.

When she finishes that and her cup of coffee an hour later, she tears out the pages, folds them, and puts them in the front of the journal. She then turns her attention to the family photo albums stored on a shelf just outside the kitchen. She casually brushes dust off the albums and is transported to the chores of her childhood, where at least monthly she dusted off the same albums, while sitting on the couch, looking at every picture, and asking herself questions about her accident that would never be answered—until now, that is.

Liz looks over the twenty or so photo album binders and

reaches for the familiar navy blue one with all the pictures of her and Carla in the year leading up to her accident. She flips quickly through the pages. There they are picking dandelions in the front yard … Carla's driving the tricycle with Liz on the back axle … they stand on the front porch in Easter dresses and bonnets on the way to church … it's all as she remembered being told. If only she could go there again with Carla—

She turns one more page and sees herself at the entrance to the barn. Where did Carla's picture go? She had an identical pose on the next page and now it's gone, leaving only an imprint of where it used to be mounted. Puzzled, Liz removes her photo from the album and caresses the front as if touching it would transport her to that time. She turns the picture over and sees "July 1964" scrawled in faded ink; it's the month before her accident.

Her heart thumps as she tucks the photo in the front of her journal near the torn-out journal pages she placed there earlier. She stands and tears out one more piece of paper. On it she writes, "Mom, I'm going to visit a few of my old haunts. I'll be back in time for dinner. I hope you're up for ice cream later."

Liz leaves the apartment determined to complete her mission. The first stop is Walmart, where she quickly grabs what she needs, barely noticing everyone's stares as she limps down the aisles.

Driving toward their old farm, she makes herself a promise toward the future: to transform any negative feelings about her accident or her leg into positive thoughts and activities, thus becoming the victor instead of the victim.

Looking through the windshield and toward the blue northern sky, she clears her throat and proclaims, "Today's for you, Dad, and also the others; I will release all of us when I declare victory."

The final mile seems like twenty, with the passing fields, gullies, and houses reminding her of her countless bus rides home from school. She remembers the dilapidated house where poor Mrs. Schotz lived; now only trees are growing where she used to sit in an old rocker on her front porch. Liz recalls with a shiver the story her mom told about Mrs. Schotz's skin coming off in layers when emergency room nurses removed the paper bags she had used for warmth during the cold Michigan winters. Rumor had it there was no heat, electricity, or running water in the old house. Liz's parents, as well as others in the community, tried to help, but Mrs. Schotz was too proud and refused their generosity. What if she had accepted their kindness? Would she have enjoyed her life surrounded by friends and neighbors rather than spewing bitterness through the community when her son was killed by a drunk driver while walking home from his job at the nearby meat market?

Liz's eyes catch something on the left. It's the field leading up to the barn and the farmhouse, a bit different than the last time she was here. She opens the window and slowly drives by the homestead, scanning the grounds to see what has changed: the house is now painted brown, the tractor garage has fallen down, and there's a new building to the left of the barn. She wants so badly to stop and explore just for a bit. However, she remembers the promise from her dream; no more victims, no more anguish. It ends today.

Liz continues to the neighbor's house next door, which is a quarter mile away. She thinks of Pete and the times on the bus when he tormented her with how he tortured and killed their barn cats. She winces hard to generate wishes for his well-being instead of thoughts of the retribution that she feels he deserves. She hopes he overcame the effects of being raised without a father.

She turns around in his driveway—as city people often do in the country when they don't know where they're going. Then she steers slowly toward the Harrises' old house, takes a long look, and keeps going. With the farm in her rearview mirror, she makes the first right onto a gravel road and stops twenty yards in.

Reaching into the plastic Walmart bag, she pulls out an American flag on a little wooden stick, along with a bunch of orange and yellow plastic flowers. She gathers the journal pages she filled earlier that day, rereads them, and replaces them in her journal. Holding everything in her right hand, she gets out of the car and limps toward the trunk, steadying herself against the side of the car.

She has a full view of the entire farm; emotions come blasting at her as the memories of living there come sharply into focus. If only she could stay here and correct life; there are many things she would do over.

In the silence of the moment, her newfound peace is the pathway to new thoughts: her accident and everything that came out of it gave her the life she has today. Yes, a tragic thing happened, but it's time to share the lessons she's learned from her life experiences with others, to help in their journey. It's time to tell the story of her strength; the tough decisions and seemingly unsurmountable obstacles that she's managed to overcome for a lifetime.

Cocking her head, she ponders the inspiration that others say they see in her; having the courage to face and overcome adversity. Emotions fill her heart as she remembers being eight years old again and having a pinch runner in softball; they ran the bases and scored the home run she never could. Now it's time for her to pay it forward—to do for others as people have done for her.

Liz looks to the heavens and says out loud, "It's time for freedom and living life to the fullest. May I daily give others access to a world of possibilities as shown through my experiences and challenges. May no child or adult ever go through the years of pain it took for me to find the peace that I have today."

She closes her eyes and makes a sign of the cross with her left hand over her face and upper chest.

Opening her eyes, she looks one last time at the farmstead. There is one seventy-foot pine by the house, surrounded by three twenty-foot maples. Speaking as if the trees could hear her, she says,

"Except for the old pine tree being one of my former playmates, your ancestors were once the only friends I had along with the barn cats."

Liz bends over and pushes the end of the flag stick into the soft ground on the shoulder of the road. She then arranges the flowers around it. She stands up and shouts, "Today I declare freedom and victory for my friends, my family, and myself over the tragedy of the past!"

Liz stares at the barn for several minutes, reveling in her feat. In a few months, it will be fifty years since that hot day in late August when she fell. What happened in the blink of an eye took almost a lifetime to reconcile; it didn't have to—she always had the power to thrive—she just needed to choose to let tragedy go and trust in the future. Ready now for that, she shouts in the wind where only the trees can hear her, "Thank you for being there when I needed it; I couldn't have made the journey without you."

With that, her inner strength rises. She looks to the heavens and says, "I've always known I was fearfully and wonderfully made. Now I have the strength and peace to live it daily."

She turns around and limps to the driver's door. Spying the pixography on the passenger's seat, she wants some type of memorabilia to remind her of the strength she feels today, so if she ever feels weak and wants to get lost in the past, she can overcome the urge and press on boldly.

Reaching through the window, she grabs her cell phone and limps back to her memorial. Bending, she takes a picture of the flag and flowers billowing in the wind with the farm in the background. She returns to the car and slides into her seat. Still holding the phone, she clicks on her Facebook page and posts the picture along with the comment: "Today is my victory over the past."

As she drives away, she no longer has tears. There's only serenity in her soul and joy in her heart for the future; knowing that although she has a few other reconciliations to make, they are short strides in comparison to what today's victory lap required her to endure.

Liz returns to her mother's apartment early in the afternoon with a bounce to her step; as if she were twenty years younger and fifty pounds lighter. She thinks, *I never realized the past was so heavy!*

Walking in, she notices that her mother has her look of disapproval that she gives Liz when she's about to point out something wrong that she did. "By the smile on your face, you must have gone to the cemetery."

"No," Liz says, feeling a touch of guilt for not checking earlier to make sure her mom was okay. "I visited the barn." She pulls the picture of little Liz from her journal and shows her. "Mom, there used to be a picture of Carla by the barn, like this one. Do you know what happened to it?"

"Your dad gave it to her," she says matter-of-factly.

"When did you see Carla?" Liz struggles to keep surprise out of her voice.

"It was before your dad died, probably ten or twelve years ago. She came up one afternoon with her children and visited for the day. We were showing them pictures of you as little girls, and your father was telling them about the trouble you both used to get into. When Carla saw the picture, she asked if she could have it. She also asked for directions to the farm because she wanted to show the kids where she stayed with you." She stops for a breath and looks at Liz. "Is that a problem?"

Liz reflects on the coincidence of her dream to Carla's actual visit. "No, that's fine." Redirecting, she asks, "Do you want to visit Dad's grave with me tomorrow?"

"You know he's not there; he's in heaven," her mom says in her judgmental tone.

Liz cocks her head and looks at the picture of her parents on wall. "I know that, but it's where I like to go to visit him."

Her mother hesitates, purses her lips, and then says, "Yes, I'll come with you. It'll be a good day to clean up around the headstone and leave flowers in the urns for the summer."

Liz perks up. "Good. Since I'm leaving for Carla's in the afternoon, we can do it on my way out of town. I already got some beautiful plastic flowers, so we should be all set. How about we have the ice cream and brownies we missed out on yesterday?" Liz uses comfort food to evade further questioning by her mother, but it backfires.

"We can't have dessert now!" her mother says disapprovingly as she pounds her fist on the table as Liz's father used to do. "We haven't had dinner yet."

"Oh, Mom," Liz sighs, frustrated. "Life is short; eat dessert first!"

Mom delays. "I guess we can—just this once. After all, ice cream does have milk in it, and dairy is one of the required food groups for daily health."

Liz smirks, knowing that she finally succeeded in getting her mother to break one of her longstanding rules about food. "That's the Harris attitude that Dad would be proud of," Liz declares, beaming at the thought of her father and his love of ice cream; he would have loved being a part of today's victory with her.

She and her mother enjoy their brownie sundaes while reminiscing about family get-togethers of yesteryear.

Mom asks, "Remember how Dad used to enjoy taking pictures when the family was together?"

"Yes," she answers with a broad smile, recalling fond memories of her dad teaching her to take pictures the day he gave her the first camera she owned, a Kodak Brownie. "He used to teach me to look for scenes no one else notices, learning to capture the ordinary in life in extraordinary photos. I miss our photo shoots."

"And I miss your father taking pictures at the dinner table, catching everyone shoving food in their faces."

They both laugh, and then Liz has an idea. "Since I have my camera, let's take a picture as Dad would have. We can make it a non-food shot and have it over by the dogwood tree in front of the building. He would've picked that spot even if there wasn't food around," Liz suggests as she points through the glass doors beside the TV.

"You're right. That's a great suggestion."

After they clean up their dishes, they walk through the apartment complex toward the front entrance. On the way, they run into the apartment manager.

"Excuse me, Mr. Sherman," Mom says. "Can you please take a picture of my daughter and me by the tree out front?"

"I would love to, Mrs. Harris!"

He follows the women to the white wooden bench underneath a blooming pink dogwood. He takes a few pictures, hands the camera back, and returns to his office. Reviewing the pictures with her mother, Liz feels a closeness she hasn't experienced in perhaps twenty years. She doesn't want the moment to end but knows it must all too soon.

Mom looks seriously at Liz and says, "I remembered something about your accident."

Liz leans forward, almost too eager to speak. "What's that, Mom?"

"When you were about ten, you were obsessed with how it happened, as well as why we didn't adopt Carla."

"I remember."

"One night at dinner, your father and I explained it to you in terms we thought you would understand. You were defiant and said it couldn't have happened that way. You even got out a piece of paper and drew a stick man standing on the ladder to graphically illustrate how you would have landed, making some argument about falling on your back."

She looks deeply into Mom's hazel, tear-filled eyes. "I remember."

"Liz, we had no answer to give you. We could only confirm what had been told to us by Carla."

Did her parents ever know the truth of her accident—that Carla pushed her? If they did, why did they lie about it? If not, why didn't they take Liz seriously when she challenged them with her stick figure drawing? Should she ask her mother about it now or let the secret she shares with Carla remain buried in the past? Although torn, she reaches her decision based her mother's most recent words.

Liz says, "Mom, there's no reason for me or anyone else to visit the past anymore. Here's what happened: there was an accident and I fell. Nothing else matters anymore except how we have lived our lives since."

Mom sighs deeply, her eyebrows and lips relaxed. "I'm glad. I'd hate for you to think your dad and I had lied to you all these years."

"I know you didn't." Liz leans over and hugs Mom.

"You know your father and I haven't always agreed with some of the decisions you made, but we have always loved you like our own child and have always been proud of you. If he was here today, he would say he was pleased by the lady you've blossomed into." Tears stream down Mom's rosy cheeks.

"I love you, Mom. I haven't said this nearly enough—I'm grateful for the life you gave me, and I've been honored to be your daughter." Liz looks intently at her. "Hey, Mom, do you want to go to the beach and watch the sunset?"

"Oh no, I'm too old for the beach, sweetheart. Besides that's always been your thing."

"Mom, no one is too old for the beach. Besides, Lake Michigan has the world's best sunsets."

Mom wrinkles her nose and shrugs. "How do you know that?" she asks.

"Well, of all the many places I've lived and traveled to, no sunset compares to the ones over the Grand Haven Harbor at dusk, with all the pinks and oranges in the sky, surrounding the bright sun as it sets over the deep blue Lake Michigan water—with the lighthouse in the background and silhouettes of people walking the boardwalk."

"Your words make it sound so beautiful. The few times we went to the beach to watch the Fourth of July fireworks, there were so many people, I guess I didn't pay attention to the sunset." Mom reflects a little more. "I'm actually surprised your dad never brought me there to take pictures. But since he worked so hard on the farm, the only thing he wanted to do by the end of the day was relax in his chair and watch TV. I guess we both were too tired to do anything else."

"I understand," Liz says, and then realizes the time. "If you don't mind, Mom, I'm going to see the sunset. By the looks of the sky, it will be a beauty."

"That's fine. I'll probably be in bed when you get back, so please lock the door when you get in. Hurry, if you don't get going, you may miss it."

Liz hugs her mom once more. Then she stands and limps to her car.

Driving, she reminisces about being confined to the farm as a young teenager, her parents acting as if it would take three days instead of twenty minutes to get to the beach. She never understood why they didn't go there more; despite chores and other activities, there's something magical about the beach that calms a restless soul.

Several minutes later, she enters the park and quickly finds a parking space close to the boardwalk entrance that overlooks the sand and water. She grabs her camera and crutch and heads for the black steel bench just a few feet ahead, at the end of the sand-covered sidewalk.

As she sits facing the setting sun, she is drawn to the body of water in front of her; it's the fountain of life that rejuvenates her with every visit. Watching the fiery orange sun sink slowly beyond the colorful horizon, Liz loses herself taking pictures of the lake she loved as a child and the sunsets she relished as a teenager.

The next morning, Liz and Mom are up early so they can visit the cemetery on Liz's way back to Carla's. Over breakfast, they share many laughs, remembering raucous stories that often starred Liz's father. By midmorning they are ready to go.

Liz follows her mom's car to the cemetery, where they pull close to the family plot to limit the amount of walking on the warm morning. As Liz walks around the back of her car, she pops open the trunk and removes two red folding chairs.

Her mom chuckles. "You came prepared with chairs?"

"Yes," she says with an impish grin. "You and Dad taught me well. It's difficult for me to stand for a long time, so I always carry chairs in case I'm somewhere I need to sit."

"That's good thinking! That dad of yours was pretty smart," Mom says seriously. "Can I carry the flowers, Liz?"

Liz smiles. "Sure." She scoops up the pink and purple roses, daisies, baby's breath, and greens from the trunk and hands them over. With the chairs in her right hand, Liz closes the trunk with her left, picks up the crutch that she leaned against the rocker panel, and follows Mom to the gravesite. Soon the urns on either side of the family headstone are filled with bright flowers.

"They look lovely!" Liz says. "And they should last all season."

The women sit overlooking the cemetery and the valley beyond; warm winds gently stir the pink blooms of the cherry trees against a clear blue sky. As she feels the breeze on her scalp, Liz thinks about how fragile life is; she could have been the one buried here. And when it's her time, will she have accomplished everything she set out to do? Probably not. But she's determined to have made a difference in the world, one day at a time, with every person she meets from now until her final day.

"This is such a beautiful place for Dad," she says quietly. "Being here with him reminds me of the times we spent together doing chores in the barn or weeding and picking the vegetables from the garden."

Mom acknowledges with a smile, nods, and stands up. "I'm going over to visit my parents. I'll be back in a bit."

Once her mother is out of earshot, Liz moves her chair next to her father's headstone. Speaking as if he was in front of her, she says, "Dad, I wish you were here for me to hug you and tell you one last time that I love you," she says softly. "We've both endured a lot of pain and done a lot of living since that day in the barn. I now understand the torment you held secret all those years. I wish you had been able to express your sorrow to me for the guilt you had over my accident. Maybe then we wouldn't have had the distance between us that existed for so many years." Liz tenderly reaches out to the white granite stone and uses her fingers to trace the lettering of his name, Norman Harris, along with the dates he was born and died. "I should have said this long ago; I know it wasn't your fault; it wasn't anyone's fault. It was just an accident."

Liz turns to see her mother walking toward her from a distance.

"Dad, you'd be proud of me. I finally see my leg as a blessing. I have you to thank for that. You gave me the courage to declare victory over the past—for both of us. Now I have to live my life for others, just as you did." Liz blows a kiss to the headstone. "Dad, it's time for me to go. I love you and miss you every day. You have always been my biggest supporter and lifelong hero."

Seconds later Mom arrives. "Did you have a nice talk with your dad?"

"Yes, and it was long overdue. I'm glad you came out here with me, Mom."

Liz looks at her father's headstone one last time. "Well, I'd better get going. I want to get to Carla's before it's too late."

"Okay, I'll say goodbye here," Mom says. "There's some things I never said to your dad that I want to talk to him about now."

Liz is pleasantly surprised. Both women rise; Mom starts to fold her chair. Liz scolds, "Mom, don't be silly. I'm not going to leave you here without something to sit on. I'll get it the next time I visit."

Mom insists, shoving it her way. "You take it."

Liz gets stern and slowly orders. "Mo-ther, take the chair, and enjoy the day. There might not be another like it for a long time."

Mom huffs as Liz shakes her head with a grin, saying "That's the Harris independence, alive and kicking!"

Mom smiles. "Liz, give Carla a hug from me, and tell her she's welcome here any time." She looks sad and adds, "We loved her as much as you and wish we had been able to keep you together with us."

"We both know that now."

Mother and daughter embrace in a way they haven't for a long time. Then Liz picks up her chair, limps to the car, and drives slowly away. Looking in the rearview mirror, she sees Mom waving.

28

Platform Shoes Are Back in Style

On the drive to Carla's, Liz's mind is racing, but one thing is clear to her: she can never use her leg again as an excuse for any circumstance or difficulty she has to overcome. If she does, she'll go back to being a victim and return to a life of imprisonment. It's only in moving forward that she'll remain the victor, having freedom, peace, and joy in her life.

Liz stares at the open road and asks out loud, "What do I want in life? Or maybe the question is what does anyone want?"

She considers her old indicators of success: Money … A big house … A good-looking husband … Children and friends … A good job.

"Damn it!" Liz yells as the sight of a police car behind a stand of thirty-foot pine trees on the left side of the road snaps her back to reality. She hits the brakes, but it's too late; the cruiser pulls out behind her with blue lights flashing. Her heart races as she pulls to the right shoulder and puts on her flashers realizing she forgot to resume the cruise control at the proper speed limit a few miles back.

The officer, dressed in a black uniform with a butt of a gun sticking out of his right-side holster, approaches her vehicle. She rolls down the window.

"Ma'am, do you know how fast you were going?" he asks.

"No, I don't," she politely answers.

"I clocked you at eighty-three; this section of the highway is a fifty-five zone," he sternly replies.

She thinks, *Oh shit. I thought I was going sixty-five.*

She says to him, "I'm sorry, Officer. I was deep in thought and didn't realize I was going that fast."

Should she tell him about her foot? Would it make a difference whether he gives her a ticket or not? In order to remain the victor as opposed to the victim of this circumstance, she decides to say nothing and instead quietly hands over her license, registration, and insurance card.

Her heart races as he returns to the squad car, knowing that a ticket could be the start of losing her license again, as it happened some thirty years ago. However, back then it wasn't just her driving privileges that got taken away but her pride as her carefree lifestyle shifted from being independent and on the move to living with a retired schoolteacher, walking to work, and depending on friends and enemies for rides to the grocery store or to go out.

She rubs her brow and sighs heavily. Since her previous situation, she has learned the technique to control her speed, since the most prevalent motion by her right foot is down. It's to set the cruise each time she gets on long stretches of road. However, she must be present in the moment; otherwise this can be just as risky for her as not setting it.

In today's situation, the real cause of her speeding was not paying attention to her driving and her surroundings. Looking around her car, she decides to take prompt action. She grabs a piece of paper from the glove compartment and writes on it, "Check Speed." She sets the note on the console where she is sure to see it every time she puts the car in gear to drive. Pleased at her positive reaction to an otherwise gloomy situation, Liz proudly proclaims, "I am the victor."

The officer returns a few minutes later holding a yellow slip of paper. She rolls down the window.

"Ma'am, I'm writing you up for eighty-three miles per hour in a fifty-five zone. If I hadn't already called it in, I might've been able to do something, but I'm bound to the rules," he says, frowning as he hands her the speeding ticket.

She graciously accepts it and smiles. "Thank you, sir. You've just helped change the course of my life."

He looks at her suspiciously. "Um, no one has ever thanked me for a ticket before."

"I'm sure they haven't, and I never would've before, either," she says, practically glowing, "but today, I realized what a blessed life I have"—she looks at his name—"Officer Glenn. You may never understand the impact of your actions today, but you saved me."

She extends her left hand, which he hesitantly shakes.

"You're most welcome, Miss Harris."

"Enjoy the day, Officer Glenn!"

He tips his hat and returns to his car.

She checks her rearview mirror for traffic, switches flashers for her left turn signal, and pulls onto the roadway. Resuming her route to Carla's, she's surprised at how easy it is to leave her frustration in the past and move in a new, positive direction. Determined to continually move forward with her life, she is committed to making the decision, one incident at a time, to overcome whatever is in front of her. She smiles triumphantly.

Before she knows it, she's parking the car outside her sister's house. Liz limps in with an air of confidence, deftly maneuvering her crutch on the stairs leading to the kitchen and toward the patio where she spies Carla reading.

"Hey, Sis!" Liz says merrily as she pulls up a deck chair beside her on the raised wooden patio, lined with pots of sprouting tomatoes, peppers, and basil, and a large hibiscus tree with coral blooms.

"Oh, hi! How was your visit with your mom?" Carla closes her book while eying Liz quizzically through her slightly tinted sunglasses.

"It was great. She sends her hugs."

Carla smiles. "Helen and Norman were always so nice to me. I always wished I saw them more often. My kids really enjoyed it when we went there."

"Yeah, Mom says you visited them several years ago. You never told me that."

"Really? I'm sure I mentioned it."

Do I bring it up? Liz wonders, knowing there will never be a better chance. She says, "So while I was there, I drove by the farm."

Carla's upper body stiffens; she crosses her legs and readjusts her ponytail. "Oh, why'd you go there?"

"It was time for me to leave the past in the past, laid to rest once and for all."

"I thought you had a long time ago."

"So did I, until recently when I realized I was still holding hostages—the biggest of whom was probably myself."

"So what did you do?"

"It didn't go quite the way I had imagined. I ended up putting a flag in the ground overlooking the farm, like a memorial. After declaring victory, I walked away."

Carla cocks her head, her eyebrows lifted high above her sunglasses as she looks quizzically at her. "What had you planned on doing?"

"Well, I dreamed I would to go up in the hayloft, and by doing so I would relive that day as it occurred, rather than from what everyone told me over the years. I figured it would be my do-over, and I would run out of the barn and walk as normally as I did before the accident happened." She looks up at the blue sky and then back to her sister. "But we both know there are no do-overs. Since leaving here a few days ago, I realized I've continued to hurt other people by being stuck in the past."

Liz leans forward and takes Carla's hand. "And it really doesn't even matter what happened all those years ago, as we all have great lives now."

She sees tears streaming from Carla's polarized lenses to her tanned cheeks below.

"What was the barn like? In your dream, that is?" Carla asks in a shaky voice.

"Just as I remembered being told: the hay piled high, grain sacks in the corner, and of course a barn cat rubbing up against my leg." Liz, sitting back in her chair, searches Carla's face for some kind of reaction; there's none.

"What about you, Carla? Do you have any do-overs you've thought about?"

Carla leans forward in her lounge chair, putting her arms around her bent knees. Pursing her lips, she says. "I'm not sure." After a pause, she says, "Yeah, I guess there is one do-over that I've wished for."

Liz takes a deep breath. "What's that?"

"It's about Dad. I often speculate whether it would have made a difference if I had reconciled things with him before he died." She sighs, looking toward the flower beds at the end of the yard.

Liz reflects on her sister's words; but since the issue is for her to figure out on her own accord, she lets it go without further comment. Instead, she's inspired by Carla's reaction, which indicates to her there's nothing more between them about her accident; the details don't matter anymore to her either.

Shifting in her chair, Liz peers towards the nearby garage with attached awning, which covers another patio set and gas grill. She envisions a future of tranquility, savoring that moment of peace in her heart as long as she can.

Her thoughts are interrupted by Carla. "What's next for you, Liz?"

"That's a great question. I was thinking about it on my way here today. I feel as if my world is a blank canvas, and I can create anything I want."

"You can if you want. It's like my faux painting on the walls. If I don't like the design, I simply wipe it off and start fresh until I have a look I like. You know, it may sound tacky, but you can have faux finish."

Both of them howl with laughter.

"On that note," Liz says, struggling to catch her breath, "shall we go to the movies to celebrate your birthday? We can take my car if you drive."

"Sure. Let me just change and freshen my makeup."

"Okay. I'm going to walk around the garden real quick. I'll meet you out front."

Liz carefully limps off the patio and through the backyard, drinking in Carla's colorful flowerbeds of pink peonies, orange poppies, purple hydrangea, burgundy hollyhocks, and yellow pansies. Over the years, the sisters have shared many gardening tips and tricks; even learning the Latin names of their favorite plants and their growing conditions. She spies their beloved one: a wisteria bush. Amazed at its gigantic size and the fragrance of the countless purple blooms that envelop the eight-by-twelve-foot wooden pergola supporting it, Liz knows hers would be that big and beautiful too—if only she hadn't moved. Although she bought their sister bushes three houses ago; like Johnny Appleseed, she plants one everywhere she moves.

Turning to head back, Liz spots a dandelion seemingly out of place near the back fence. She bends down and plucks it from the dirt, like so many others she and Carla picked as little girls. Then she heads to the car. When Carla joins her behind the wheel, she looks at her sister and says with a grin, "I see you're still picking dandelions."

"This one was hiding from you," Liz answers, as she twirls the stem, entranced by the bright yellow swirl. "Carla, do you remember picking dandelions at Helen and Norman's?"

"Of course! It brings back happy memories."

"I feel like we're there again today." The sisters smile, eyes connecting through their sunglasses as they quickly get lost in conversation.

On the way home from the movies, they stop at the grocery store. Liz looks around as Carla drives through the parking lot. "Damn it, there's no handicap space left," a tired Liz says. She points to the entrance. "If you drop me over there, Carla, I'll grab one of their zippy carts as I'm not walking well today. Perhaps you can take my crutch since it never fits well on the cart."

"Sure." Carla pulls in the loading zone near the front of the gray brick store, puts on her flashers, and follows Liz. "I've been meaning to tell you, not everyone shares your light attitude about the powered scooters. I used your term 'zippy cart' in the store once and a woman about took my head off. She told me it wasn't a toy, and she had a medical right to use it in the store."

"Oh my gosh. What'd you say?" Liz asks while she steps onto the scooter and hands Carla her crutch.

"What could I say? I just smiled and granted her a little grace for being uptight about it."

Carla points to the left as she returns to the car, "I'll be right over there waiting. I'll see you when you come out, and I'll pick you up right here."

"See you in a few." Liz waves as she takes off in the massive store and heads toward the bakery section.

A few minutes later, a young lady with a large birthmark in her left check and a pierced lip ring greets her. “Hi. Can I get something for you, ma’am?”

“Yes, thanks. Do you have a small white cake with raspberry filling and icing?”

“Sure do! Would you like anything written on it?”

“Great idea! Let’s do, ‘Happy thirty-nine again, Carla.’ And can you put a few flowers or some other decorations on, too?”

The clerk agrees. “If you want to continue shopping, I’ll have it ready in about five minutes,” she says.

“Perfect. That should give me just enough time.”

An exuberant Liz steers over to the baking section and gets halfway down the aisle before seeing the birthday candles high on the left side. Frustrated that she can’t reach to get them, she struggles to stand up and then loses her balance on the awkward cart, almost falling into the middle shelf loaded with boxes of cake mix and cans of frosting. She quickly snatches a pack of candles as her legs give out under her, and she plunks down in the seat. She looks up at the top shelf. How do people in zippy carts shop, or do they just never buy things that are out of reach?

Liz returns to the bakery counter to find the young lady standing in front with the cake box. She places it in Liz’s basket and says, “I hope your celebration is a good one!”

“It’s going to be the best in years!” Liz declares.

She then drives to the front of the store and gets behind a lady purchasing cat food, in the only checkout line with a cashier. She thinks of Ruby and Abbey, hoping they’re doing well in their new home. She puts her purchases on the conveyor belt as the customer ahead of her takes her groceries and leaves.

Liz glances at the cashier and then his name tag. “Hello, Eduardo.”

He nods, rings up the candles with a scanner, and says, “Doesn’t look like there’s anything wrong with you that you need to be using that cart.”

She thinks, *Does a person with a disability need to look a certain way to warrant use of the cart?* She explains, "I just wanted to save my energy. It's been a long day."

He rings up her cake and continues to observe her every feature.

"Walking has been difficult for me lately. My crutch is in the car," she adds trying to convince him of her legitimate need for the scooter.

Without missing a beat, the young man looks at her feet and says, "Nice shoe. What do they call those, platforms? I didn't realize they were popular again."

Liz is speechless; but seething. She looks at her feet; the difference in her shoe heights should be clearly visible to him.

He says, "That will be twelve dollars and twenty-three cents."

She quickly swipes her debit card and enters her PIN.

He continues, "What medical term do they call it when you have one leg shorter than the other?"

Victim or victor? Choose, Liz.

She retorts, "I'm not sure, but I can tell you're jealous. You want to be riding in this 'zippy cart' and wearing this platform shoe, now, don't you?"

His mouth drops as she grabs her receipt from the tips of his long, skinny fingers.

"Have a nice day, Eduardo. Oh, and maybe you want to ask your manager for a different way to greet shoppers so you don't offend them, causing them to shop elsewhere."

He just stares, mouth open, as Liz puts the bags in her basket and zooms away.

Carla pulls up to the curb as Liz exits the store. "Great timing, Carla," she says through the open passenger's window. "If you weren't here, I might have gone back in and made a scene."

"Oh no! What now?" Carla asks.

"Let's just get out of here before I do something I'll regret."

"Yikes. You get in, and I'll drive the cart back."

Liz loads the bag into the back of the car and climbs into her seat while Carla returns the cart, screaming as she takes off. Fixated on her tussle with the cashier, Liz debates whether she should report him to HR, write an anonymous letter to the manager, or inform the editor of the local paper in order to spread awareness of the proper way to treat people with disabilities.

Carla returns to the car still a little shaken. "Boy, that has pickup! Now I understand why you call them 'zippy carts'!"

Liz smiles but still can't shake Eduardo's comments.

"So tell me, what idiot thing did someone do back there?" Carla asks.

"It doesn't matter. We all say stupid things." Liz looks at her right foot and says, "I guess it does kind of look like a platform shoe from the 'seventies."

"Someone commented on your shoe?" Carla stares at Liz, looking shocked.

"The cashier thought they were hip. I suggested he should maybe try a pair out," Liz says drily.

"No way!" Carla exclaims.

They discuss the incident briefly before pulling into Carla's driveway, filled with billowing smoke from the back patio. Patrick walks over to the car and leans on Carla's open window. "So, uh, ladies," he asks slyly, "need a strong man to carry in groceries?"

"We sure do, handsome," Carla says with a grin.

Patrick faces the backyard and bellows, "Brandon, come here! Your Aunt Lizzy needs you!"

The three laugh as Brandon, the oldest, arrives and says, "Go ahead, Mom and Aunt Lizzy. Walk with the old guy. I've got your bags!" They head into the house to begin celebrating Carla's birthday.

While setting around the fire pit later that night, Liz can't help but admire the strength of her sister. Carla was able to put the past behind her to raise a beautiful and caring family. She had a worse childhood than Liz did, yet Carla believed she could give her children a better life—and she has. Liz may have been the one out on the edge, taking risks and following adventure, but Carla has truly been the source of everything Liz has done. She loved her when Liz couldn't love herself.

With the cooling of the night air, Liz signals her nieces, Arielle and Sophie, who head into the house. They come out a few minutes later with cake, complete with lit candles. Sophie places it in front of the birthday girl, while Arielle lays out the blue paper plates and black plastic forks.

"Everyone around the table!" Patrick shouts. "Time to sing!"

As the last "Happy birthday to youuuuuu" fades, Bryce, the youngest of the four, yells, "Make a wish!"

Carla hesitates and blows out her candles.

As Sophie dishes up pieces of cake, Liz says in tribute to her sister, "Carla is the best sister and friend anyone can ever wish for. Although our life paths have taken us in different directions, she's always been there for me, and on that I can always depend. It's great to have her and all of you as my family and to be here celebrating on her special day."

Patrick interrupts, "Before we have cake, you have to open your presents."

He pulls two bright packages out from behind the nearby grill and hands one with a blue ribbon to Carla and a matching present with a purple ribbon to Liz.

"Um, Patrick, it's not my birthday," Liz says, confused.

"Ah, but it will be soon," he says cryptically.

The sisters look at each other and tear open their packages at the same time.

"Oh, Patrick!"—Liz starts.

"It's a book of *The Sister Adventures*!" Carla finishes.

The sisters are giddy as they flip through the books, laughing and smiling and occasionally tearing up.

Patrick explains, "After Liz left the other day, I was telling the kids it was unfortunate that you two didn't grow up together or live close by like my family does. So when I came across some pictures of the two of you, it gave me an idea: I had the kids gather as many as we could find and we made an album for each of you, so you're always with each other."

Now the tears really start to flow from both women.

"That's it!" Bryce says. "If you two are going to get weepy, we're going to leave."

Everyone laughs. Carla brushes away her tears and with a loving smile says, "Now, let there be cake!"

A few days later Liz is on the homeward drive to Pennsylvania. Passing each freeway mile marker, she puts closure on another chapter of her life, until she reaches the Ohio Turnpike. There, she realizes there's nothing left to reconcile; just an awareness of the wasted opportunities caused by previously held limitations in her thinking.

Without the agony of her past holding her back, she begins to plan for the future. She gets the notion to create a legacy that gives back to others as people have given to her. But what will it be? Although she ponders many approaches, like fundraisers or selling rubber bracelets with slogans for disability awareness, nothing concretely strikes her fancy; so she lets her thoughts aimlessly drift.

An hour or so later, Liz turns in for a break at a rest stop along the turnpike. Sitting in the car with a fresh cup of coffee and the warm breeze coming through the sunroof, she opens her pixography to a certain page and stares until the image is etched in her mind; it's her at the beach building sandcastles with Brandon, who was five at the time, and Sophie and Arielle, a little over three.

She puts the car in reverse and looks in her rearview mirror to back out of the parking spot; she imagines that day when the three kids were in the back of her flaming orange Pinto. Her sunglasses are similar to what she now sees in the mirror, the hat is close to a match, and the smile is dead on.

Studying the age lines in her reflection, she thinks, *Gosh, I'll be fifty-five this year. At the rate I'm slowing down, I may only have ten or so years left to be fully mobile. What's there left for me to do in that time?*

Her mind floats to the dream she's always had to own a business and the reality that she couldn't make it successful when given the chance. Although her most recent venture was a solid business idea as proven by her competitors, who make millions with the same model, their full house of money and people trumped her pocket aces of information and content. Although it's time for her to move on with a new career, she's confused whether to return to human resources, where she was professionally successful, or to start in a different line of work.

Personally, Liz still feels a degree of emptiness from her failed marriage and being childless. As she starts spiraling downward, she catches herself and begins an upward climb. Her inspiration comes from knowing that her worth extends beyond the crutch that she carries, the age lines of her experience, or the scar on her forehead; it's the fabric of everything she does—the manner in which she chooses to rise above her daily obstacles. It's not easy, but it *is* simple; it's all a matter of choice. She thinks long and hard, knowing there's a certain comfort in the familiar but surging potential in the new.

She sees mile marker 166 at the side of the road. With only a few more hours to go, she starts listening to some Bob Seger and quickly gets lost in 'seventies rock as she puts the last couple hundred miles behind her and gets safely home.

29

Five Months Later

Having closed her business, and in the process of looking for a new career, Liz digs through her files for work accomplishments to list on her resume. Buried in the midst of client project notes, she finds the manila envelope containing Rhonda's questions, which she never touched again since their last face-to-face meeting. She knows there's one more reconciliation for her to make; it's time to tell Rhonda the truth.

She dials her work number, which is answered on the second ring. "Hi, Mrs. Taylor. It's Liz Harris. I'd like to talk to Rhonda if I could, please."

"Liz! It's been a long time," says Mrs. Taylor. "Rhonda actually isn't scheduling clients anymore."

Astonished at the news, Liz gulps. "I didn't realize that, Mrs. Taylor. Can you see if she'll meet with me on a personal matter?"

"Please hold. I'll check with her." Liz bobs her head as she listens to the hold music played in the background.

Rhonda's voice breaks in sharply. "Liz. I'm surprised to hear from you after all this time. What personal matter do we need to discuss?"

She inhales deeply and says, "Rhonda, first I want to apologize for the way I acted in the past. I really have no good excuse for my actions."

Rhonda snipes, "Okay."

"And I'd like to tell you the truth about my past."

"I've thought about it," Rhonda says, "and decided it would be best for you to work with someone else. I met my obligations as a course mentor when last we talked, and—"

Liz cuts in despite the curveball from Rhonda. "I know I've hurt you and betrayed your trust. It may be too late to fix that. However, I want to meet and tell you about the breakthrough I had because of you."

"It would be best for you to start fresh with someone else," Rhonda says, unwavering. "I will email you the name and number of an associate as soon as I hang up."

"Please, Rhonda, I am begging you! Please meet with me one last time. After that we can go our separate ways, I promise."

There's a long silence until finally Rhonda says in a curt tone, "I'll give you ten minutes. Although I haven't been there in ages, meet me at Coco's tomorrow morning at ten."

"Thank you! I'll see you then."

Liz disconnects the call and punches in Justin's number. He answers. "Hi, Justin, it's Liz. I know it's been a while, but I was hoping you could meet me for a few minutes tomorrow morning so I can complete my final assignment for the Visionary Course."

"Sure, Liz. What do you need to do?"

"Well, I need to review my pixography with someone and come up with a plan for what's next in my life."

"Isn't that something you can do with Rhonda?"

"Um, I don't think that's a good idea." She hesitates. "We sort of haven't talked for months. I'm still on her bad list, and I don't think there's even a chance for coal this year."

He laughs. "I understand, totally. Been there myself more than once."

"Besides, it sounds like she's not meeting with clients anymore," Liz says in a low voice.

"Yeah, that's what I heard. Say, can you meet at about nine thirty?"

"That works. I look forward to seeing you again."

The next morning, Liz is at her usual table near the back of Coco's by nine twenty, reviewing her latest journal notes, when Chloe comes over with a cup of coffee, wearing a blue apron with a matching ponytail scrunchie.

"Good m-m-morning, Ms. La-La-Liz. It's ga-ga-good to see you again. Can I ask you s-s-something?"

"Sure, Chloe."

Liz observes Chloe's intense look as she closes her eyes and struggles to voice her thoughts. "Ma-ma-my grandfather lives in the n-n-nursing home down the st-st-street. I d-d-don't like the way he's treated by s-s-some of the staff. How d-d-do I get it to st-st-stop?"

Liz pauses and says in a light tone, "What do they do that bothers you?"

Chloe bites her lip and blinks, "Tha-tha-they're not na-na-nice to him."

Liz offers, "I could visit with you if that would help."

"C-c-can we go to-to-today?" Chloe pleads.

Liz purses her lips and looks up. "Well, I have a lot of things scheduled for today—"

Chloe hangs her head and sighs. "Oh, I'm s-s-sorry I ah-ah-asked."

Liz's internal voice is not having it. This smacks of the time that introduced her to Rhonda. She needs to stop being an idiot and help Chloe, despite her to-do list.

"Chloe, what time do you finish work today?"

"Ta-ta-two o'clock."

"Okay. I'll meet you then, and we can go from here."

"Thank you, Ms. La-La-Liz." Chloe's face lights up as she leaves, and Justin approaches.

"Hi, Liz," he says as he slides into the booth. "I don't mean to rush, but something came up that I have to address. Hey, your hair has grown in very nicely."

"Thanks. I really appreciate you squeezing me in. I'll get right to it. Do you think if I tell the story of my past, it could prevent others from going through the same suffering that I did?"

"I think it depends on whether the other person is willing to listen and learn, or if they're too prideful to accept help from someone else." Justin scratches his chin. "The tough part is that not everyone's ready to learn when the teacher is there to teach. What exactly are you thinking of?"

"I want to help others break through their limitations—perceived and real. When I started the Visionary Course, I thought of becoming a speaker and telling my story. Since then, I've come to understand that it doesn't have broad relevance, as not everyone has had an injury like mine, and there are only so many parking lots I can patrol for handicapped parking violations."

He laughs. "Yep, your chiding has made converts out of many in the community."

She blushes.

"Seriously, Liz, the way you handle life amazes and inspires me. The lessons I've learned from you, I've tried to implement in my life. It's all starting to make a difference."

"Really?" She is stunned. "What could you ever learn from me? We have totally different lives and challenges."

"Yes, we do. But watching as you fearlessly overcome challenges gives me the strength to move forward and face the unknown. I'm not there yet, but I've recognized that the inability to make difficult decisions has been my Achilles' heel for many years."

"Justin, you have it all wrong. I don't do that."

"You're too hard on yourself, Liz. With your disability, you could have easily given up years ago and been dependent on our social system. But you got an education and a job; you've owned businesses and had relationships. You should bottle whatever inspires you to get over hurdles. You'd make a fortune!"

She hangs her head. "You don't know how often I've wanted to quit or blamed others for my difficulties."

"We all do at some point. The real test of resilience is where you end the journey—not the number of detours you've had along the way. Watching you press on makes me wonder what might have happened if I had decided to go after what I wanted." He pauses. "Liz, I've never told this to anyone—not even my wife. When I was in the Air Force, my friend and I applied to helicopter school on a dare. We were both accepted; I never reported, so I lost that opportunity."

Liz sighs, feeling what she perceives is the weight of his regret.

He looks at her over the top of his black-framed reading glasses. "Anyway, back to you. I admire your courage to continue despite adversity."

"You're very kind, Justin, but I don't feel courageous. I feel like I'm always running, always trying to prove something. I'm tired of being the poster child for handicaps."

With outstretched arms, he says, "Liz, you are a poster child—but it's for possibilities and opportunities. That's what I see in you."

She leans back in her seat. "I guess I see it differently. When I returned from my visit home last spring, I made the commitment that the future would be different. I would no longer be held victim by a past that I can't change; rather, I would choose to enjoy each moment I'm in and make choices rather than fall victim to circumstances."

His eyes widen. "Wow. How does that make you feel, Liz?"

Without hesitation she says, "Victorious."

Justin then turns to face the front register. "Well, it's time for me to go. Did I help you with your assignment?"

She smiles, "Yes, you did, Justin. You've given me a lot to think about as I decide the next step in my journey. Thank you for meeting me on such short notice."

"It's I who owe you the thanks. This conversation confirms it's time for me to face the Huey, only this time it's deciding whether to tuck and run or just quit and accept my current position as the best it's going to get."

"Justin, I hope whatever you decide, it works out for the best."

Justin gets up and leans over to hug Liz. "Thank you for your friendship, Liz."

"You're welcome, Justin." She watches him disappear into the kitchen.

As she muses over his words, Liz spots Rhonda rushing to the café entrance. Her red hair is pulled back to frame her face, and she's wearing black yoga pants and a yellow running jacket. Liz waves her over.

"Hello, Liz. Your hair looks very nice," she comments in a cool, guarded tone.

Liz shakes her outstretched hand. "Thank you, Rhonda. It's good to see you."

Rhonda sits as Chloe arrives with her cart of steaming coffee mugs and an orange plate of sticky buns.

"I d-d-don't mean to interrupt, la-la-ladies. Mr. Justin asked me to d-d-deliver this." Chloe sets the items on the table.

"That's fine, Chloe. Tell Mr. Justin we'll take his buns anytime," Liz says.

Chloe blushes as she turns to face Liz. "I th-th-think you mean s-s-sticky buns." The three women laugh.

"You are absolutely right, Chloe. I'm glad you corrected me, as that was clearly inappropriate to say," Liz says with a grin of embarrassment.

Chloe limps away.

Liz takes a sip of her coffee and says, "Rhonda, I don't want to waste your time. I'm going to get right to what I came here to say."

"Please do," Rhonda replies as she places a bun on her plate and begins to eat.

"I appreciate your willingness to meet. Since we last spoke, I've been able to resolve the guilt, anger, and hopelessness about my accident and leg. I have both you and Tony to thank for that. The pixography and collages helped me confront the past and declare victory over it."

She looks Rhonda squarely in the eyes. "I'm not going to tell you the details of what happened; there's no need anymore."

The sternness in Rhonda's face breaks slightly as she asks, "Then why are we talking?"

"Please hear me out," Liz continues calmly.

Rhonda nods. "I'm listening."

"Here's what I can say. My sister and I were playing in the hayloft, and there was an accident. I fell to the concrete floor below and landed on my head, suffering severe head trauma. I was rushed to the hospital and remained in a coma for several weeks. When I awoke, I had to relearn everything from walking to talking. During my hospitalization, I was adopted by the distant relatives who had been serving as our foster parents. I was raised by them, and my sister was raised by our biological mom, dad, and another relative. It took years, but we have developed a sisterhood and friendship that thrives despite our separate tragic pasts and the miles and lifestyle that separate us."

"That's it?" Rhonda asks, sounding annoyed.

Liz pulls out her journal notes with the details of her dream and hands them to Rhonda. "This is the true story as I believe it happened."

As Rhonda unfolds the pages to read, Liz is unsure whether telling her the truth is the right thing to do. Will it put closure on their past, or will it prolong the contention between them?

When Rhonda finishes, she says, "Perhaps our work wasn't wasted." Refolding the pages she hands them back to Liz. "Why couldn't you be honest with me from the beginning?" she asks, looking intently at Liz, who searches her eyes for a connection.

"As private as this writing is, that's how deeply I buried my feelings." She pauses. "I had to first be honest with myself. Over the past months, I realized I was secretly holding on to everything I ever heard, knew, or thought about my accident. The only thing that did was keep the emotions in place. It's been a long journey, but I've finally reconciled it and can let go."

Liz feels her confidence practically radiating, and Rhonda seems to warm up to her.

"What about your leg?" Rhonda asks softly. "How do you go forward and not regress as life happens?"

"That's a great question. I've got a lot of work ahead to keep me focused. Since I've spent much of the past chasing what I didn't have, what I wanted, and what I thought I needed. Now it's time to give back. I've got a lifetime to pay forward."

"What's that look like?" Rhonda asks, concern and curiosity in her voice.

"I'm going to share how I overcome the hurdles in my past. I believe this can illuminate an approach that works for others to follow, thereby making a difference in my corner of the world."

Rhonda announces, "I accept your apology." She asks, "Now, may I say a few things?"

"Turnabout is fair play," Liz responds with a smile.

Rhonda cocks her head and asks, "What happened that you are willing to talk about your leg or accident now?"

Liz points to her head and speaks from her heart. "The turning point was when my head was shaved; it revealed the cornerstone that had preserved the past—the scar. As I confronted the truth through my pixography and collages, over the days and weeks that followed, I was able to break the connection between my leg and all my tragedies or shortcomings in life—losing my family, walking with a limp, failing at my marriage, getting fired .... Then I was able to shift my perspective to gratitude for the blessed life I have, rather than sorrow for what's missing. It's taken time, but now when things are bad—like having increasing pain that will eventually lead to hip replacement surgery—I can be at peace knowing that I choose the life I have by my reaction rather than because of the circumstance I'm faced with."

Rhonda says, "That's a great approach and one I hoped we would have been able to get to with our work. However, I'm happy that your life has turned upward in a different direction." Her lips purse. "And I'm sorry to hear about your hip."

Liz shrugs. "No worries. I've known for thirty years that it was inevitable; I just never expected it would mean using two crutches or that I would be limited to only walking fifty feet or so without needing to rest."

"Is there anything else?"

"Yes. I'd like you to be my friend; someone whom I can confide in and trust, or laugh with, who doesn't want to fix me."

Rhonda looks up. "That would be different, but I'm willing to try," she says.

"Me too. And I'm thinking if I build it with you, I can do it with others I want in my life. Perhaps my next Mr. Wonderful." Liz winks.

"Oh, Liz, you've done an amazing amount of work in a short time."

Liz smiles. "Actually, it's been a lifetime in the making. It simply came together when I was receptive and willing to express my thoughts and emotions in a positive rather than a hurtful way.

I've realized that by doing this, there's less likelihood I'll have a lot of future hairballs to get rid of."

Rhonda laughs. "How did you remember that? It's been so long since I've talked about hairballs, I had forgotten my own analogy."

"I didn't. It stuck with me every day, especially as I remembered the girls." Liz's eyes moisten.

"Do you have any regrets giving them up?"

Liz thinks of the consequences her biological parents must have faced when they decided to give her up for adoption. She winces, knowing she will never know their agony or the demons that tormented them over their pivotal decisions.

With a hint of melancholy in her tone, Liz looks at the table between them and says, "I miss them dearly, but I gave them the best life I could. The way my life's been heading, it wouldn't have worked to take care of the girls. It's going to be challenging enough just to take care of me for the next few years, given my hip."

Rhonda nods. "I understand."

Liz sinks back in her seat. "You know, as I end this part of the journey, I realize everyone has some form of hurdles in their life. Kind of like my leg, only different. I know what worked for me may not be the same for another, but the key is to keep moving forward and to enlist others who can support you over hurdles."

"Liz, I want to be included on your support list for whatever you do going forward."

"Thank you, Rhonda. That means a lot to me."

Rhonda reaches to touch Liz's hand. "I want you to know that through our work together, you have helped me grow also. However, that's a story for another day. How about if we catch up over dinner someday next week? I can tell you all about my hurdles and hairballs then."

Liz grins from ear to ear. "I would like that!" The women stand and embrace; Liz gathers her things to leave.

"I'll get our bill—or what's left of it since Justin took care of his buns." Rhonda winks, and they both hoot like school girls. "Speaking of whom, I'm going to catch him for a quick hello. I'll email you on dinner for next week."

Rhonda sits looking out the front window and reflecting on how much Liz has changed since they last spoke. She starts planning where next to meet that will be convenient for both of them and outside of Coco's.

Suddenly, there's an arm on her left shoulder; she jumps and inhales deeply. Seeing a familiar face slide into the seat across from her, she breathes and covers her chest to check her heart rate. "Oh! You scared me, Justin! I didn't hear you coming!" She looks intently at his oblong face; black hair frames his dark eyes and million-dollar smile with offsetting dimples. For the first time since they met, she doesn't have pangs in her heart as she watches him.

"Yeah, I'm stealthy that way," he says with a grin. They both laugh. Before she can respond, Justin blurts out, "Rhonda, there's something I should have talked to you about a while ago."

Bracing herself for the worst, she inhales deeply and exhales slowly.

"A lot has changed since that day we spoke about your business; it seems we don't see each other anymore, and I've heard you're moving on—at least with your career, that is."

She warmly smiles and nods in agreement.

"I miss our friendship, but I understand, as there are reasons on both our ends for the distance. If you haven't heard, I'm in a nasty custody battle with my wife over the kids."

"I'm so sorry, Justin. I hadn't heard."

"So am I. Although I gave it my all to get her back, I failed. However, I can live with the fact that I tried my best. Now it's just down to the final settlement with the lawyers." His eyes fill with tears. "Anyway, I hope that someday you and I can put the past behind us and enjoy each other's company again—and without business between us."

His comment catches her by surprise. For her, a large part of her interest in him was business; without it, who would he be? What would they talk about if not their dreams for business—certainly not his wife's kids!

She muses, knowing there's nothing left at Coco's for her anymore. Like Liz, she found the strength to get past what was in front of her: the heartbreak that was holding her back. She reaches near his hand and says, "Let's just take it one day at a time and see where life takes us."

His brown eyes meet her green stare, which radiates confidence and clarity of direction. He nods to her; she stands to walk out of Coco's, leaving the past and him behind.

30

Courage to Face the Unknown

Justin walks out from the kitchen and sees Liz at the baking display counter by the front register. He hurries toward her, and they share a tight hug.

He says, "Chloe told me you were here, and I didn't believe it!"

Liz beams.

"You look fantastic," he says. "And your hair—it's long again! And blond! What a pleasant surprise. It's been ages."

"Probably a year and a half or so. I've tried your cell but never get an answer."

"Yeah, a lot of people say that. The short version is I have a new number."

He hands her a card from his pocket. "Here it is. Gosh, I'm so glad you stopped by. Do you have time to catch up for a bit?"

"Sure, but it'll have to be quick. I have an appointment with the shoe guy, and I can't be late."

They walk to the brown bistro table near the front entrance and sit. "So much has happened so fast, Justin. I've got some big news."

"What's that?" he asks in an upbeat tone.

She summarizes: "Last we talked, I had closed down my business and was looking for a job. Well, after months of searching for the right opportunity, I landed a great job in human resources working for a large automotive manufacturer."

"Wow! I'm so happy for you," he says.

"That's the good part." Her head dips.

"There's a bad part?" he asks slowly.

"Sort of. The job is in Tennessee."

"Oh." His brow creases. "Who do you know there?"

"Besides my new boss—no one. But I've thought of moving south for years to get out of the cold and snow. When this job came up, everything seemed to come together—so I figured it's God's way of opening the door to the next chapter in my life."

"Wow. That's great! Are you scared?" he asks with eyes wide open.

She taps her fingers on the table. "A little. But I'm excited at the same time. And I've started moving on that speaking thing. You know, the one I envisioned when I enrolled in the Visionary Course?"

"Yes, of course I remember. When are you speaking?"

She hesitates, silently debating how much of her vision to reveal for fear that it won't come true and he'll think she's a failure. She presses on, slightly embarrassed. "Well, that part isn't ready yet, but the book is coming together nicely."

He scoffs, grinning. "Book? Why a book?"

"I've researched becoming a speaker, and it seems every good speaker has a book that tells their story. If I want to be one, I need all the tools."

"Makes sense. And you've always been super prepared for anything," Justin says. "I'm so happy for you, Liz! Sooo," he continues with a smile, "what about a man in your life?"

She wishes she had left before he asked that question, as her love interest—or lack thereof—is not an area of her life she feels empowered by just now. She bows her head and slowly answers, "I'm just starting to put myself out there again. I've gotten past my guilt for Timothy and others, and I know what I want out of a relationship."

He rests his chin on his hand. "Oh? What's that?"

She confidently says, "It begins with friendship and mutual respect. It involves family and community activities that help others. It's being aligned on a future path and making a collective dream become reality. Last, but most important, it has to be God-centered."

"How'd you come up with all that?"

She shifts in her chair. "I guess I've always known those things, but I was too impatient to hold out for what I wanted. Y'know, Justin, life is short, and there are no guarantees. I may not find that relationship, but I'm going to enjoy the journey."

"That's beautiful, Liz." He leans forward. "I can tell your heart's at peace."

She smiles brightly. "Yes, it really is. And I have you and a few others to thank for that."

He asks, "Why me? I didn't do anything special."

Taken aback by his question, she hesitates to formulate the right thing to say. In a warm tone, she responds, "Yes, you did. You held out your hand of friendship and accepted me as I was. There's so much I learned from you, I don't know where to begin or end. I only know that my life is deeply imprinted by the grace of who you've been to me."

He winks. "Just give me some credit in the book, and we'll call it even." They laugh.

She leans in and asks, "So what about you?"

"I guess I have my own big news. My divorce was final almost a year ago."

"I didn't know. I'm sorry, Justin. I was hoping it would work out for you."

"Don't be. I have you to thank for it." He leans back, stroking his chin.

She retorts, "Hey, I only helped you with some human resource matters; I was never a marriage counselor!"

"No, but you gave me the courage to face the copter. Remember that day when we sat at Coco's and pored over our pixographies?" he slowly asks.

"Yes—"

His lips pucker. "That night I went home and began my own journey. I looked at my two beautiful kids and my wife. I realized I could let life happen the way it was headed, or I could be the pebble thrown into the water to forever change the surface and the current beneath." He chuckles. "Actually, now that I think of it, I probably was the boulder."

She laughs and quickly resumes her seriousness to listen.

He looks past her shoulder toward the sidewalk. "I fought to get her back, to clean up my side of the street; it didn't work, and for that I'm sad. However, I have no regrets because I gave it my all. In the end, she chose not to commit to our marriage or love me anymore. It's been better to live without her than live a sham out of separate wings of the house and deceive the kids about everything."

He turns back to face her and the surrounding café and points to a nearby photograph a few feet behind her on the wall. It shows a young boy and girl embracing each other on a wooden dock overlooking an inland lake at sunset. He says, "Ever since our separation, I've worked on my relationship with my kids. We're closer than ever before. They mean everything to me."

"They're beautiful, Justin. I see you've also been enhancing your photography skills while I've been gone."

"Yes, I have. But as far as what I do with any of it, I won't know until the dust settles. I need time to get my head together and decide what else I want for my life. For now, I'm simply keeping myself afloat."

She bites her lip. "Aah, unfortunately I remember all too well what that feels like, but that's a story for another day—on both our parts." She looks at the clock above the register and starts to gather her things. "I wish nothing other than your peace and happiness. When the time is right for you, let's reconnect. I miss talking to you and laughing."

"I will, Liz," he promises.

With a twinkle in her eye she adds, "Now I have to scoot to pick out my new shoes. Then I'm off for the twenty-plus-hour drive to Tennessee with a day to rest before my new job starts on Monday."

"Wow! So soon?" His head tilts.

"My mommy always said, 'No rest for the wicked!'" She winks.

His eyebrows lift as he smiles. "I think you may have taken that out of context."

They laugh, and he walks her to the front door. "Let me know when you finish the book. I want the first copy hot off the press—signed by the author."

"I will," she promises as they hug.

A few minutes later, Liz drives by the prosthetic shop, hopeful to get handicap parking out front; however, no such luck. She pulls around the corner to a parking lot at the end of the next block. There are puddles everywhere from two days of rain. There's a break in the dark skies, and she hopes the threatening clouds will hold off long enough to secure her new shoes and get on the road. She walks toward the building with her purse strap over her shoulder and across her chest.

As she nears the entrance, the mailman is coming out, and he holds the door for her. "Thank you!" she says gratefully and walks toward him.

Peering at her crutches, he says, "Oh my, when did that happen?"

Liz blurts, "It always happened."

"Oh, I'm sorry! I thought you might have had surgery."

"I have."

He's speechless.

With a bounce in her step, Liz turns her head as she passes him, still holding the door, and says brightly, "Have a great day, Mr. Postman. I gotta run and see the shoe guy."

Once inside, she's ushered to a private room. As she waits, Liz remembers the times her mother would take her to the brace shop following her annual visit to the orthopedist. It always started with her longing looks at the pretty black or white shoes with open toes and heels. Then Mom would give the clerk her prescription, and he would disappear behind a green curtain and emerge with exactly one box of shoes. They always looked the same, just a newer version of the same ugly oxfords Liz had worn to walk in. She choked back the tears when she tried them on, and the shoe clerk said to Mom, "You're lucky this year; although her right foot is smaller than the left, it's not enough to require two different sizes."

On the ride home she always tried to figure how long it would be until she got new shoes again—hoping that next time they would have pretty ones for her to buy—just once—so she could feel the way Cinderella did at the ball. Outgrowing her youth, Liz realized this would never happen; she then viewed this annual event on a par with having all her teeth pulled in one sitting.

She returns to the present when Tommy, her shoe clerk, walks over with two boxes. He sits down and begins to open them—two identical pairs, only one is black and the other, pewter. He starts to remove her current shoes and she smiles. Shoe styles might have changed significantly for the rest of the world these past forty-plus years, but not so for Liz. There's still a limited selection, and they cost a fortune including the price to build up her right shoe. She sighs. At least now she can find shoes a tad sexier than when she was a kid. After all, she'd hate to spend the rest of her life crying over shoes.

"This Mary Jane I wore last year looks great and works well for both casual and dressy looks. And I especially like this floral decoration," she says, leaning forward to point to the top of the shoe near the base of her middle toe. Liz puts on the new pair and stands up to awkwardly walk a few steps, trying her best not to scuff the shoes up or to trip. Although the limp in her gait is greatly exaggerated by the absence of a two-and-a-half-inch buildup on the sole of the right shoe, she tries her best to act as graceful as possible. She asks Tommy, "What do you think?"

He smiles. "They look great on you!"

"Good. I'll take both pairs. A gal can never have too many shoes, even if they all look alike."

He takes the new shoes off and puts her old scuffed-up black pair back on her feet. He tags each right shoe with notes of the height needed to build up the soles and bags the left shoes for her to take. When she finishes paying, Tommy hands her the bag of shoes and walks her to the door. Holding it open, he says, "I should have those done in a week. I'll FedEx them to you. In the meantime, be careful out there. It looks like it's gonna start raining any minute."

Liz limps towards the car as fast as she can with two crutches, an awkward shoe bag dangling off her wrist, and a clutch purse slung over her shoulder. The damp air quickly turns into a steady downpour.

She stops near a parking meter to reposition the shoe bag but drops a crutch, which of course hits the curb and lands a few feet away in the street. She looks on helplessly. How's she going to get it without falling or tripping on the curb? She hates the obvious thought of using someone's car to balance herself as she bends down, below the curb, for her crutch. While she tries to figure out her next move, she's being pelted with rain and splashed by cars whizzing by. She's soaked, frustrated, and really agitated at the fact that she had to walk two blocks in the rain because there's no damn parking by the shoe shop.

Suddenly a red Mazda 6 stops near her. The young man in the passenger seat jumps out, grabs her crutch from the street, and hands it to her. The driver, another young man, yells out the window, "Can we drive you to your car?"

"Well, what do you know?" Liz says, as rain drenches her smiling face. "Young men, I would be most honored by your assistance."

31

Forgiveness Is One Conversation Away

The following New Year's Eve morning, Rhonda is jogging back from the gym when she runs into Justin as he's cleaning off the walk into Coco's from last night's snow. He invites her in for a cup of her favorite chai latte, but she declines, blaming it on the arrival of company and needing to get the house cleaned by noon.

She arrives home to an empty house. The Taylors are with their children out of state, and her other renter is celebrating the holidays with her fiancé, which leaves her alone to spend the time as she sees fit. After grabbing a cup of freshly brewed coffee, she heads to her study, intent on formalizing personal and professional goals for the upcoming year. Taped to her office door is Liz's Christmas card, an important reminder to Rhonda, especially today, that there's one last thing she needs to do. She sits in her charcoal leather chair, picks up her journal, and begins writing:

> Dear Phillip—Years have passed since the last time I held you close in my heart. I'm so sorry for the anger, resentment, and jealousy I felt toward you for taking Mom and Dad's attention all those years. You were Number One, and you needed to be. As your sister and your twin, I should have understood that and been there to support you, and I wasn't. I want to make it right—with you, with Mom and Dad, and with others I could have helped over the years and didn't.
>
> Beyond the Disability is a company founded for young adults with disabilities. In your honor and memory, I will devote resources to it to create programs for youth with disabilities and their families, so every child with a disability can lead a life of full inclusion, respect and opportunities. I love you, Phillip, and I'm proud to be your sister. ~Love, Rhonda

She turns the journal page and visualizes the way her parents looked the last time she saw them: her mother was paper thin, her spine curved from years of hunching over to care for Phillip, and her father had dark circles under his eyes and a muscular build from working several construction jobs to pay their bills. Although they were only fifty-two when they were killed; their hard lives had aged them well beyond their years.

She writes:

> Dear Mom and Dad—I should have said this years ago: thank you for inspiring me and being magnificent parents to both of us. I'm sorry I reacted like a spoiled brat to your constant care for Phillip. I was too angry and self-absorbed to recognize the

> strain that his needs put on your lives and your marriage. How could I have been so selfish to think you loved me less because Phillip needed all of you just to stay alive? I now understand you loved us both equally.
>
> Because of your love and devotion to us, I'm going to honor my brother, Phillip, by devoting my resources to services for young adults with disabilities. Through this work, I hope to help every family get the support they need to provide their loved ones with a respectful quality of life outside of the home. I love you, and I'm grateful for the life that you provided to Phillip and the lessons you taught me, even though I wasn't ready to learn them at the time. ~Love, your daughter, Rhonda

Putting aside her journal, Rhonda closes her eyes and imagines being with her family. She envisions Phillip, with his reddish curly hair and green eyes, smiling at her as he rises from his wheelchair and walks toward her. He stops directly in front, holds his arms out to embrace her, and says, "I forgive you. I love you too, Rhonda." Then he bows and returns to his chair. Her parents, smiling and embracing each other as they move toward her, give her a long-overdue hug and express how much they love her. They then return to his chair and wave as they wheel him away, fading from her vision.

"Blessings until we meet again," Rhonda says, as tears fall freely down her cheeks.

32

Every Scar Tells a Story

In October of the following year, Liz flies into Philadelphia to be the guest speaker at a local university in honor of Disability Awareness Month. After her presentation, she and her agent attend a book signing at the university's book store.

One of the attendees from the conference approaches the table and says, "You mention that your book is inspired by your life, so I'm curious: what parts are true?"

Before she can answer, she hears a young boy shout excitedly, "There's Miss Lizzy!"

She looks up and recognizes a few familiar faces: Mrs. Taylor with her curly gray hair, her face framed by her glasses and wearing a high-neck royal blue tunic; Mr. Taylor, with his hands in his pockets as always; and their not so little grandson Ayden, standing a tad more than waist high to Mr. Taylor, with shoulder-length brown hair and glasses, wearing blue jeans and a black T-shirt.

Liz smiles and turns back to the young man to answer his question. "I believe your perspective is more important. What really matters is based on your values and beliefs that people can overcome very difficult circumstances, even if they are born from tragedy." She continues, "Any story involving multiple people will be told differently based on each person's perception. You see, Liz's story is her view of how life's events contribute to and shape who we are."

He nods his head in agreement.

"Your capacity to deal with the tragedy Liz suffered will determine whether you believe in people's ability to rise and become who they want to be," she concludes.

"Thank you, Miss Liz, for that insight," he says.

Liz answers, "You are most welcome." She takes the book he's holding and asks, "How would you like me to sign it?"

He says, "Make it to Antonio, please."

She finishes writing and hands the book back to him.

The Taylors are next in line. Ayden runs to Liz and hugs her waist. "Miss Lizzy, I missed you!" he exclaims.

He looks at the cuff on her crutch propped by the side of the table and says, "And you too, Steve!" He turns slightly to the other crutch leaning on the chair behind her, cocks his head, and asks, "What's your name?"

Liz leans slightly back to grab the crutch and moves the arm cuff while saying in a squeaky voice, "I'm Stephanie. Liz needed extra support, so I came to help. Now my break's over, so I better get back to work."

The small group shares a laugh, while Liz smiles fondly at Mrs. Taylor and says, "I am so glad you came by the book signing. Thank you!" She reaches under the table for a pre-signed copy and gives it to her.

"Oh, we wouldn't miss it for anything," Mrs. Taylor says as she brushes her fingers over the front cover. "Especially now that you live in Tennessee. Keeping up in Facebook just isn't the same as seeing you in person. Do you have time to stop by Rhonda's for a cup of coffee? You really should see what she's done to the place."

"I'd love to, but unfortunately I can't today. My flight leaves in a few hours, and I still have to return the rental car. Where is Rhonda, anyway? She texted me last night that she'd be here."

"An urgent matter came up, and she needed to go to the office to meet with her staff this morning. She said if we brought you by this afternoon, she would find a way to break for a bit to come home."

"That's too bad. Tell her I'll take a rain check, and the next time I'm in town, I'll stay over if that's okay."

"We'll look forward to that, Liz. Let us know the date as soon as possible so we can get it on the calendar."

One by one, the Taylors hug Liz. As they walk away, Mrs. Taylor turns, waves the book in the air, and shouts, "I can't wait to read it!"

Liz inhales deeply. "Oh, that reminds me. I should have mentioned about page two hundred sixty-seven—"

Putting her hands on her hips, Mrs. Taylor curtly asks, "What did you say about us this time?"

Liz laughs as her eyes twinkle. "Remember, the names were changed to protect the guilty."

Her friend laughs again, and the Taylors leave. Ayden trails slightly behind his grandmother, who is preoccupied with leafing through the pages as she walks.

Liz helps her agent finish packing up their book display and covers a few details for their next signing. She slings her purse over her shoulder, slides both arms into the crutch cuffs, and limps toward the elevators to exit.

While she's waiting, a man approaches her and says, "It's great to see you again, Liz. I especially loved the part in your story where you told about people who have trouble accepting your disability." The words linger before he continues. "Do you remember when we met?" he asks.

She cocks her head to study him more closely. He stands tall, with a medium build, sandy brown hair, and hazel eyes. He wears a gold university class ring. She thinks back on men she's met over the last few years, between work and travel. She answers, "No. I'm sorry, I don't."

"It was a long time ago at a hotel bar. You were writing; I joined you by the fireplace."

It all comes back in a flash—every single detail of their night together. "Ah, now, I remember. You stood me up for breakfast."

He bows his head and sheepishly says, "Yes, and I have regretted my behavior ever since. I'm a gentleman, and normally I don't act that way. There's no excuse. Something triggered inside me when I saw you in the lobby that night, and I reacted. I have begged God every day for the chance to apologize. Will you please forgive me?"

She swallows and recalls a recent Facebook post from one of her friends. "Forgiveness doesn't excuse their behavior; it saves you from destroying your heart."

She smiles gently. "I forgive you."

As the bell rings to indicate an approaching elevator, he says, "I'm so glad. I also want to know if I can call you sometime and we can pick up where we left off. I find you very attractive."

She looks to the green lit arrow above the shiny, steel elevator doors. "I'd love to chat, but I'm going up. Besides, I already have a date waiting."

His mouth drops.

She steps inside, turns around and pushes her floor number, looking him in the eyes as the doors shut in his face. How did she muster the strength pull that off, and with a straight face to boot? A year ago she would have fallen for his charm and been back in the same trap as before, but he's one of those people who was in her life for a reason. Facing his rejection that morning in the hotel lobby turned everything around for her.

Speaking to the ceiling, she says, "Thank you, God, for the

jerks in the world. Without them, we wouldn't know how we're supposed to be respected as human beings."

Liz's plane lands in Memphis around four o'clock that afternoon.

On the two-hour ride home, she mentally plans her immediate future. In light of the overwhelmingly positive reactions to her speech and the book signing, she figures it's time to start on her next manuscript. But first, she has a date with the guy from the online site at six at the coffee shop; she figures she'll be there until seven or so, and then get her hair cut.

Liz arrives at her destination at 5:52 p.m., leaving her eight minutes before her date is set to begin. Parked in a handicapped spot, she spies a man in a car a few spaces to her right. Their eyes meet; she likes the fullness of his face, his black mustache, and black-silver wavy hair.

She thinks, *That's him, and he's driving a good-looking but muddy Buick Encore. Maybe there's hope.*

He smiles and nods at her.

She gets out of the car, opens the back door to get her crutches, and meets him at the restaurant door. "You must be Larry," she says, looking up at his six-foot four-inch frame and into his brown eyes.

"Yes, ma'am," he says in a husky tone. "You're Liz?"

"Yep!" She limps through the door he holds open for her, and they are seated promptly by the perky hostess.

"Have you been waiting long?" Liz asks her date as she peers up at him.

"No. I just got here a minute before you."

The waitress arrives with a white carafe and two big white mugs. She asks, "Can I interest you in some coffee?"

"Yes!" they answer in unison. Liz smiles as the waitress pours their drinks. He quickly grabs his mug, adds two packets of sugar and a creamer, and takes a big gulp.

"Are you ready to order?" she asks them both while tapping her black pen on the green order pad.

Liz turns to Larry and asks, "Are you eating anything?"

He pulls on his mustache and in a soft Southern drawl says, "No, ma'am, but feel free to get something if you're hungry."

"Okay, I will! Other than airplane peanuts, I've haven't had a chance to eat since breakfast. I'm starved." She scans the menu, turns to the waitress, and orders a blueberry muffin. As the waitress walks away, Liz asks him, "So what do you do for a living?"

"I'm a retired firefighter."

"That sounds interesting."

He's gripping his coffee cup. "Yeah, it was until a few years ago when I began having chest pains while responding to emergencies. I figured it was time to quit rather than become a casualty of the job."

The waitress arrives promptly with Liz's muffin and the check. "That was smart," Liz says, sipping her coffee.

As she breaks off a piece of muffin, Larry says, "I didn't know you were disabled."

She keeps chewing as she considers his comment and thinks, *Apparently he can't read. I mentioned in my profile that I walk with crutches.*

She takes another sip. "I'm not," she says simply.

"So what happened?"

For Liz, his question this early in their relationship is a deal-breaker. If he can't wait to get to know her a bit before she divulges one of the most tragic details in her life, he's not worth her time, and he'll never understand a smidgeon of who she really is.

She curtly answers, "Oh, that's a story for another day." She takes another bite, looks at her watch, and in an Oscar-worthy performance feigns surprise and claims, "Oh, my! I almost forgot,

I have a hair appointment! I'd better get going. Please excuse me. How could I have been so forgetful that I double-booked?"

He stares at her and stammers. "I'll, uh, get the check. It's the least I can do."

She stands up, grabs her crutches, and smiles at him. "No, Larry. You're wrong. It's actually the most you can ever do for me. Have a great day."

She limps out the door and to her car. As she pulls away, she can still see him sitting in the green booth with that dumfounded look on his face; however, she's still smiling.

Liz arrives at the hair salon almost an hour early, so she waits in the car and taps out a message to Carla:

> Liz: "Landed safety, had my date, and now I'm waiting to get a haircut."
>
> Carla: "Sooo, how was it??"
>
> Liz: "Hmm … perhaps I should have stuck with that Facebook guy who wanted me to 'tickle his pickle' … LOL!!!"
>
> Carla: "Oh, no way! Gross. I am so sorry."
>
> Liz: "It's OK. I'm actually good."
>
> Carla: "You can tell me more when we talk this weekend."
>
> Liz: "K. Luv u. Off to get my new hairdo!"
>
> Carla: "Later, sis!"

Liz decides there's no reason to tell Carla what Larry said since that would be living in the past for both of them. She dismisses him and the incident without further thought. She gets out of the car, grabs her crutches, and limps into the beauty parlor.

A young girl with short black hair and blue streaks greets her at the front counter. "Can I help you?"

"Hi. I'm Liz. I'm a bit early for a haircut with Sarah."

"Oh, I'm so sorry, Miss Liz. Sarah had an emergency and had to rush her little girl to the hospital."

She gasps. "Oh my gosh! Is everything okay?"

"It should be. It seems she fell and broke her arm."

Liz winces. "Poor little girl."

"I know, right? I'm sure she'll be fine. Oh, and Sarah said I could cut your hair if you're okay with that."

Liz looks at her brown name tag with white lettering. "Well, Tatum, how long have you been cutting hair?"

She gulps. "I just graduated from beauty school. But I've practiced on plenty of women at the jail!"

Liz smirks at her. "Did any of them have hair like mine? You know, the kind that grows back?"

Tatum grins and says in a bubbly tone, "Probably all of them."

"Great answer! You passed the test. I'd be delighted for you to cut my hair!"

Tatum escorts Liz to her chair toward the back of the salon and puts a black cape over Liz's shoulders. She says. "Your hair is gorgeous. How do you want it cut today?"

"Just a trim please, and thin the top out a little," Liz says as she pulls absently on the blond-gray strands that frame her face.

Tatum begins to dry cut Liz's hair, starting with her bangs. She lifts them back to reveal a thick line of gently raised running skin along her hairline.

"My mother told me that every scar tells a story," Tatum says mysteriously. Holding Liz's blond hair back, she looks at her client's reflection in the large rectangular mirror and asks, "What's yours?"

Liz senses the beautician's interest in her life is genuine as compared to her date's earlier inquiry, which she interpreted as his judgment on her abilities based on flaws he perceived in her. She smiles and warmly answers. "Once upon a time there were two little girls—"

Afterwords

For some of you, it may have been a short journey. For others, it may have taken months, decades, or even a lifetime to resolve past issues. Whether you see your life, or the life of a loved one, in that of Liz, Rhonda, Justin, Sam, or any other character, know that with each tale we tell and every day we live, we can begin anew. May you discover quickly what took Liz a lifetime to uncover—that we can never remove ourselves from our stories because they are us. At the same time, we need not allow our story to rule the way we live into the future. The past, once understood, never has to be repeated.

Everyone can generate a powerful future through their generous gift of words, and grace in daily actions, that show they care for all of humanity—friends, family, lovers, strangers, and even enemies. Live each day powerfully. Speak and act as if it were a new day, a new circumstance, a new opportunity to positively change the world—one word at a time, one person at a time, one choice at a time. For it is only in living into the future that we can be victorious over the past and experience true freedom, peace, and love.

~Victoria K. Mavis

We have been blessed, and cursed, with the freedom of choice and the knowledge of our own mortality. We therefore get to choose how we use whatever time we have. Liz and Rhonda struggled with their choices, going from self-centeredness—to fear—to an awakening about the impacts of their decisions.

Daily we must choose how we will use the gifts given to us. Above all, we must use them to benefit one another. Life is difficult, but we are sustained by the wonder of all that we see and feel, the warmth of friends, and the love of family. We have the freedom to make friends, embrace those we love, find joy in the beauty all around us, and serve others. Use the time wisely.

~Dr. Angelo R. Senese

Acknowledgments

Every Scar Tells a Story, inspired by the life of the author, Victoria Mavis, would not have been possible without the contributions of thousands of people she met along a five-decade journey, encompassing the United States, and occasionally reaching beyond its borders. Everyone played a part. She may not remember their faces or names, but she remembers how each of them made her feel.

Some of you will bow your head in shame, realizing that you could have acted differently toward her or others like her; others will be brought to tears in humility by the realization that your interaction shaped the life mission of those less fortunate than you. You see, Victoria just wanted to be like everyone else; she wanted to fit in and never could. That is, until she realized the essence of her life as she lived it is her greatest gift: to inspire others, regardless of circumstance.

Preparing to publish this book, the authors received an email from a childhood friend of Victoria's who captured it the best when he wrote, "You've been such an inspiration for me and I've used you to inspire my children as they grew up, telling them of your strength and grace. I just wanted you to know that you have touched and are touching lives in so many ways. I am proud and honored to call you my friend."

Those listed below are not necessarily the people who gave the most to create this story. They are, however, the ones Victoria believes were pivotal in its becoming a platform to inspire others, and she is grateful to them for its completion: Winston Baugh, Jim

Becker, Margie Becker, Shirley Brown, Brian Chappell, Josiah Chappell, Micah Chappell, Ronni Chappell, Roxanna Chappell, Audrey Gambino, Steve Gambino, Shelbi Holland, Sarah Kent, Karen Maten, Betty Mavis, Russell Mavis, Terry Mavis, Dr. Ivan Misner, James Peter Quinlan, Jr., Ed Raarup, Kristan Roehrs, Bonnie Schulze, Larry Seibert, Angelo Senese, Jr., Tom Shilander, Billy Staples, Mary Stuart Martin-Sklar, Cade Peter Swartzentruber, Dottie Wagner, Doris Wehe, Robert L. Wehe, Jr., Regina Whitmer, Mark Willey, Irene Yoder, and Marv Yoder.

About the Authors

Victoria K. Mavis, SPHR – In 1964, Victoria had a tragic accident at the age of four that resulted in brain trauma and left her partially paralyzed. Facing a grim diagnosis, she fought for her life and relearned how to perform basic functions such as walking and talking. Within a year of her accident, she would be the first physically handicapped child to enter a school system that wasn't equipped physically or culturally for her special needs. She was a pioneer for equality of treatment in an era when people who were handicapped were considered social misfits that should be institutionalized, were openly ridiculed, and were discriminated against for access to public systems. Victoria paved the way for others who "didn't fit in" long before the Americans With Disabilities Act (ADA) was ever signed into law in the United States or before "bullying" was a community epidemic to resolve.

Victoria grew professionally and thrived in a world where her handicap was the "pink elephant" in the room which no one spoke about—including her. Details of her disability did not exist in a public dialogue or open conversation, as few outside her immediate family ever knew the story of what happened and knew even less of the horrific discrimination that she faced over the years by those who judged her abilities only by the gait of her walk. Friends, coworkers, and everyone she encountered would only be left with the power of her presence and her sheer will and determination to succeed.

Victoria is a speaker, author, and human resources (HR) professional who has owned her own businesses, as well as been employed by private industry ranging from privately held companies to large international manufacturing corporations. She holds an MBA, is lifetime certified as a Senior Professional in Human Resources (SPHR) by the Society of Human Resource Management, and is also certified as a behavioral specialist. She has held memberships in Rotary International, BNI, and other business, professional, and community organizations.

Victoria currently resides in Arkansas. She is developing programs for disability agencies, educational institutions, and healthcare providers to help individuals with disabilities gain an independent lifestyle through art.

Angelo R. Senese, Ed.D. – Dr. Senese has forty-five years of experience as a teacher, coach, and school administrator in rural and suburban settings, beginning as an urban-schooled student himself. Growing up in Brooklyn, New York, he graduated from Tilden High School and attended Central Connecticut State University majoring in English. He began a master's degree program in special education and then moved to New Jersey where he switched to supervision and administration, earning his master's degree from Kean University.

He worked with students of differing abilities and gained a strong sense of accomplishment helping those with many challenges. He earned his doctorate from Nova Southeastern University in educational leadership. He served as an assistant principal, principal, and assistant superintendent, and was superintendent of the Northampton Area School District.

After leaving the K–12 system, Dr. Senese became an associate professor in Professional and Secondary Education at East Stroudsburg University in Pennsylvania. Dr. Senese consults for public and private schools in strategic planning, service provider analysis, curriculum design, leadership, and professional development. He has presented at local, state, and national conferences. He published an article about alternative education programs and continues to be an advocate for all students.

Lightning Source UK Ltd.
Milton Keynes UK
UKHW011830191120
373696UK00009B/668/J

Peter Havranek
Illustrations by Naomi Stearn

Too Many Mothers

Bumblebee Books
London

Dedication

Alice Milena Culverwell

A long way from here and ages ago
Lived a poor Chinese man named Yip Han Lo.
He'd a beautiful wife who gave him a hand,
To work the rice fields on his master's land.

His master was rich but not very kind.
The work was boring, but Yip didn't mind.
From dawn to dusk in the same paddy field,
Yip had to work hard to increase the yield.

He grew rice for himself an hour every day
To feed his family and supplement his pay.
He needed the work, so he tried his best,
And worked every day, never given a rest.

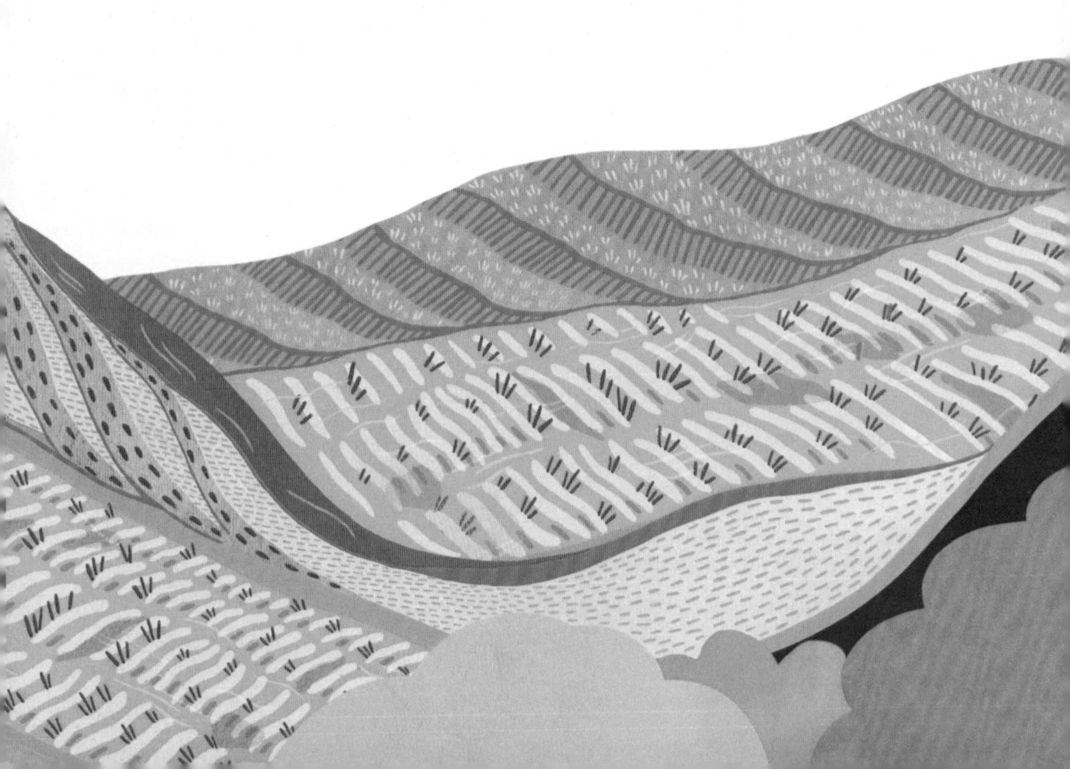

His life was dull, his prospects were bad.
Always happy and never seen to be sad.
Coping with problems as they came along,
With a smile or a grin and a cheerful song.

He'd three little children, a mum but no dad,
Who'd died very young, making them sad.
The nearest town was a long walk away,
So going to market took most of the day.

His wife kept his master's house very clean,
For scraps of food as the man was so mean.
They lived in a hut and were incredibly poor,
Had few possessions and slept on the floor.

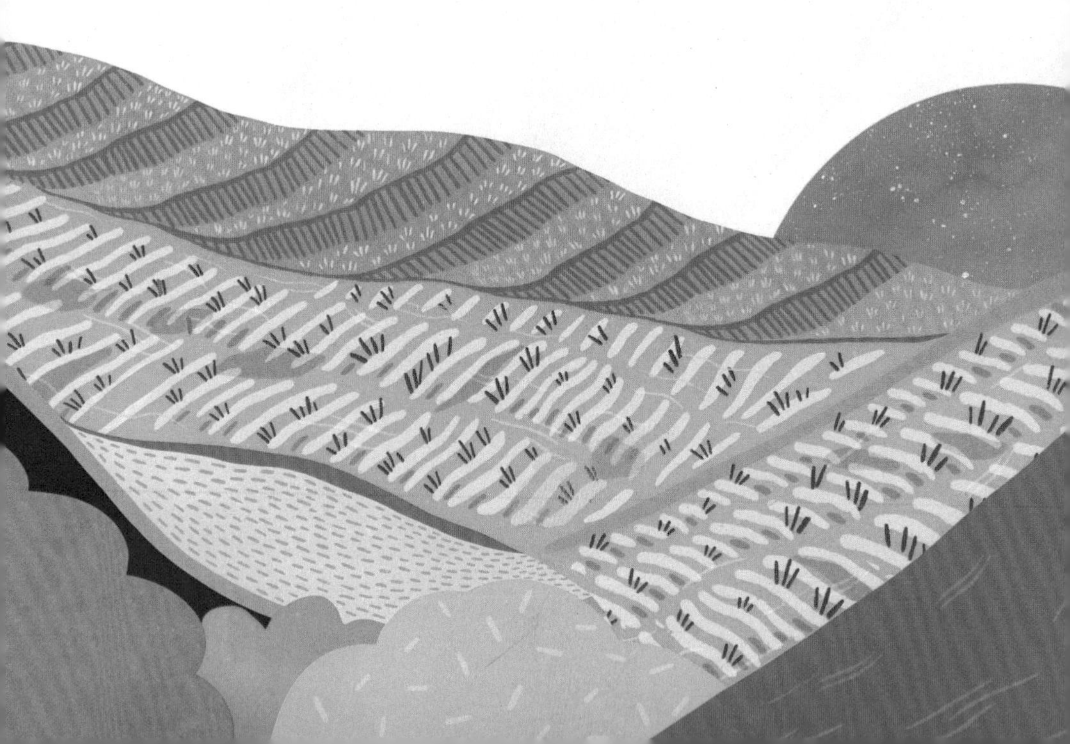

Yip was pleased with life, and what he had got.
He was happy, fulfilled and content with his lot.
A more fortunate man you never could meet.
He had a place to live and enough food to eat.

When planting out rice, you need to know
That it needs deep water to help it grow.
Rice only grows in a country that's hot,
With plenty of water, in fact quite a lot.

In a field full of water, you stomp up and down
Turning the soil muddy, a deep shade of brown.
All day Yip would labour, and he would toil
Up to his knees in water and deep muddy soil.

His trousers rolled up and his feet quite bare,
Mud squidged through his toes. He didn't care.
The very worst thing was to tread on a stone
That might cut his foot right down to the bone.

One day while working a new piece of ground,
He trod on something hard. What had he found?
Put his hands in the mud to see what he'd got.
It felt round and smooth, like a very large pot.

It had been there for ages, buried very deep.
If he could dig it up it would be his to keep.
How long to release it he just couldn't say
But it took him hours, the rest of the day.

A beautiful jar worth the labour and toil
And very heavy, packed full of wet soil.
A wonderful present to give to his wife.
The first one he'd given her in all of his life.

He continued to work past the end of the day
Then carried it home, didn't stop on the way.
The pot was decorated with flowers and trees.
The perfect gift, he was sure it would please.

His wife was happy with what he had found,
Except for the mud from it being far underground.
"Emptied and cleaned it will look very nice.
We'll use it to store our best cooking rice."

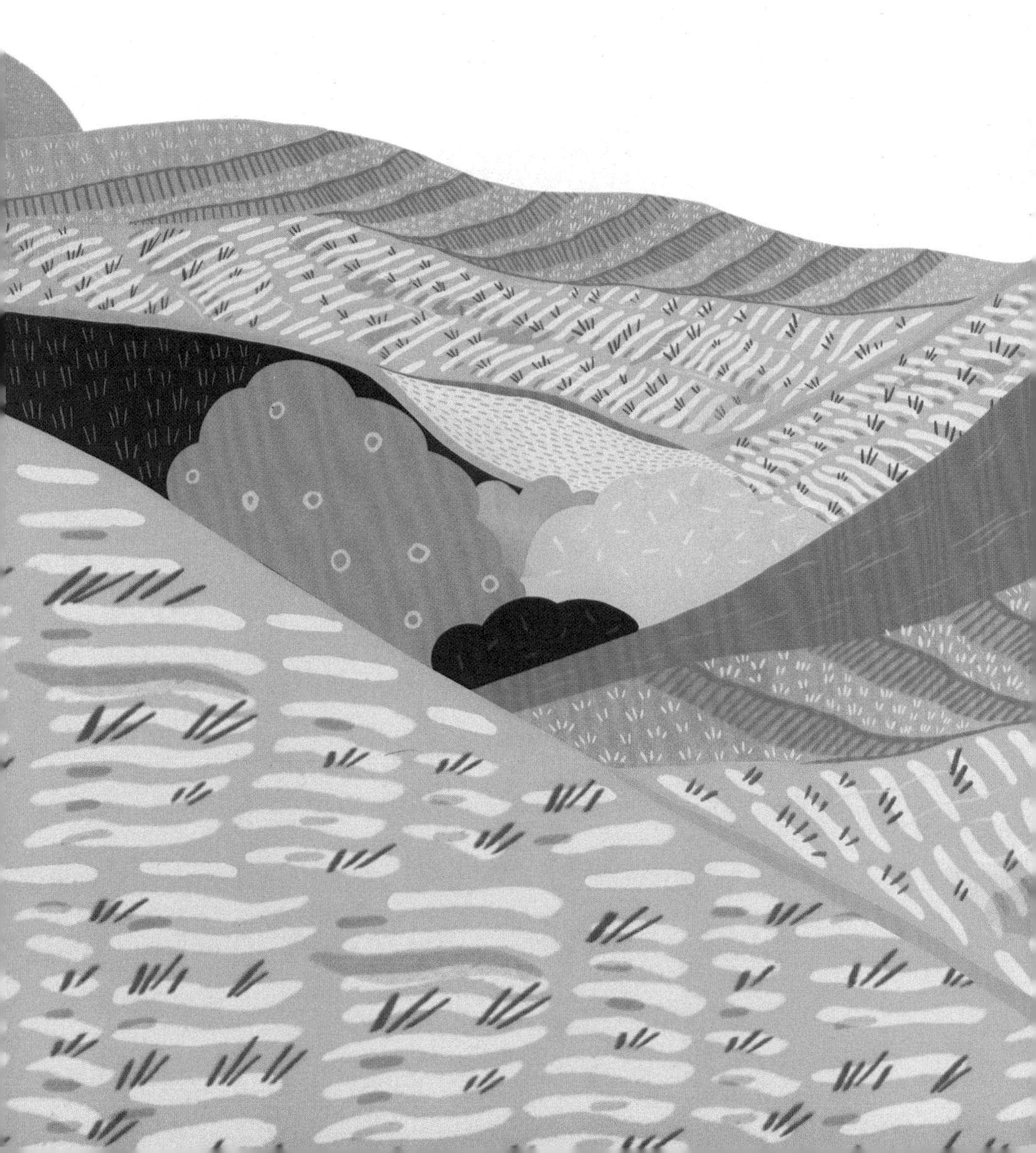

Much water was used to wash the outside.
It looked amazing and filled him with pride.
It was graceful, slender, nearly tall as his wife.
Not seen anything like it in all of his life.

The outside was polished, all shiny and bright.
Could it be emptied without much of a fight?
He dug at the mud. The time seemed to fly.
The pot stayed full, and the mud pile grew high.

"The pot will not empty!" He said with a shout.
"It's packed too hard, and I can't get it out."
Suddenly a thought popped into his head,
"I could perhaps use a scrubbing brush instead."

His idea worked and the mud started to clear,
But working this slowly could take half a year.
Something happened that he hadn't planned.
The now muddy brush fell out of his hand.

Fell into the pot where the soil had been.
Not a trace of the mud could now be seen.
The pot wasn't empty, but what startled him,
Was a jar full of brushes, right up to the brim.

A mountain of mud from his labour and toil
Surrounded his hut, good plant growing soil.
He planted some peas and all kinds of beans,
And rows of radishes and plenty of greens.

He'd rows of potatoes and lots of sweet corn.
Started working his garden long before dawn.
He had plenty of rice and vegetables as well.
What food he had over, he might as well sell.

The veg started growing in no time at all.
His dutiful wife opened a small market stall.
With all the money he would buy a hen.
He'd be very rich. He just couldn't say when.

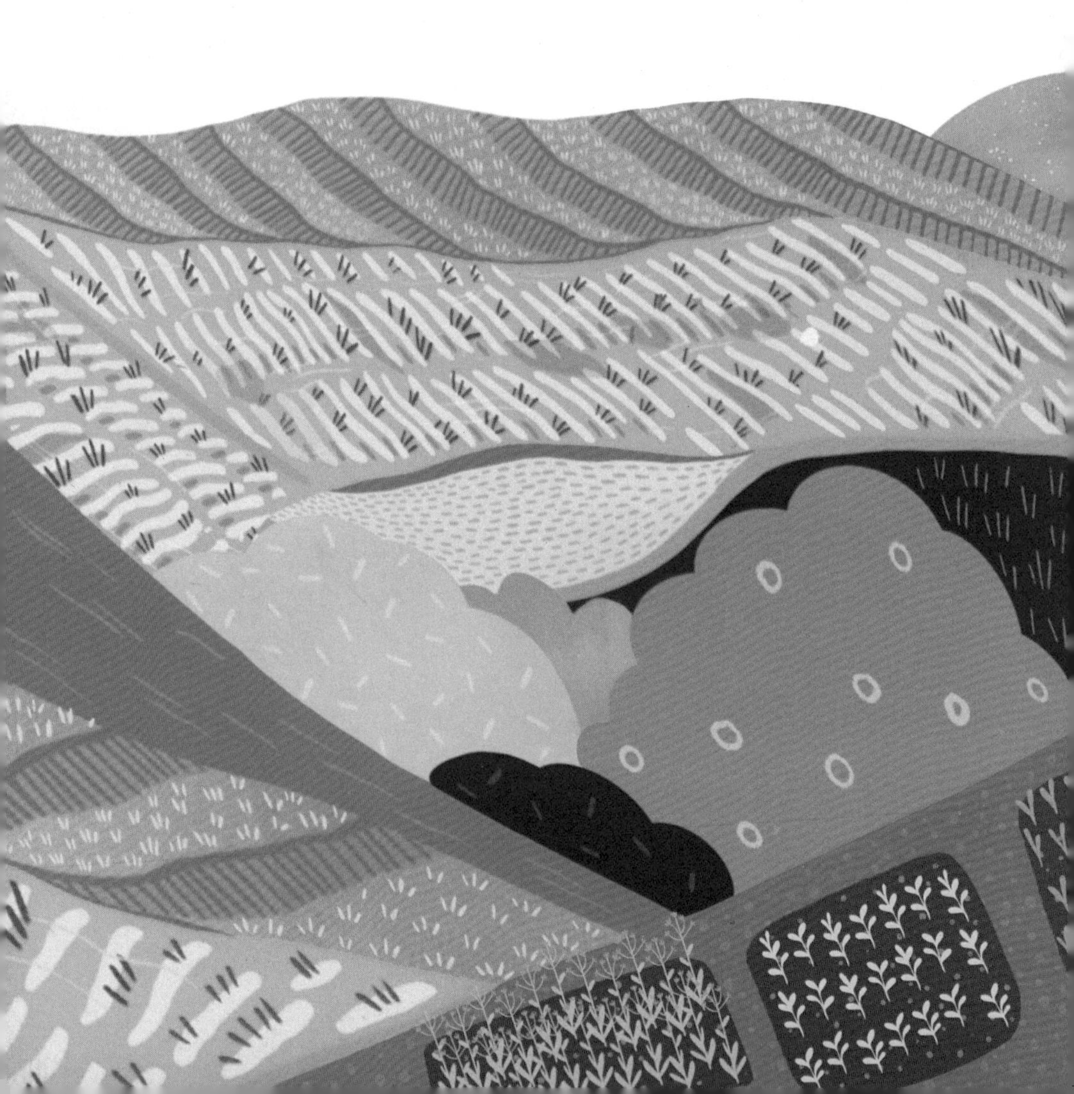

Later that day a thought came to him.
"I've a pot full of brushes, up to the brim.
By selling vegetables I'm now not so poor,
Selling brushes though will make me much more.

He went to the pot, now filled to the top.
He knew it was greedy. He just couldn't stop.
It would refill with brushes of that he was sure.
Fill up his barrow till it couldn't take any more.

Emptying the pot, brushes covered the floor,
Filling the room till it couldn't take any more.
With his barrow full, and more in his pack,
He was going to be rich. No looking back.

He made his wife take two loads in a day.
A long trip to market, a very long way.
He'd worked all his life, tired of being poor.
He'd got lots of money, but he wanted more.

He spent all his free time emptying his pot.
He'd plenty of money, spent what he'd got.
He'd three little children who liked to play,
But he set them working on very little pay.

Carrying brushes to market was just a start.
With all the money came a horse and cart.
At first the brushes were very easy to sell,
But after a time, they didn't do so well.

He'd sold lots of brushes and had loads of cash,
But his empire wobbled, then fell with a crash.
He'd sold brushes to people from miles around.
Needed new customers, but none could be found.

At first it was easy to empty the pot.
Working fast, he could empty the lot.
He'd go to bed, put the last brush away,
Woke to a full pot at the start of the day.

He worked all night and early one morn,
Before sunrise at the start of the dawn,
Emptying his pot, and not making a din,
A gold coin from his pocket simply fell in.

By now I'm sure you don't need to be told
That the pot was full of coins made of gold!
Yip was delighted and jumped up and down.
He'd be the richest farmer in all of the town.

He went to his master and was heard to say,
"I'm quitting my job as I don't need the pay.
You paid very little. I was poor as a mouse.
I'm leaving your old hut to buy a fine house."

The best place for his gold, he was now sure
Was stored in a bank, to keep it secure.
He quickly became an unhappy old miser.
Wouldn't have happened if he had been wiser.

Travelled to town, over five times a day.
Gold is heavy. The horse died on the way.
Put his wife to work in place of the horse.
It worked quite well, but slower of course.

It didn't last long and by the end of the day,
His wife and children were taken away.
Yip was happy, and he just didn't care.
With them now gone he didn't have to share.

Without a wife to cook, his food would be cold.
Less people to feed, meant more room for gold.
Banking by day and emptying the pot by night,
The heaps of gold were an incredible sight.

He lost all his friends now he'd become rich.
Better watch out. Might end up dead in a ditch.
His old clothes were burned or thrown away.
He now wore new clothes and shoes every day.

Being very rich didn't go down at all well.
Nobody liked him. It was easy to tell.
Yip didn't care. He was now a rich man.
"I'll move to town just as fast as I can."

From rags to riches, what a message to send.
For Yip the beginning, and not a happy end.
Hang on a minute! What about his mum?
Perhaps happiness might eventually come.

Greed and cruelty were now buried deep.
It didn't worry Yip. He didn't lose any sleep.
He fretted little, but what made him frown?
Who'd empty his pot when he went to town?

His mum had a thought that couldn't be said.
"I don't like my son!" So she took to her bed.
Going to bed made Yip come up with a clue.
"I've solved the problem. I know what to do."

His mother liked to knit as she lay in her bed.
Her son made her empty gold coins instead.
Propped her up with a pillow behind her back,
Then watched her secretly to see if she'd slack.

His mother was sitting bolt upright in bed.
A blanket around her, nightcap on her head.
A little old lady, now covered in gold,
With her hair in curlers, was a sight to behold.

Emptying coins at the top was easy at first.
The ones at the bottom, probably the worst.
To reach the last coin, she had to dig deep.
With her head in the pot, she fell fast asleep.

Gravity took hold, and she gracefully slid in.
The pot was narrow. It was good she was thin.
She needed help as she couldn't get out,
First calling quietly, then started to shout.

Blood rushed to her head. She was upside down.
The house was now empty. Her son was in town.
She was there for ages, probably most of the day.
Could she survive long? It was impossible to say.

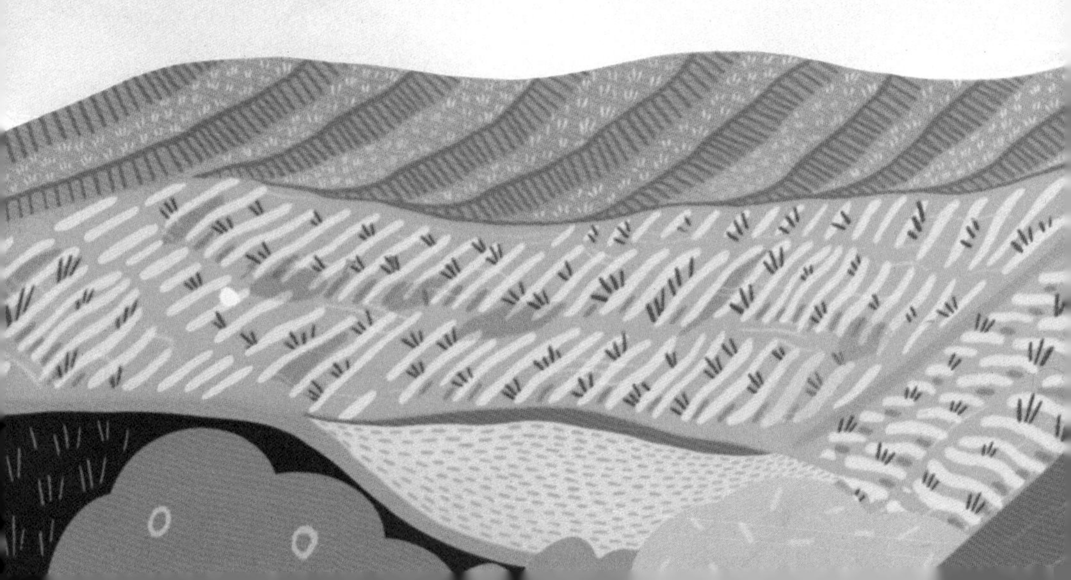

Yip spent the day buying clothes in the town
And didn't get back till after sundown.
Spending the day upside down on her head
Resulted in her being unsurprisingly dead!

Yip expected to see his mum covered in gold.
Instead, what he saw made his blood run cold.
He tried to speak but he couldn't even shout.
Saw his mum in the pot with legs sticking out.

In ancient China when a mum's laid to rest,
The family's fortune is put to the test.
Everyone's invited and expected to come,
And given lots of money. A very large sum.

There'd be a party. A magnificent affair
With scores of people all gathered there.
If it wasn't grand what would people think?
Must be plenty of food and lots to drink.

You had to dress smartly, in your best attire.
Showing your status. Your wealth to admire.
Fashion dictated clothes covered in gems.
Silk or velvet, with gold around the hems.

Looking at his old mum, most definitely dead,
Yip started to panic, stilled by a voice in his head.
"Invite the whole town. A vast, mighty throng.
People think you are poor. Prove them all wrong."

Buried in a coffin all covered in gold,
Tastefully decorated, the best ever sold.
A tall black headstone with her name all in white
That must look expensive - a magnificent sight.

Give them plenty of food, with delicacies galore!
Nothing running out. There must always be more.
And loads of barrels of best Sake wine,
And silk covered tables from which to dine.

The funeral director came the very same day.
Pulled her out of the pot and took her away.
With his mother dead, you'd think he'd be sad.
She'd not emptied the pot which made him mad.

For days he was too busy to empty the pot.
Something had changed, in fact quite a lot.
He spent all his time perfecting a plan,
To prove to the world, he was now a rich man.

People had noticed since his mum had died
He'd not looked unhappy nor even cried.
So, at the funeral when people came near,
He pulled a sad face and shed a crocodile tear.

The funeral happened just as he'd planned.
They saw a rich man who was ever so grand.
It cost him a lot, but he had plenty to spare.
Made a dent in his fortune, but he didn't care.

"I've spent lots of money," he suddenly thought.
"Need more gold from the pot, mustn't run short."
But we both know that he was in for a scare.
Another dead mum, feet sticking up in the air.

When he opened the door, what did he see?
The part of his mum, from her foot to her knee.
"I've buried my mum," he wailed in his grief.
The funeral director's a vile, wicked old thief."

He grabbed this dead mum and pulled her out.
"I'll bury her properly," he said with a shout.
As he carried her out, a neighbour dropped by.
Making Yip Han Lo jump and even stifle a cry.

"The woman that we buried was the wrong one.
We'll have another funeral and get the job done."
The second funeral would cost him much more.
Bury this mother. Open the coffin to make sure.

"I'll take her to town in my own horse and cart
And watch the coffin nailed down, just for a start.
I'll guard the sealed coffin all day and all night.
I'll bury this mother, and this time do it right."

Money was no object, easily meet the expense.
His determination and drive were truly immense.
He'd be rid of this problem and have her put away.
He'd be free of this mother by the end of the day.

A person he knew, said while scratching his head,
"Have you more mothers that are not yet dead?
You've spent a fortune. Must have made quite a dent
I dread to think how much money you've spent!"

"I have gold in the bank. How much I'm not sure.
What will happen if I can't get any more?"
Holding his head high as he entered the bank,
They'd dark looks on their faces and his heart sank.

What he heard next made his blood run cold.
"You've spent too much and run out of gold!"
"I've plenty at home so I can easily get more."
But we all know he had a surprise in store.

He hurried home just as quickly as he could.
Galloping faster than he knew he should.
Opening the door his mouth gawping in fright.
Yet another dead mother. A terrible sight.

He gritted his teeth and started to shake.
What he did next was a terrible mistake.
Rushed outside and took an axe from the shed.
"She's ruined me by being three times dead."

He swung his sharp axe to chop off her head.
Missed the target smashing the pot instead.
The pot seemed to explode, bits flying around,
Falling in pieces, scattered all over the ground.

Yet another funeral would finish him he feared.
This third mum vanished. She just disappeared.
He was delighted and relieved and started to cry.
He was blissfully happy but didn't know why.

With the axe in his hand, the penny finally dropped.
The pot was no more, so his income had stopped.
Now surrounded by pieces that covered the floor
They were just bits of pottery, not a pot anymore.

That magical pot had destroyed his life.
It had lost him his children and a beautiful wife.
He would lose his house, as he'd have to sell.
He'd upset his master and lost his friends as well.

He should have been happy with what he'd got.
Greed had consumed him and taken the lot.
He left the village and walked the lonely track.
Held his head in shame. He couldn't look back.

Do you feel sorry and sad for Yip Han Lo?
Do you find yourself saying, "I told you so!"
He made a mistake. It didn't cost him his life,
Only his home, his kids and his beautiful wife.

We've all made silly mistakes in our time,
For us things have usually turned out fine.
Should we forgive him if he shows remorse?
If truly sorry and repentant, then **YES, OF COURSE.**

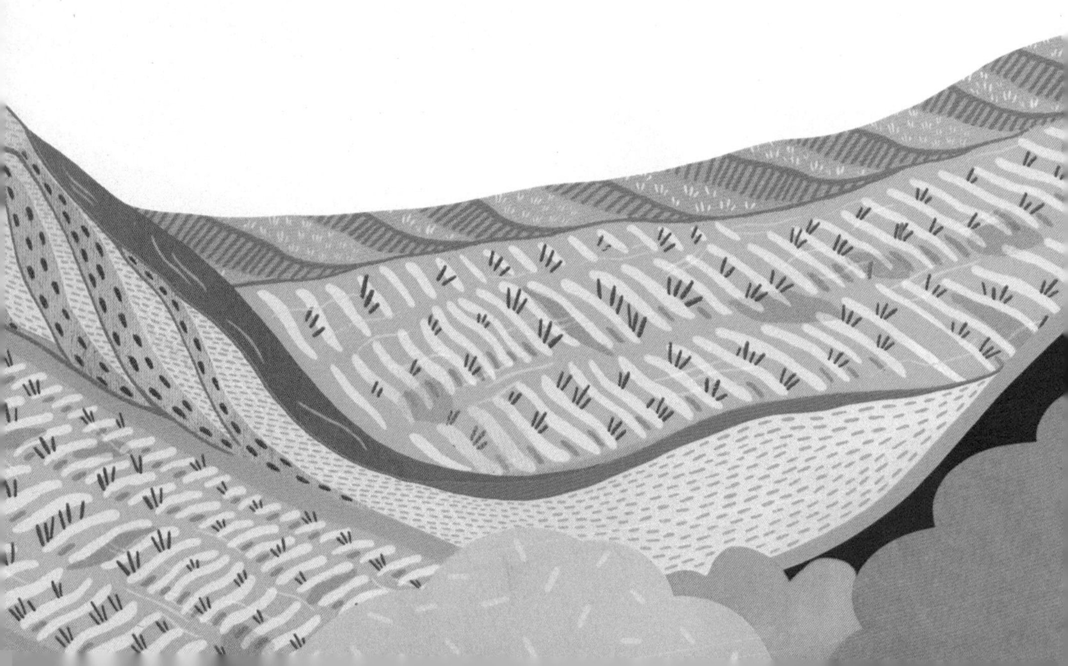

About the Author

Peter Havranek was born and brought up in East Africa to a Czech father and English mother. He went to boarding school on the Isle of Wight while his parents worked and lived in the Middle East. He started his teaching career teaching English to Iranian Airforce pilots. He trained as a primary school teacher and taught in Wiltshire primary schools for thirty years. His story telling skills were developed when he led large groups of primary children in History Through Drama projects. He finished his career as headteacher of a Wiltshire Primary school near Chippenham.

Acknowledgements

To my wife Susan, my sister, Maggie, and friends who have helped with proof reading, especially Alan and Marilyn.